SANTA'S DRAGON

C. R. STOBO

CRANREUCH PUBLISHING

For Robert and Ruaidhri, who always believed in the funky dragon living beneath the sofa.

And in memory of Scott McMurray (1972-2021), who I hope would have enjoyed this story, and especially chapter eight.

The greatest feat Santa Claus ever achieved was convincing the world (of grown-ups) he didn't exist...

CONTENTS

PROLOGUE

Father Giuseppe Antonelli did not hear the dull thud of the cellar door to the church hall being forced as he did his regular evening rounds of the Chiesa del Natale. Evening rounds was stretching a bit at this time of year, he thought. He watched the last rays of the weak December sunlight filter through a stained-glass depiction of the late Signora Repry. In that moment, the dust that played on the fading, coloured beams was far more beautiful than anything he could recall the church's late patron ever having done.

Now, now, Giuseppe, he chided himself. There is always some beauty everywhere and in everyone – even in the late Signora. Without her very generous gift, the church would have closed long ago. By now, he was deep in thought. He mulled over the late Signora's many interventions in the church's life. Indeed, he was so deep in thought that he failed to hear several creaks on the stairs leading from the cellar to the nave of the church. But then, it was an old building, indeed an ancient building, and old buildings are wont to create clusters of creaks and groans at any given time, almost as though they were alive themselves. Which they never are. Well, almost never.

As Father Antonelli continued his rounds, he was feeling the usual mix of faint nervousness and excitement that built in the weeks before Christmas. The infant group last Sunday had really triggered it, with their enthusiastic singing of the carols and the high point of the morning, the annual Nativity play. It was just a pity no one had told him this year's donkey had been recently rescued by an animal welfare centre. It turned out it was not a fan of either being tethered nor of enclosed spaces, having been held hostage in just such a way for the past two and a half years.

Still, he mused, it had been quite comical when it announced its bid for freedom with five minutes of non-stop braying just as the shepherds arrived in Bethlehem, before making a bolt for the front door of the church and skittling the three wise men into a rear pew.

Fortunately, there had been no injuries, and the kids had thought it was hilarious – even if several of the many Christmas trees that festooned the church's interior now looked a little the worse for wear.

He gazed intently at the two tallest trees in the Chiesa to make sure they were still vaguely symmetrical. It would not do to disappoint the hundreds of visitors who would visit the Church 'where Santa Claus lay in rest' before Christmas Eve. Even though he had occasional doubts about whether the remaining relics were truly those of St Nicholas, Father Antonelli had long understood that they attracted the tourists. For a man of the cloth, he didn't mind the whole Santa myth as much as he should have done: for every child who just wanted ever more material things from Santa, there was another who wanted to give to others in the true spirit of Christmas.

Now, the adults, that was a different story. Every year it was the same: rushing around, overeating, over-drinking, paying for everything on credit cards and then worrying about the bills for the next eleven months; barely ever a thought for anyone other than themselves and their own wants; the need to buy the latest toys so they could curry favour with their kids; the 'must have' latest gadgets, the latest home makeover, the latest car.

If only they would learn to spend some time with their kids, with people, thought Father Antonelli, then they would find many of these 'things' unnecessary and they could get off the merry-go-round of working ever longer hours to buy ever more things and stuff. He told them this every year, in a different way each time, in his sermon. And every year, they ignored him and kept on behaving in precisely the same manner as the year before, anyway.

He stopped for a moment to chuckle to himself about the donkey once more. As he did so, he noticed a stray bauble hiding under one of the pews. Must have been a refugee from last Sunday's antics, he thought, bending down to pick it up. At this, the blood rushed to his head and he felt a little dizzy. I'm getting old, he thought, as he grabbed the nearest pew and gradually eased himself upright. His own involuntary grunts and groans as he did so masked the sound of the sizeable iron door handle to the nave being turned and the scraping sound of the door slowly being eased open.

There was a loud crack from Father Antonelli's spine as he neared being vertical again and he winced. I am definitely too old for this, he thought. His mind floated off to consider retirement for a moment, but as always, when he considered this, he scolded himself for negative thoughts.

"They gave this job to you for life, Giuseppe," he muttered to himself, "and for as long as you are able, you shall do it. There is nothing more important in the whole of Italy than the guardianship of the Chiesa del Natale and its most famous resident."

He felt for the large golden key under his cassock once more and as his fingers touched the cold metal under his robe, he recalled the words of the late monsignor on the day he entrusted him with it:

"You must remember that the key which you wear around your neck is a very serious responsibility, for only this key unlocks the casket that contains the most important relics of St Nicholas himself; they must never leave this place."

Father Antonelli gave a small sigh of relief. It was still there. It was always there and for as long as he was alive, it would always be there.

The gloom within the church grew as the shadows throughout it merged into the darkness. All except for one particular shadow, which was slowly creeping its way along the wall that ran from the nave to the altar.

As Father Antonelli walked around the edge of the inside wall of the church, checking each door was locked and bolted, he wondered if it would snow at Christmas this year. It never snowed as much as it used to. At least, that was how it seemed. He wondered if his memory was playing tricks on him or it really was less snowy. People always said that you remembered the winters of your childhood as snowy and the summers as hot and sunny, and that such memories became more pronounced as you aged.

There was no doubt about it: he was an old man now. Even with his new glasses, his eyesight was not as sharp as it had once been. Fortunately, for his evening ritual of locking up the church, he had no need of them. He had been doing this for so many years now that he often joked he could do it with his eyes closed.

However, had he been wearing his glasses, it is possible he may have noticed there was one shadow which was moving more quickly than all the others as the very last slivers of daylight within the church faded in the seeping darkness of the cold December night. This shadow had eyes, and these were following Father Antonelli's every move.

He finally reached the door to the crypt; it was ajar – which was strange. He could have sworn the door had been closed earlier. He fished out another set of keys and began singing his favourite Christmas song to himself as he looked for the large cast iron key that fitted this particular ancient lock, "Jingle bells, jingle bells, jingle all the way…"

This was the door he always locked last. It was the heaviest lock, and it needed twelve turns to secure it: one for each month of the year; one for each day of Christmas. He turned the key.

Clunk. One. Clunk. Two. Clunk. Three…

I wonder how many turns I have given this key over the years…

Clunk. Four. Clunk. Five. Clunk. Six…

it must be thousands, maybe even tens of thousands…

Clunk. Seven. Clunk. Eight. Clunk Nine…

actually, it must be hundreds of thousands… ach, I am such an old man…

Clunk. Ten. Clunk…

Father Antonelli heard the creak in the floorboard directly behind him a fraction of a second before his brain registered the crack to the back of his neck. Then, it all went black.

Inside the church, in the darkness by the crypt door, the one moving Shadow lifted Father Giuseppe Antonelli's head slightly and removed a large golden key from around his neck.

The Shadow tiptoed towards the old wooden door. He turned the key in the lock twice more and tried the cast iron handle. The door creaked its way open, revealing a small stone staircase behind it. The Shadow pocketed the bunch of keys, flicked the switch on his head torch and picked his way down the narrow stairs. His steps were careful and efficient – just as he had planned. He touched the walls. Damp. Water leaking into them from down the centuries. The stairs stopped. He had reached the interior of the crypt itself. Its dank air filtered into his nostrils and he scrunched up his face. He would not be spending any longer in here than he had to.

He glanced around the cramped stone-enclosed space. There, in its centre, was his target: an unremarkable marble tomb, the top of which was the same height as his waist. He brandished the golden key in front of him, his eyes darting around, looking for the tomb's lock. On the far side, he located it, halfway down and with a partly worn inscription:

… giace San Nicola

"… lies Saint Nicholas," he muttered. "Good. Just as expected."

He fitted the key into the tomb's lock and turned it methodically six times until he heard what he had been waiting for:

CLICK

He was in. He lifted the lid, and there, resting on a long-discoloured stone slab within, were a collection of bones, fragments of bones, and other assorted objects, some of which appeared to be broken pieces of wood.

He had no time to consider what these were (or might have once been). Reaching into his jacket pocket, he pulled out a small piece of paper with a short list of words on it, written in black ink and which only made sense to him. A coded list of all the objects which now lay before him.

He silently checked off each one in his head and then grabbed them, two or three at a time, and stuffed them into a rucksack. As he did a final sweep of the tomb's interior, he checked his watch: ninety-two seconds had elapsed since he had sent Father Antonelli into a deep sleep. It was time to leave.

He sealed the tomb once again. Then, reversing his earlier actions, he took out the bunch of keys and replaced the large iron key in the door of the crypt; it was ready to lock the door once again when the good Father awoke. He retraced his steps back to where the unconscious priest lay.

The Shadow took the golden key and gently replaced it around the priest's neck. Now for the tough part.

The good Father was not the lightest victim he had ever come across, the Shadow thought, as he strained in silence to replace the slumbering priest onto one of his church pews. As he arranged the priest's limbs into a more natural sitting pose, beads of sweat trickled down his face. He could taste the salt on his lips. He glanced one last time at Father Antonelli and silently asked for his forgiveness.

And then, he was gone, a shadow slipping back into the night.

By the time Father Antonelli started to come round, several minutes later, his first act amidst his confusion was to feel for the key around his neck. Still there, he thought, and relief swept over him. He sat for several moments, wondering what had happened to him and considered whether he should tell anyone about it, lest the suggestion he should retire be made once more. On balance, he mused, there was no immediate need to rush such a momentous decision.

By this point, the Shadow was already a couple of miles away from the Chiesa Del Natale, driving towards the next stage of his assignment in an anonymous car. No one seeing his car sleeking past that evening would have even given it a second look. A dark, bland saloon car that was efficient and discreet, in alignment with his life. He smiled thinly at his night's work and, for a moment, allowed himself to feel pleased.

The transient smile vanished, and a slight grimace took its place. It was time to call his employers. He pressed a button on the steering wheel and the car's speakerphone sprang to life. The phone rang once, twice…

"Yes," said a toneless voice at the other end.

"Is the line secure?"

"Of course."

"Good. Stage four is complete."

"It went smoothly?"

"Yes, exactly as planned."

"Excellent. She will be most pleased, especially as it is now well into December."

The Shadow's grimace tightened at this last comment, given that today was the sixth of December.

"Don't worry. I haven't forgotten your deadline: all of them by Sunday 23rd December at 6pm…"

"Or your bonus is void."

There was the slightest of pauses. The Shadow took a deep breath before he spoke again.

"You will hear from me again soon."

"Make sure we do, Monsieur," said the atonal voice. "Goodbye."

The line went dead.

And a Merry Christmas to you, too, thought the Shadow, as his foot pressed down on the car's accelerator and it sped off into the night.

CHAPTER ONE

Tom Brightly was sitting at a desk in a dimly lit room, lined with endless books, with his eyes tightly closed, awaiting the worst. The only sound was the steady tick-tock of the grandfather clock which stood, sentinel-like, guarding the outer part of the room, which was cleaved in two by an ancient door of frosted glass. He shivered again, though he wasn't sure if this was because of the draft of cold air blowing under the old wooden outer main door to the room or the fear of what was about to happen next. An older lady approached his desk. Tom heard the clack-clack of her boots on the wooden floorboards and could picture her, dressed in tweed from head to toe, her shortish black hair immaculate as ever, and looking serious as always. He heard the rustle of papers being placed on his desk and the older lady spoke.

"Much, much better. See, I told you that you could do it."

Tom opened his left eye to peek at the paper on the desk in front of him. His right eye remained tightly shut.

"A B minus?" he said in disbelief.

He didn't believe the evidence of his one open eye, so he unscrunched his right eye as well, which confirmed the matter.

"Wow - I got a B minus! I didn't fail! I actually didn't fail!"

"Well, of course you didn't," the older lady replied. "All these weeks of extra lessons and hard work are paying off. You did it. Well done."

"Thank you – you're a legend, Auntieprof. I thought I was going to fail maths for sure, but I might still have a chance."

The older lady drew herself up to her full height and peered straight at Tom over the top of her half-moon glasses with her piercing green eyes.

"Thomas Brightly, how many times have I told you this? You must have more faith in your own ability. You are a clever boy and perfectly good enough at mathematics." She paused. "You simply have an eejit of a teacher at that new school of yours, who clearly only has one method of teaching – and a limited one at that. I mean, honestly, what kind of teacher schedules a test for the last day of term before the Christmas holidays?"

"I know, Auntieprof. It totally sucks. It's just that Mr Hurndall has gone on and on at me so much about how rubbish I am that I thought I'd never get it."

Professor Octavia Merryweather sighed and sat down next to Tom.

"What have I told you before? Pay no attention to grown-ups who behave like eejits. They're not worth listening to – and that Mr Hurndall of yours is a prime candidate. You've only been in his class five minutes and he's made your life a misery. He's the worst sort of teacher: wants a quiet life and hassles any of his students who 'underperform' because that means extra work for him."

She looked at Tom with her most serious face now and took his left hand in hers. Her eyes wrinkled as she looked at him and her mouth hinted at a smile.

Tom squirmed in his seat and ran his free hand through his unruly mop of dark blond hair, messing it up deliberately. He was about to receive another lecture.

"Tom, you must believe in yourself and not let folk like him knock your confidence. Don't let him undermine you – it's not on and *whatever* you do, do not start repeating his language as your own. Never forget that we become what we think about, so do not let anyone else transplant their negative words or thoughts into your head and do *not* start parroting them, either. Do you understand?"

Tom met her gaze and nodded.

"Good. Now, pack up your things and get on home. You've a busy day of it tomorrow."

Tom picked up his mock test papers and questions and reached for his rucksack, before stuffing them and his textbook into it. He gathered his pens and pencils and shovelled them in, too.

Merryweather spoke again.

"So, what's on after your maths test? The annual sledging race?"

"Yep."

"Ah, good old Playfair - never changes. How's the weather looking? Snow?"

Tom shook his head.

"That's a pity. The artificial slope then?"

Tom nodded again.

"Are you nervous?"

"A bit."

Merryweather gave Tom her over-the-rims-of-her-glasses-look once again as she spoke.

"Don't be. You're excellent at sledging. Fearless, even - just like your father."

"I'll try my best, but the sledge is pretty ancient now."

"Raw ability, that's what you have. Runs in the family. Took your father three years and two rather spectacular crashes before he won it for the first time, if I remember correctly. Once he'd done it the first time, though, he kept on winning every year afterwards. Didn't matter if it was on snow or not."

"I know, I know, Auntieprof, but he was much better than I'll ever be."

Merryweather shot Tom another stern look.

"Young man, no more chatter like that. You have every chance. Just do your best and do it your own way and you'll be grand."

Tom nodded again and began putting on his coat, buttoning it up against the chilly night air which awaited him, before pausing.

"Did he really crash twice before he won it?"

"Yes. Yes, he did, and both times were dramatic in their own way. It never put him off, though. He just tried even harder the following year."

There was a rap on the door. Merryweather bustled over to open it. As she did so, Tom could make out two men, one older and besuited, one younger, with a beard and dark, longish hair and more casually dressed, standing in the corridor beyond.

"Oh, hello, Atticus, Nicky. Goodness, is it that time already?" said Merryweather.

The older gentleman spoke.

"Indeed it is. May we come in?"

Tom thought he looked rather stern. He certainly wasn't smiling. Nor was the younger man. Indeed, he looked even more grim-faced as he nodded his head in acknowledgement at Merryweather.

"Of course, come away in and I'll make us some tea."

"Thank you, but that won't be necessary. Unfortunately, this is not a social visit. Oh, I didn't realise you still had company."

The older, stern looking man had spied Tom.

"Ah, that's Tom, my courtesy nephew and maths tutee. He's just packing up now."

"Hello, young man," said the stern man.

"Hi," mumbled Tom and carried on gathering his things.

"Let's go through to my office," said Merryweather, as she ushered the pair of visitors in. "Tom, good luck for tomorrow and do well. I'll see you again after Christmas. Just let yourself out - and have a Merry Christmas."

"Thanks. Merry Christmas to you, too," replied Tom.

Merryweather and the two visitors went through to the back of her office and she closed the frosted glass door, which separated it from the front office space, behind the three of them.

Tom put on his rucksack and made his way to the outer door, heading out into the corridor. It already felt chilly as he closed the door behind himself. He had taken only a few paces when he stopped.

"Calculator," he muttered and silently facepalmed himself. He took off his rucksack and opened it to check. There was no calculator to be seen in amongst the jumble of books, papers, pens and pencils that comprised the innards of his schoolbag.

"Rats."

He turned around and knocked lightly on the door. From inside, he could hear the muffled sounds of Merryweather and the stern-looking man's voices. They hadn't heard him knocking. He quietly opened the door and crept back into the outer office. The two voices were now louder and raised. It sounded to Tom as though they were in the middle of an argument.

"... Octavia, I have told you both that I've done everything I can to prevent these cuts, but the University Court was quite clear: no more funding in the next calendar year - and they are not at all happy about this extra project that you've taken on, either, Nick."

"Oh, come on, Atticus. It's not as if it's interfering with any of my day-to-day work," said the third voice, which Tom figured out must belong to the younger, bearded man.

"That is as may be, but it's how it looks to the powers that be which matters."

"Atticus, I must agree with Nicky. The university cannot have it all ways." It was Merryweather, and she sounded angry.

"Octavia, be reasonable," said the stern-looking man.

"No, Atticus, I will not be 'reasonable'". Merryweather spat the last word out. "The university has been cutting our budget for years; Nicky's found another source of income and now the university doesn't like this either. It's hardly fair, is it?"

Silence.

"Well, is it?" Merryweather repeated.

Her question went unanswered. There was a further pause, and Tom held his breath as he reached onto the desk for his calculator before placing it carefully in his rucksack.

The stern man spoke.

"For the last time, Nick has to drop this extra-curricular stuff once and for all. No more arguments. I am trying to protect you both."

"Protect us?" shouted the younger man. "How is telling me to stop doing extra work – work that is necessary to supplement my research funding – supposed to protect us?"

Tom made his way to the door and gently turned the handle.

"Because if you don't, you are giving them the perfect excuse to get rid of you – and believe me, they've been looking for a way to do that for months now. There simply isn't the money…"

"Rubbish!" snorted Merryweather.

Tom didn't think he had ever heard her as angry as she sounded right now.

"Octavia, you may not like the truth – goodness knows, I don't much like it myself – but that's what it is. Nick must drop the work for Gris Corp right now or else… well, you know the consequences. I'm here to warn you that it's out of my hands. There's nothing more I can do. Nothing. At. All."

There was the sound of a hand hitting a wooden desk.

"I am NOT standing for this," shouted Merryweather.

Time to go, thought Tom, and he slipped out the front door of Merryweather's office and set off once more into the chilly corridor, leaving the three grown-ups to their not very Christmassy argument.

CHAPTER TWO

The Shadow walked down the street, checking in passing shop windows that there was no one who was taking a similar route to his own or who was zig-zagging along the street as he traversed it. He walked like this for two blocks, dodging the puddles forming on the pavements, his collar upturned against the howling wind that was chasing the nocturnal raindrops through the Parisian streets.

He grimaced once again at this most foul of evenings: the once vertical rain was now increasingly horizontal and turning heavier by the minute. He took a sharp right turn into a narrower street and paused about a third of the way down it, next to a small, bashed-up scooter, and began fiddling with its ignition.

Hoisting a backpack over both his shoulders, he jumped onto the spluttering scooter. He shoved it backwards with his feet and the machine rolled onto the road. Given that it was mid-evening, the traffic had quietened down from its rush hour peak. He hoped he could complete the next part of his journey in under five minutes.

He revved the throttle, and the bike sped off, droning and buzzing like an angry metallic wasp. The Shadow weaved in and out of the cars that still semi-blocked the road ahead and kept his speed at a steady 35 miles per hour. There was no point in attracting any undue attention. He stopped at the two red lights en route and thought ruefully to himself that this was typical: always red when one needed them to be green.

He rode for four blocks in this stop-start manner before rounding a sharp left-hand corner onto a road that diverged in two in a Y-shaped junction. The Shadow took the left-hand fork and rode on into the darkness. There were few streetlights on this backstreet and the only light he could rely on was from the puny front headlamp on the scooter, and even this barely illuminated his way. As he rode on, semi-blind, his eyes were already tiring from following the small spotlight which was picking out the road ahead of him.

The Shadow knew he did not have long to reach the rendezvous point he had arranged, were Plan B for the fifth stage of his contract to become the sole option. Which, earlier this afternoon, it had. Once more, he cursed the over-zealous security guard at the Bibliothèque de St. Nicholas who had prevented him from entering the building with his rucksack. Such diligence was always irksome, but in this instance, it had also foiled the Shadow's original plan to procure an archaic floor plan of the Basilica de Noël, in which lay another batch of the relics of St Nicholas. Rumour had it that a clutch of the Saint's long-lost gold coins were also secreted somewhere inside the ancient church. Which, had he been able to locate them, would have represented a decent bonus payment that his current employers need never have known about. Now, however, because of the extra time he had had to spend setting up his alternative break-in plan, he was unlikely to find the coins.

As he sped on, he wondered how long his associates would wait for him. Always work solo, he reminded himself, and shook his head at ignoring his own sound advice.

The sole headlight continued to bob up and down as the Shadow made his way down the pot-holed backstreet, with the scooter jolting and jarring him as he did so; its light was so puny that the Shadow almost parted company with the scooter when a man dressed completely in black, swarthy, unshaven and with a swathe of unkempt curly hair stepped out from behind one of the crumbling buildings on the pock-marked side street and directly into the Shadow's path.

"Gomez! Good grief, I nearly hit you," the Shadow exclaimed as his ride skidded to a halt.

The man shrugged.

"But you didn't. Leave that thing and follow me. We don't have much time."

The Shadow turned off the scooter and propped it up against a nearby wall, making a half-hearted attempt to cover it with a couple of cardboard boxes lying nearby. Gomez was already striding towards the door in one of the tumbledown buildings.

"Quickly, in here." He motioned the Shadow to follow him inside. The Shadow did so and closed the door behind him. It was pitch black. Gomez produced a torch and flicked it on. The Shadow could pick out nothing much other than puddles and the sounds of something – indeed, many things - scurrying across the empty floor.

"Rats," he muttered. "Oh good." But this was no time to be squeamish. Gomez had broken into a jog and was heading for the other side of the building.

"Shortcut," he whispered at the Shadow, as his footsteps echoed off the graffiti-covered walls.

They reached the other side and exited the room into a corridor. The Shadow could make out a tangle of pipes on the wall and surmised that they must be in the building's basement, near the heating plant. Which was good because it meant they were going in the right direction towards the sewer system.

Sure enough, at the end of the corridor, Gomez motioned for the Shadow to follow him through a smaller wooden door, through which the Shadow had to duck, and then down a set of old and slippery stone stairs.

The sounds of their footsteps were more muffled now as they made their way down the stairs at speed. Gomez drew to a halt at the foot of the stairs.

"Slowly now," he said, pointing the torch at the ground. "One slip and you will fall in there."

The Shadow took the point. They were now next to an underground water culvert of some sort, which in the darkness looked icy cold, black and unwelcoming.

The pair of them inched their way along the path until it turned into more of a ledge. In fact, it became so narrow that the Shadow felt sure he was going to slip off and into the water with each step he took.

No rats now – please, he thought to himself.

Just as the Shadow thought the ledge couldn't become any narrower, Gomez disappeared around a corner. The Shadow hesitated. Had Gomez fallen in? He had heard no splash; then again, the sounds in this place were disorientating and playing tricks with his mind. He received his answer in a matter of seconds as Gomez stuck his head back around the corner and motioned towards the Shadow urgently.

"Come on, Monsieur. We are nearly there."

The Shadow hugged himself to the wall as he slid his way around the corner and found himself on a much wider path on the other side.

"See, it is easier," said Gomez.

"Yes, yes, it is," the Shadow replied.

They proceeded for another fifty yards when Gomez halted.

"We wait here," he said.

The Shadow did not need to be told twice. The two men were now far beneath the city centre of Paris, waiting in an old, dank tunnel that the Shadow hoped was part of the underground sewerage network. Otherwise, he had endured this descent into the dark, dank gloom for nothing. The two men stood silent in the tunnel, each counting the seconds and then the minutes to the steady sound of drips from the tunnel's slimy moss-covered ceiling and the shuffling and scratching of various rodents as they hurried around their underground lair. It was not, the Shadow reflected, the sort of place one would wish to find oneself in for any length of time; he had already been there far too long.

The drips continued to fall into the inky water below, interspersed with scrabbling noises when Gomez grabbed the Shadow's arm and pointed. Straining his eyes, he peered through the darkness and saw a more irregular series of ripples disturbing the surface of the water. The ripples drew closer to the edge where he and Gomez now perched. The Shadow thought he could make out a shape moving under the water and was peering over the edge of the ledge to obtain a better view when a diver's head popped out of the murk as he swam the final few yards towards the pair of them.

"Quick," said Gomez. "Help me lift him out."

The Shadow almost gagged as he did so. The smell surrounding them was a mixture of cold, semi-stagnant water and the harsh stench of dilute sewage. It was not a place for any kind of swimming.

The Shadow and Gomez hauled the diver up onto the ledge and helped him take off his breathing apparatus and mask.

"Well," asked The Shadow, "do you have it?"

"Yes," the diver replied. He reached inside his suit and produced a small package wrapped in black plastic.

The Shadow suppressed a grin as he took the package. It looked intact.

"May I?" he asked the diver.

"Of course."

The Shadow took out a knife and sliced the adhesive tape binding the package together. He unpeeled several layers of thick black waterproof wrapping until he reached a solid plastic capsule, snapped tightly shut. He undid the clasp fastening it and saw his prize: he had the Loci map, the map that would take him to the precise spot where the Parisian relics lay.

He reached inside his jacket and handed a bulging envelope to the diver.

"Your fee, Monsieur."

The diver nodded, placed the envelope inside his diving suit and nodded a thank you towards the Shadow. He replaced his air tank and mask before he slipped back into the dark water and disappeared from view.

The Shadow's phone buzzed. Again. That was the third time so far this evening. He was brief and to the point as he answered it.

"I have it. Now I wait for the chimes."

From the other end of the phone came one word. "Good."

The Shadow ended the call, switched the phone off and turned to Gomez.

"Where's the car?"

"Around the block." Gomez indicated with a nod of his head in the general direction of the car's location.

"Let's go."

The Shadow had never felt happier leaving a place – not even prison – as they had made their way out of the sewer. The stench of the sewers and the echoes of the scrabbling rats lingered in his mind. He reminded himself of the gold that awaited him and decided that it would all have been worth it. Just about.

The Shadow and Gomez reached the car in a couple of minutes: a black nondescript saloon – complete with tinted windows - and, as the Shadow recalled, not an especially fast model, but it was inconspicuous, and exactly what he needed. The pair of them got into the car. Gomez drove. They travelled for just over half a mile before stopping on a side street opposite a side door of the Basilica de Noël – the fifth target. The church was in darkness, exactly as the Shadow had expected. It was a Thursday night; mass was long since over and there was no reason for the church to be lit up any longer. He checked his watch. Almost 10.30pm.

"What now?" asked Gomez.

"We wait for an hour," replied the Shadow.

"Why an hour?"

"You'll see shortly."

Gomez sighed and looked out the windscreen of the car down the road ahead. It was deserted. He looked across at the dark, hulking shape of the gothic church once more. It was unchanged: still in darkness. Gomez fidgeted and blew bubbles with his chewing gum. The Shadow ignored him and stared impassively directly ahead, straight down the street in front of him. Gomez stole the occasional glance at him, before eventually plucking up the courage to ask the question that was bugging him.

"What are you looking at?" Gomez asked.

"Not looking at; looking for – and who," the Shadow replied.

"Ok, *who* are you looking for?"

"No one – yet." The Shadow was curt. Then he added, "I'm waiting for someone in particular to arrive, okay?"

It was not a question that demanded an answer nor any further enquiry.

Gomez paused and shrugged his shoulders.

"Whatever you say."

The silence in the anonymous car resumed.

The Shadow and Gomez sat there, in the cold and the dark, the rain lashing off the car's windscreen the only sound, for a further hour. The more Gomez fidgeted, sighed, and blew chewing gum bubbles, the more grateful his companion became that he would not be spending very much longer with him. The Shadow's eyes darted like a lizard's, stealing a glance at the church's clock. 11.30pm. Any moment now.

And there he was. The church's night-watchman, ambling along the street after an evening drinking whisky in the local bar. Not, as the Shadow had noted over several months, the most careful nor punctual of men, but he usually made it to the church each night around this time and was always gone by midnight.

"There he is," said the Shadow.

Gomez looked up.

"Him? That's the guy you were waiting for?"

"That's him. Now, do exactly as I said: wait here. I'll be back in 30 minutes. And stay out of sight."

The Shadow silently opened the car door and slid out of the car into the rain and the shadows, where he waited. Gomez slunk down in his seat so as not to be seen, though given the car's current location and its darkened windows, this risk was minimal.

The nightwatchman sauntered his way up to the side door of the church and fumbled in his pockets for a bunch of keys. Having produced these, he then spent several seconds going through the keys one by one until he alighted on the one for the side door, put it in the lock, turned it and the door opened. Had he perhaps had a couple of whiskies fewer that evening, he might have noticed that the door failed to make its usual rustic creaking sound as it swung open. The Shadow silently congratulated himself once again as the door opened without a sound.

The nightwatchman closed the door behind him, and the Shadow began counting to one hundred. As he reached the ton, he made his move and hurried to the side door. With his eyes darting in all directions almost simultaneously, he opened the door and disappeared from sight.

Inside the church, it was no longer dark, but the light was so dim as to be useless. This suited the Shadow perfectly, as he crept his way into an anteroom in the nave of the Basilica. There, he waited in the pitch black.

There was no sound for a further ten minutes and then he heard it. The steady pad, squeak, pad, squeak of the night-watchman's shoes, accompanied by a faint whistling and the jangling of keys. He was returning to the side-door. On this occasion, the Shadow was content to let him leave unhindered.

He heard the church's side door handle being turned and then the snapping shut of the door and the locking of it. The whistling grew fainter and fainter, before being replaced by silence.

The Shadow slipped out of the room and put on his red beam torch. He brought the Loci map out of his inside pocket and glanced at it, before setting off down the passage of the church which lay towards its rear. He arrived at the first of three wooden doors leading down into the crypt. He had picked the lock of the first one in fifteen seconds flat and continued along the corridor to the second door, trying its handle. As he expected, it opened first time. Ah yes, he thought, our night-watchman is a creature of habit, is he not? Do not bother with any effort which is more than is strictly necessary. Only lock the primary door.

The Shadow paced his way along the old corridor, the red light picking out the ancient stone. The corridor was airless but dry; at least this time, he consoled himself, it wasn't full of rats. He reached the third door, turned the handle and once more, it opened first time. Oh, my friend, the Shadow thought, you will have no small amount of explaining to do to your masters as to why these doors were not forced.

He looked at the tattered map in his hands to confirm his next move before proceeding down the stairs into the crypt. As he had expected, the crypt itself was rather more damp than the upstairs corridor. He shone the torch towards the stone inserts, counting these from left to right, looking for one particular tomb amongst those of many ancient long-forgotten French merchant families, until he alighted on one with a small, discoloured stone, barely discernible from the others. He stepped towards it and pressed the stone. It swung sideways to reveal a small locking mechanism that the Shadow knew would be more of a challenge to pick. The prize for successfully doing so would be access to the tomb that contained the next batch of relics. The beam of the torch flashed on the inscriptions of the ageing stones all around him and as he ran it along the back wall of the crypt, he picked out a wooden sign bearing the legend, "St Nicholas".

The Shadow walked around the tomb. His mouth was dry. He had been a professional criminal all his life but, until this assignment, he had never yet had cause to rob from a grave. He reminded himself that this was not a true grave or that if it was, it was only one of many, and in any case, how could any man have more than one grave? But this was no ordinary man. This was the tomb of a saint and, even for the Shadow, breaking into churches and pilfering from ancient tombs represented a crossing the Rubicon moment. Or rather, moments. Even though this was the fifth instance of him doing so, it did not become any easier. He compromised: closing his eyes, he crossed himself and muttered "amen" under his breath, vowing to do something vaguely good with whatever gold he found inside the casket and consoling himself that this was the penultimate stage of this job.

Taking the Loci map from his pocket, he paused briefly to wonder at how such an ancient lock could be so impenetrable, but stopped before he thought for too long. He had turned this over and over in his mind and had run the gamut of many thoughts, ranging from 'had some ancient genius designed the lock?' to whether there had been some sort of magic or holy act involved in its creation. But now, he had the map, complete with instructions about the lock on the tomb itself. He began his work.

Several minutes passed, and the Shadow was now sweating. This lock was difficult and stiff – it had not been designed to be opened easily and nor had it been. For centuries. Finally, he managed to twist the key into place. The lock's mechanism gave and started opening. The Shadow turned it a full six times before he heard the satisfying clunk that told him the lock was now fully open.

Ok, he thought, let's see what we have in here.

He opened the lid of the tomb to reveal a lead casket within. With some effort, he slid the top of the casket aside enough to reveal its interior and turned the torch on it. There were a few bones, some scraps of what looked like paper and a large piece of ornate cloth. The Shadow took this to be St Nicholas' bishop's cowl. He began to lift them out and place them into his rucksack.

As he moved the remnants of the cowl, it was surprisingly heavy. He weighed it in his hands. This was too heavy simply to be cloth alone. He felt around the seams at the edge of the robe and picked at it. The stitching gave way easily and several golden coins tumbled to the floor, clanking as they hit the stone below. The Shadow bent down and picked one up. He rubbed it and revealed its true face to the world for the first time in centuries. It was true then: someone had indeed buried St Nicholas with his gold – at least in this tomb.

The Shadow hurriedly tore at the rest of the cloth until he had all the gold coins from it; he placed them into a separate compartment in his rucksack. His secret bonus was secure. He ran his hand around the tomb. Nothing remained. Time to leave. Replacing the tomb lid to leave it as he had found it, he began retracing his steps out of the crypt and along the corridor back to the front of the church, carefully closing each door behind him as he went, including the first door to the corridor which he locked behind himself. There was, he reasoned, no need to leave any clues which would raise the alarm any sooner than was necessary.

With this door secure, the Shadow turned towards the back of the church. There was no point in trying to break out the front. Too obvious. He could pick the lock readily but would then be exposed in the street as he tried to relock the front door. No, there was a better way.

The Shadow darted around the back of an ornate font and into another of the church's small anterooms. This one looked like some sort of kitchen, insofar as it had a sink and a bin. He stood on the bin to reach a small window, which was on nothing more than a snib, and wedged it open as far as he could. He dumped the rucksack through it and prised himself through the gap and onto the ledge below. Catching his breath, he unwedged the snib and let the window slip back into place, wondering how long it would be before anyone noticed that someone had tampered with it.

He jumped down from the ledge, collected the rucksack and made his way towards the railings that enclosed this part of the Basilica's grounds. He then hoisted himself over the railings and dropped onto the pavement below. He glanced quickly up and down the deserted street. It had been a good evening's work.

As he rounded the corner of the street and strode towards the car, Gomez switched on the engine. The Shadow opened the passenger door and got in the car.

"Everything okay?" asked Gomez.

"Fine. Go," replied The Shadow as he reached into his jacket for another stuffed envelope.

"This is for you. For your help. And now, you will forget all of this ever happened. Do you understand?"

"Of course, Monsieur. Who are you again?" asked Gomez, cracking a nervous smile.

"Good. To the airport. I've a jet to catch."

The Shadow pulled out his mobile phone and punched in a phone number, grinning broadly as he did so. This call was going to give him a lot of satisfaction.

The phone rang once before the lifeless voice answered.

"Yes?"

"Stage five is complete."

"Good."

"Is the transport ready?"

"Of course."

"I'm on my way."

"Good. You have only a few more days."

The line went dead.

The Shadow smiled again. He was back on schedule and tonight had also increased his fee. For the first time in months, the end was now in sight.

CHAPTER THREE

Tom slammed the front door of the wee house shut as he announced his return.

"Hi Mum. Hi Nan."

"Hi there. How did you get on?" came a shout from the other end of the house.

Tom dropped his rucksack onto the floor and traipsed through the hallway to the kitchen, where his mum was in the middle of making dinner.

"B minus."

"See, I told you," said his mum.

"Well done, Tom. You're a clever boy," chipped in his nan. She was sitting at the big, round wooden table at the faraway end of the kitchen, sipping her usual cup of tea and watching the small television in the corner. Tom went over and gave first his nan and then his mum a hug.

"Well, Auntieprof said the same thing. She says I need to have more faith in myself."

"Well, you do. That's good though, especially seeing how worried you've been about it."

"I know, Mum."

"How was Octavia anyway? How's she doing?"

"Fine," said Tom. "She was just busy as usual. Had a meeting after I left."

He didn't think that this was the right time to share that he had overheard a huge row between Merryweather and the other two gentlemen, mainly because he knew he wasn't meant to have heard it.

"Hope you passed on my best wishes to her for Christmas," said his mum.

"Mine, too." said Mrs Brightly senior.

"Er, yes, I did. She said Merry Christmas, too."

"Didn't you forget to take something with you?" asked his mum.

"Er…" mumbled Tom.

His mum nodded her head towards the kitchen dresser next to the table. On it, sat a Christmas present with a white envelope propped up against it.

"Aw no," sighed Tom.

"Octavia's Christmas card and present?"

Tom rolled his eyes.

"Sorry. I'll drop it off to her after school tomorrow."

"Good lad. Now, go get changed and come and have your tea. You look frozen."

"It's Baltic all right."

"Is that you all ready for the big race tomorrow?" asked Tom's nan.

"Think so, but I'm still not sure about the sledge. It's pretty ancient now."

"I remember your dad's first race. He was so nervous before it." said his nan. "Then, he crashed – oh, it was awful. Thought he'd broken himself, but he was fine of course."

Tom had heard this tale about half a dozen times already this month, but his nan was on a roll now.

"'You need to be more careful,' your grandpa and I told him, but it was no use. He only had one way of racing – full speed. You make sure you take care tomorrow – and wear a helmet."

"Yes, Nan," said Tom.

"Right, you two. Tea's being dished up. Tom, go and get changed."

Tom headed out of the kitchen and up the stairs to his bedroom.

"And Tom," his mum continued, "have you packed your things for staying at Jack's?"

"Yes, Mum."

"Are his mum and dad still okay with it?"

"Ye-es, Mum."

"Good lad. That's your soup out."

Tom was halfway up the stairs and paused on the landing to look out the window.

"Rats. Still clear – come on snow, where are you?"

He really did not want to race on the artificial ski slope the next day, but the first snowfall of the winter seemed as elusive as ever.

CHAPTER FOUR

"Brightly…"

Tom tried his best not to look nervous as HH (short for Horrible Hurndall), his maths teacher, half dropped, half threw his test paper onto his desk.

"What a pity it is, Mister Brightly, that when it comes to maths, you cannot live up to your surname. C plus, a slight improvement upon your previous performance. MEF."

"MEF, sir?"

"More Effort Required, Brightly."

Tom's face burned red, to the accompaniment of sniggers from the rear of the classroom. HH continued his post-test rounds, dispensing his own brand of Christmas cheer to Tom's classmates, one by one (and in random order).

"Wanless…"

Jack Wanless, sitting at the desk next to Tom's, braced himself for the worst.

"Well, Wanless, you have surpassed yourself this term. You have clearly been spending too much time with Mister Brightly."

"Or playing that stupid game," came a heckle from the back row of the classroom.

"Yes, thank you, Branning."

The owner of the heckle, an untidy, sharp-faced boy with greasy black hair, lounged back in his chair, a smug smile spreading across his thin-lipped mouth, as HH threw Jack's paper onto his desk.

"D minus, Wanless. *Worse* than October. In fact, rather pathetic. Well adrift."

Cue more sniggers.

Jack Wanless shook his head of curls, puffed his cheeks out and looked skywards. He turned to Tom, who was still blushing, and gave a huge roll of his eyes. Tom silently nodded and pointed with his pencil to the clock at the front of the austere classroom, which ticked on as HH zig-zagged from desk to desk. Jack understood his friend's signal and glanced up at it: in under a minute, their maths torture would be over for the term. He smiled at the thought.

"Branning…"

"Yes, sir," the still-lounging youth smirked. His surrounding pals joined in the sniggering.

"A minus. MBE."

"MBE, sir?" Branning's voice was full of the fake curiosity of someone who already knew the answer to the question.

"Much Better Effort, Branning."

"Why, thank you, sir," Branning replied with fake sincerity.

Jack turned to face Tom. "No way," hissed Jack. "He must have seen the questions."

"I know," said Tom, "he's going to be even more insufferable than usual."

"Quietly now," HH instructed. He had returned to the front of the classroom and gazed over the heads of the entire class, into the middle distance.

"Sometimes, I wonder how many of you are paying attention in class. These results would suggest not very many. Those of you who have scored badly, and we *all* know who you are, have work to do over the Christmas holidays."

The bell marking the end of the period began clanging.

HH continued with a shout over the noise of the bell and the twenty-five chattering schoolchildren who were bundling their possessions and themselves towards the door,

"Make sure you do it and I'll see you back here in a few weeks. A Merry Christmas to you all."

"Merry Christmas, sir," responded most of the class (Branning and his acolytes didn't bother).

Tom and Jack had stuffed their papers and textbooks into their rucksacks at speed and led the charge to the door.

"Thank goodness that's over," said Tom.

"You've got that right. What a *total* 'mare. Mum and Dad are going to flip when they find out I got a D minus," said Jack, "and how did Branning - *Branning* of all people - get an A minus?"

"I know. That makes no sense. He's never worth an A minus."

"At least it's over now. Race time! You ready?"

"Sort of," said Tom, but in a way that suggested he was anything but prepared.

"You okay? Want a sweet?"

Jack thrust a small paper bag of sweets towards his friend.

"McCrindall's finest buttery toffee gooballs," said Jack with a gleeful smile.

"No thanks. Bit nervous to be honest. Feel like I'm gonna puke.

"You'll be fine. You're good at this. Here, take a bag for later. I've got loads."

Jack produced another small paper bag, similarly bulging with gooballs, from his other pocket to make the point.

"Thanks," said Tom as he took the first bag of sweets. He stopped and turned to Jack, looking very serious. "Thing is, everyone always says I'll be fine, but I'm worried: the sledge is ancient now."

"How ancient?"

"As in, it was my dad's."

"What, his *actual* sledge?"

Tom nodded.

"You never told me that before. That's epic! Where is it?"

"In my locker," Tom replied.

"Can I see it?"

"S'pose so." Tom shrugged.

They walked down the corridor to the lockers. Tom fished around in his pocket for his key and opened his locker door. There, lying under the heaps of detritus that only young boys can keep in their lockers, including football cards, magazines, various out-of-date foodstuffs and muddy clothes, was an old-looking wooden sledge.

Tom reached under the pile of gubbins and yanked it out.

"Woooowww," said Jack. "The sledge of legend."

"The one and only Ptarmigan Mark II," said Tom, but with little enthusiasm. He had had this conversation before.

"What's this at the front?" Jack pointed at a small handle that didn't appear to be attached to anything.

"It was the brake."

"What happened?"

"My dad took it off. He figured he wouldn't need it."

"Your dad sounds epic."

"Yeah. He was cool."

"And how does this work?" Jack was now twisting the twin skis at the front of the sledge back and forth.

"That's the steering. You know the luge in the Winter Olympics?"

"What, the tea tray on ice thingy?"

"That's the one," laughed Tom. "This is a variation on it from the late 1970s – before it all went fully plastic and modern."

Tom started putting on his ski kit over his civvies (a traditional concession for the last day of term for those participating in the Annual Sledging Championship). He went to stuff the bag of sweets into one of the pockets of his ski jacket and then realised it already contained the Christmas card and present for his aunt, so he quickly shoved the bag into an alternative pocket. He was in the middle of zipping up his jacket when the locker door slammed shut. Tom whirled around to see Branning's sneering face as he and his entourage sloped around the corner, blocking Tom and Jack's path.

"All right, losers? On our way to the race, are we?" asked Branning, looking even more snide and smug than usual. By his side were two of his fellow back row hecklers, Willis and McDaid. Each looked more unpleasant than the other.

"Get lost, Branning," said Tom.

Branning turned to the mini-fan club surrounding him and repeated Tom's words in a mocking tone.

"Oooh, did you hear that, lads? 'Get lost, Branning'... listen to the tough guy," he hissed. His acolytes laughed at the non-joke.

"How'd you do it, Branning?" asked Jack.

"Do what?"

"You know – the A minus? How did *you,* of all people, manage that?"

"Hard work, Wanless. You should try it sometime," sneered Branning.

"Aye, right," snorted Jack.

Branning grabbed Jack's blazer by the lapels and hoisted him up to his rat-like face.

"What are you insinuating, Wanless?"

"You know full well…"

"You'd better watch your mouth, trog."

Tom intervened, "Let him go, Branning."

"Oooh, what have we here, lads? Listen to the scholarship boy."

Branning released Jack and turned on Tom.

"What's it like to be poor, Brightly?"

"Shut it, Branning."

"Yeah?" sneered Branning. "Are you gonna make me?"

"You're not worth it," said Tom.

"I'm worth more than you, poorboy. What have you got for the race then? A bin bag?" This remark brought more derisory laughter from Branning's two-strong fan club.

Tom's face turned red once more, but this time, the look on his face wasn't one of embarrassment. He was fizzing.

"My dad's sledge," said Tom.

Jack shot his friend a look. He could sense when the red mist was about to descend on Tom, and it was dangerously close now.

Branning was unrelenting.

"That thing? It must be an antique by now. You sure it'll make it to the end?" Branning, Willis and McDaid laughed at another non-joke once again.

"Yeah, well, we'll see, won't we?" said Tom.

Branning stuck his face directly into Tom's and hissed his reply, "Yeah, pauper boy, we'll see. My family's held this title for five years straight now and you'd better not do anything to end that run – or I'll end your run. Your sledging run. Geddit?"

He turned to Willis and McDaid, who, after a brief satellite delay, laughed excessively at Branning's latest attempt at humour. The three of them shouldered their way past Tom and Jack and wandered off down the corridor, before Branning gave a last shout.

"Good luck, poorboy. You're going to need it!"

Jack took one look at his friend's face and saw that he needed to deploy soothing words.

"Ignore him. He's a muppet."

"A cheat, more like," replied Tom. "Think I'll have one of those gooballs after all."

He reached into his jacket pocket and pulled out a now less than bulging bag.

"Aw no, they've fallen out and gone down a hole in my pocket."

"Least you've still got some left for the race. Come on, we'd better move it. We've got ten minutes."

Tom locked the door to his locker and hoisted the ancient sledge over his shoulders and the pair of them set off down the corridor. People were bustling in the same direction, all heading towards the sports field and the dry ski slope which stood at the end of the field which was farthest from the school itself. Tom picked up his pace, so much so that Jack was almost having to break into a run to keep up with him. As they neared the end of the main corridor and dived down a side-corridor, they went past the

Sixth Form Common Room. The door was ajar. This was a room into which the juniors in the school were never allowed to enter under any circumstances.

Jack spotted the door first.

"Oooh look, the door's open."

They both stopped stock still.

"Shall we have a quick peek?" asked Jack. "I've always wanted to know what they do in there all day."

"Just a quick look then."

Tom set down his sledge and they edged their way in through the door. The scene inside made it look as though the place had been burgled. There was rubbish everywhere: bulging black bin bags, old takeaway boxes, newspapers, magazines, bowls and plates of mouldy food, random items of clothing, shoes (mainly muddy) and trainers (ditto) throughout. In the centre of it all, half-buried was what looked as though it had once been a three-piece suite and presiding over the entire dump was a massive widescreen television, with the News Channel blaring away to an invisible audience.

Tom and Jack stood open-mouthed at the sight that confronted them.

"It's like my locker," said Tom finally, "but worse."

"And bigger," said Jack, with authority.

"How do they get away with it? If my room was like this, mum would totally be on my case all the time."

"Dunno, maybe Old Hendo just turns a blind eye – wait. Look!"

Their eyes fixed on the television as it began playing dramatic music, which announced that *something-very-important-was-about-to happen.*

"THE HEADLINES AT 11 O'CLOCK… and we have some Breaking News: Gris Corp has just announced that, with the Christmas Eve deadline fast approaching, the winner of Apotheosis has yet to be found. The virtual gaming sensation has swept the globe, capturing the imagination of children worldwide as they strive to become the All-Time Global Gaming Champion and win their own instant social media platform and £100 million to set up their brand. Here's what Max Gris herself had to say just a few moments ago."

Tom and Jack stood, transfixed, as a tall, willowy woman, dressed in a sharp power suit, styled for her individually and with slicked back, curly hair, brought firmly under control with a ton of hair products, and wearing a shock of red lipstick, began looking directly into the camera and spoke.

"Good morning, everyone. Well, this is our regular daily update, and I can report that…"

Max Gris let the words hang in the air for several seconds before she continued.

"… we do *not* yet have our winner. However, there are still a few days to go before the Christmas Eve deadline and I am *certain* we will find the ultimate girl or boy gamer – our new global superstar."

Tom and Jack both simultaneously fist-pumped.

"Yeeeeesssss!" they shouted in unison.

The news cut back to the studio, where the presenter paraphrased the very words that had just been uttered as part of his 'analysis'.

"C'mon, we'd better move it before we're late," said Tom, looking at his watch.

"It's still up for grabs!" shouted Jack as the two of them exited the sixth-formers' indoor rubbish dump and began running down the corridor. "TRAAAAAAA!"

The television continued blaring away as the news rolled onto its next item.

"Now, scientists are warning that the biggest solar storm since the Victorian age could be about to hit the Earth. What does that mean for us, and is it really going to happen? Our science reporter spoke to me earlier…"

CHAPTER FIVE

Tom fiddled with the strap of his crash helmet for the umpteenth time in the past five minutes. It was still chafing into his jaw and generally annoying him. His mouth was dry, he felt as though he was going to puke and, as for his stomach, it simply felt weird. He checked the zip on his jacket once again and buttoned and unbuttoned his jacket pockets several times in quick succession. In short, he was fidgeting. Lots. Trying to take his mind off the race. Which was proving difficult, given he was currently sitting on his dad's ancient wooden sledge at the very top of Playfair School's very own custom-built dry ski slope, a feature unique to the school and one it had prided itself on for decades. Likewise, the Annual Sledging Championship, which had been a tradition in the school from the days when it used to be held on actual snow (most years).

At this precise moment, Tom wished he was anywhere else other than where he was: lined up with five other pupils from his year and the year above in the first of the four heats to determine the semi-finalists, and ultimately, the finalists for the championship. His head was swimming; all he could see were rows and rows of cheering faces, his fellow Playfairians, several deep, lining the slope all the way down from its top to the flattened stopping area at the very bottom that backed onto the rugby pitches. In their midst, dotted throughout, was the school's entire complement of teachers, with Old Hendo (Mr Henderson, the headmaster), on PA duty as usual, ready to give his annual, much-loved commentary on the proceedings.

Right now, Tom couldn't hear much other than the sound of his own heart pumping furiously as his eyes went out of focus. He loved sledging, but this was awful. Everyone was looking at him and his five fellow contestants, one of whom was, naturally, Branning. Two places along the starting line from him, black-helmeted, jacketed and trousered, and ready to hit the slope on the latest Snowscooter Deluxe.

Through his wooziness, he heard Old Hendo's booming tones.

"Good morning, everyone, and welcome to the running of Playfair's 98th Annual Sledging Championship, one of the school's most ancient and much-loved traditions and a sure sign every year, snow or no snow, that Christmastide will soon be upon us.

"Now, I want you to welcome the six competitors in the first heat of this year's competition, drawn from the very best sledders from the first and second forms of the senior school. Please give them all a very warm round of applause if you would and especially as for four of them, this is their first ever appearance in the Championship and it is a proud moment for all concerned – a true sign of being in the 'Big School'.

The assembled crowd lining the slopes clapped and there were sporadic whoops and cheering as Old Hendo began reading out the names of the first heat's contenders in alphabetical order.

"Branning....

A mini roar went up from the acolytes and a few other stragglers over the general hubbub.

"Brightly....

"Come on, Tom!" Jack's voice pierced the air, and there was a ripple of laughter from the crowd at his enthusiasm and loudness.

"Harrington... Smithson minor... Tempest... and Verigula."

The list was complete. The crowd was still looking very blurry to Tom's eyes and the next announcement sounded as though it came from a long way away.

"S1 and S2 contenders, please take your marks."

Tom stood up and shuffled Ptarmigan II and himself forward, before digging his boots into the artificial slope, with the sledge to his right, and both hands gripping its steering bar.

There was a brief pause.

"*SET…*" Tom flipped down the visor on his helmet.

The next pause felt interminable, though it only endured for a few seconds.

And then…

CRACK!

Old Hendo had fired the starting pistol. Tom lunged forward, both hands grabbing for the steering frame at the very front of the sledge to shove it as far as he could as quickly as he could before the first tricky manoeuvre. He had one chance to nail this, sprinting aside the sledge as the slope fell away underneath him. He jumped sideways as it did so and landed head-first and on his stomach on the main board of the sledge. He was racing.

Headfirst, with his head lifted upwards and tilted back as far as it could go, all he could see in front of him was the artificial slope. It looked endless. But there was no one in the corners of his eyes. Was he in the lead? His thoughts raced as he fought the sledges steering, using all his strength to keep it going in a straight line as it buckled and jolted and tried its hardest to veer first one way, then the other. Tom was winning the battle against his sledge and the race itself. He was flying down the slope.

And then, he wasn't.

He felt it first as a jolt running through the part of the sledge that was underneath and beyond his right leg, a jolt that ricocheted through the whole of Ptarmigan II, instantaneously jerking the steering from his hands, and spinning the sledge sideways. At high speed.

The last thing Tom saw as his world imploded around him was a flash of black streaking past, laughing as it did so.

His race was over in under a second as he and Ptarmigan II combined into a spinning, roiling mess of boy and wooden sledge and the mix of the two of them birled their way directly off the side of the artificial ski slope around halfway down it and into the crash barriers which lined the slope from top to bottom.

Tom didn't move. He opened his eyes first. They were still working. Then he heard the noise of the crowd being more muffled and subdued than it had been previously, and there was no longer any cheering. It took Tom several seconds to realise that there were shouts of concern, screams and gasps – all in his general direction.

"Brightly… Brightly…"

HH was huffing and puffing towards Tom, who still hadn't moved.

"Brightly, are you all right? Brightly, can you hear me?"

He was standing directly over Tom now, his face looking as though something awful had just happened.

Tom opened his mouth.

"Sir…"

To Tom's relief, his mouth still worked.

"Brightly, can you move? Does anything hurt?"

Right now, thought Tom, everything hurts.

"I think so," he replied as he levered himself up onto an elbow and then, with some effort, raised himself up towards a more vertical position.

The crowd started cheering and hollering at his resurrection.

Then, he saw Ptarmigan II – or what remained of it. The old sledge had endured the impact, but it had not ended well for her. The steering was smashed and a chunk of the rear of the sledge was hanging off, connected by only a couple of metal rods that had once been part of the steering system.

"Can you walk, Brightly?"

"Think so, sir."

"Come on then. Best get you off here and make sure you're okay."

Tom looked at his battered sledge and then glanced around at the crowd, who were now breaking into sympathetic applause. He clenched his fists.

"I want to finish, sir."

"What? Don't be daft. Pick up your bits and pieces and let's get you checked out."

Tom stopped, span around and looked straight at HH.

"No."

Wincing with each step, he limped towards Ptarmigan II, hoisted what was left of her over his shoulders and started tramping his way down the slope, picking out each footstep with care.

"Brightly, come back here!" shouted HH.

"See you at the finish line, sir," shouted Tom in return as he continued his trudge.

The entire school was now cheering and going nuts with applause, whooping and hollering. And then, the chanting started.

"Brightly, Brightly…"

With each step Tom took, the chanting became louder.

Clenching his teeth, Tom stared straight ahead and plodded on through the second half of his race. Meanwhile, at the finish line. Branning and his acolytes, who had been laughing and celebrating his win, noticed the mood of the crowd changing and that it was not in their favour.

"Huh. Cheering on a loser," muttered Branning. "Come on, let's get the Snowscooter ready for the final." He, Willis and McDaid slunk their way out of the finishing arena and disappeared through the crowd.

Tom finally walked across the finish line to loud cheering; he was immediately engulfed by Jack and a crowd of people who had barely acknowledged him in his first few months at the school, all of them slapping him on the back and saying how well he had done and that he had shown the true spirit of the school.

From the PA system came Old Hendo's booming voice.

"Finally, in sixth position, Brightly, in the slowest time ever recorded for the race – but also one of the bravest. 6 minutes, 39.72 seconds. Well done.

"And to confirm, after the first heat of this year's competition, the course record remains at 1 minute, 1.32 seconds, set in 1981 by the late David Brightly.

"Now, contenders for the second heat, please make your way to the starting line."

Next year, thought Tom, as he gazed back up the slope at the next group of sledgers assembling.

Next year...

CHAPTER SIX

"Hark! The herald angels sing... Glory to the newborn Kiiiiing."

The last note lingered as the pupils and teachers of Playfair school - and parents and grandparents – resumed their seats in the Grand Hall of the school. The room was old, with dark wooden panels on the walls, and ancient wooden floorboards, scuffed by several decades' worth of pupils' feet. It was a room which had its own atmosphere and Tom had thought it almost eerie when it was empty, but this wasn't the case today: it was packed.

Old Hendo stepped forward to the lectern and microphone (not that he truly needed one) at the front of the stage at the far end of the hall, illuminated in semi-silhouette by the winter half-light of a gloomy late December afternoon as it petered in through the stain glass windows and their images of the schools' founders, the three brothers Playfair. As the fidgeting and general hubbub subsided into a thick, clinging silence, the lights in the hall gradually brightened, until Old Hendo was fully visible, complete with extravagant handlebar moustache and his festive waistcoat shimmering beneath his teacher's gown. He gave the pause just long enough to ensure it had maximum dramatic effect, and that he could be sure that the whole of the audience's attention was focused on him.

"Ladies and Gentlemen, boys and girls, welcome to our annual Christmas assembly, a very special time of the year for old and young alike, as we mark the long autumn term drawing to its close. In so many ways, this is the turning point of the wheel of the year as we arrive at the shortest day and the light starts, almost imperceptibly at first, gradually to return, though we often have several months of the cold and snow to traverse before we notice this. And we are, of course, here to celebrate Christmas, too, before the school breaks up for the holidays. We began our service with the traditional singing of 'Hark the Herald Angels', and I now move onto the next part of the day's business: the crowning of the school's sledging champion for the year."

There was a murmur in the crowd at this point.

"Now, as has often been the case in recent times, this year's championship was, once again, held on our artificial slope. However, as those of you who were able to attend this morning will, I'm sure, agree, this did not detract from the quality and the bravery of all our sledgers."

At this, Old Hendo paused and looked over his half-moon spectacles at the crowd before him. The pause for dramatic effect once more.

"This is an unusual departure, as this part of our Christmas assembly is normally all about the winners, but I wish to single out one young man in particular for the manner in which he raced and conducted himself this morning. Tom Brightly, will you stand up, please?"

As he heard his name being spoken aloud, Tom wanted to do the precise opposite of standing up; indeed, had he been able to, he would have melted into his seat. As it was, Jack was prodding him into responding to Old Hendo's request.

"Get up."

"Aw no… total nightmare…" muttered Tom. He could feel his cheeks burning up as he prised himself out of his seat until he was the only person standing in the entire audience. Indeed, in the whole room. Apart from Old Hendo, who now continued.

"Ah, Master Brightly. I wanted to note your outstanding performance and spirit in this morning's first heat. For those of you who were not there this morning, young Brightly here was streaking ahead in his heat when there was a most unfortunate 'coming together' with the sled of one of his fellow competitors around the halfway mark, which caused him to crash rather spectacularly."

Tom was now scarlet. He didn't know where in the room to look and just wanted the ordeal to be over – but Old Hendo had not finished yet.

"Alas, this was the end of his sledge, but not, thankfully, for young Brightly, who, despite being badly shaken up, got up, dusted himself down and carried his broken sledge down the rest of the course to the finishing line. It was an act of true determination and entirely in the spirit, both of the Championship and the school itself, and one of which his father would have been very proud."

Make it stop - please, was all Tom could think, as every pair of eyes in the place bored into him.

"Tom, very well done indeed. You sledded an exemplary race and showed the grit and spirit that will I'm sure one day see you emulate your father's record."

Old Hendo began the applause and the teachers on stage behind him as well as the entire audience in front of him all enthusiastically joined in.

Tom acknowledged them with a half-wave before he sat down in his chair again as quickly as it was polite to do so.

"No pressure then," said Jack.

"Total. Nightmare," Tom replied as the applause subsided.

Old Hendo continued reading out the winners of the various heats and the semi-finals, before he announced the result of the final.

"And once again, it is a familiar name on the winners' board: Branning. Branning major, to be precise. A round of applause for our winner please."

The crowd applauded once more, but it was more of a polite smattering, rather than the enthusiastic clapping which had greeted Old Hendo's recounting of Tom's earlier crash.

A taller, even more unfortunate looking version of Branning took to the stage, with a swagger and an air of nonchalance which suggested that this was all a matter of some routine to him. Alastair Branning was the elder brother of Douglas Branning, Tom's tormentor, and the family trait for being unpleasant was clearly a strong one.

Old Hendo passed over the winner's trophy and gave Branning major a desultory handshake before having a quiet word in his ear, over the polite applause which was already fading. There was a tiny cluster of whoops and hollers: Alastair Branning, much like his youngest brother, had his own fan club in the crowd, a select band of sycophantic hangers-on, who were by now the only ones making much noise. Branning brandished the trophy aloft as though he had won the World Cup, which, in his own mind, he had.

"What do you think Old Hendo said to him?" asked Jack.

"Dunno. Maybe told him to stop cheating to win," replied Tom.

"Ouch. Truth hurts though."

The younger Branning, as it transpired, had learned many of the dark sledging arts from his older brother, for whom winning was the only thing that mattered; popularity clearly did not.

Old Hendo continued the assembly with a brief review of the highlights from the past term, before announcing the final Christmas song, O Come All Ye Faithful. The assembled company sang the carol with gusto and as it drew to a close, the lights in the Great Hall were blazing away at full blast. The old place looked impressive as the colours in its curtains and ceiling, not to mention the windows, were finally revealed in all their glory.

As the audience resumed their seats for the final time, Old Hendo wrapped up.

"Finally, I wish you all a very Merry Christmas and a Guid New Year when it comes. May it be a peaceful and prosperous one for us all. I look forward to welcoming you back on the ninth of January – see you next year!"

He ended, as ever, with a flourish and a cheery wave and began his slow march down from the stage and out to the front of the Grand Hall, ready to greet every departing pupil and parent and to wish them all a very Merry Christmas.

Tom and Jack stood up and Jack spotted his mum, several rows back.

"Come on, it's home-time!" he yelled to Tom as they made their way towards her.

"Hi Mum."

"Hi Dr Wanless."

"Hello boys – and well done you." Dr Wanless gave Tom's elbow a wee nudge.

"Thanks," said Tom, hoping he wouldn't blush again.

Jack took a deep breath. "Mum, remember I said Tom was staying over for the weekend? Is that still okay? It's just that we've nearly finished that big game I told you about and…"

"Jack, it's fine. I'm working all weekend anyway, so your sister's in charge."

At this news, Jack rolled his eyes.

"Try not to annoy her."

"We'll try. Thanks, mum."

And with that, Jack gave his mother a flying hug and he and Tom bundled their way towards the doors of the Grand Hall.

"Make sure you do! See you on Christmas Eve," Dr Wanless shouted after the pair of them, and after they paused their half-walk, half-run, to exchange festive pleasantries with Old Hendo, the boys were off and out the door, and heading straight into the Christmas holidays.

CHAPTER SEVEN

Tom and Jack waited in the aisle of the number fifty-nine bus as it wheezed its way up to the corner of Byres Road, before it shuddered and juddered its way to a halt. The boys hopped off and onto the crowded pavement. Streetlights were blinking into life, some of them still the old-fashioned kind, spluttering the ruddiest red before gaining in strength and glowing orange. They were the perfect lights to watch on the type of cold winter's evening when it was threatening to snow, although this happened even less often in Glasgow these days than it did out in the countryside, where Tom lived.

The streets were rammed with people, old and young, many of them laden down with endless bags of shopping as they made their way around the west end's festive shops and markets. This made navigation both slower and trickier than usual for the two of them.

"Seriously, how many folk are here?" asked Tom.

"You think this is bad? This is only Friday. Just wait 'til the weekend. After 10 o'clock, it's game over if you want to do anything quickly. C'mon, shortcut."

Jack motioned Tom to follow him up one of the old lanes that led away from the main thoroughfare, behind the old, stately tenement flats and their mini-back yards and gardens. The boys picked their way along the lane, dodging the wheelie bins peppering their way, before eventually popping out onto Killermont Drive proper, one of the oldest streets in the city and with some of the few remaining houses left that hadn't been divided up into endless flats.

As they walked along the considerably less busy pavement, their focus shifted back to the weekend ahead.

"Good grief, it is cold. Hope you've got some snacks in," said Tom, blowing on his hands yet again.

"But of course. Winning Apotheosis is going to be hungry work. Always have provisions, that's what I say. Speaking of which…"

Jack produced a half-packet of milk chocolate digestives from his jacket pocket.

"Want one?"

"Yeah, go on." Tom laughed. "Do you ever *not* have snacks on you?"

"Good choice. Always carry snackables. This is a Wanless rule. You know this to be the truth!"

Tom laughed again and chomped down on the biscuit.

"Skills."

Then he looked more serious for a minute.

"Do you think we could, y'know, actually do it?"

"What? Win it?"

"Yeah."

"Course we can. We'd've won it by now if we hadn't lost Haggis 1."

"Ah, poor old H1. I miss H1. She was a good ship."

"Ah yes, but now we've got a better one." Jack stopped at a gate outside an ancient-looking sandstone ramble of a house.

"Here we go. Time to deal with the *Sistermonster*…"

"You mean Katie."

Jack eye-rolled.

"Oh yeah… let's get it over with."

He pressed the doorbell for several seconds and it rang with the type of olden bell sound that suggested the doorbell was the original one which had been installed during the house's construction.

The boys heard footsteps approaching the door.

"All right, all right, I'm coming…"

The door was flung open by a teenage girl, blonde-haired, her hair scrunched up almost as much as her face the second she saw her younger brother.

"Oh, it's *you*."

"Hi sis, we're home!" chirped Jack, wearing his biggest and most fake (Tom thought) grin and doing jazz hands.

"I'm going to my room. I don't wanna hear a single word from you."

"What, us?"

Katie Wanless's face expressed precisely how she felt about her stupid brother as she gave the biggest combined 'tut' and mini-harrumph she could muster, before turning on her heel and marching back along the long hallway and clumping back up the stairs.

"NOT. A. WORD."

"Love you, too, sis."

"Hi Katie…" mumbled Tom.

Jack took a beat and looked at his friend. "Mate, you're scarlet again."

"Shurrup."

"She's my *sister*. My very annoying sister. Honestly…"

"Yeah, I know…"

"C'mon, sack your coat here, we've got a game to win."

Tom and Jack chucked their coats and bags in a heap and galloped up the stairs, two at a time; as they reached the landing, they heard the slam of a door from the other end of the top floor of the Wanless house. Katie Wanless was ensconced in her room, earbuds firmly in place and lost in her phone, bemoaning her babysitting chores to her pals online, and she did *not* want to be disturbed.

CHAPTER EIGHT

"So, is Katie always this grumpy about babysitting?" asked Tom as they entered the huge, ornate living room in the Wanless family home.

"Pretty much," Jack replied. "Mum works nearly every weekend now, so Katie's always got to stay home and look after me when she does."

"Who looked after you before?"

"Well, we used to have Mrs Roberts – she looked after us for years – but she was getting on a bit and wanted to retire, plus Katie turned sixteen a few months ago, so mum and dad figured she could look after the pair of us when they were both working."

"She wasn't too happy about it tonight," said Tom.

Jack shrugged. "She's just annoyed 'cos she's stuck inside with the pair of us, and all her pals are out enjoying themselves. When she's like this, I keep out of her way. Sorta works – she usually leaves me alone and I just make some dinner, do my homework and then play the QuadCube – not always in that order."

"Doesn't she get on your case about that?"

"Nah, she couldn't care less. She thinks Apotheosis is a total waste of time anyway, so unless I do something totally stupid, like blowing up the microwave or setting the house on fire, she stays in her room, chatting to her friends online."

"So, what happens if someone comes round looking for your mum and dad when they're not here?"

"Hardly ever happens, mate. We don't really know our neighbours and the only people who come round the doors these days are the odd charity tin-rattler, delivery drivers and the postie – and he always rings the doorbell during the day. Speaking of delivery drivers," Jack picked up a brown cardboard package and brandished it in front of Tom's face, "have-a-look-at-this."

"No idea."

Jack tore open the cardboard box and thrust his hand into it, extracting a long black plastic stick. He pressed a button on its side and a small blue light blinked at the top end of the stick before turning a solid blue.

"This, my friend, is the Gris QuadCube 360 e-wand – the last piece of kit we need so we can win Apotheosis once and for all!"

Tom looked at him, and then at the e-wand. "How?"

"Remember how last weekend we narrowly lost out against that proto-Purple Blob?"

"You mean when we were annihilated by it in that 'battle' that lasted less than a minute?"

"That's the one, and this," he said, swishing the plastic stick around his head, "is what we were missing. Any Purple Blob takes us on tonight and it's toast. So, shall we?"

"Totally," replied Tom.

Jack switched on the QuadCube, and Apotheosis booted up. A giant, virtual 3-D head of Max Gris appeared in the centre of the room. Tom reckoned it was at least six feet tall. The head span round slowly and started speaking.

"Welcome to Apotheosis! Congratulations on reaching level forty-one. You have played excellently so far to reach this point, but time is running out – it will soon be Christmas Eve! Will you reach Apotheosis before it is too late – and will you even know it when you find it? Time to find out. Goggles... ON! Strap yourselves in!"

Both boys snapped on their VR headsets smartly & buckled up in the Quadcube's two D-seats, designed to simulate the deck of whichever mode of transport players picked for each level.

Then, Max Gris's robotic voice bellowed out a final instruction: "Good luck. Now, UNLEASH THE GIANT SPACEWEEVILS!"

"Aw no, not these bozos again," groaned Tom.

A massive buzzing hum filled the entire living room. Tom and Jack unstrapped themselves from their seats and stood up, back-to-back, in the centre of the room and waited.

As the noise increased, Jack barked some last-minute instructions, "Now, remember, each bar of gold is worth three dinosaurs, but a barrel of oil and a box of gems are worth a space-jet each."

Tom nodded. "Okay, okay, what's printed money worth again?"

"Depends who printed it. Usually starts off being worth loads – at least a couple of galleons – but after a few decades, you'll be doing well to pick up a couple of sacks of eco-protein for it and after a century, it's only useful for lighting the fire in the cave you'll be living in."

"So, best to avoid it then?"

"Not completely, just don't keep it too long. Buy valuable stuff. That's the best way to make it work for you."

Jack bent down and flicked the switch marked 'Quad3D' on one of the Cube's twenty faces. (Gris Corp had deliberately misnamed their best-selling console to add to its coolness. This was part of that which marked it out as the ultimate gaming console.)

"Pirates in the room, here we come! Aaaaaaarrrrrrrrrrrrrrrrrrrrrrrrrrrrrrrr!"

And with Jack's war-cry, all hell broke loose in the Wanless living room as a 3-dimensional hologram of a 17th century pirate galleon burst through the wall as though it were still sailing the high seas. Which, in the world of Apotheosis, it was. Powered by its 22nd century booster rockets.

"Nice touch!" shouted Tom over the combined noise of rockets, the sea crashing, pirates going, "AAAAAARRRRR!" and their own virtual spaceship, Haggis 2, telling them to "WHOOP WHOOP PULL UP! WHOOP WHOOP PULL UP!"

And then, there were the promised giant spaceweevils.

"Uh oh," said Tom.

"What? What is it?" shouted Jack.

"Look at the deck, there's hundreds of them!"

"More like thousands – it's a swarm. Hit the plasma anti-gravs."

Tom flicked the controller he was holding as though trying to remove something that was sticking to his fingers and a holographic electric blue screen buzzed into life, completely encircling both boys.

"Shields are up!" shouted Tom over the din.

As the galleon crashed around the living room, Tom and Jack realised that not only were there scores of pirates lined up and spoiling for a fight, but they had trained their 'pets' – cosmic mandrills – to brandish laser cutlasses. Judging by the way the mandrills were waving these around, it looked as though they knew what to do with them.

The living room exploded with light: the first waves of spaceweevils had swarmed towards the hull of the boys' virtual spaceship and were promptly being vaporised by the plasma anti-grav shields – but at a cost. Amidst the chaos, the living room turned a deep red colour and a high-pitched voice announced impending doom:

"WARNING... POWER DRAINAGE ACCELERATING... WARNING... POWER DRAINAGE ACCELERATING... WARNING..."

"Aw no, not again... we're gonna crash," shouted Tom.

"Not this time. Here, grab this."

Jack threw Tom the e-wand.

"What do I do with this?"

"Point it at the Purple Blob when it shows, then ram it into its blowsnout. Hard."

"We'll crash before then."

"Doesn't matter – hit it right in the gob with that and we've got a chance."

"What are you gonna do?"

"Stop us crashing."

Jack's hands and fingers moved quicker than he had ever moved them before in his life, pressing buttons, twisting and turning the controllers, and grabbing at virtual weaponry to defend the boys' spaceship from the triple threats of the angry pirates, the cosmic mandrills and the spaceweevils. He had just dived over the sofa to take on the first incoming mandrill when the entire room appeared to lurch.

Tom was swatting the swarm of spaceweevils with his laser forker when the ship let out a groan of creaking metal as it thudded towards the ground.

He shouted at Jack, "We've lost power. We're gonna crash onto the ship's deck. Get your laser cutlass ready!"

"I know!"

The initial thud was followed by the sounds of shearing metal and of the turbo-boosted galleon's mast cracking in half and falling deckwards, taking out several hapless pirates on its route to earth.

"Hah!" cried Jack. "They're not going to like that!"

The pirates were, indeed, less than ecstatic about the damage which had just been visited upon them by the 22nd century's leading ultra-modified space jet and expressed this displeasure by turning to face Tom and Jack en masse and screaming:

"AAAAAAAAAAAAARRRRRRRRRRRRRRRRRRRRRRRRRRRRRRRRR R!!!!!!!!!   KIIIIIIIIIIILLLLLLLLLLL THEEEEEEEEEEEEEEEMMMMMMMMMM!!!!"

"They're angry!" warned Jack.

"No kidding! Aw no, it's here!" Tom shouted as he pointed towards the front window of the room. In the corner of which, a gelatinous purple mass was expanding – rapidly – while making a noise that was the laughter of pure malevolence.

"The e-wand," shouted Jack, the colour draining from his face.

Tom leapt from his chair and ran towards the evil-sounding Purple Blob. In the few seconds it took him, the Blob had already expanded to fill a good quarter of the living room, its evil, honking laugh drowning out the rest of the mayhem.

Tom leapt up towards the source of the Blob's foul noise, brandishing the e-wand and tried to stuff it into its source - but missed, collapsing in a heap, and rolling out of the path of its purple goo just in time.

"We're not finished yet. H2. Gimme, triple laser bomb ducts. Gimme them now!" shouted Jack at the ship.

Seven different lights on Jack's controller lit up as he pointed it straight at the Blob.

"LASER BOMB DUCTS… CHAAAAAAARGED!" boomed a voice that sounded very like Brian Blessed from the left-hand cushion of the sofa.

Jack blasted the laser beam bombs directly at the Purple Blob's lead antenna and blew it straight off. The Blob howled in pain and for a couple of seconds stopped expanding – and then began laughing again, resuming its encroachment. Meantime, the pirates were circling the room, readying themselves for a secondary attack.

"It worked!" shouted Jack in disbelief. "It can't see where it's going! H2, quadpods boost. Tom – DO IT!"

H2 announced, "QUADPODS BOOOOOOSTED!"

Tom ran towards the Blob, waving the e-wand. Jack was now hopping around on the left armchair, thrashing at pirates with his laser cutlass. And the Purple Blob was still laughing like a maniac trapped down a well, with a bump growing where its antenna had once been.

Jack pointed and shouted, "It's growing a new one!" as Tom bounced on the other armchair and lunged towards the Blob, arm outstretched, and banged the e-wand directly into its blowsnout. As it hit its target, the Blob's laughter changed into the type of howl a space banshee might make and as it did so, its colour also altered, turning deeper purple at first, then becoming redder and finally darkening to black, at which point, the howl became a nasty laugh once more.

"HUHUHHUHHHHHHHUHHHUHHHUHHHUHHHUHHUH HHHRRRGHHH…."

"Oh no…" Jack's voice trailed off, "it hasn't worked… Maximum solar warp. NOW! NOW! NOW!"

"That's going to blow up the ship!" Tom exclaimed.

"Don't care – it's all we've got left!"

Haggis 2 intoned yet another alert:

"WARNING… WARNING… NUCLEAR SPACEWEEVILS FORMING IN STARBOARD TANK… WARNING… WARNING… NUCLEAR SPACEWEEVILS FORMING IN STARBOARD TANK…"

The room was now entirely a shade of darkened blood red and the ship's holographic warning system began shutting down all but its most essential features.

"We've got spaceweevils!" yelled Tom.

Jack blanched.

"Throw the proton lasso. If we're going down, let's take as many of these eyepatch wearing dingbats with us as we can," he motioned towards the pirates, "and especially that thing," he continued, pointing at the still laughing Purple – though now technically Black - Blob.

"RED CONTAGION ALERT… RED CONTAGION ALERT…"

"Hit the quarkfoam. Drench them! Now!"

Tom punched further buttons and clouds of virtual fine white mist flooded from every nook and cranny in the room.

"RED CONTAGION ALERT. SHIP BREACHED. PURPLE BLOB APPROACHING."

Recent experience had taught Tom that there were three phrases you never wanted to hear in Apotheosis: 'red contagion alert', 'ship breached' and most especially, 'Purple Blob approaching'. This was not good. This was very not good indeed.

He shouted at Jack, "Solar warp engaged."

"Fire it."

"You sure?"

"DO IT!"

Tom poked the e-wand into the Quadcube's right paddle, and the countdown began.

"FIVE... FOUR... THREE..."

"This is going to be messy," cried Jack.

"TWO... ONE... DETONATION IGNITION ENGAGED."

It began with a low humming sound, as though Haggis 2 had momentarily forgotten itself and become distracted. The pirates' chants and shouts became more and more muffled. Even the noise of the Purple Blob seemed far away.

Then – finally – the Purple Blob stopped laughing and resumed its screeching and howling.

"It's working!" shouted Jack.

The humming became a low whine, which grew louder and louder. Tom covered his ears as it turned into a cacophony of white noise, drowning out even the Purple Blob.

"My ears!" cried Tom

"Here it comes!" shouted Jack.

And then…

KABOOOOOOOOOOOOOOOOOOOOMMMMMMMMMMMMMM M!!!!!!!!!!!!!!!!!!

The room erupted into thousands of points of light, of gold, silver, red, orange, yellow and white. And lots and lots of blackened debris from the erstwhile Purple Blob, most of which was now adorning the walls of Jack's parents' formerly pristine living room as virtual dripping black and purply goo, sliding down the walls.

Several parrots flew past at high-speed, squawking their virtual last. Bits of galleon had embedded themselves in the living room walls. The pirates had been thrown into the middle of next week and one of them was hanging from the lightshade directly above Tom's head. He didn't look very well.

Then, all was quiet and the only sound that could be heard was the gentle swish of the sea as the lads' antagonists gradually faded from view.

Tom and Jack looked at each other, then Tom spoke.

"Is that it? Have we done it?"

"Dunno."

In the centre of the room, the giant spinning head of Max Gris was reforming and began to speak.

"Well, congratulations. You're quite the little adventurers, aren't you? Who would have thought that level forty-two would be the answer? Well done! You now have one puzzle left to solve to win the game… good luck!"

As Max Gris's head disappeared back into the virtual ether, it was replaced in the centre of the room by a small golden orb, about the size of a tennis ball, which rose from the floor and started to glow.

"What now?" wondered Tom.

"Have the lasers ready," said Jack.

"Look, it's changing. It's growing and getting bigger."

"It's beginning to look like an egg – an Easter Egg."

The golden egg-shaped object continued to grow larger until it was taller than both the boys. Once it had reached around seven feet in height, it stopped. The outline of a door appeared in the front of the egg and a handle protruded out of its front shell.

As the boys watched, open-mouthed, the handle turned, and the door opened. They raised their lasers.

A man, well over six feet tall, with a mop of curls and a huge, toothy smile, appeared in the doorway. He was dressed in late Victorian era clothes and wearing a battered old hat and the most ridiculously long striped scarf either of the boys had ever seen.

"Hello there. I say, don't shoot. I'm not armed."

At this, he held both sides of his jacket open and the toothy smile became even toothier.

"See? Now, would you like a jelly baby?"

At this, the grinning man rummaged around in the pockets of his burgundy-coloured jacket and produced a small, white paper bag of virtual jelly babies which he proffered to the boys.

Tom and Jack lowered their lasers and stared in sequence at the man, slack-jawed, and then at each other.

The man replaced the paper bag.

"Perhaps later on then, eh? They are an acquired taste, I suppose."

Momentarily, the man stopped smiling and looked overly thoughtful, considering he was contemplating a bag of jelly babies.

"Now, have you met Freda?" The smile snapped back on, as he gesticulated towards his left shoulder, sitting on which was a small golden bird – which also appeared to be on fire.

"I know, I know, you're thinking she can't possibly be enjoying that, but she is, you know."

"Is she a phoenix?" asked Tom.

"Yes, she is. Clever lad. That's exactly what you are, isn't it, Freda?" said the man, turning to the golden bird, which seemed to puff itself – and the surrounding flame – up a little more.

"Now, we've travelled through all of time and space to bring you good news: you've won. Well, nearly. Just one more puzzle to solve now and Freda has it for you."

At this, the small golden bird produced a tiny envelope in its beak and fluttered its way towards Tom and Jack, settling on Tom's shoulder.

"Oh, she likes you all right. Well, take the envelope, there's a good lad."

Tom gently took the envelope from the golden bird's beak and opened it. He drew out a small golden card and stared at it for a moment.

The man gestured towards Tom, "Well go on, read it out."

"It says 'To win, you must be like me.'" Tom looked blankly at Jack, then asked the scarf-wearing stranger, "What does that mean?"

"Ah yes, that's the thing. What indeed?" the man said, as he tapped his nose. "You have to figure it out to win. Good luck to you, lads. Come on, Freda, we've got work to do."

The phoenix fluttered back onto the man's left shoulder and he turned and went back inside the large golden egg, closing the door behind him, with a final "Cheerio!" as he did so. The egg faded away.

Jack stood there, open-mouthed. "Woooooahh, no way. That was him. Really, really him."

Tom nodded, smiling.

"The original, you might say," both boys said in unison and started laughing.

"So, we've to be like him then?" asked Jack.

"But that makes no sense," said Tom. "Besides, how could we do that, anyway? No, it must be something else."

His brow furrowed, and he paced the floor, mumbling to himself.

"Be more like me… more like me… who's me? Cannot be him… the bird? Be like the bird? The phoenix?"

He stopped pacing and looked at Jack.

"It's the phoenix. We need to be like the phoenix."

"How? What does it do?"

"It dies and then comes back to life. We need to kill something off that'll come back to life and then we'll win. That's how we do it."

"But we've massacred everything in the game. There's nothing left to beat."

"No, it can't be one of the baddies anymore. It must be something of ours."

Tom was thinking. Hard. Racking his brains, trying to figure out what else this could mean.

"Is it our weapons we have to destroy? 'Cos I'm not doing that; it took ages to gather this lot."

Tom only half-heard Jack as he murmured his reply to him, "It's not our weapons… it's the ship."

"What?"

"It's the ship. To win, we have to nuke the ship."

"No way."

Tom sighed. "Don't you see? It's the one thing left that we have to do to win, but it's the hardest thing as well. That's why it's the final puzzle."

Jack looked at Tom in disbelief.

"It has taken us *months* to get this far. Every night – since the game started back in the summer – hours and hours *and hours* of work to build it up to this point…"

He held his arms outstretched towards Tom, imploring him to see sense.

"… and… and this is our second ship! We had to do it all over again after the original Haggis crashed into the molejinks! No. No way. I'm not doing it."

Tom gave an even deeper sigh.

"I get all that, but it's the only thing left. It's the thing we have to destroy."

Jack was exasperated now. "What if it's a red herring? Then what? Start all over again?"

"It's not…"

"We'd never win then. We wouldn't have time! No. I'm not doing it."

"But Jack…"

"*NO!*"

Tom sighed. Again. This time it was more a sigh of exasperation.

"*Jaaa-aack…*"

"No."

"But we have to do it to win. It's the ultimate test. Besides, if it's like the phoenix, it will come back to life."

Haggis 2 continued to hover and hum as the boys argued over its future.

"How? How exactly will it come back to life if we've nuked it?"

"'Cos it's a game, so anything's possible."

It was Jack's turn to pace the floor.

"No, no, no, no, no, no, no, no!"

Tom said nothing and stood on the prow of Haggis 2, silently watching him.

"Maybe it's something else we haven't found yet?" suggested Jack.

"There's nothing left to find. This is it: the final level. The ultimate test. We have to have faith…"

Jack looked at Tom. He hated the idea of voluntarily blowing up so many months of work, but he already knew that his friend was right. Tom's face was calm and certain, and Jack could tell that the point was beyond argument as far as he was concerned.

Jack closed his eyes, lifted his head back and opened them once more, to stare at the blood red ceiling.

"If you're wrong…"

"Yes!" Tom clenched his fist and gave a victory pump with his arm. "You won't regret this. We, my friend, are about to win."

"You'd better be right."

Tom was now hopping about all over Haggis 2's bow.

"Right, what do we do again?" he asked.

"We have to punch in the three codes in sequence."

"Like we did the last time? When we wrecked Haggis?"

"Yes, but this time… this time, we're doing it on purpose." Jack grimaced at the memory of their previous ship imploding from underneath them because of a misunderstanding about the best way to take on shoals of prionstarfish. As it turned out, causing the original Haggis to self-destruct by ploughing into the molejinks had not been the way to reach level fourteen, though it had successfully taken out most of the offending space vermin which had covered ninety-eight per cent of the ship's surface, as Haggis's onboard computer had kept reminding them.

The two boys grabbed their controllers.

"Let's do it," said Jack, as he began punching in a sequence of codes into his controller. As he did so, Tom made several swirling motions around his head using the other controller.

Haggis 2's booming onboard voice barked into life.

"WARNING... YOU ARE ACTIVATING ONBOARD SELF-DESTRUCT PROGRAMME... WARNING... YOU ARE ACTIVATING ONBOARD SELF-DESTRUCT PROGRAMME..." And its emergency sirens stared whooping their very loudest whoops.

"We know, H2," muttered Jack as he punched in the last of the numbers of the first code. "Okay, done. Over to you."

At this, Tom ceased whirling his controller like a dervish and typed further combinations of letters and numbers into his own controller. As he did so, Jack resumed the swirling around his head and gradually worked his way down through the air until he was swirling his controller around his feet.

Tom punched in the last combinations of letters and numbers.

"13, A, B, A, C, U, S, 25, C, H, R, I, S, T, M, A, S, 1, S, A, N, T, A!" he announced in triumph. "Done!"

"SELF-DESTRUCT PROGRAMME: ACTIVATED," announced Haggis 2, "COUNTDOWN STARTING. 10, 9, 8. 7..."

"Get off the seats – get behind the sofa. This is going to be messy," shouted Jack.

Tom bounced off his D-seat and tumbled over the sofa.

"6... 5... 4..."

Jack came flying over the top of the sofa and landed in a heap next to Tom.

"3... 2... 1... GOODBYE..."

The low steady state hum which Haggis 2 had been making for the past several minutes was replaced by the sound of its engines revving up as though for take-off, but instead of reaching their usual top note, they kept on whining and screeching their way through several more octaves, accompanied by electric white flashes and blue sparks zooming from every nook and cranny of the ship, until the room changed from its blood red colour into a brilliant whiteish-blue haze of light.

By now, both Tom and Jack had their eyes scrunched tightly shut.

Just as it seemed that the ship could not make its displeasure at its imminent destruction any more obvious, the room erupted into a mixture of all the colours of the rainbow and an explosion of white noise as Haggis 2 was torn apart into hundreds and thousands of pieces which bounced off the walls and rained down all around the two boys.

And then, the storm of wreckage, light and noise stopped and was replaced by silence.

Tom edged his way up and peeked over the top of the sofa to be confronted by the giant head of Max Gris once more.

"CONGRATULATIONS! You have done it! *You* are the Global Apotheosis Champions, the greatest online gamers of all time! Fantastic work! Now, I'm going to disappear, but make sure that you report your victory as soon as possible to Gris Corp HQ, where worldwide fame and riches await! See you soon!"

And with that, she disappeared. In her place was a small spinning globe-like golden trophy emblazoned with "Apotheosis Global Champions" on one side and "Santa Lives" on the other, which was spilling virtual golden coins onto the floor as it span around and around.

Both boys stood stock still, in shock, gazing at this spectacle for several seconds.

Then, they began whooping and hollering, as well as jumping around as though they had trampolines built into their shoes and high-fiving for all they were worth.

"We've won it! We've won it!" they were both shouting.

Then Tom yelled,

"Quick, get your phone – grab a selfie!"

Jack dived for his mobile phone and the pair of them moved next to the spinning globe.

"Ready?" Jack pressed the screen of his phone and looked at the results. There both boys stood, bathed in golden light, with the globe, somewhat out of focus and fuzzy, between them.

"That one's rubbish. Take another."

"Okay, okay." Jack raised his phone to take a second selfie, but just as he was about to press the button, the entire room fell dark and silent.

The phone's flash went off in complete, instantaneous darkness.

CHAPTER NINE

The dark car inched its way along a road that was barely wide enough to be called a road, occasionally dipping to the left and then to the right as it splattered its path through the puddles and mud. Its driver muttered under his breath once again. Not for the first time, he wondered why the fates had brought him to this place at all. Last of all. In the middle of the darkness, the car driver noticed – belatedly – that it was raining - no, sleeting. There were occasional blobs of melted snow appearing on the windscreen. He muttered some more non-repeatable words and considered turning on the car's headlights. His hand hovered over the switch for the dipped lights for a few seconds before he replaced it on the gearstick.

No, this was not the time to break with his plan, for he was the Shadow, and if there was one thing he had learned, it was not to deviate from a well-made plan other than through dire necessity. To be as unseen as possible was the key, especially here in the middle of rural Ireland, a place with which he was unfamiliar, a place where he did not know who, if anyone, could be watching on such a foul night, and the place to which he had come in order to locate and acquire the final objects of his mission: the County Kilkenny relics of St Nicholas.

He had been driving for almost half an hour with no light at all. Even before it had begun sleeting, it had been cloudy and before that, moonless: the perfect night to come to such a place and precisely why he had planned this as the final acquisition. For this was how the Shadow had viewed this particular contract: a series of acquisitions. Not robberies. No, that was such a vulgar term. He was merely engaged in the re-appropriation of items which had once belonged somewhere else, in a different country in most cases, and to many people over the centuries. All he was doing now was facilitating their passage to a new owner, who, happily enough, was prepared to pay him handsomely for his meticulous planning and skill.

The car's front left wheel lurched into another puddle that was actually a pothole in disguise. I am glad this is not my car, thought the Shadow. The windscreen was becoming even more obscured with the half-melted snowflakes which were now battering it. The Shadow turned the speed of the windscreen wipers to their fastest setting. Truly, he would be glad when this job was over once and for all.

The road had ceased to be even a pretence of a road and was now a mere muddy track. As he rounded yet another tight corner, the Shadow finally saw the outline of the landmark his eyes had been straining for in the darkness: an ancient and long ruined abbey. He was – literally – on the right track. As he edged the car towards the scattered, moss-covered rocks that may have once been a wall of the ancient ruin, its back wheels started spinning and the rear of the car slid away from the direction in which he wanted it to go. Time to quit whilst he was ahead. He drew the car to a stop and cut the engine. In the darkness and desolation, there was nothing but the sound of the continuous sleet bouncing off the vehicle now; this foul winter's night and its weather was on the turn: he could see more and more wet flakes of snow in the wintry mix.

He pulled on his jacket – all-weather and waterproof, naturally. This would help, for a short while, but now the hard part began. The Shadow got out of the car and opened the boot, bringing out a large bag of tools.

He trudged his way up the short incline - all that remained of the road now - until he reached the ruin. He was close. He flicked on his phone and opened its compass app: twenty-two paces to the south-southwest. Trudging his way through the grass and headstones, the remnants of a once grand churchyard, he nearly tripped over the long stone slab marking the tomb.

Here it was. His last challenge. He set to work, prising at the slab, using all his might gradually to gain some purchase on it. After several minutes, there was a slight grinding sound as the large block of stone moved for the first time in several centuries. It was only the tiniest shift in its position at first, perhaps only a couple of inches, but it had moved. The Shadow collapsed in a temporary heap and let out a brief cry of triumph. This was *most* unlike him – he always prized discretion as much as possible – but the moment merited it. He had moved the tombstone ever so slightly; the final task was achievable after all.

The sleet was now more wet snow than sleet, which encouraged the Shadow to gather himself up from the grass at the side of the ancient tomb and refocus on the matter at hand. With each heave, the old stone slab gave a little more and shifted further. As he prised and levered it, first an inch or two one way and then, the same but from the opposite side, the gap which exposed the ground below, and the interior of the ancient tomb itself, gradually grew wider. After several more minutes of effort, the opening into the gloom below the tombstone was big enough to poke his head into for a look around.

He flashed a torch on and peered into the darkness. All he could see was mud, water and half-embedded rocks in the walls of the tomb; even with the torch on full beam, he realised he would have to go down into the tomb itself to do a proper search. He reached down into the darkness and with his fingertips, wiggled a stone out of the side wall of the tomb and dropped it into the blackness. There was a splash below: clearly, nothing about this part of his mission was going to be easy.

He delved into his bag, brought out a harness and slipped it over his head, before securing and tightening it in place. Then he looked around the abbey's former graveyard in search of a solid object on which to secure one end of a long rope. He walked across to a shape hulking out of the darkness: an old yew tree. That would do. The Shadow looped the rope around a thick, gnarled branch, knotted it tightly, and then ran the rope back to the edge of the tomb.

Before he clipped himself onto it, he realised he would need to wedge the opening wider before he could drop into it himself to have a thorough look around. With several more heaves, he moved the stone sufficiently for the opening to accommodate him - just. It would be a tight squeeze but needs must. He did not have any time to spare – and the weather was deteriorating. He strapped a headtorch around his hood, flicked it on and pointed it – and his head - into the darkened tomb. There was definitely water at the bottom. Fortunately, it didn't look like it was too large a drop. He clipped on, tugged the rope one last time, and lowered himself into the mud and the dark, his feet scrabbling for footholds as he inched his way downwards.

His boots sploshed into the water as he hit the bottom. It wasn't deep enough to cover them; just deep enough to be irritating. He flicked on the torch and kicked his feet around in the water, but felt nothing. He pivoted around, scanning the walls of the tomb, but all that he could see was mud, earth, and the ragged edges of stones. Nothing else.

The tomb was empty.

The Shadow cursed his luck for deserting him at the very end. He fished the map out of his inside pocket and turned the torch on it once more. The map was clear, and it was the only one he had. The map that had been given to him by his current employers and verified by specialists in their field as authentic. He checked it and rechecked it. There could be no doubt: he was standing in a large puddle at the very bottom of the Irish tomb of St Nicholas – only, it was empty.

The Shadow shouted another curse at the top of his voice this time, given how sure he was that there was not another living soul within ten miles of his current location. Then he let out an enormous sigh and muttered aloud.

"Oh well, nothing else for it. Time to break the news."

He reached into his inside pocket again for his mobile and flicked it back to life, hitting the speed-dial for the only number stored in it. He lifted it to his ear and waited… and waited… and waited – but the ringtone never came. Silence.

He took the phone from his ear and stared at its screen. There was no service. He redialled, with the same outcome. At this, he cursed loudly once more and, replacing the phone back into his pocket, heaved his way back above ground. As he did so, the falling wet snow was settling on the grass surrounding the empty tomb. He hauled himself back out into the night, collapsing on the wet ground, the snow peppering his face. Of course, the phone hadn't worked underground, he thought. He pulled off his gloves and reached into his pocket once more. He could feel his fingers turning numb as he leadenly punched the speed-dial button once again, but still there was nothing. No ringtone. Just dead air. As he looked at the screen and realised that the phone's signal was still non-existent, the Shadow led out his loudest curse yet and flung the useless object to the ground. It was time to leave. He would have to find another way to make contact – and quickly.

CHAPTER TEN

"Jack!"

"Jaaaaaacccckkkk!"

"JAAAAAAAAAAACCCCCKKKKK!!"

Tom and Jack heard the sound of stomping footsteps approaching the living room door before it was flung open with such force that it bounced back off the wall, nearly parting company with its hinges in the process.

In the darkness, Katie Wanless was making her displeasure known.

"What have you *done*, you annoying little muppet?"

Jack and Tom were both hyper.

Jack went first.

"HeySishaven'tdoneanythingwejustWONApotheosisthenwewerecelebra tingandtakingselfiesandthenallthelightswentout!"

Jack paused to take a breath.

Katie launched into another salvo.

"WHAT-IN-HELL'S-NAME-HAVE-YOU-DONE-TO-THE-LIGHTS?"

"Nothing!" protested Jack.

"I told you: we won the game and then all the lights went out."

"It's true, Katie. We didn't do anything," Tom chipped in.

Katie Wanless was having none of it. Pulling the best look of disdain on her face she could muster, she began talking to the two boys as though they were five-year-olds.

"I was in my room, minding my own business and chatting to my friends on my phone and all I could hear from in here was thumping, banging and crashing…"

"That was us winning the game," said Jack, with a look of pride on his face.

Katie was not to be deterred from her rant, though.

"Then, just as all the banging stopped, ALL the lights went out and whatever you two bozos did, you managed to wreck the phone signal as well. So, you'd better figure out…"

"What?" said Tom. "Did you say your phone was off?"

Katie turned her fire on her annoying younger brother's equally annoying best pal.

"What?"

"You said your phone went off."

"Yeah, dingbat, look: no signal." Katie thrust the glowing screen in Tom's face. There was indeed not a single bar of signal.

Tom pulled out his own mobile.

"Look! Mine's gone as well."

Jack reached for his phone and a quick glance at its screen confirmed it was in the same state.

"Snap."

"What *have* you two idiots done?" demanded Katie again.

"Nothing!" shouted both the boys in unison.

"There must be something wrong with the electricity," said Tom. "Quick, check the sockets."

He and Jack used the light from their phones to find the remaining lamps that were standing and tried flicking the plug socket switches on and off. The room remained steadfastly in darkness.

"Maybe something's wrong with the fuses," suggested Jack.

But Tom was already at one of the living room's very tall windows and throwing open the curtains.

"Look…"

Jack and Katie picked their way over to the window.

"It's pitch black out there," announced Tom. "All the streetlights are off and the houselights. Must be some sort of power cut."

Jack was now wearing a look of renewed triumph on his face, the sort of look that was expressly designed to cause maximum irritation to one's siblings.

"See, I told you it wasn't us." He hurled the words, laced with smugness, in Katie's direction.

Had there been any light in the room, both boys would have been able to see Katie's face scrunching up in a look of utter disdain, though as it was, her voice conveyed her mounting annoyance.

"You have got to be joking," said Katie, as she peered out the window at the darkened streets below.

Jack was still grinning.

"No joke, sis. It's a proper, bona fide power cut. Best go find some candles."

Katie Wanless tutted and harrumphed. Again. This evening had already been bad, but having to be responsible for two pre-teenagers without even her mobile phone to distract her was a total nightmare.

"I'm going to my room. I don't want to hear a peep from either of you two."

She turned on her heel and stormed back out of the living room, slamming the door shut behind her with full force once again.

"And the door is still there... just. She's going to be in terrific form now," said Jack, with more than a hint of sarcasm.

"What do you mean 'going to be'...? Anyway, we've got bigger problems than your stroppy sister to worry about. What are we going to do about winning the game?" asked Tom.

"What do you mean?"

"Well, we need to tell *someone*," said Tom.

"We could just wait until the power comes back on and the internet's back up."

"That could take hours. It looks like the entire street is out."

"Fair point. What are you thinking?"

"We need to find someone to tell about our win in person – before somebody else beats us to it."

"Yeah, but who are we gonna tell? And how?" asked Jack.

"We-elll," Tom began, "we could head down to Gris Corp and report it in person – before anyone else wins it."

"You mean, go into Gris Corp ourselves?" asked Jack.

"Yep."

"And say what?"

"That we won it. They'll have back-ups and all sorts. They'll know. Plus…"

"Plus what?"

"We've got proof." Tom was waving his phone at Jack.

Jack slapped his forehead.

"The selfie! Of course!"

"C'mon, let's have a look," said Tom.

Jack fished his phone out of his pocket and brought up the photos.

There, next to the last photo of the two of them looking puzzled in the darkness, was a blurry photo of the two boys, looking elated, with a golden, fuzzy object in between them.

"Well, it's not exactly going to win any awards, is it?" said Tom.

"I – we – were excited," said Jack in mock indignation. "Anyway, it's the only thing we've got. If we explain what happened and how we won it, we can convince them."

Tom had already decided. "It's worth a shot. C'mon, get your coat. Let's get a move on."

Jack stuffed his phone back into his pocket and the pair of them sprinted for the living room door, once again nearly removing it from its hinges.

"Do you know how to get there?" asked Jack, as they bundled along the hall and down the stairs.

"We'll find it. It's massive." replied Tom.

"Bye, Katie! We're off out!" yelled Jack as he and Tom careered out of the front door.

As they half-walked, half-ran into the street, the odd flake of snow fell gently out of the darkness.

Katie Wanless heard the front door of the house slam – just – above the music playing in her ears. She pulled out her earbuds. There was silence.

"Jack. Jaaaaacccckkk? JAAAAAACCCCCKKKKK!"

Silence was the only reply.

"Humph, good," she muttered. "Peace and quiet at last." And then stuffed her earbuds back into her ears, tuning out the silence once more.

CHAPTER ELEVEN

"This is weird," said Tom. "It's so dark."

The two boys had now been walking for over an hour in the cold and darkened city. Not a single streetlight lit their way, and now only the odd car was venturing about. Gradually, the snow had turned heavier and was being whipped up by the wind. It was now settling on grass and on stationary cars.

"I know – and it's Baltic," replied Jack. "It's well creepy without any lights. Well, except the tree lights. And the torches. Look, over there, there's another one." He pointed to his left.

Tom glanced over at the flat Jack was pointing at. From inside it, the only lights were those of the Christmas tree in the window, complete with random beams zig-zagging their way around inside the flat's interior.

"Must be the whole city that's out. What a total nightmare," said Tom.

"You think?" asked Jack.

"Well, we've been walking for ages now and all we've seen are some cars and the odd person wandering about with a torch. Christmas trees will be all right if they're on batteries, but nothing else electrical is working. Think about it."

"That's a point," said Jack, as he reached into his pocket for his phone and flicked on its screen.

"Anything?"

"Nope. Still dead."

"This is weird. It's like everything's down. You'd think that they'd have some sort of back-up."

"Imagine if they don't get it sorted soon. It'll be chaos."

"Don't..."

Jack stopped.

"Are we almost there?"

"I think so."

"This is far too much walking. I need a snackable."

With this, he fished into his pocket and pulled out a packet of milk chocolate digestive biscuits.

"Want one?"

"Oh yes please," said Tom. "I'm freezing." He took off his left-hand glove and grabbed the top biscuit, stuffing it into his mouth. "Mmmm – ta – that's better."

"Where are we now then?" asked Jack.

Tom went into his pocket, took out his phone and flicked it on.

"Cool – the map is still working offline. According to this, we've only got a few hundred yards to go to the main gate of Gris Corp."

"It's kinda hard to tell; it's so dark!"

The two boys walked on. They had long since left the West End of the city and had walked for long enough now to be nearing one of the city's reclaimed former industrial areas nearer to the river. In this case, it was the relatively new Mackintosh Innovation Park, a vast sprawling green area that had sprouted out of the city's former shipyards and docks over a decade ago and which was peppered with futuristic buildings and spaces in between them. The park had been the first of its kind and – in a far-sighted leap of innovation – had brought together arts and sciences in an all-encompassing 'space of the future which symbolised regeneration'. This, Tom mused, as he and Jack reached a large sign announcing the park and its 'mission', was the sort of wordy guff that adults came out with all the time, often to justify the completely obvious or a huge amount of money being spent.

In the middle of the Park was the giant Gris Corp headquarters, a massive labyrinthine structure of whiteness and glass which didn't so much sit at the centre of the park as erupt from it, throwing jutting crystalline structures into the sky during the day and after dark, blazing light shapes and sculptures into the night sky.

Except tonight, it wasn't.

As the two boys walked through the park's entrance, what was most striking was the absence of light. It was eerily dark compared to its usual brilliant state. They could see the Gris Corp HQ was lit up, but it was as though someone had found a giant dimmer switch and turned it down.

"Well, at least we can see the entrance," said Jack.

"Come on, let's see if we can find someone."

They approached the huge, curving glass front doors of the building and then stopped. They waited for the door to open, but nothing happened.

"They're not working. Try the one at the side," said Tom.

Jack moved across the entrance to another single glass door, less impressive than the non-budging doors, but one which was ajar, or strictly speaking, wedged open. With a large piece of folded-up cardboard.

"This one's open."

The pair of them edged their way inside Gris Corp. It was still dim inside the building, and they could hear the sound of many people flapping and running around. There were voices – lots of them – shouting and echoing through the building's vast atrium.

As they made their way inside and walked towards the other side of the atrium, Tom and Jack spied the occasional shape running around in the upper parts of the building and could decipher snatches of the shouting.

"… whole of east Asia…"

"… what about the north-eastern back-up in the States…"

"… no, I don't know how many we lost there… we've got nothing…"

"… what do you mean it's ALL down? How can it still ALL be down?"

"… where is she? When?"

Tom grabbed Jack's arm and motioned upwards. There, in the half-gloom, was someone who was having an especially huge shouting fit.

"NO! You're not listening to ME! I DON'T CARE WHAT *THEY* TOLD YOU! There is NOTHING working! DO YOU UNDERSTAND?!"

"And *how* did you two get in here?"

Tom spun around. A short, somewhat rotund, bald man stood in front of them. He had a youngish face and round glasses, and was wearing a trendy suit and clutching a walkie-walkie, which kept squawking with ever more shouting. Tom thought he looked stressed and in a hurry.

"Erm, we…" Jack stuttered.

"Well?" The man stared at Jack.

"The door," said Jack, pointing.

"We've won," Tom blurted out.

"Won what?" asked the man.

"Apotheosis… the game."

The man gave a sigh.

"Have you now?"

"Yeah, earlier on. We completed level 42, and then we won – and then just after that, all the power went."

"Hmph, not just the power," said the man. "Try ALL the power AND the phone networks AND the entire internet."

"Oh flip…" said Jack.

"Well, that's one word for it, sonny. Now, as you can see, we're a little busy here right now, so you two need to get lost. Now."

He motioned back towards the door.

"Move it. Before I call security on you – and I can tell you, they're already pretty grumpy. As am I."

"Wait! We've got proof, haven't we?" Tom motioned to Jack.

"That's right. Look at this."

Jack reached into his pocket and brought out his phone.

The man pursed his lips impatiently as Jack flicked the phone on and pulled up the blurry victory selfie, before brandishing it in front of the man's face.

"See. That's the photo we took when we won. It's proof!" exclaimed Jack.

The man peered at the screen for a few seconds, before pulling himself up to his full height and speaking with complete condescension dripping from his voice.

"Nice try, sonny, but we all know how to use Photoshop and filters now, don't we?"

"No, we…"

"OUT. NOW."

He grabbed each of them by the arm and began shepherding them back across the atrium and towards the one functioning front door.

"But, but…"

"Before I call security…"

"But we really won!"

"Course you did."

They reached the door, and the man opened it and bundled the pair of them back outside into the snow before giving them some advice.

"If I were you, I'd get yourselves home. It's a tad chilly out. Nighty night."

With this, he removed the cardboard wedge from the door and slammed it shut, giving the two boys the fakest of smiles, before turning on his heel and heading back across the atrium, with the walkie-talking re-clamped to his ear.

Tom and Jack stood on the front steps of the Gris Corp HQ and looked at each other.

"Did… did… did… you see what he just did there?" spluttered Jack in shock.

"Yep," replied Tom.

"No way! What a total trumpet! He totally didn't believe us!" Jack was now in full indignation mode.

"I k-k-know…" Tom was involuntarily shivering. "C-c-come on, let's go home and figure out what to do next."

"But… I mean… he… how… it's just…"

"I k-k-know," Tom said flatly, "but we're not gonna solve it here. It's too cold to figure it out now. Let's get home and then sort it. Maybe they've got back-ups or something."

"So unfair," harrumphed Jack one last time.

The boys trudged back along the snow-covered path away from the building, their heads down against the driving snow and their hands thrust in their pockets. It was going to be a very long walk home, plodding one foot in front of the other in the deepening snow. They walked in silence, nearing the edge of the park, disconsolate and cold. The snow was muffling the world now, a world that already had been unusually dark, though with the blanketing of the snow, it had lightened a little more.

The snow had already dampened the usual city sounds so much so that Tom noticed the headlights of several cars heading towards them before he heard them. He grabbed Jack.

"Look out, cars incoming."

Jack looked up and in the middle distance, both boys could see lines of car headlights snaking their way through the snow along the front road to the main entrance to the park.

"Not just one or two," said Jack, "there's loads of them – and they're big. More like SUVs…"

"Must be someone important – probably to do with the power cut or something."

"Hey, do you think maybe it's Max Gris herself?" asked Jack.

The procession of large black SUVs drew nearer.

"I dunno, but I'm not sure they'll be happy to see us. Quick, get behind here," said Tom as he grabbed Jack behind an old, gnarled tree which stood on the edge of the park at the start of the long drive to Gris Corp HQ.

The SUVs swept in through the park's gates at a speed not usually associated with driving on snow.

As they did so, there was an enormous flash in the night sky above.

"What the…" exclaimed Jack as he jumped.

"Settle – it was a flash of lightning," shushed Tom.

"Eh? It's snowing – we're not having a thunderstorm," Jack whispered back. "And why are we whispering?"

"It's thundersnow."

There was a loud, booming crack above them.

"See, told you," said Tom. "Look, they're all getting out." He pointed to where the SUVs had all drawn up and stopped directly outside the front doors of the Gris Corp building.

Tom counted six of the SUVs, from which at least a dozen heavily built men had emerged and were swarming around the vehicles. From the SUV third from the front, there stepped a tall, more slightly built figure, wearing a long, flowing coat that was billowing almost as much as the snow.

Jack pointed towards the group of people and exclaimed, "It's *her*!"

"Shut up," said Tom.

"I'm telling you, it's her. That is Max Gris."

"How can you tell?"

"'Cos she's tall and always wears big coats. Look!" Jack was now gesticulating and bouncing up and down. "Maybe she's here 'cos she knows we've won."

"Doubt it. More likely because there's a total power and Wi-Fi meltdown, doofus."

"We should go tell her. Seriously, I mean, what have we got to lose? She'd soon sort that idiot out from earlier. C'mon, let's go talk to her…" Jack was looking at Tom, imploring him and then made to head out from behind the tree and towards the group of figures, but Tom grabbed him and brought him down in the snow.

"What are you doing?"

"Look," hissed Tom.

The two boys looked back towards the group in front of the building. Several of the men appeared to be in conversation with the tall woman in the billowing coat, whilst several more were unloading crates from the SUVs.

"Yeah, they're talking. So what?" said Jack.

"No, look... there," whispered Tom, pointing, one at a time, towards two lone figures, standing on either side of the cluster of vehicles and people, scanning all around them, and wearing guns around their necks. Guns they were toting in readiness for something.

"Woah... what the..." said Jack.

"Somehow, I don't think now would be a good time to approach Max Gris," said Tom.

"What are they up to? What's with those guys being armed?" asked Jack.

"I don't know... it looks like they're moving something inside."

Several of the figures were now manhandling the crates in through the one functioning glass door, whilst the two sentries continued to scan all around themselves, peering into the snowy darkness.

"Whatever it is, I think we should get out of here," said Tom.

The sky above them flashed white again, lighting up the entire park and all the snow falling around them.

Jack grabbed Tom's arm.

"D-d-did you just see that?" he stuttered.

"Huh? What?"

"Over there..."

Tom looked at his friend's face.

"Are you okay? You look like you've just seen a ghost?"

"N-n-not a ghost... s-s-something worse."

CHAPTER TWELVE

The inside of the long, glass-panelled room was darker than normal. At one end of the room, a giant television screen was uncharacteristically silent and switched off. The light from the interior lights was inadequate for the size of the room – and this was no ordinary room. It was the Boardroom at the very centre – literally – of Gris Corp HQ and it was full of a lot of very miserable-looking people, sitting around a very long wooden table which ran for most of the length of the room. The tabletop was black and had been picked to be so in order to contrast the rest of the room, which was usually glimmering and shimmering bright white. Another two people were in the room: one - the tall be-caped woman who Tom and Jack had seen arriving a few minutes earlier - was striding around, gesticulating and being furious and shouty; the other, a gaunt, severe looking man, dressed entirely in black – suit and tie – save for a white shirt, stood impassively in the corner of the room closest to its only door, staring at the assembled company sitting around the table.

The Boardroom itself had been specially designed to be placed at the very centre of the Gris Corp HQ and, in so being, was the very heart of the Gris Corp empire. The use of natural light to make the room a brilliant white during the day had been, as Max Gris herself declared, a stroke of genius. Mainly because it had been her idea. The same was true of the bespoke glass which surrounded the entire room: this acted like a one-way mirror, in that from the outside, it appeared cloudy (and therefore no one could see inside the room), but those in the room could see out of it and into the rest of the building. That was the theory when there was enough light; right now, no one could see anything much, but they could hear Max Gris, that was for sure. The entire building could hear her (the Boardroom had been designed to be soundproof, but the architects and builders had reckoned without Gris's temper tantrums – and right now, she was in the midst of an epic one).

"What do you mean, 'all the back-up generators are working at full capacity?' It's so dark in here that I might as well be in a cave!"

This part of the rant was being directed at a nervous, older man, bald and in need of a looser suit, who was sitting at the far end of the table. The colour had drained from his face after Gris's tirade.

Max Gris put both her hands down on the table and leaned on them.

"Well?" she shouted as she banged its surface.

The older man opened his mouth to speak.

"W–w–we didn't quite… anticipate… an event of this scale… I mean, it's unprecedented…"

The older man picked up a glass of water in front of him and took a gulp from it.

There was a pause.

"Novits, what's your job title?" asked Gris, her voice now barely registering as audible.

"H–h–head of Contingencies," Novits replied.

Gris turned on him with full force.

"NOT ANYMORE IT ISN'T, YOU FOOL. NOW, GET OUT!"

A gigantic oak of a man in a dark suit, with an earpiece in his ear and a huge beard, paced towards Novits' chair and stood directly next to it. He was 'security'.

"B–b–but I… I… I…" Novits stammered.

The walking tree in a suit yanked the chair out from underneath him and then grabbed the hapless Novits by the collar to encourage him to stand up. He then propelled him towards the door. Mainly by dragging him there by the scruff of his neck.

Novits' protests dwindled to a series of whimpers as the man mountain with the earpiece ejected him with considerable force out of the Boardroom. Once outside the room, other enormous men in matching dark suits escorted the cowering Novits from the building. Permanently.

The Boardroom was silent as the original man mountain re-entered it.

Gris addressed him.

"Thank you, Grunk. At least someone around here knows how to do their job."

Grunk grunted an acknowledgement.

Gris turned towards the gaunt, severe-looking man who had stood in the corner of the Boardroom, impassively, throughout her rolling tantrum and Novits' exit.

"Slymington, who do I shout at now?"

Slymington replied in a nasally whine of a voice.

"This one here, ma'am." He pointed at a now terrified looking middle-aged woman in a smart suit. "Ms Beets. Mr Novits' former deputy."

Gris span around to face Ms Beets.

"Beets, you're now the new Head of Contingencies. So, what's the story?"

Ms Beets took a deep breath.

"Well…"

"Yes, yes, yes, come on. Come on. What's happened? What's happening? Now. Right now. What's broken? What's fixed? What's going to be fixed? When? What's the plan? When is this whole shebang going back online? And when – for the sake of all things – can we get some light in here?"

Ms Beets took a deep breath and began.

"It appears…"

Gris interrupted her.

"It appears? What do you mean 'it appears'? I don't want your opinion. I want facts. And action. Now."

She whirled around towards Slymington.

"Slymington, where do we *find* these people? I'm not interested in their opinions. You do make that clear to them, don't you? I want facts. Data. IN-FOR-MAT-ION!"

"We make that very clear, ma'am. Always."

He turned towards the now blushing Ms Beets and oozed his words at her in his best condescending tone.

"Ms Beets, if you would be so kind as to continue your report for Ms Gris and if you would indulge us all by sticking to the facts this time…"

Ms Beets took another gulp of air.

"The data we have shows that this was a once in a century solar storm, similar in scale to the Carrington event of 1859, but with a significantly larger impact, because of the world's dependency on global telecommunications and power networks. Information is still being gathered, but at this stage, we estimate that over 75% of the globe's power networks are not functioning or malfunctioning."

Max Gris's facial expression changed to one which suggested she was now musing over this new information, rather than simply being angry.

"Hmm. Wow. Well, that's a biggie. What about telecoms? And the internet?"

"Essentially, non-functional as of now," Ms Beets replied.

"What, all of it?" Gris asked.

"95% of it, so essentially, enough of it is broken…"

"… to render it useless." Gris finished the sentence.

"Yes."

Gris gave a huge smile, walked over to Ms Beets and gripped her by the shoulders.

"Ms Beets, I *like* you!"

"Th-th-thankyou, ma'am."

Gris drew herself up to her full height and threw her cape over her shoulder, before pacing backwards and forwards, up and down the Boardroom.

"So, Ms Beets, how are we going to fix this?"

"We have teams across the five territories, working with national utility companies and governments to get everyone back online."

Gris shot her a look.

"Everyone?"

"Well, the most developed countries will naturally have greater resources to deploy in order to repair their networks…"

Gris slammed the table.

"EXACTLY! Fix the rich countries back up first. They're the ones who make us our…"

She left the statement hanging in the air.

"Money…" chorused the entire company around the table, if it were possible to chorus in a mumble.

"Money!" cried Gris triumphantly, throwing both her arms up in the air, "Money-money-money-money! Love it! Love it! Love it!"

She turned to face Ms Beets again.

"Continue."

"The Tier One countries' networks are expected to be functional again before Christmas…"

"*What? Noooooooooooooo….*" howled Gris.

"That is a realistic assessment of the time…"

"NonononononononononoNO!" On the final 'no', Gris slammed the Boardroom table once more. "It must be *before* Christmas. Well before Christmas, because…"

She took a step towards Ms Beets.

"Christmas…"

Another step.

"will be…"

Another step and Gris bent down to put her face right in front of Ms Beets.

"too late!" Gris was now grinning like a maniac, right in Ms Beets' face.

"Understood?"

"Yes," squeaked Ms Beets.

"So, Beetsy, whaddya need? Eh? To have this whole shebang working again?"

"Well, if we doubled the teams…"

"You got it! What else?"

"More kit…"

"Done. It's yours. Double… no, quadruple the equipment, the teams and the money and…"

"And?"

"When will then be now?" asked Gris, raising an eyebrow.

"Well, I…"

"Come on, come on, come on! Stick your neck on the chopping block, Beetsy. I'm either going to promote you or fire you. Your choice."

Gris flashed all her teeth in a fake smile towards Ms Beets.

Ms Beets, who now realised she was being made the proverbial offer she could not refuse, spluttered out a date.

"December 23rd."

"A.m. or p.m.?" the still fake-smiling Gris enquired.

"P.m...."

"Final answer?" The smile floated in the air, with all its teeth bared, a shark wearing lipstick.

"A.m. I meant a.m," Ms Beets quickly corrected herself.

"Great! So?"

"So?" asked Ms Beets.

The smile vanished. "So, why are you ALL still sitting here? Get to it!"

All the employees around the Boardroom table scrambled to their feet and rushed for the door. All barring Slymington, who remained impassive (though his face appeared to be locked in a permanent sneer) and Grunk, who gave a low growl as some of the terrified Gris Corp employees scuttled past him on their way out.

As the last of the hapless Gris Corp executives exited and the Boardroom door closed, Max Gris flopped down into a chair at the head of the Boardroom table and put her feet up on it.

"Slimey, what news of Ireland!"

"Nothing, ma'am."

"*What?*"

Max Gris whizzed around in the chair and was now sitting fully upright and completely alert, like a meerkat on sentry duty.

Slymington continued as dispassionately as ever.

"All the grids failed around the same time as our contractor should have been making the last acquisition."

"And you've heard nothing?"

"Not a single thing. We've tried all the channels. They're all down."

"There was a plan B, right?"

Slymington gave an especially oily reply.

"Of course, ma'am. It's ready for your activation."

"Activate it! Now!"

Gris paused.

"Hang on, what is it?"

"Our contractor was to make his way to Dublin and await further instructions at your favourite hotel.

"That's the plan?"

"Yes."

"What, all of it?"

"Not quite," Slymington pointed to Grunk. "Grunk's going to fetch him back here, so the next update will be in person."

Gris was now up on her feet and pacing around again. And gesticulating. Wildly.

"How long's that going to take? It's Christmas Eve in three days, Slimey!"

"We have the speedboats ready."

"Grunk," said Gris.

Grunk nodded at Gris.

"Go. Go now. Get him."

"Yes, ma'am."

Grunk made for the door, walking like a man whose trousers were now on fire.

"And Grunk?"

Grunk half-turned back.

"Quick as you can, there's a good boy."

"Yes, ma'am."

He was out the door and gone.

Gris slumped back down in her chair and sighed, slightly dreamily, a big grin on her face.

"I like Grunk. He doesn't answer back or say too much. He just does stuff."

She paused. Then she stood up again, looking anxious.

"Slimey, do you think he'll get the last consignment to us in time?"

Slymington's face remained impassive. Sometimes, Gris wondered if he'd ever experienced an emotion in his life. He opened his mouth, paused, and closed it again as he considered an appropriate response. After a further few seconds had passed, he opened his mouth and this time, words followed.

"He's a professional. We gave him the very best intelligence regarding all the locations."

He paused again. "He will deliver the final piece on time."

Max Gris's face was, for the first time this evening, contorted into an expression that was not one of her own choosing. Whereas before she had veered between gleeful, playful, angry and plain psychotic as it suited her, now she merely looked drawn.

"He better had. We need it by Christmas Eve. In daylight. You do realise what happens if he misses this deadline, don't you? I mean, we were cutting it fine as it was."

"I am very aware of the pressing urgency, ma'am." Slymington sounded almost weary, as though he were addressing a small child.

"Slimey, I don't want to wait another year," wailed Gris. "Especially not when we've gone to all this trouble, and…" she grabbed his arm, "we are *so* close." She looked plaintively into Slymington's eyes. It was like staring at the eyes of a cold, dead fish. There was nothing there.

If Slymington was uncomfortable about Max Gris now literally hanging off his arm, nothing registered on his face. Not even a flicker of a feeling.

"He has never let us down before, ma'am. This is only a slight and temporary delay."

"You had better be right. He's got less than three days left. He'd better deliver."

"He will. Grunk will bring him in."

Gris released Slymington from her grip and veered away, towards the other end of the Boardroom.

"And then there's this!"

She waved her arm towards posters of Apotheosis at the far end of the Boardroom.

Gris looked at one of the clouded panes of glass, staring into the middle-distance.

"Slimey, what time is it?"

"It's past 7 o'clock, ma'am."

"SEVEN? Have we heard from our winner by some miracle?"

"No, ma'am. Everything is down. We have heard nothing since just after half-past five when it all happened."

"Get Rudderts in here."

Slymington walked to the door and motioned to one of the other monster men in suits, standing outside it.

A few seconds later, the short, fat, bald man with the round glasses, who had turned Tom and Jack away, bundled his way into the room.

"Hello, ma'am. How are you this evening? That is a most striking outfit indeed," he fawned.

Max Gris's face was as flat as the tone of her voice.

"Yes. Thank you, Rudderts. Apotheosis. Update. Now."

"Ah, yes, well, we have had a few little problemos…"

"What, like the whole internet being fried?" asked Gris, as though she were talking to a complete idiot.

"Well, yes, ma'am, there is that…"

Gris marched straight towards Rudderts, who was now trembling slightly. She grabbed him by the lapels of his jacket and snarled into his face.

"Where. Is. Our. Winner?"

Rudderts gulped. Then he squeaked.

"Don't know."

"Well, how are you going to find her?" Gris threatened. "Or him – or maybe one of each."

Rudderts smiled weakly. As of approaching seven thirty this evening, this was not a question to which he had, as yet, an answer.

"Erm…"

"THAT is not an answer, Rudderts!" Gris was bellowing now, in full flow. "They were *supposed* to win it this evening."

"All the systems are down, ma'am."

"I know that, Rudderts! Tell me something I don't know…" She was directly in Rudderts' face now.

"Well ma'am, before everything broke, we know that several hundred players around the world had reached level forty, thirty-seven had reached level forty-one and twelve were on level forty-two. Look, here."

He produced a crumpled piece of paper from the pocket of his overly florid jacket and proffered it, as one might a peace offering, to Gris. Max Gris shot Rudderts a look of pure disdain and swatted the crumpled paper from his hand.

"I don't want to see your paper offcuts, Rudderts. I want to see a winner in this building. NOW! They were meant to have won by 8 o'clock this evening *at the very latest* and that's not going to happen now, is it?"

"No, ma'am. It is not." Rudderts was squeaking again.

"Well? What are you going to *do* about it?"

Rudderts had been ready for this one.

"We'll interrogate all the systems so we can pinpoint the locations of the players who were really close, and I'll have our snatch squads ready in all of those areas, so we can bring them in as soon as we're all back online."

"Rudderts…" Gris rolled her eyes.

"Yes, ma'am?"

"They're not 'snatch squads', you imbecile! They are the Customer Acquisition Teams – the CATs – these winners are children, for goodness' sake… 'snatch squads' indeed. Honestly, for someone who is *supposed* to be my PR wizard, you let yourself down sometimes, Rudderts, you really do."

By this point, Rudderts couldn't really work out whether Gris was still furious with him.

"Now, get out and find my winner!"

No, she was still incandescent, he concluded. He scuttled out of the Boardroom, relieved to have survived the encounter.

Max Gris sighed as she propped herself up on the table and leant on it. She turned to Slymington and sounded weary.

"Slimey, make sure Grunk brings in our man. Do whatever it takes but have him here by the morning."

"Yes, ma'am."

Gris stood up and stretched her arms upwards as though re-energised. Right, she thought, who can I shout at next?

CHAPTER THIRTEEN

"Tell me again *exactly* what you saw." Tom was looking at Jack sceptically, trying not to let too much of a tone of disbelief enter his voice.

Jack sighed (again). This was the third time they had had this conversation in about as many minutes.

"I told you, it all happened so quickly. I'm not sure, but it was sort of... like a monster or something. Like a dinosaur."

Tom raised his eyebrows.

"Right. A dinosaur. In a snowstorm. In Glasgow."

"I know it sounds bonkers, but I'm telling you that's what I saw!" protested Jack, throwing his arms out in exasperation.

"Except... you're not entirely sure what you saw. I mean, first, you said you didn't know what you saw, then you decided it was either some sort of monster. Or a dinosaur." Tom paused.

"I think we'd better get you home, mate. You've been out in the cold too long."

"I feel *fine*," protested Jack. Again.

The two boys stood in the snow, which was deepening by the minute, staring at each other in a wintry stand-off. The flakes were billowing everywhere now and had covered the pair of them in snow from head to toe. Tom cracked first.

"Look, maybe you saw something, maybe you didn't. Perhaps it was just a trick of the lightning and the snow, but whatever it was, it'll have to wait. We shouldn't be out in this: it's getting worse. We should go home."

Tom moved out from their hidden position behind the trees and walked back towards the entrance to the park. Jack stood stock still, refusing to budge. Tom turned and pleaded with his friend.

"Jack, seriously… it's Baltic out here. We have to go home."

"You don't believe me, do you?"

Tom was shivering by now.

"It's not about whether or not I believe you… if we stay out here, we're going to freeze. Stop being so stubborn. We need to go. We can figure it out once we've got home and thawed out. Come on."

As Tom finished speaking, there was another massive flash of lightning, which lit up the whole park once again in an eerie, unreal light of temporary daylight and snowflakes. It also lit up a very large silhouette against the profile of an old semi-ruined building on the edge of the park's woods, a few hundred yards from where Tom and Jack were standing, shivering.

"There! There it is again!" Jack cried in triumph, grabbing his friend's arm, and pointing towards the building.

Tom was silent.

"Did you see it? Did you see it this time? You must have seen it? It was totally massive that time!" said Jack. All in one breath.

Tom replied slowly and quietly.

"What the… Yep. I saw it."

"See! I told you I saw something! It's like a monster or something, isn't it?"

Tom was still staring at the place in the darkness where the building and the silhouette had been revealed. He nodded.

"Now do you believe me?" asked Jack.

"Yeah. Sorry," said Tom.

"We need to go figure out what it is!" exclaimed Jack, shaking his friend by the shoulders.

"I think that would be a *very* bad idea..." Tom replied, emphasising every word deliberately. "It's none of our business..."

"Come on, we need to go investigate," urged Jack.

They were both peering into the darkness. From the area where the building had briefly flashed into view, they could now see what looked like muted, orange-coloured lights flashing on and off for a split second.

"What on earth...?" muttered Tom.

"Come on!" cried Jack.

"No, wait..."

But Tom was too late. Jack was off and running towards the old building and the strange flashing lights sparking away inside it. Tom rolled his eyes and set off after his friend, talking to himself as he sprinted after him.

"This... is... none... of... our... business..."

After a few hundred yards, Tom caught up with Jack, who was standing at the edge of the old building. The strange, muted lights were still flashing randomly from somewhere inside it.

"You're a maniac," panted Tom, as he caught Jack.

Jack raised his finger to his lips, motioning his friend to be quiet.

"What? What is it?" whispered Tom.

"I thought I heard something moving inside. Look at this place."

Jack gesticulated at the old, semi-derelict building as it stood hulking in the snowy darkness. Its snow-flecked stone walls were caked in moss and there were boards covering the gaps in the structure where there had once been windows. It did not look safe, nor, in Tom's opinion, did it look like a building one would want to stand too close to, let alone venture inside.

"It must have been here for centuries. Come on, there must be a door somewhere," Jack said quietly – and with this, he was off again.

He edged his way around the outside of the building. By now, Tom was shivering so much that his teeth were chattering. He had been worried that they were making a big mistake, even by staying in the park to watch the comings and goings outside Gris Corp's HQ, but this was taking it to a whole different level.

"Jack…." Tom hissed, "Jaaaaack…."

But it was no use. Jack had headed into the gloom on a mission to find an entrance to the ruin. Tom knew his friend well enough and whilst he'd always liked Jack's spontaneity, on those occasions when it tipped into impulsiveness, it usually ended up with Jack – and Tom – landing in trouble of some sort. Tom sensed that this could be one of those times.

He set off after Jack, who had by now almost disappeared into the darkness. The zig-zag of his headtorch was barely visible. Tom was muttering to himself about his friend.

"… total eejit… freezing… can't even see two steps in front of… OOOFFFTT."

Tom faceplanted into the snow and his headtorch flew off his head, its light going out in the process. He was now ready to curse Jack. As he dragged himself up, he saw the cause of his trip and fall: an enormous stone, which had been semi-covered by the snow. He reached for his headtorch. Gone.

"Brilliant…" he muttered, in a tone which suggested it was anything but.

He peered more closely, his eyes adjusting to the darkness, trying to locate the missing light. As he felt for it in the snow, he saw another stone, next to the first one. Again, it was only semi-covered by the snow. Then, he made out an uneven shape a few feet away, a whole pile of the old, massive, cuboid-shaped stones, scattered all around the base of the ruin, some of them with barely a dusting of snow on them at all.

That's odd: it's been snowing for ages, but these look as though they've only been here for a few minutes, he thought.

And then, he realised.

"Oh no… Jack," he hissed. "Jaaaaccck." This time, more loudly.

Tom set off, blundering his way through the darkness, trying to keep as far away as he could from the edge of the building. He needed to find Jack and warn him.

"Those stones… not enough snow on them… must have fallen… d-d-dingbats… I'm cold…" he muttered to himself. The snow was relentless, and it was being whipped up by occasional gusts of wind, birling in small, snowy white tornadoes. Tom now understood a little of what people meant when they talked about snow blindness. He caught his breath as he reached the far corner of the building, the furthest point from both the front of Gris Corp HQ and the entrance to the park. Tom realised that there was a small risk that as he moved around the corner, he would (at least in theory) be in plain line of sight of the Gris Corp building, though whether anyone would actually be able to see him in the midst of a semi-blizzard was questionable. He stood, frozen and out of breath, the cold air scorching his lungs, and wondered what to do next. He needed to find Jack. Quickly.

He felt the weight on his arm a fraction of a second before the words.

"Arrrrgghhh!" Tom cried.

"SSSSSSSHHHHHHHHHH!" It was Jack.

"You nearly gave me a heart attack, you eejit," Tom hissed at him.

Jack put his fingers to his lips again and indicated to his friend to be quiet. He beckoned him towards the building.

"Jack, not a good idea. It's not safe… some stones fell…"

Jack tapped his finger furiously on his lips, to emphasise that Tom should stop talking. Now.

"What? What is it?" whispered Tom.

Jack crept forwards in front of Tom, beckoning him to follow, and neared a different coloured shape set in the wall of the building. He pointed at it with the thumb of his left hand, all the while keeping the index finger of his right hand firmly pressed against his lips.

The shape was a door. A very old, broken and rickety door, with lots of gaps riddled up and down it, but a door nonetheless.

Jack reached for where the handle should have been, but where there was now just a hole in the wood. He stuck his gloved fingers into the door and yanked at it. It gave a tiny bit, but no more than the width of a twig. Jack indicated for Tom to help him. Tom shook his head and opened his mouth as though to speak, but Jack simply motioned at him to stay quiet and to help him pull at the door. Tom threw his hands up in exasperation and rolled his eyes. Then, he sighed, grabbed the part of the door next to the hole where the handle had once been and both boys pulled at it.

The door shifted again, this time by a little more than it had done before.

"It's working," whispered Jack. "Come on: pull."

The boys put all their strength into it and this time, the door properly gave way and fell open with such suddenness that Tom landed in a heap – again – clutching part of its ancient wooden structure. Jack bent down to help his friend up.

"You okay?"

"Yeah, just about."

Tom dusted the snow off himself as he got to his feet.

"What's happened to your headtorch?" asked Jack, noticing the lack of the wearable headgear on his friend's head for the first time.

"That's what I was trying to tell you. I fell over some stones and lost it in the snow back there. They looked like they had just fallen."

"Eh? Hmph, don't see how that could've happened."

"Jack, I'm telling you, this place isn't safe. And anyway, what are you doing?"

"Remember I said I thought I heard noises coming from in here?" whispered Jack.

"Yeah…"

"Well, I definitely heard *something*, but it's stopped now."

"Maybe it was more stones falling."

"And there haven't been any more of those weird lights, either."

"Look, Jack…"

"C'mon, let's just take a quick look."

"Jaa-aack, this is a really bad idea…"

"Two minutes. I promise."

Jack went to the doorway and beckoned his friend to follow him inside. Tom dutifully did so, though with little enthusiasm. As he stepped into the interior of the building, he was grateful that at least it wasn't snowing in there as well.

Jack was already off and hunting around the building.

"Look, look at this." He had taken off his headtorch and was pointing it at an ornate-looking carving on the wall.

"Looks like some sort of ugly cartoon."

"It's a gargoyle, Jack."

"And look at this: looks like churchy stuff – all crosses and angels."

Jack was flashing his torch around the walls of the building, picking out the various objects and symbols carved into it.

"It's like some sort of ancient church," said Tom. "That's weird. How come it's here?"

Jack was still flashing his torch from side to side, across the blackened space inside the church, when this time, as it swept across the walls, it picked out an eye. The beam from the headtorch stuck to the eye like a magnet. Only the eye wasn't carved into one of the walls. And it was an enormous eye indeed. Which then blinked.

And then, it moved.

And then, from somewhere very near the eye, there was a bellow which turned into a roar.

The light from the headtorch disappeared.

Tom yelled out in fright and made to run. There was just one slight problem: as he tried to move, he realised something rather heavy was weighing down on his feet. Glancing downwards, he could just make out Jack lying sprawled across them in an unmoving heap.

The roaring stopped. It was replaced by a series of thumping footsteps and loud sniffing noises, which grew louder as whatever was making them drew nearer to Tom.

The heavy footsteps and the sniffing stopped.

And then, a gruff voice spoke in a broad Scottish accent.

"Are you a knight?"

CHAPTER FOURTEEN

Max Gris was pacing around the Boardroom of her HQ. She had been doing a lot of pacing around it for the past quarter of an hour, stalking an invisible prey like a trapped tigress. With occasional outbursts of shouting in her lair. She had not directed these at anyone in particular. Well, not except her faithful number two, Slymington, who sat, as impassive as usual, letting her verbal volleys wash over him. Slymington had become inured to Max's flare-ups down the years. Temper tantrums, as he occasionally described them to a select few others. She had been prone to these since she was a little girl and Slymington had seen them develop into a typical mode of behaviour she deployed, often to get her own way and especially with her employees.

Personally, he blamed her father for this. Slymington had been his faithful number two for decades, but the one thing he had learnt never to disagree with Max Gris Senior about was his daughter. Maxine was 'special', as the older Gris had told him frequently. An only child, a true daddy's girl throughout childhood, and one who had always got whatever she wanted and whenever she wanted it. Which was frequently 'everything' and 'now'.

Slymington had realised very early in her childhood that she was becoming spoilt, but also that she was being brought up and educated by her father to take over the family business from him one day. Saying anything to contradict her father had become increasingly pointless whenever it concerned the young Maxine, particularly if he wanted to continue being her father's right-hand man. Max Gris senior did not receive any kind of criticism – even if it was constructive – very well. Like father, like daughter, Slymington thought to himself.

However, when the young Max (and she had been young – too young, in Slymington's opinion) had taken over the running of the business, her pre-existing traits of being spoilt, bossy and prone to occasionally epic outbursts of vitriol had become amplified – especially in the workplace. This was something that had initially been a cause of some worry to Slymington, particularly as the one person who could have moderated her behaviour - her father - was no longer there to do so.

But over the months and years, Slymington had realised several key points about Max's volatility: one) it was never aimed at him (other than in the most superficial of ways when she was having a general rant); two) he could manipulate Max into having an outburst or two with relative ease, through the judicious deployment of particular triggers; and three) her behaviour or the threat of it – or even the threat of the threat of it – was a very effective weapon with which to control the rest of her employees. The subordinates, as Slymington delightfully referred to them.

It was a weapon which he secretly enjoyed deploying whenever it suited him. Which was often. Not that anyone would have known that Slymington was deriving any covert joy from this, as his face defaulted to its permanently impassive state and his voice rarely varied from a monotone as he instructed people what to do next, and accompanied this with the hint of a threat of an explosion from Ms Gris if they didn't do exactly as he had ordered them to do, in precisely the manner in which he instructed them and precisely when he had ordered them to do it.

This evening, however, even Slymington was slightly taken aback at just how on edge Max seemed, and with the increasing ferocity of her outbursts. Tonight, he mused, she appeared to be genuinely stressed and angry. And what was worse, the cause of her anger wasn't taking her calls.

"Try him again, Slimey," snapped Gris, pointing at the Boardroom's speakerphone.

Slymington leant forward to type in the number on the machine's touchscreen. He may have sighed, ever so slightly. Gris bent forwards over the table, resting her arms on it, her face a contortion of worry and stress. She spoke again.

"You don't think he's bailed on us?"

"No, ma'am, I don't, he replied flatly as he began tapping in the number. The speakerphone's dial tone was replaced with silence.

"What if he's holding out – because this is the last haul? Maybe he has a second burner?"

"Ma'am, he's a professional. There is likely to be a reasonable explanation for his unavailability."

As Slymington punched in the final digit, all that could be heard from the phone was the not-quite-silence of modern communications, before the familiar, neutral voice of the mobile phone network spoke once again.

"It has not been possible to connect your call. Please try again later."

"Arrrrrggghhh!" Gris howled in rage and slammed her fists on the table. "Where IS he?"

She resumed her pacing, her mind whirling.

Slymington paused for a few seconds and then spoke once more.

"The likelihood is that the network is still not working properly because of all the power cuts, ma'am, and therefore we cannot reach him. We'll just have to be patient. He will be in touch."

"Yesyesyesyes… I know all this. The power cuts. The STUPID, IDIOTIC POWER CUTS!"

She was shouting again. Never a good sign, thought Slymington. He made a suggestion.

"Why don't you take a break for ten minutes and we can try him again then?"

Gris paused, considered the option for a nanosecond, and then whirled around, back towards the centre of the room.

"No," she said firmly and pointed at the speakerphone. "Try him again. Now. "

Slymington did as she instructed.

This time, as he punched the final number in, the not-quite-silence hung in the air for a fraction of a second longer than in previous attempts, before a faint-sounding ring tone began.

"Yes!" Gris exclaimed, and launched a celebratory fist into the air.

A fractured French voice answered the phone.

"Hello?" It was him.

Gris nodded at Slymington. He dispensed with any pleasantries.

"We were becoming slightly concerned we hadn't heard from you."

"I have had no phone signal. There have been power cuts, as I'm sure you are aware."

"Yes, we have them here as well."

Slymington cut straight to business.

"Was your trip successful?"

The not-quite-silence returned to the phone line. Finally, the recipient of the call spoke.

"No."

"No? What do you mean, 'no'?" asked Slymington.

"Monsieur, your intelligence was wrong. There was nothing at the site."

Slymington glanced at Gris. He could sense an eruption was coming.

"Our intelligence has never been incorrect before," said Slymington.

"Well, this time it was. There was nothing there. I checked the whole site. Thoroughly. The tomb was empty."

There was a pause. Gris grabbed the speakerphone. Strictly, this wasn't entirely necessary, as this model was a high-end device, capable of picking up voices at a range up to ten metres, but Gris wasn't thinking rationally, as the Shadow was about to find out.

"What do you mean… empty?" she hissed.

"Ah, Ms Gris, it is good to hear your voice." The Shadow actually meant this; he had grown tired of always having to listen to Slymington's monotone.

"As I said, Ms Gris, empty. There was nothing in it."

"Impossible," retorted Gris.

"Ms Gris, there was nothing there. No bones nor any other relics."

"You had better not be lying to us."

"Madame, I am not lying."

"Or holding out for more money." Gris was glowering at the speakerphone.

"I am a professional. We have an agreement. The fee is perfectly sufficient."

The Shadow was calm and measured as he spoke. He had dealt with characters like Max Gris before. In such situations, it was always best to state one's truth calmly – and to repeat it, if necessary.

"Why should we believe you? How do we know you don't have the relics and are just holding out for more money?"

"Madame, I do not have the relics. We have an agreement, and you have my word when I say that the tomb was empty – as was the rest of the site. I am as disappointed as you are by this turn of events."

"Your word," Gris snorted derisively. She looked at Slymington and raised her hands and eyebrows, as though asking him a question.

Slymington interjected and spoke into the phone.

"You are quite certain that you could not be *mistaken*…"

"Monsieur, I followed your instructions to the letter. Beyond this, I searched the whole site to ensure I had not missed anything, but there was no trace of them anywhere. I say again, your intelligence was incorrect this time."

"I see," said Slymington. "One moment, please."

He hit the mute button on the speakerphone.

"Well?" asked Gris. "Do you believe him?"

"I'm not sure that, right now, we have any other choice other than to believe him."

"Dammit!"

Gris slammed the table with her fists again.

"Slimey, we have two days left to do this. What are we going to do?"

"I strongly advise that we recheck the intelligence to confirm whether it is possible that Dr Auld could have been incorrect."

Gris paused, thought for a few seconds, and then spoke again.

"How soon can you bring Auld in?"

"As soon as you give the word, we can have him here within the hour."

"Do it."

"And what of our friend?" Slymington nodded towards the phone.

"He stays where he is until we figure this out. And if he's lying…"

"Grunk shall deal with him." Even in Slymington's monotone, this sounded like a threat.

"Put him back on. He stays where he is – for now." said Gris.

Slymington took the phone off mute and spoke.

"Hello, we have discussed what you have told us and have some new instructions: you are to stay where you are until we issue fresh orders. Understood?"

"Understood, monsieur. I shall wait to hear from you again."

"Good." replied Slymington. "Make sure you do."

He hit the button to end the call. Gris spoke first.

"Take some men and bring Auld here immediately."

"Understood, ma'am."

Max Gris sighed, closed her eyes, and kept them closed for a few seconds, as though trying some sort of speed meditation. As she opened them again, a false smile flashed onto her face.

"Right, I have a press conference to do," she exclaimed with a flourish, and turned and strode towards the Boardroom door.

CHAPTER FIFTEEN

It had been an evening of firsts for Tom Brightly. It was the first time he had won a global gaming competition. It was the first time he had walked across the city in the middle of a snowstorm – and a blackout. It was the first time he had visited Gris Corp's HQ. It was the first time he had ever broken into a building (even if it was a derelict one). And now, it was the first time he had ever had a strange creature's snot dripping onto the top of his head. And it was very gross indeed.

However, it was not as foul as the breath from the afore-mentioned creature, which was so noxious that it was making Tom want to barf. At least he thought that was what was making him feel sick, but given the way his stomach felt right now, that he was shaking and could feel the blood draining from his face, it was possible it was sheer terror that was leading to this feeling of nausea. Tom glanced down at his feet. Jack was still sprawled in a heap on the stone floor. He had had the right idea when he fainted. He was missing all this – including the creature's unfortunate personal habits. And its chat. And the questions…

The creature loomed in front of Tom in the darkness and started again.

"Are you sure you're not a knight?"

Tom spluttered out an answer.

"D-d-d-definitely sure."

"And your pal there?"

"D-d-d-definitely sure he's not a knight, either."

"Hmph, just as well. 'Cos he'd be a rubbish one if he was."

The creature clumped away from Tom and rummaged around in the gloom. Tom could hear it moving things around.

It spoke again.

"If you're not a knight, then what are you doing here?" It paused. "Come to think of it, what am *I* doing here?" Then it moved further away from Tom and started scrabbling around again, moving objects hither and thither in the darkness. A crash occasionally punctuated this general noise as it threw something away.

Tom seized the moment to bend down and try to shake Jack awake.

"Ja-a-a-ck... Jaaaacccckkkk... c'mon waken up..." he whispered as he shook Jack's shoulders. Nothing. Jack was still out cold.

The footsteps rumbled back towards him.

"What's up with your pal? He's not saying much for himself."

"I-I-I think he fainted."

"Fainted? Eh? He really would be a rubbish knight."

Tom bristled, despite being terrified. He had had enough.

"He's not a knight. He's just a boy. And he fainted 'cos you made him."

There was a pause.

"Eh? How'd I make him do that?"

"Because... because... you... whatever you are, terrified the wits out of him, that's why. And me!"

The creature stopped its scrabbling and rummaging.

"Are you sure neither of you is a knight?"

"Totally!" said Tom in exasperation.

"Well then, laddie, if you're not knights, then I mean you no harm."

Well, that was a start, thought Tom.

He could now hear strange crunching sounds.

"So..." the creature began, CRUNCH CRUNCH CRUNCH "... iff you'me---CRUCH... notmm... MUNCH MUNCH... ahhmm... knighttt... CRRUUUCNCCCH... whatfmph ur you?" CRUUUNNNCH CRUNNNCH CRUNCCHH.

"Sorry," said Tom, "I didn't catch any of that. What are you doing? Are you *eating* something?"

"Yesspmh... CRUNCH CRUNCH CRUNCH... Aaaaaahhh."

The creature let out a sigh of satisfaction as the last of the crunching and munching noises subsided. And then it let out an enormous burp.

"What on earth are you eating that makes all that noise?" asked Tom.

"Wood, mainly. But there might be some other stuff in there, too. Coal perhaps. Maybe a wee dash of peat as well. Then again, probably not. Hard to tell. It's been a wee while since I had a slap-up feed like this."

"You eat *wood*?"

"Aye. Well, usually. Mainly because it's always lying around somewhere. Easy to find and easy to chomp. Mind you, some of the stuff in here's a wee bit chewy."

The creature brandished the remains of what looked like some sort of chair in Tom's face.

"What was that? And what are *you*?"

"That, laddie, was a pew. No idea what they've done to it, but it was all covered in something that made it extra-chewy. Got it down in the end. It'll take a minute or two before I know if it's worked."

"What do you mean, 'if it's worked'?"

"Hang on…"

The creature let out another massive belch.

"Aaaaaaah, that's better."

Tom tried not to keel over from the stench of the huge burp. He covered his face with the sleeve of his coat.

"I don't think whatever it is you've eaten is agreeing with your stomach much."

"Och, that's just because it's still waking up. Like me. I'm still half-asleep. Right!"

The creature stood bolt upright and took a deep breath.

"Here we go…"

It let out the breath, making a noise that sounded half like a sneeze and half like a roar. At first, a few sparks flew out of its nose and then a pop or two of flame. It opened up its mouth as well – mid-breath – and there was a further flash or two of orange-coloured flames and then came the smoke… an awful lot of smoke. And coughing – from both Tom and the creature, which was, by now, lost in its self-created fog of smoke and in the middle of a giant coughing fit.

As the smoke (and the coughing) gradually subsided, it spoke again.

"Och… that's annoying. Still not awake."

It appeared to be addressing its stomach.

Once he had drawn breath, Tom asked the question again.

"What on earth are you and where did you come from?"

"Well, laddie, since you ask, I'm Gus, short for Angus. I'm a dragon – the last one on earth… probably… and I came from right up there – via somewhere else a long time ago."

Gus was pointing towards the roof of the building with one of his winged arms. At least Tom thought they were arms, though he wasn't entirely sure, having never met a dragon before.

"At least I think that's what happened. Or maybe it was all a dream. Maybe I'm still asleep and dreaming. That would explain a lot." Gus now appeared to be talking to himself. He pivoted back towards Tom.

"So, what's your name then?"

"Tom. I'm Tom. And this is Jack." He pointed at Jack's still comatose form.

"And you're a *dragon?*"

"Aye, are you deaf or something?"

Tom couldn't believe his ears.

"So, you're an actual, living, *talking* dragon?"

"Well, I'm certainly not a dead one."

"And you, like, breathe fire and everything?"

"Can you not see I'm trying to do that? It's just I'm a little sleepy after being woken up and my stomach's still in hibernation. Takes time, all this waking up stuff. Managed it for a wee while, though. Just not got enough oomph to do it again yet."

Tom nodded as though he understood what Gus had just said – whereas he had no clue what the creature - or, rather, the dragon - was talking about. Then, he had a lightbulb moment.

"Of course, that was what the orange lights we saw were…" said Tom, and he facepalmed his forehead.

"And I'm *still* absolutely starving," said Gus.

And with that, he began scrabbling and rummaging around again, moving what sounded like more pieces of furniture.

"What are you doing? Are you looking for more things to eat?"

Gus stopped, mid-rummage.

"Yes, sort of, but I think I've lost something as well. Or at least I remember losing something a very long time ago. And that I need to find it."

"What is it you've lost?" asked Tom.

Gus rumbled back to Tom and put his face right in Tom's. And thus it was that Tom finally got a good look at his first ever dragon. He had a dark green, scaly face, with huge nostrils and prominent triangular ears at the very top of his head – a head that was the size of a beach ball - and large, heavy-lidded eyes, ringed in deep purple, with golden-flecked eyeballs and prominent, strangely shaped pupils at their centre. There were sharp vertical scales all over his face as well. His mouth and jaw were huge and angular – and then Gus spoke again. Tom could see his very long, olive-green and pink, slightly forked tongue as he opened his mouth, but most of all, what he saw were the large, white and very sharp teeth that adorned the dragon's mouth.

"Well, laddie, if I could remember that, then I likely wouldn't still be looking for it, would I?"

"Uh huh," said Tom, unconvinced.

As Gus rumbled back into the darkness, Jack started making noises, which suggested he was coming round. Tom bent down to check on him.

"Ooooh... monsters... stop the monsters... all the snow... snowballs... throw the snowballs at the monsters..." Jack murmured.

"Jack," Tom whispered, giving Jack a gentle shake. "Wake up."

"Ow, my head... what happened? Where am I?"

"Jack, Jack, it's me, Tom. You fainted, but I'm right here. We're in some sort of building. At Gris Corp – remember?"

Jack hauled himself up onto his elbows.

"Tom? What are we doing here? Why's it all dark?

"We're in some sort of old building and you went looking for something..."

"The thing!" Jack sat bolt upright. "There was a huge scary thing!"

"Yep, there was – well, is - a thing."

There was a crash from several feet away as Gus threw something else away.

Jack grabbed Tom's arm.

"What was that?"

"That's 'the thing'," said Tom, "although actually, he's a dragon."

"A dragon?"

"Yep."

"Am I having a nightmare or something?"

"No, you're definitely awake."

The sound of further crashing and bashing echoed off the old stone walls of the building, punctuated by occasional shouts of delight.

"Oh, this looks tasty. But I couldn't eat all of it."

And more noises of crunching, followed by those of satisfaction.

"Mmmmm, not as chewy. Aaaah, that'll go down a wee treat."

Tom spoke again.

"Where's your headtorch?"

"Think it must've fallen off when I passed out."

"Do you have another torch?"

"Hang on…"

Jack fished around in his pocket and produced a long, thin torch.

"Here you go."

"Ta."

Tom switched it on and pointed it in the general direction of the rummaging.

"Hey, what are you doing? Are you trying to blind me?"

Gus clumped back over to the two boys.

"I see your pal's woken up then?"

For the first time, both boys could see Gus properly. He was big and solid. Huge, in fact. Tom reckoned he was at least eight feet tall. His winged arms were enormous enough, but they were dwarfed by another pair of wings on his back, which looked even more massive. He stood on his hind legs and was covered from head to tail in scales, the same darkish green colour as his face. And then there was his tail, which looked like a lethal weapon in its own right. It went on forever and was serrated with ridges, finally tapering, at its very end, to one big scale, shaped like the ace in a deck of cards.

Tom and Jack could see Gus's face more clearly now and he looked terrifying. Mainly it was the teeth that produced this effect, but also his eyes, with their dark lids and their piercing, glittering irises and massive pupils. Which were staring directly at both boys. The rest of his face looked quite scrunched up as he spoke again.

"Would you put that flame away, the pair of you. You're wrecking my night vision."

"Aaaaarrrrrgggghhh!" screamed Jack. "It's going to eat us!"

"Eh?" said Gus, now looking bemused. "I heard that. Who's going to eat you? I'm not going to eat you. Hmph, what an insult."

"B-b-but you're a monster," spluttered Jack.

Gus looked indignant.

"Well, that's not a very nice thing to say to someone you've just met, is it?"

He bent his long neck down to put his face right in front of Jack's and spoke slowly and deliberately.

"I am definitely *not* a monster, laddie. Got that?"

"Yes," squeaked Jack.

"Good! Now, I'm looking for something, something very important and I need to get on with it. Need to find it… got to protect him…"

His voice trailed off as he headed back into the darkness.

Tom shone the torch after Gus as he thumped and clumped his way around in the darkness. He could see that Gus was searching and moving indistinct objects around again, most of which looked rather large. He would occasionally stop, bend down and inspect something he'd found in more detail, and then either eat it or throw it away.

There was a further crash as Gus chucked yet another wooden chair aside. And then, a cry of delight.

"Aha!"

Followed by the sounds of more crunching and munching.

"What are we going to do?" whispered Jack.

"Either we stay and help him, or we go," replied Tom.

"I vote we go," said Jack. The urgency in his voice told Tom he meant it, but Tom was curious.

"Gus, can we help you?" asked Tom.

"What are you *doing*?" asked Jack, as he threw his hands up in exasperation.

Tom continued.

"You said you had to protect someone. Who?"

Gus put down his latest snack and clumped back over towards the two boys.

"Can you two keep a secret?"

Tom nodded. "Yes."

"Are you sure? You really want to help me?"

"Yes."

"St. Nicholas."

"Eh?" said Jack.

"I'm here to protect St. Nicholas."

"St. Nicholas?" said Tom. "Do you mean Santa?"

"Who's Santa?" asked Gus.

"That's another name for St. Nicholas. Well, one of them," said Tom.

Gus looked puzzled.

"I must have been asleep longer than I thought this time."

He paused and looked thoughtful for a moment, and then stared down at the two boys.

"Are you sure you really want to help?" Gus asked.

"Yes," said Tom.

"Grand! Only, I still cannot remember precisely what it is I'm looking for, but I'm sure it's in here somewhere."

"What is this place, anyway?" asked Tom.

"It's his church. Well, one of them."

"Whose church?"

"St Nicholas's. The one and only."

"What's it doing here?"

"St Nicholas is everywhere, laddie," said Gus.

Gus was trundling around, picking up – and mostly throwing away – everything he could lay his hands on. Pieces of wood, old benches, stones, old chairs, bits of masonry. He was a dragon on a mission. He paused in front of an ornate marble slabbed tomb.

"Hmmm, this looks promising."

And prised its marble lid open. Even for an eight-foot-tall dragon, this took some effort and as he heaved it aside, it crashed into the sides of the rest of the marble structure, with an almighty smash, creating a further heap of slabs and debris.

"Oops... aha! Here we are."

Gus began rooting around in the mess he had just created, throwing things aside, occasionally inspecting some of the objects buried within it, and even more occasionally, eating one or two of them. Tom noticed him chomping on another piece of wood and then what looked like some stones.

"What have you found now?" asked Tom.

"Dunno, but the wood is tasty. Not sure about these stony things. Bit chewy. This one looks okay though."

Gus held up a polished, black stone that sparkled as it caught what little light there was in the old ruin; Tom reckoned it was about half of the size of his hand as Gus brandished it in front of him, before he promptly scoffed it. Then belched. Again.

"Dunno what it was, but it seems edible enough."

Tom looked bemused. "I think – hope – it was maybe a piece of coal?"

Gus shrugged. "Well, whatever it was, should help the rest of it go down okay."

He took another deep breath. Tom knew what was coming next. The dragon let out another half-roar, half sneeze and sparks, brief flashes of flames and an awful lot of smoke followed.

Jack stood open-mouthed at this display. Which wasn't a smart idea, as when the smoke hit him, he started having a major coughing fit.

"What's he doing?" he gasped between coughs.

Tom had put his face into his sleeve to stave off the worst of the smoke.

"Trying to breathe fire," replied Tom.

Gus was by now in the middle of his own self-created smoky fog – and having his own, very loud, coughing fit. Tom had realised by now that Gus wasn't exactly a quiet individual.

"Och, I nearly managed it that time," said the dragon with a sigh.

And off he went, this time heading for the far corner of the church, searching again for his next snacks.

"We have got to get out of here," hissed Jack. "He's making enough noise to wake up the whole of Glasgow."

"We can't just leave him," said Tom. "We said we'd help him."

"No, *you* said you'd help him," protested Jack.

There was a further almighty crash as Gus shoved yet another large, heavy marble lid from atop the tomb where it had rested for centuries onto the floor of the church.

"*See?*" Jack said in exasperation. "He's a lunatic – and he's going to get us caught."

Tom was about to reply to try to persuade Jack that Gus wasn't a lunatic and was just a bit sleepy, confused and possibly over-exuberant when both boys heard the sounds of barking in the distance.

"What's that?" Jack asked. "Did you hear it?"

"Of course I heard it," said Tom.

He picked his way through the trail of debris left by Gus and towards one of the church's windows and peered out into the snowy darkness.

"Uh oh…"

"What? What is it?" asked Jack. There was now a tone of slight panic in his voice.

"We have to go. Now," replied Tom. "Gus, we have to leave."

"What did you see?" asked Jack

"GUS!" Tom shouted and then turned back to Jack. "Dogs, and people with torches heading our way from Gris Corp."

"But those guys we saw earlier had guns…" Jack's voice trailed off.

"Exactly."

Jack peered through the window to take a look for himself. In the distance, he could see several small dots of light zig-zagging their way towards them in the darkness.

Tom had bounded over to Gus.

"Gus, we have really got to go. Now."

Gus was in the middle of inspecting what he suspected was going to be a particularly tasty piece of wood.

"Eh? Go where, laddie?"

"Anywhere. And we're leaving. Now. There are people coming here with guns and dogs and they're not going to want a friendly chat."

"But I haven't found it yet. At least I don't think I have."

"Gus, found what?" Tom asked again, throwing his hands up, with more than a hint of exasperation.

Gus paused, cocked his head to one side, thought for a moment, and then replied.

"Nope, still cannot remember."

"We have to go." Jack had scooted over to the pair of them from the window. "They're going to be here any second."

"Who is?"

"The guys with the dogs and guns!" Tom shouted. "Gus, if they see you, they'll probably shoot you first and ask questions later."

"Well, that would be rather rude," replied the dragon.

"Come on!" Tom shoved Gus. Which was pointless, given how huge he was.

Gus was still mulling this instant turn of events over in his own mind and semi-talking to himself.

"But this is my home. Well, at least temporarily, and I've got to find it."

"Look," said Tom, still trying to move Gus's hefty body, "we'll take you somewhere where there's loads of snacks and you can rebuild your strength and then come back here."

"What kind of snacks?" Gus asked, as he chomped down on another piece of wood.

Tom continued, "Wood. Loads of wood. And coal. And peat… anything you like…"

"And firelighters!" Jack chipped in.

"Eh? Firelighters? What are they?" Gus sounded puzzled.

Tom shot Jack a look.

"Never mind," said Tom.

"Lots of snacks?" asked Gus.

"Yes," replied Tom.

"Are you sure?"

"YES!" both boys shouted in unison.

"And we can definitely come back here?"

"YES!"

"Okay – hang on, one last try before we go," replied Gus, as he took another deep breath, before breathing it out in a half-sneeze and half roar.

It produced the same results as before: a load of sparks, a couple of flickers of flame and a lot of smoke. And a new side-effect: hiccups.

"Well – hic – it was – hic – worth a try – hic… maybe I can fly now…"

With this, Gus unfurled his enormous wings and started flapping them. This had the effect of clearing away a lot of the smoke quickly, but he remained steadfastly stuck on the ground.

"Och, that's no use. They're still waking up, too," the dragon sighed.

Tom had run out of patience.

"Come on! This way," he said, scurrying towards the door he and Jack had come in. They prised themselves out of it again, but it was trickier for Gus. He just about squeezed his head and neck through it – but that was all. The noise of the barking dogs was growing ever louder.

"Take a run at it!" urged Tom, gesticulating at the doorway.

Gus shuffled backwards and his giant head and neck disappeared back inside the church. Tom moved back instinctively and hauled Jack with him.

There was a rumbling sound and then another crash as Gus didn't so much exit through the door as take out rather a lot of the wall surrounding it. He stood in the new mini-heap of rubble and rubbed his head.

"Owya, that stuff's harder than I thought."

Tom dived back towards him and shoved Gus in the back to get him moving.

"Come on! We need to move it!"

The two boys, followed by the eight-foot-tall dragon, quickly made their way into the trees at the edge of the park and back into the snowy darkness.

As they did so, on the other side of the ruined church building, half a dozen Gris Corp security operatives, complete with several large, barking and very lively German Shepherd dogs, arrived at the main door to the church.

Their leader, a tall man, built like a tank and with an extravagant beard, spoke to two of the men. It was Grunk, and he was annoyed.

"Take the dogs in and check it out. We'll sweep the perimeter. You two, that way. You, with me. Make it snappy. I've a boat to catch."

The six men split up into three groups of two.

Grunk shouted one last instruction, "If you find anyone, let the dogs have their fun, and if that doesn't work, shoot them."

CHAPTER SIXTEEN

Gris Corp's headquarters was full of activity. A lot of energetic, frantic activity. People were scurrying up and down its many pristine corridors, clutching walkie-talkies and shouting. There was a great deal of shouting. Some of the scurrying about people would join other stressed-out looking people who were gathered in rooms, scribbling and drawing on whiteboards, both of the paper variety and the electronic kind.

They were grouped in huddles, in many of its plush, open plan 'playbubbles' (a name Max Gris herself had devised for what most other corporations called breakout areas). This name was supposed to reflect Gris Corp's history as a toy-making firm as well as its present (and future) as the world's dominant company in all matters connected with childhood. Everything from toys and games to electronics and tech; from books and movies to education and consoles. From cradle to leaving school, Gris Corp's mission was to be at the heart of childhood – and to make money. Lots of it.

For its employees, these playbubbles were often places of terror, as senior people shouted at their juniors to 'inspire' them to come up with ever more and better ideas and products in endless meetings and idea sessions. Occasionally, even the senior people would be terrorised in such sessions, when either Slymington or Max Gris herself 'dropped in'. However, as terrifying and stressful as their normal day-to-day employment could be, nothing had prepared any of Gris Corp's employees for what was happening this evening.

The whole place was simultaneously in meltdown – and in lockdown – as hundreds and hundreds of people tried to achieve the impossible: fix the internet, get Apotheosis back online globally – and keep Max Gris happy.

Currently, the first two of these three aspirations appeared to be far more achievable than the third, because as of now, Max Gris was striding around the centre of her empire, looking for reasons to shout at people and to fire them on the spot.

The building itself had quickly come back to life after the initial power cut had occurred as its extensive emergency generators had kicked in, but it had soon become clear to the many teams of engineers who had been carefully shepherding the progress of Apotheosis as a global phenomenon for months and months that this power cut was more than a mere local issue.

As the true gravity of the wider global situation had become apparent, Slymington had assumed overall control of the effort to resurrect the Apotheosis IT architecture, the systems and networks that were at its very heart. It was also he who, very early in the evening, had made the phone call to Max Gris to report they had a major problem. The one which led to her arrival at Gris Corp's headquarters in the middle of a snowstorm shortly afterwards – and to the ensuing wave of terror sweeping its way around the building in her stead.

For this evening, Max Gris was in the heart of her empire – and she was furious. Truth be told, she had a low-level anger simmering away in her most of the time, but tonight, she was scaling new peaks of fury. As she strode down a minimalist corridor on the first level of Gris Corp, its pristine white walls occasionally changing to show Gris Corp's latest products – or Max's face herself – on their newly nanocloud paint-covered surfaces (product marketing slogan: 'now all your walls can be pictures'), she spotted an underling and made ready to shout at someone once more (or, as Gris herself occasionally put it to Slymington, "It's like a reflex: I see someone wandering around HQ, establish that she or he is not a member of the public, nor a representative of the media, and then I shout at them. It's a remarkably effective management technique.").

Gris walked briskly up to the unfortunate Gris Corp worker and took a deep breath.

"You. Yes, you. What do you do?" she barked at an ashen-faced man in a casual shirt and glasses who was clutching a tablet and urgently tapping at its screen.

"M-M-M-M Ms Gris. I-I-I'm trying to work out what's gone wrong with the main servers," he spluttered.

Gris gave him a long, icy stare and leaned in towards him, sticking her face way too close into his personal space. And then she flashed that smile of hers, the one that every Gris Corp employee dreaded.

"Well, speccy, I'd say it's extremely likely to be something to do with the solar storm that's wiped out at least three-quarters of the globe's power supply and pretty much all the internet, wouldn't you?"

The man nodded and squeaked out a "Yes."

Gris drew herself up to her full height, which this evening was over six feet tall given she was wearing boots because of the rather inconvenient semi-blizzard outside, and asked her favourite question.

"What is your job title?"

"S-s-s-erver engineer, Ms Gris."

"Not anymore. You're fired."

"B-b-but it's Christmas…"

"Go sing some carols then."

With this, she turned on her heel and strode on, with all the care of someone who had briefly encountered something mildly irritating, like a bug landing on her jacket, which she had now brushed off and from which she was now walking away. Quickly.

Gris Corp was crawling with engineers this evening, all frantically trying to restore enough power to reboot its entire server system. Meanwhile, further teams of boffins were in intermittent contact with their counterparts all over the world, and manically working on the not inconsiderable problem of the entire internet. Or rather, the lack of it. All of them in fear of their jobs should Max Gris suddenly decide to pay them a visit. Or videocall them. Or communicate with them in any way.

Unbeknown to all these Gris Corp workers, they were safe for the next thirty minutes as Gris had something more urgent to attend to – as Rudderts was scuttling towards her general direction in order to remind her.

"Hello, ma'am. Are you remembering?"

"Oh, Rudderts, it's you."

Gris sighed. A long sigh. And then spoke again, as though lecturing a small child.

"Am I remembering what? That it's my mother's cat's birthday the day after tomorrow? That I'm the richest woman in the world? That, going by this evening's events, I'm considerably smarter than all my employees and I don't know why I pay most of them? Or that I have a press conference with half the world's media in two minutes' time?"

Rudderts pulled his face into a nervous smile.

"Oh ma'am, you are *soooo* funny. That's why the children and the media love you so much."

"No, Rudderts, it isn't. The children love me because I oversee the creation and manufacturing of games and toys to which they become hopelessly addicted, and the media love me because I give them ready-made stories on a regular basis - and because the vast majority of journalists are – like most human beings – ultimately very lazy and also lack any critical thinking."

Rudderts was still grinning vacantly at Gris. She shot him a look of pure disdain.

"I rest my case."

Then sighed again.

"All right. Go on. Tell me in which one of my very expensive interior spaces they're all waiting."

Rudderts paused at a handless door and punched a code into the tablet, to which he was permanently attached.

"This one here," he said, looking very pleased with himself.

Gris glanced at the tablet, then at the newly opened door.

"Is that still working?"

"Yes, ma'am."

"Hmph, I'm better than I thought."

Rudderts paused, unsure if this was anything close to a compliment or not. He decided on past experience that it was best to err on the side of caution and assume that it had been an insult.

"Thank you, ma'am. Now, just a quick run-through of the briefing…"

Gris held up her hand to silence him.

"We were supposed to be announcing the winner of Apotheosis tonight, but now it's an update – as well as an outline of how we're dealing with the wider contingency."

Rudderts opened his mouth to speak.

Gris placed a finger across her own lips.

"Sshhh!"

And carried on talking.

"I'll flesh out the update, give them a broad revised timeline – that's hopelessly optimistic – for everything being back to normal and finding a winner, take a few questions – which will demand all the brainpower of a gnat – and then wrap up. Does that about cover it, Rudderts?"

Rudderts realised he had permission to speak again.

"Yes, ma'am."

"Good. Well, get on with it. Someone's got to introduce me to that lot."

Gris gesticulated at the packed room, full of reporters, cameras and microphones.

Rudderts fumbled for the walkie-talkie in his pocket and whispered into it, with a hint of urgency.

"Run the film!"

At one end of the room – again pristine white –, there was a screen. A Gris Corp promotional film all about Apotheosis started playing. And simultaneously appeared on the three other glass walls bordering the rest of the room.

A narration began booming out.

"APOTHEOSIS: the ultimate game, the ultimate education, the ultimate experience…"

Gris grinned to herself. The game angle to sell it to the kids; the education angle to sell it to their parents (along with the never-ending upgrades) and as for the experience, well, for the winner, it would be one that he or she would never forget…

The film boomed out across the semi-darkened room, extolling the virtues, fun and playability of Apotheosis and ramming home why it was *a good thing* for all children the world over to be playing it, with many images culled straight from the game's higher and most difficult levels.

"APOTHEOSIS: the game that can be whatever you want it to be…"

And now for the finale, thought Gris.

"One game. One world. One vision. The future of edugamement is now. APOTHEOSIS."

Gris strode onto the stage and oozed charisma.

"Ladies and gentlemen, thank you so much for all coming along this evening, on such a wild and wintry night – and on such an extraordinary day. And what a day it has been!"

Gris was in her element now: the centre of attention and grinning as though she had been on laughing gas.

"As you know, this evening we were due to announce the first ever global winner of Apotheosis, but sadly, because of the small matter of a mega-solar storm wiping out half the globe's power supplies and most of the internet," she flashed an even bigger grin and rolled her eyes, producing a slight murmur of laughter from the crowd, "we are going to have to wait just a little longer for the big announcement of our winner."

She paused for effect.

"But not too much longer…"

Ah, Gris thought, and this is where I give them what they want: an easy story.

"Tonight, ladies and gentlemen, I can reveal that, despite all the power and technological difficulties we have faced today, we have several dozen youngsters around the world who, after many months of battling through the ever-ascending levels of the game, are within touching distance of the ultimate prize itself. They have all done amazingly well and as of this evening, they are extremely close to solving and winning the overall game, and to claiming their ultimate prize: Gris Global Gaming Champion. Which, lest I need remind you, brings lots of further goodies," the smile flashed again as she continued, " - a huge prize of one hundred million Bitpounds, to be used to fund their own edugamement projects and institutions, instant global fame across all Gris social media accounts, a contract for ten years to work at the Gris Gaming Lab – once they've finished school, obviously – and a guaranteed e-credit from my own personal account worth a further fifty million Bitpounds to spend on whatever they and their family like.

"In short, ladies and gentlemen, for the girl or boy who ultimately wins Apotheosis, this will not just be a game-changer, but a *life-changing* experience.

"And we really will have found the best of the very best of our youngsters, our children, our world's future."

Gris was now dolloping sincerity over each word she spoke. Fake sincerity, but, as she reminded herself daily, as a wise man once said, 'once you can fake sincerity, you have it made'.

"For Apotheosis is more than a mere game, it is the first truly global gaming phenomenon, specifically designed for children under sixteen, to test them to the very limits of their mental, physical and, dare I say it, spiritual abilities. Only the very best, the very brightest, the most resilient and the wisest will prevail through its many tests of physical and mental endurance. We wanted to find the most intelligent children – mentally and emotionally. Those who could solve a problem and understand its impact on others as they did so. Those who could think about the options in front of them and make a rounded decision when they made their choices."

She paused for effect and then began emoting again.

"We wanted to discover the most persistent and resilient children, those who would never give up in the face of adversity and who would try and try again to crack the most difficult of problems, scenarios and situations."

Another pause. Maximum fake sincerity engaged.

"And we wanted to find those physically agile children, because Apotheosis is a new form of experience: immersive, stretching, hyper-realistic, virtual reality taken to the *max* until it *is* reality. It is more than a game. It truly is edugamement and we at Gris Corp firmly believe that all children need to be healthy and should exercise as they play. Which is why Apotheoisis has been designed to be the most physically demanding experience children have *ever* been able to stream in real-time."

Time for a joke, thought Gris.

"And to all the mums and dads out there who may have suffered the odd breakage around the house as the youngsters were tearing around trying to solve a level here or ward off space pirates there, I can only apologise." Gris grinned what she hoped was a goofy, apologetic grin.

"But we are helping to keep your children fit and active, so I hope that is some consolation for the odd broken lamp or two!"

Another attempt at a guilty and apologetic grin. And then she switched on her most sincere and yet determined facial expression.

"So, in summary, despite the difficulties today has brought, we have teams of the very best engineers and specialists working round the clock all over the globe to help get the world back online as quickly as possible."

She paused once more for dramatic effect.

"And I can assure you, ladies and gentlemen, that with so many amazing youngsters so very close to solving Apotheosis, we *shall* have our Gris Global Gaming Champion by Christmas Eve."

Gris finished her speech with a flourish, as though the entire day's events were a mere constituent part of the overall 'ultimate test' that Apotheosis represented.

Now for the fun part, she thought, before her next utterance.

"I'll now take any questions you may have."

A flurry of hands shot up from amongst the assembled journalists. Gris pointed to her favourite tame reporter. The one to whom Gris Corp regularly 'leaked' stories and updates whenever they wanted some favourable media coverage.

"Yes, Moira Schlessler from Brit News."

The chosen journo, noted for several scoops in recent months about Gris Corp and Apotheosis, straightened herself up as though someone had pulled her vertically upwards with strings and asked her question.

"Ms Gris, you've said tonight that you are very close to announcing a winner for Apotheosis and that you have teams of engineers helping to sort out the internet around the world *right now,* but how can you be so sure that you'll be successful in time for Christmas, given the sheer scale of the power outages and disruption caused by the solar storm? And can you be more specific as to the exact timings for any of this?"

The grin was fixed on Max's face now as she readied her prepared answer.

"Thank you, Moira. Great question, as ever. To expand on my earlier announcement, we know of several children who had reached the penultimate level immediately before the storm caused its havoc, so when I say we are close to having a winner, I mean it: we are very, very close indeed.

"Once the damage from the storm became apparent this afternoon, we immediately activated our specialist Gris Corp global contingency recovery teams to work with governments and other specialist emergency agencies in over ninety per cent of the countries around the world with one express objective: to re-connect everyone to the internet as quickly as possible.

"This is an event for which we have run drills and simulations for over a decade, so whilst the precise timing of it was not something which – unfortunately – we could accurately predict more than a few days in advance, we were aware that there was a heightened risk of a solar storm of this magnitude occurring at some point in the next decade or so and we have, therefore, prepared for it over the past several years and as of this afternoon, have now put those plans into full and immediate effect.

"I'm very pleased to say that our offers to assist however we can have been universally accepted by governments all around the world and this spirit of global co-operation is what will win through and see us all re-connected and back online within... forty-eight hours. At the most."

There were further murmurs at this last point. Gris pointed at another journalist with a raised hand. Not one of her especial favourites, but he had a huge presence on traditional and social media, mainly thanks to his eccentric style and louche approach to questioning and life.

"Yes, Richard Lister from Independent News."

This time, the journalist, with his floppy fringe of hair and laid-back pose, oozed and rambled his way to his question.

"Thanks, Max," he began, to show how well-connected he was.

Gris bristled at this over-familiarity, but kept her grin fixed.

"Would you say, given the circumstances, that Apotheosis, has, in fact, been a success, and what happens, in the event we have another solar storm before you can fix the entire internet and we're all offline again, and the game cannot be completed and how do you respond to the growing criticism from parents and teachers about the game itself, that it's eating up too much of children's time, affecting their school work, costing them all their pocket money and more, and ultimately, it's all going to be for nothing as only one of them can actually win it?"

The usual: multiple questions in one sentence, thought Gris.

"Thanks, Richard," she began, though she didn't mean it.

"A lot of very incisive questions there! To take them one at a time, I do view it as a success. We've already heard heartwarming stories of children helping other children around the world with tips and insights on how to solve puzzles, reach the next level, unlock some of the amazing Easter Eggs we've placed throughout the game and all of this whilst learning how to be emotionally intelligent, to be resilient and to really stretch themselves mentally and physically, too. That, I would argue, is more than just a game, hence why we developed the term, 'edugamement'. It is *so* much more than a mere game.

"I am *very* confident we will both succeed in helping to re-connect the world *and* in finding our winner before Christmas Eve; in fact, in the next forty-eight hours. Now, should there be another solar storm, we will deal with whatever effects it throws at us, as and when they arise, because we are prepared for it.

"And as for the criticism, well, there will always be doubters, but I would simply refer them to the point I made a few moments ago: unparalleled global co-operation amongst children around the world as they all strive to make the very best of themselves – something that the game itself encourages throughout its many levels. Children from vastly different backgrounds helping each other out, from the west to the east, the north to the south, the rich to the poor, all working together towards a common goal.

"And as for Apotheosis being blamed for using up children's time, costing them pocket money, schoolwork and the likes, all I would say is this: the United Nations itself has highlighted the many beneficial aspects of Apotheosis and in the end, no one is forcing any child to take part in it. They do so because they want to and, in any event, we have ensured that there a myriad of safeguards in place to prevent over-participation, because, in the end, the welfare of the world's children is paramount to everyone at Gris Corp for they are our future."

Gris paused, very pleased with herself and her rhetoric. Of course, that it was as far removed from the reality of Apotheosis as a squadron of pink elephants was neither here nor there. She had a report from the UN stating it was 'a good thing' – one that had cost her a lot of money and favours to obtain – and that trumped all the critics.

The questions continued for several more minutes, growing ever more puerile, in Max's opinion, until she was asked how she would be spending Christmas this year. She resisted the temptation to say, "as far away from you lot as possible"; instead, doling out the usual platitudes about family, opening presents and looking forward to turkey with all the trimmings. She smiled her secret smile.

Oh, if you but knew how I was *actually* going to spend Christmas this year, that would be the scoop of the century, she thought. Then, corrected herself. Actually, it would be the scoop of the millennium. No point in selling it short.

It was time to wrap up.

"Well, ladies and gentlemen, it has been a delight to see you all, as ever, and to reiterate, we will have a further update for you all very soon, won't we, Rudderts?"

She turned towards the hapless Rudderts.

"Yes, ma'am," gulped out Rudderts, as though his job – and pretty much everything else in his life - depended on it, which judging by the false smile Gris was glaring in his direction, it very much did.

Gris turned back to the throng of journalists.

"Trust me, we need our winner by Christmas Eve, and we will find her - or him! Thank you all once again for coming along on such an inhospitable evening and we'll speak again very soon no doubt."

At this, she departed the stage, leaving Rudderts to end the press conference. As she left, Gris flashed her best smile for all the cameras one last time, but her eyes were not smiling. They were cold, dark, and deadly.

CHAPTER SEVENTEEN

The streets all around Gris Corp's HQ were, by now, thick with snow. No cars ventured along them and the normal sounds of the city were absent amidst the ongoing power cut. Such occasional sounds as there were had been muffled by the ever-deepening blanket of the white stuff – including the snuffling and hiccupping noises emanating from underneath an eight-foot-tall walking – or to be more accurate – shuffling tarpaulin, which was being led around by two miniature arctic explorers.

"Gus, do you have to make so much noise?" asked Jack for the umpteenth time in a few minutes.

"I'm doing my best, laddie, but these hiccups are lively," the dragon replied.

As if to prove his point, Gus proceeded to snort, which was then punctuated by another hiccup.

Tom had had enough. This had been going on for at least ten minutes now. He raised his hand, drawing them to a halt, and turned to address the pair of them.

"Will you two stop bickering. Jack, Gus has the hiccups. Deal with it. Gus, could you at least *try* to keep the noise down until we find somewhere to hide you?"

The three of them had paused on the corner of a semi-suburban street a few blocks from Gris Corp. In the distance, Tom heard some shouts and cries coming from further along the road. He strained his eyes, trying to peer through the whiteout, but it was no use.

"Quick, in here," he said, as he motioned the other two to follow him.

The two boys led Gus into a dark alley, full of bins, behind the row of neat little bungalows that lined the street as the shouts and cries grew closer.

"Quiet…"

"Sounds like students," whispered Jack.

"Yeah, hopefully, they won't notice us…"

The chattering voices drew closer, and some were singing. Christmas carols. Badly. As they neared the entrance of the alley, Tom, Jack and Gus held their breath, which, in Gus's case, was a considerable feat.

"Hang on, ladsh, I jusht need to make a pit-shtop," shouted one student to the rest of the crowd as he stumbled into the alley.

Which was the moment when Gus hiccuped again. Loudly.

"Hullo… hullo… whosh there?"

Tom acted quickly.

"Merry Christmas!"

The student was swaying backwards and forwards in the snow, not sure whether or not he could believe his ears.

"Whatsh you doing in here? Itsh Baltic."

Great, thought Tom, he's had a few beers too many. Time to go for it.

"Merry Christmas! My friends and I are just on our way to a Christmas fancy dress party, but we got a bit lost. You having a good night?"

Whether any of Tom's words registered in the student's addled brain was a moot point, because he was now staring at the eight-foot-tall tarpaulin immediately in front of him.

"Whatsh that?"

"Ah, that…" said Tom, stalling for time. "That is part of our costumes. We're arctic explorers and that's a yeti."

There was a pause as the student now swayed from side to side, considering this new information, before he eventually grinned.

"Thatsh epic."

Relief swept through Tom.

"Yes, it is, isn't it? Took us all day to make it."

"Epic get up. You ladsh have a good night, y'hear. And Merry Chrishmash."

"You, too, mate," replied Tom as he elbowed Jack.

Jack blurted out a swift, "Merry Christmas," and dragged Gus towards the entrance of the alley. As they bundled their way back out into the side street, the student saw Gus's very long, scaly tail sticking out from underneath the tarpaulin, shook his head and muttered to himself.

"Some coshtume…"

Tom, Jack and Gus didn't hang about to find out whether the student's critical faculties would kick in.

"Come on, let's move it," urged Tom and they picked up the pace, hastening through the snow and down the street.

"We've got to do something," said Jack. "We can't stay out here much longer. We're bound to bump into some more people."

"I know," replied Tom, "but where can we go? Yours?"

"Katie would freak," said Jack. "Besides, it would be too busy on the way there – even on a night like this. What about taking him to the police? They'd know what to do with him."

Tom stopped and looked at his friend.

"Seriously? The police?" Tom raised a quizzical eyebrow.

"Who are the police?" Gus piped up.

"They're, er, sort of like knights. In a way..." replied Tom.

Gus threw back the tarpaulin and looked indignant.

"What? You're going to take me to a bunch of knights? I thought you said you were going to help me?"

"Gus," interjected Tom, "we are going to help you. We just dunno where to take you that's safe, that's all."

Gus wasn't listening. He seemed to be talking to himself.

"Hundreds of years... so cold... and dark... I've waited and waited... freezing... cannot make fire... no knights... St Nicholas... don't know where or why... I'll find it... I know I'll find it... just need time... make fire... fly away again..."

"He's rambling," said Jack.

"It's probably because of the cold," replied Tom.

"What are we going to do?" asked Jack. "There's nowhere we can take him, and we can't stay out here all night. Katie's gonna go ballistic as it is."

Tom had had enough. He was cold, tired and exasperated. Gus was still chuntering away to himself and Jack was looking at Tom plaintively, as though this would spark some sort of idea. Tom threw his hands up in the air.

"I don't know, Jack. I don't know where we're going to take him. I don't know where's safe to take him and if we were stupid enough to take him to the police, we'd have to explain to them how we found him, wouldn't we? That's if we even managed to get in through the front door of the police station... with a dragon! Think it through!"

"All right, all right, don't have a go at me. I'm just trying to figure it out as well," Jack shouted back.

Tom sighed.

"I know. Sorry. I'm just freezing and well, I dunno what to do."

He thrust his hands deep into his jacket pockets. As he did so, he felt something. Something squidgy, wrapped in paper and another object, with pointed corners. He drew them out and looked at the two of them, an envelope with a card inside it and a Christmas present, wrapped carefully, with a bow and gift tag on its top.

"Aw no, Aunt Octavia's Crimbo present... I totally forgot about it – again."

"Who's Aunt Octavia?"

"Aka Professor Merryweather."

"What, as in, your maths tutor?"

"That's the one," said Tom. And he grinned.

"Oh, look out, I know that face," said Jack.

"Hah!" cried Tom. "That's where we can go."

"To your maths tutor's?"

"She's not just a maths tutor. She's a professor. And my courtesy aunt. She'll know what to do. She knows about ancient stuff as well as maths. And physics. If anyone knows what to do with a dragon, it's her!"

"Are you sure this is a good idea?" asked Jack.

"'Course I'm sure. She's the smartest person I know. She'll help figure it out."

"Okay..." said Jack, though he was unconvinced.

"Gus, come on, this way," said Tom, as he draped the tarpaulin back over the dragon's head and began leading him briskly along the street, with Jack scampering beside him. Gus was still producing a mixture of rambling, chuntering, snorting and hiccupping noises, now with the occasional sneeze thrown in for good measure. He did not sound very well…

"How far to her house?" puffed Jack.

"Not far; in fact, only a few more blocks. She lives in one of these huge old sandstone houses up the hill. It's pretty quiet up there. Gus will be safe."

The boys, with Gus in tow, made their way along several more streets before they reached Merryweather's street end.

"Here it is: Strathgailes Road. Come on, it's up the hill a bit yet."

The three of them huffed and puffed their way up the hill through the snow, with Gus contributing his continuing symphony of drowsy dragon noises to boot. Near the very top of the hill, they reached the front gate of a very long drive, at the end of which was a huge, old sandstone house, most of which appeared to be in darkness. As the boys peered through the snowy evening towards it, there appeared to be some sort of dim light coming from one downstairs window.

Tom opened the gate and guided Jack and Gus in. He tugged on the tarpaulin.

"Gus, Gus…"

The dragon popped his head out. He looked confused.

"Are we here? Are we safe?"

"Yes, we're here and we will be. I just need you to hide here in these bushes for a few minutes, okay?"

"A few minutes… you sure? I'm cold, laddie, and tired with it…"

"Gus, I swear, it will only be a few more minutes."

Tom parted more of the shrubbery and levered Gus's considerable heft into it with Jack's help.

"Now, don't move, okay?"

"I might just have a wee nap," replied the dragon, as he settled down and made himself comfortable in the snow.

"Jack, come on. This way."

Tom headed towards the front door and pulled on the old doorbell lever outside.

"And I thought our house was ancient," muttered Jack as he did so.

There was no reply. Tom yanked on the doorbell lever again.

This time, there was the sound of footsteps clacking their way across a wooden floor to the front door. The inside door opened with a creak and then there was the sound of bolts being unbolted and the key in the outside door lock being turned, before it, too, opened with a slow creaking noise to reveal Octavia Merryweather's somewhat puzzled face.

"Tom? What on earth?"

"Hello, Aunt Octavia. Merry Christmas!"

Tom thrust out his hand with the card and the present. Merryweather took them both with a bemused smile.

"Thank you. Who's this with you? You must be freezing. Come away in."

With this, she threw open the door and ushered both boys inside.

"This is Jack, Aunt Octavia."

"V-v-v-ery pleased to m-m-meet you..." shivered Jack, whose teeth were now chattering uncontrollably.

"Lovely to meet you, too, Jack," replied Merryweather. She then shifted into concerned auntie mode.

"For goodness' sake, how long have you been out in that snow? Did you come all the way over here in it just to give me the card and present? That was very good of you, but it could have waited until tomorrow. You must both be freezing. Here, I'll get you some towels so you can dry yourselves off."

With this, she was off, bustling about in cupboards, whilst still shouting instructions.

"Go into the living room. The fire's on. Warm yourselves up. I'll bring the towels and get some tea and hot buttery things on."

Tom and Jack headed straight into the living room, which was bedecked with candles and a large roaring fire.

Thank goodness, thought Tom. Everything was going to be okay. Well, once they explained to his aunt the minor detail about there currently being a dragon hiding in the bushes in her front garden.

The two boys moved into the room and towards the fireplace, standing as close as they could to it to thaw themselves out. The fire in the hearth crackled and sparked and threw strange shadows and light on the wall, as though it were remembering long-forgotten secrets of its own, old stories that were not yet ready to be told.

CHAPTER EIGHTEEN

Doctor Nicholas Auld was working late. On the Friday before Christmas. In the middle of a snowstorm and a power cut. For most people, this would have been a sign that their so-called 'work life balance' was out of kilter, but not for Nick (which is how nearly everyone except his mother referred to him). Rather, he was lost in the flow of his work, oblivious to the wider events going on around him. He was, in this respect, what many people referred to as a workaholic, though Auld had always rejected this label. He simply enjoyed what he did and where he worked at the university. He loved what he did to such an extent that he would have happily worked on his areas of research for free. He was also ambitious, some felt too ambitious, and whilst he was generally highly regarded in his field, there were those among his peers who considered him to be somewhat overly concerned with publishing his next paper as he worked towards his life's objective of becoming a professor.

This evening, he was so engrossed in his latest research that he failed to notice the trio of large, black vehicles drawing up outside the elegant Victorian townhouse in which the university had located his office. And so, it was with a start that he responded to the subsequent loud knocking on the door of his building.

"Goodness, who on earth can that be?" he asked himself as he lifted his head up from his papers for the first time in several hours and padded over to the intercom.

"Hello, who is it?"

"Dr Auld, please would you be so kind as to open the door? I need a word with you."

Auld blanched as he recognised the thin, monotone drawl emanating from the intercom's speaker.

"Yes, one moment please."

In those few seconds, he knew he would have to open up the door and let his visitor in. And he also knew that such a visitation so late on an evening such as this was unlikely to be anything good.

Despite his trepidation, he pressed the button anyway and heard the loud clunk of the lock on the building's ancient wooden door opening, followed by the thud of the door itself. He waited nervously at the interior door to his office. It clicked open and Auld was confronted by Slymington and three other men he didn't recognise by name, but whom he surmised, given their size (which was huge) and their attire (all were dressed from head to toe in black) were security employees from Gris Corp.

"Good evening, Dr Auld."

Slymington dispensed with any further pleasantries. He wouldn't have known where to begin in any case.

"Evening, Mr Slymington," Auld replied thinly. He could already feel his mouth going dry.

"Do you recognise this?" asked Slymington, as he brandished a clutch of papers in front of him.

"I, well, I think it's, er, the research that I undertook for your company."

"It is indeed your research, Dr Auld. The research you undertook for Ms Gris on St Nicholas and his relics. The research for which we paid you handsomely, well in excess of anything you could ever have earned... *here.*"

Slymington's voice dripped with disdain as he waved the papers around Auld's rather tired looking office.

"What about it? What do you want?" asked Auld nervously.

"It's wrong."

"Sorry?"

"You heard me, it's wrong."

Slymington threw the papers onto Auld's desk.

"But it can't be. I spent months and months on it," protested Auld.

"And yet, it is," Slymington replied flatly. Then he switched into interrogation mode.

"Who else has a copy?"

"No one. This is the only one. As we agreed."

Slymington bored into Auld with his dark, menacing eyes.

"What about your boss? Did you run anything by her? Does she have a copy? Or any notes?"

"Octavia? N-n-no, she doesn't. I kept it confidential, as we agreed. Just between us."

"Are you sure about that? Very, very, sure?"

"Yes, of course, I'm sure." Auld was now becoming indignant at having his integrity called into question.

There was silence. Slymington let his last question hang in the air whilst staring straight at Auld. This was, he had found over the years, a very effective technique by which to elicit answers.

Auld spoke again. The heavies were pacing around the office, looking at various shelves and ruffling through papers.

"Look, ask her yourself if you don't believe me, but I can assure you that what you're holding is the only copy in existence."

Slymington smiled thinly.

"What an excellent idea."

He turned to one of the three besuited brick outhouses who were rummaging around in the office and gave the instruction.

"Have the cars ready for a visit to Professor Merryweather's house. And wait for me."

The particular outhouse to whom this instruction had been addressed gave a grunt and departed the office. Slymington returned his attention foursquare to Auld.

"You need to come with us, Dr Auld."

"What? Where to? Why?" Auld was now panicking slightly.

"We need you to accompany us to Gris Corp HQ. We have work for you to do. To correct one critical final aspect of your research. As I'm sure you will understand, this is very important to Ms Gris herself."

"I can't come with you... I have things to do, to look after... at home..." Auld's voice trailed off as his eyes focused on the smartphone Slymington was now brandishing directly in front of his face. On it was a picture of a black Labrador.

"Dakers... what have you done with him?" asked Auld.

"Your dog is safe," Slymington intoned in a manner which suggested precisely the opposite.

"I can't just come with you. I need to go back to my house," protested Auld.

"No, you don't. We've already been to your house and have collected everything you need. Now, if you would be good enough to gather your things from here and accompany us to HQ, that would be most helpful."

Auld looked at Slymington, who was still looking straight at him - and through him - and realised he had little choice in the matter.

"Will it take long?" he croaked.

Slymington leaned in towards Auld.

"It will take as long as it takes, Dr Auld, but you will be done well before Christmas."

Auld grabbed his coat and laptop and was ushered out of the office by one of the two remaining outhouses, and into one of the waiting SUVs.

Slymington turned to the remaining Gris Corp security operative and issued a last instruction.

"Get two of the others in here. Tear this place apart – carefully – and find whatever you can. Anything to do with St Nicholas and the relics, bring it straight to HQ. Understood?"

"Yes, boss."

"This time, make sure you leave it as you found it. We don't want to attract any unnecessary attention…"

With this, Slymington walked calmly out of the office, through the corridor to the front door and exited the building. He then hurried up to the middle SUV and opened the door.

There, wedged between two more of Gris Corp's finest security operatives, was a rather pale looking Nick Auld.

"Ah, Dr Auld, sitting comfortably, I see. Good. These gentlemen will ensure you make it safely to HQ."

"Mr Slymington, I must protest. What's so urgent about all of this that you're dragging me into Gris Corp in the middle of the night? You've burgled my house, kidnapped my dog and you've threatened me. I mean, I know Ms Gris is an avid collector of ancient relics, but this is taking things way too far."

"Dr Auld, we had an agreement and Ms Gris is *very* keen that you honour your obligations under it. You'll be free to go as soon as you have done so."

"But Mr Slymington…" Auld protested.

Slymington held up his hand to silence him.

"Take him to HQ," he instructed the driver, before turning once more to Auld.

"I'll see you again shortly."

With these parting words, Slymington slammed the passenger door shut and the SUV roared off into the snowy night.

CHAPTER NINETEEN

In Professor Octavia Merryweather's candlelit living room, Tom and Jack were munching their way through several warm buttery things - in this case, crumpets - in between slurps of hot, sweet tea. They had dried themselves off and were now wearing an assortment of spare clothes that Merryweather had fetched for them, as their own soaking clothes were drying out on a makeshift clothes airer next to the fire. They had gradually stopped shivering and were even warming up a little now. Tom had realised just how cold he had felt as his aunt gave the pair of them a gentle scolding.

"I mean, honestly, Tom, I'm very grateful that you came over all this way to give me my Christmas present, but you should never have been outside on a night like this. It's utterly freezing out there and what with the power cuts and everything, I mean, what on earth were the pair of you thinking?"

Jack shot Tom a quizzical look as he wondered whether he should answer this question. Tom returned his silent query with a subtle shake of the head and noticed Jack was fidgeting as Merryweather continued talking. Meanwhile, all Tom could think about was the elephant in the room – or rather, the dragon outside in the bushes.

"Well?"

Tom realised Merryweather had actually been addressing a question to him and that he needed to come up with an answer.

"Um…"

"Did you really make a special trip over here just for this?"

She was pointing to the Christmas present once again.

"I mean, it's a lovely thought, but it could have waited until tomorrow morning, you know. And what about your poor mother? She must be worried sick. I should call her – if the phones are working properly again."

"No!" Tom realised he had perhaps over-emphasised his reply.

"No? What do you mean, 'no'? She'll be wondering where on earth you are, laddie. And what about your mum and dad, Jack? Do they know you're out in this?"

Merryweather gesticulated towards the tall curtains in the living room, and to the snowstorm beyond them, still billowing away.

This time, it was Jack's turn to foul up his answer.

"Um, it's okay. They're both at work."

Tom rolled his eyes. This was not the type of answer that was going to make his aunt change her topic of inquiry.

"Working? Well, who's looking after you then?"

"My sister."

"And where is she?"

"At home, most likely."

"And will she not be worried about you?"

"Shouldn't think so," replied Jack. "Doubt she'll even have noticed we're not there."

Tom realised he had to intervene to change the subject.

"I was staying at Jack's for the weekend after school finished today, after the big race."

Merryweather paused.

"Oh yes, of course. The race – it was today, wasn't it? How did it go? Did you win?"

"Not exactly…" Tom's voice trailed off.

"He had the most epic smash!" Jack interjected.

"Oh, Tom, what happened? You were so looking forward to it."

"One of the older boys cut me up about halfway down and totally took me out. Still finished though," said Tom, with a hint of defiance.

Merryweather gave a wise smile.

"Just like your father. He crashed – a lot – before he eventually won it. Oh, that's such a shame on your first run, but good for you for finishing it."

"Yeah, it was really cool," Jack butted in. "Tom's sledge was totalled, and Horrible Hurndall wanted him to get off the course, but Tom totally ignored him and walked it down the rest of the way."

"You did not," said his aunt.

Tom was reddening.

"Yep, did."

"Well, good for you, Tom. Never give up; never give in." Merryweather paused.

"You're more like your father than you could ever know. He always persevered, even when the odds were stacked against him and everyone else would have quit."

Tom never knew what he was supposed to say when his aunt (or anyone) mentioned his father, so he ended up giving his usual reply.

"Um, thanks."

"He was a total legend. The whole school was cheering him on," announced Jack.

"Shurrup..." Tom muttered back at his friend.

"Well, I'd say 'like father, like son', but then I believe you already know that. Deep down." Merryweather gave Tom a warm smile.

"S'pose so," Tom mumbled.

"But you need to have more faith in yourself," Merryweather continued. "No more of this playing down of your talents. You're too modest."

"It's just... it's embarrassing, that's all," said Tom. "Everyone always goes on about my dad, but I barely even remember him."

"But Tom, it's important that you do..."

The clanging of her ancient doorbell cut Merryweather off in mid-sentence.

"Now, who on earth could that be? Hmph, twice in one night... like buses," she mused aloud and was out of her chair and bustling towards the living room door.

"You two stay here and keep thawing out. There's plenty more tea in the pot."

Her instructions hung in the air as she left the room. Tom and Jack looked at each other. Tom cracked first.

"When are we going to tell her?" he asked.

"You mean, *how* are we going to tell her?" replied Jack.

"Do you think someone's seen him?" Tom's face was now contorting into one of worry.

"Who's seen him?"

"Whoever's at the door, you doofus," replied Tom.

"Aw no, I hadn't even thought of that," said Jack.

With this, Tom was up and out of his seat and diving towards the very tall curtains which were draping the long bay windows of the living room, with Jack following him. He inched open a gap between the heavy, lined curtains just enough so he could see through it and out towards the front door in the porch.

"Oh no…"

"What? What is it? Let me see." Jack barged Tom out of the way and peeked through the crack himself. There, on the front doorstep, stood two of the massive bruisers who they had seen earlier that evening at Gris Corp. Same build, same uniforms and the same grim expressions etched on their faces. Only this time, there was another man with them: a thin, balding, gaunt-looking man who appeared to be engaged in conversation with Merryweather.

Jack whipped back his head and let the gap between the curtains close together again.

"Oh ratfinks… they must have followed us here!" Jack gasped.

"But how could they have?" Tom was mid-reply when the same thought hit both boys' brains at exactly the same instant, and they spoke in unison.

"Gus!"

Tom prised open the curtains at a different spot again and peeked out towards the front garden.

"Can you see him? Can you see anything?" Jack was behind him, itching to look for himself.

Tom withdrew his head.

"Can't see anything except snow."

"Let me have a look." Jack barged his way past Tom and put his eye towards the crack in the curtains himself before withdrawing it several seconds later.

"Nope, nothing. What are we going to do?" Jack was looking at Tom to see if he had any answers. Tom was already up and moving about the room.

"Need to find something…" he was saying to himself, as he scouted the entire living room, before alighting on an object on one of the many bookshelves that lined the room.

"These'll do," he said, brandishing an old khaki-coloured case which he opened before extracting the prize inside it.

"Bins!" he exclaimed triumphantly and dived back over to the window. Jack moved out of the way as Tom slowly opened the curtains once more and stuck the binoculars towards the window. Several more seconds passed.

"Well?" implored Jack. "Can you see him?"

Tom eased his head slowly out from between the curtains, allowing them to fall back together again, and turned to Jack, his face as white as the snow outside.

"There's nothing there. He's gone."

CHAPTER TWENTY

Merryweather walked along the hallway of her house and towards its front door as the ancient doorbell clanged for a second time in quick succession.

"Yes, yes, I heard you the first time."

She unlocked the door and stepped outside into the porch, undid the large bolt on one of its outer doors and pulled it open. There, standing on the doorstep, were three men. Two of them looked huge and were dressed from head to toe in black and wearing trapper-style winter hats. Their faces suggested they were not enjoying being outdoors on a snowy evening. In their centre was a thin, balding, gaunt looking man, who was around a foot shorter than his two companions. He, too, did not look happy to be there.

"Hello, can I help you?"

"Professor Merryweather?" asked the thin man.

"Yes, I am she. What can I do for you?"

"My name is Slymington. I am a representative of Gris Corp and am here at the request of Max Gris herself. Would you mind if we ask you some questions?"

Slymington proferred a business card to Merryweather, which she took from him rather tentatively.

There was a pause as Merryweather considered this request.

"Yes, of course, but what on earth is so urgent that it's brought you here on a night like this?"

"A matter has arisen," Slymington intoned as though he were reading a very dull set of terms and conditions for a new consumer product.

"A matter? What kind of matter?" Merryweather was by now thoroughly bemused.

"A matter concerning your colleague, Dr Nicholas Auld."

"Dr Auld? What's wrong? Has something happened?"

It was Slymington's turn to pause briefly.

"Nothing has happened... yet." He chose his words carefully as he continued. "As you may know, Dr Auld has been working on a confidential project for us for some months..."

"I knew he was working with Gris Corp, but not the specific details," Merryweather interjected.

Slymington continued without acknowledging this statement.

"Unfortunately, the project has now suffered a snag, a rather *significant* snag and one which we need to address urgently."

Merryweather shuddered inwardly. The way in which Slymington spoke was giving her the creeps.

"Well, I'd love to help you, but I'm afraid I know nothing about the project Dr Auld was working on."

"Really?" Slymington was staring directly at Merryweather now as he left the question hanging in the snowy night air.

"Yes, really. Dr Auld is working on many research projects at any given time and I'm not involved with all of them."

"I see," replied Slymington.

Merryweather did not like the way this conversation was developing and took the initiative.

"What is the research concerning? And what is the snag to which you're referring? Is it something to do with the blackouts?" she asked.

Slymington drew himself up to his charmless, corporate, bureaucratic best.

"As I mentioned, the project is confidential, Professor, and if you are not involved in it, we should not keep you any longer." Slymington half-turned as though to leave.

"Well, it must be very urgent if you've come all the way to see me in the middle of a snowstorm," Merryweather fired back.

Slymington turned back towards Merryweather and paused once more; it was time to end this particular conversation.

"Ms Gris herself requested to speak to Dr Auld. During our conversation with him, he suggested we speak to you personally to check whether you knew anything else about the areas of interest on which he was working. This we have now done. Thank you for your co-operation."

By this point, Merryweather had formed the view that Slymington spoke like a robot. A terrible robot.

"Mr Slymington, I can assure you that I have no clue about whatever it is that Dr Auld was working on for Gris Corp and if it is confidential, then it is entirely proper that I should *not* know anything about it."

"Indeed."

"Besides, I have my own areas of research to focus on and they keep me busy enough without poking my nose into my colleagues' work."

"That is a very healthy approach, Professor. Thank you once again for your assistance this evening. Goodnight."

This time, he was leaving, along with the two goons by his side.

"Goodnight, Mr Slymington," said Merryweather, as she retreated inside to the warmth of the house.

Slymington half-turned back in the snow to utter one parting shot.

"Oh, and Professor, if anything *should* come to mind, *do* get in touch. You have my details."

Merryweather was hesitant.

"Yes, yes, of course. Goodnight."

She closed the porch door once again, and this time double-bolted it as well as locking it. She looked at the business card and shuddered, unsure if it was from the cold alone. Her instincts were telling her that something was very wrong here.

As she tapped her fingers on the card, she stared into the middle distance and murmured to herself.

"Oh Nicky, what on earth have you got yourself involved in this time?"

CHAPTER TWENTY-ONE

Merryweather closed the heavy wooden front door to her house, turned and lay against it, and briefly shut her eyes. She became aware that she was biting her lower lip, an old habit from childhood that occasionally resurfaced in times of stress. She opened her eyes and took in the barely lit hallway before glancing down once again at Slymington's business card. She placed the card hurriedly on an occasional table. It reminded her of Slymington and that man had given her the creeps; something about his manner and his eyes, the way they bored right into you, almost as though you weren't there. She shuddered once more and drew herself up, taking a deep breath.

Right, Octavia, phone him, she thought. Quickest way to deal with this.

She reached for her landline, which, in an act of defiance, she still insisted on keeping in the hall. Well, the base unit at least; regarding phones, her concession to the never-ending tide of modernity had been to acquire (eventually) a basic mobile handset for the landline, though even after doing so, she had continued to hold out against using a mobile phone for several years, and even now, her mobile was as basic as a phone could be.

Merryweather tapped the button on the landline handset that was the speed-dial for Nick Auld's mobile and pressed the receiver to her ear.

Nothing. No sound whatsoever, other than the slight electrostatic hiss that accompanied the silence of modern telecommunications. She waited... and waited, but there was no dial-tone.

She cancelled the call and tried again. Still no sound, other than the same electrostatic hiss once more.

She tried a third time, this time tapping the speed-dial for his home number, with the same result – and it was then she realised.

"Of course; you idiot, Octavia, all the networks are still down."

She sighed as she replaced the handset in its holder and walked back towards the living room. She opened the door and strode in.

"Well, that was an unexpected visitation…"

Merryweather paused and looked around the room. The fire was still crackling merrily away; the candles were still throwing their golden light across the room's many antique pieces of furniture, endless bookshelves and assorted objects and knick-knacks from Merryweather's lifelong adventures, and the long, elegant curtains remained firmly shut, warding off the cold outside.

However, something was missing. Or rather, someone. Or, to be even more specific, two someones. Of Tom and Jack, there was no sign.

"Tom? Jack? Where are you?"

No reply.

"Boys, if this is a prank, I have to warn you in advance that my sense of humour is diminishing as this day wears on."

Still nothing.

"Come on, you pair of wee rascals, what *are* you up to? Where are you?"

From behind the sofa, ever so slowly, a mop of tousled blonde hair slowly emerged. It was followed, further along the sofa, by a sea of brown curls as Jack followed Tom's lead and tentatively inched his way out of hiding.

Merryweather stood, looking quizzically at the pair of them, half amused and half bemused. Her bemusement won out.

"What *are* the pair of you doing?"

Tom peeked his head above the top of the sofa, his face looking serious.

"Have they gone?"

"Have who gone, Tom?"

"Those guys who were at the door."

Merryweather noted at this point that, even in the dim twilight of the candlelit room, both Tom and Jack, whose head had also now fully emerged from hiding, looked worried, possibly even scared. She put on her best bedside manner voice.

"Yes, they've gone. Now, what is the matter with the pair of you? Why were you hiding behind there?" Merryweather gestured towards the sofa.

Jack looked at Tom imploringly.

"Tell her."

Tom remained silent, and then took a deep breath, as though he was winding himself up to speak. He half-opened his mouth and then closed it again.

"Tom?" his aunt asked, looking directly at him. "What is it? What's wrong? Sit down, the pair of you and tell me." She pointed at the sofa.

The boys sat down; there was a pause and then Tom launched into his (semi) prepared speech.

"Those guys... the ones at the door..."

"Yes?" said Merryweather gently.

"Well, we... we saw them earlier on this evening."

His aunt's face now took on a more serious expression.

"Go on."

Tom, with occasional interjections from Jack, explained the boys' months long quest to fight and solve their way through the many levels of Apotheosis, the trials and tribulations of losing their beloved Haggis One spaceship, the hard work that they had both put into rebuilding their quest via Haggis Two, the further tests they had endured and passed as they proceeded upwards through the levels, until finally, he reached the events of earlier on Friday afternoon and evening: winning the game and heading out into the snowstorm to report their win, only to be given short shrift by the Gris Corp flunky who had met the pair of them when they reached the company's HQ.

Merryweather had only vaguely heard of Apotheosis. The media had been obsessing over it for months now, so it had been difficult to avoid it completely, given the proliferation of media sources scattered throughout normal, everyday life. As far as Merryweather could figure out, the media zealously reported Max Gris's every utterance and seemed generally to be obsessed with her and the activities of her corporation.

However, she had paid this particular strand of reporting practically zero attention, other than noting that it was likely exploiting children in some manner that probably wasn't good for them, that it would be their parents who would be paying for everything anyway and that Max Gris would be even richer by the end of her latest PR blitz. Oh, and that it was books, which remained, as far as Merryweather was concerned, the best source of information and entertainment for children (and their imaginations) that humankind had yet invented.

Despite her disinterest in the game itself, Merryweather listened patiently as Tom and Jack poured out their adventures from earlier on this evening – right up until the part when they were hiding behind trees as Max Gris herself and her security detail roared up to the HQ in their huge SUVs.

"And then what happened?" asked Merryweather.

"Well, this was when they began unloading some sort of crates into the HQ, with Max Gris giving them instructions. And that's where we first saw those guys who were at the door. They were there. Standing guard…" Tom's voice trailed off.

"With guns and everything!" interjected Jack, flapping his arms. "They were totally tooled up!"

Tom shot his pal a look.

"I was just about to get to that part, Jack."

"Guns? What on earth?" asked Merryweather.

Sometimes, Tom wished Jack would just occasionally try to process information before blurting it out to grown-ups – and this was one of those times. He was going to have to downplay this now. Bigtime.

"Well, we *think* they *might* have had a couple of guns, but to be honest it was so dark and snowing so heavily that we…"

"They *definitely* had guns," said Jack with total certainty.

There was a pause. Tom shot Jack another look.

"What?" asked Jack indignantly. "We saw them; they had them around their necks. Properly armed, they were. And huge."

"I see," said Merryweather. "Is that why you were hiding just now? Did you think they were here for you or something?"

Tom shifted uneasily on the sofa.

"Well, yeah, sort of."

"Sort of?" Merryweather raised a quizzical eyebrow.

Silence. Tom was looking down at the floor.

"Tell her," urged Jack.

Still silence.

"Tell me what? Tom? What's happened? Are you in trouble?"

Tom looked at Jack and took yet another deep breath.

"So, er, *we* waited behind the tree until they had all moved inside and then… one of us saw something near an old building and *we* went to investigate it…" Tom was making it very clear that this had been a joint effort.

"And anyway, we saw some lights coming from this old ruin and found our way into it and… and…"

"And?" Merryweather's face was now looking deeply serious, and her eyes were like those of a hawk as she waited for Tom to finish the story.

"And…" Tom scrunched his eyes closed and began babbling.

"And-we-found-a-dragon-and-at-first-it-was-scary-but-it's-okay-he's-quite-friendly-and-not-going-to-eat-us-and-we-had-to-get-him-out-of-there-because-those-security-guys-heard-all-the-noise-and-were-coming-over-to-investigate-so-we-escaped-and-then-had-to-hide-on-our-way-here-and-we-brought-him-here-'cos-we-thought-you'd-know-what-to-do-and-then-we-saw-them-through-the-window-and-thought-they-must-have-followed-us-or-something…"

"And breathe," interjected Merryweather.

Jack was looking at Tom, unsure whether to admire what he had just said or be terrified of how Merryweather was about to respond.

There was a silence as Merryweather paced around the living room.

"A dragon?" she asked.

Tom realised the question was for him.

"Yes. Well, that's what he told us he was."

"In a ruin?"

"Yes."

"Next to Gris Corp?"

"Yes."

"And you brought him here?"

"Yes," squeaked Tom.

"And where is he now?"

"Well, we left him hidden in the bushes in the front garden."

"Yes?"

"But it looks as though he's not there now..." Tom's voice trailed away.

Another silence as Merryweather paced some more.

"Right, well, you two had better get your jackets on."

Tom and Jack looked at Merryweather questioningly. She stopped pacing as she addressed them both, her face breaking into a broad grin.

"Well, come on. Jackets on, Get a turn on you! We have a dragon to look for."

CHAPTER TWENTY-TWO

Nick Auld could feel the sweat trickling down his back as he was frogmarched into Gris Corp's HQ. Given how cold it was outside in the snow, he was putting this physical symptom down to pure fear, rather than any possibility of overheating.

The two security men accompanying him had said nothing on the short but slow journey from his office to Gris Corp and upon their arrival, had issued a perfunctory, "Get out", followed by an even more perfunctory threat of, "Come with us", as he exited the vehicle.

He had not been restrained in any way on the short journey (other than his seatbelt); no handcuffs nor blindfolds or suchlike - but nor was he going anywhere other than wherever it was his captors determined he should go. Judging by their size and general demeanour as he sat squished between the pair of them in the back of the middle SUV in a convoy of three of the vehicles, they would have snapped him in two had he so much as tried to unbuckle his seatbelt, let alone open a window.

Auld had never been frogmarched anywhere in his life before – not even at school – so this was a novel experience for him, and his face flushed as the three of them made their way through Gris Corp's vast atrium. Fortunately, those few Gris Corp employees who were also present in the atrium appeared preoccupied and too busy to notice his arrival and were dashing around in all directions in barely concealed blind panic as far as he could work out.

Auld and his personal security detail headed towards one of the many lifts connecting the glass-covered centre of the HQ to the web of inner meeting rooms and offices which spiralled off into the building beyond.

"Get in," grunted one guard as the doors to the glass doors of the lift opened.

Auld did as he was told. The guard punched in a number, pressed his thumbprint on a scanner, and the lift doors closed as they began their ascent. As the doors glided shut, Auld briefly shut his eyes and tried to slow his breathing to calm himself down. It didn't work. He was too nervous and his mind was racing. He knew Max Gris could be difficult – very difficult, if truth be told – but he had only met her twice before.

Each time it had been a brief encounter: the first when he had formally agreed to work with Gris Corp on what Gris had called 'Project Saturn'. She had seemed pleased that day, he remembered. Although he also remembered her shouting at various members of her staff over relatively trivial matters. After that particular meeting, Auld had been relieved when his subsequent project update meetings were with her number two, Slymington, albeit he gave Auld the creeps.

The second time he had met Max Gris, it had been a similar encounter to their first: again, it was a milestone meeting, this time upon completion of the project and, once again, given there had been a successful outcome and that he had delivered his findings on time and on budget, she had seemed pleased with him and his work. There had been lots of smiling from her and a brief chat, peppered with her, once more, shouting at people, this time mainly via her mobile phone, which never stopped buzzing and ringing.

In truth, Auld had been glad to collect his fee for completion of the work and to leave her office – and the building itself – for good. Or so he had thought - until this evening.

He snapped out of his thoughts as the lift gave a metallic ping to announce it had reached its destination; this was followed by another (human) grunt.

"This way."

Auld duly followed the lead guard as they walked down a very long, well-lit corridor which, as with most of the building, incorporated more glass than a decanter set in order to reflect every available photon of light that strayed into it. Auld thought it looked as though it had been transported from fifty years' hence.

They arrived at a doorway. The lead guard punched in another number and then, as previously, placed his thumb on a scanner. The door slid open.

Auld felt his mouth drying up and a lump forming in his throat as he wondered what kind of mood Max Gris would be in this evening. As he stepped through the doorway into the large office beyond, it turned out he did not have to wait for long to find out.

"Ah, Dr Auld, please, do come in. Coffee? Tea? Take a seat."

Max Gris swept her arm around in the general direction of the coffee and tea-making facilities on a table in one corner of the room and ended the sweep by pointing towards a specific chair on the far side of the boardroom table from her.

It was her. Solo. She was wearing her best fake smile, thought Auld, as he sat down in the chair and answered her.

"Coffee, please."

"Coffee it is. You – name?" Gris was addressing one of the two security guards.

"Simmons, ma'am."

"Be a good boy and make Dr Auld a coffee. Milk? Sugar?" She was grinning at Auld again.

"Just milk please," replied Auld, his throat drying up again.

Simmons busied himself trying to get to grips with the delicate china of the coffee cups, which, for a man who had hands the size of dinner plates, was not the most straightforward of tasks.

Eventually, he planted the coffee - with reasonable care - on the table in front of Auld. Simultaneously, Gris began walking around the room.

"So, Dr Auld, you're probably wondering why you're here. Again," Gris began.

Auld paused and took a sip of his coffee as he considered how to answer.

"Well, yes. It was all rather rush…"

Max's smile evaporated as she strode towards the table and leaned over it, sticking her face way too close to Auld's for his liking.

"I'll save you the time. Your work was wrong. We only found five of the six batches of relics we were looking for. The last batch wasn't where you said it would be in Ireland."

"Oh," said Auld, unsure of what else to say. He then made a tactical error: he contradicted Max Gris.

"Are you sure?"

Gris went silent and leaned in closer towards Auld as she growled her answer back at him.

"Oh, we're completely sure, Dr Auld. We had the best man in the world go looking for them, and he was successful at five of the six sites you suggested, but at the last one – the one in Ireland – there was nothing. Not even a hint of anything remotely resembling a tomb, let alone a relic."

"I see," said Auld, even though he didn't.

Gris didn't waste any time.

"We had an agreement. You would research these, decipher them, and give us all the locations you could identify – six, you said. For which, you would be paid a very generous fee."

She snapped her fingers and Simmons brought forward an old wooden case which he placed on the boardroom table, before unfastening its locks, opening the lid and spinning it around so Auld could see its interior. He recognised the contents immediately.

"The scrolls…"

"Yes, Dr Auld, the scrolls. You remember them?"

"Of course, I do. I spent months researching them."

"But not quite accurately enough."

Gris stood bolt upright and stared directly at him.

"So, you're going to try again. Starting now."

"But, but it's the weekend before Christmas and there's a snowstorm going on outside."

Gris leaned back into Auld's personal space once again and raised her voice.

"I. Don't. Care. *We* had a deal. *You* have not delivered on that deal. Therefore, *you* will now restart the final piece of the work and this time, *you* will get it right."

Auld was now realising why most of the Gris Corp workforce looked as though they were perpetually walking around on eggshells.

"I-I-I'm happy to redo the work, Ms Gris. I just don't see why it's so urgent that it needs to begin immediately," he spluttered in reply.

Gris began pacing again. She was frowning.

The door opened, stopping her mid-pace, and Slymington entered.

Immediately, Max's face lit up.

"Ah, Slymington, good of you to join us."

Her opener sounded more sarcastic than she intended, but Gris didn't care.

"I was just explaining to Dr Auld here about the need for him to redo the final piece of the project he recently undertook for us and Dr Auld was questioning why it was so urgent that it had to be restarted immediately. Do you have anything you wish to add that could *help* Dr Auld?"

Slymington looked at Gris dispassionately and shook his head.

"Unfortunately, ma'am, I have been unable to glean any further useful information, so it does appear it is going to be all down to Dr Auld to remedy his error."

"Well, that all seems straightforward, if somewhat disappointing."

Gris wheeled back towards Auld, her pretence of professionalism now disappearing quickly.

"Right, Nicky boy, it's all on you. Here's the gen: need six batches of relics; currently have five; last site you identified in Ireland held nothing of interest. Zip. Zero. Nada. You're the only one who can figure this out – and believe me, we've checked – so it's all on *you*."

Gris prodded her long, bony index finger into Auld's chest to emphasise the last part of her statement.

"We need this now, because we already have boots on the ground in Ireland – very expensive boots, as it goes – and we need to recall our man to wherever it is that this last batch of relics is actually located.

"Oh yeah, and we need them *at the latest* by Christmas Eve, preferably sooner. Got all that?"

Auld was reeling from this verbal volley of invective from Gris, but he had had enough. He knew his rights. He pushed out his chair and stood up to leave.

"I'll do it, but not tonight." He walked to the door of the room, but it was blocked by Simmons and the other security gorilla. They subtly edged together to form a two-man human wall through which no one was getting past.

"Excuse me," said Auld, as he tried to reach for the door handle.

"I think you should sit down, sir," said Simmons, before adding, "for your own good."

Auld paused and looked at Simmons and his pal. Both remained stock still, staring straight ahead of themselves, towards the wall opposite the door. Neither had altered his gaze throughout the exchange. Auld retreated back to his chair, looked at Gris and Slymington again, and considered his choices. He decided to argue. Again.

"I just do not see what is so urgent that I have to begin this work tonight," he threw his hands up in the air in protest.

Slymington stepped forward and produced his mobile phone from his pocket.

"Perhaps this will help you decide. Again."

He showed the phone to Auld. On it was a photo of a black Labrador, but it was a different one from that which Slymington had previously brandished at him in his office.

"Dakers…" Auld's voice trailed away. "You'd better not have harmed him."

"He's safe," replied Slymington, before adding, "for now."

Slymington took his turn to approach Auld and stick his face far too close to Auld's for his liking.

"When I say, for now, I should really be more specific. For twenty-four hours."

He stood up and fished out a small red and green plastic device with the slogan 'Christmas Countdown' emblazoned across it and pressed a button on its front. The device's display started counting down.

"One of our most popular pieces of Crimbo tat – one in two families has one!" Gris said triumphantly, as Slymington placed the small countdown clock in front of Auld.

"And ever so appropriate, too, don't you think?"

She didn't wait for the answer to her question as she strode towards the security detail once more and snapped her fingers (both hands) as though they were castanets for some sort of exotic dance.

"Simmons, take Nicky boy here to his new office, along with this." Gris picked up the wooden box containing the ancient pieces of parchment and thrust it towards the security guard.

"Don't let him out until he has the answer for us."

Auld looked firstly at Gris, then at Slymington and finally towards Simmons and his pal, trying to work out if this was really happening. Simmons approached his chair.

"Dr Auld, if you would come with me, please."

He eased Auld out of the chair and lifted him up by the arm and towards the door. Gris gave Auld a huge grin and a little wave as Simmons forcibly guided him towards the exit.

"Twenty-four hours, Nicky boy. Lovely working with you again. See you soon."

The door closed.

"Well?" asked Gris turning to Slymington. "Who else knows?"

"No one, ma'am."

"You checked? With his boss, that Professor woman?"

"Yes, ma'am. She didn't have a clue."

"And what about Auld's office? Anything in there?"

"We should know that shortly, ma'am. I left a few of our best operatives there to search it. Thoroughly."

Gris looked pensive. She was chewing her bottom lip.

"Do you think he's hiding anything, Slimey?"

"No, ma'am, I don't. He doesn't suspect the true nature of what it is we're asking him to do."

Max's face set into a look of grim determination.

"Let's ensure we keep it that way. Oh, and Slimey, if he hasn't delivered the goods to us by this time tomorrow…"

Slymington gave a look of satisfaction.

"I shall dispose of the animal, ma'am. In order to focus his mind."

"Good," replied Gris, as she began grinning again. "I sense we're back on track!"

CHAPTER TWENTY-THREE

Tom, Jack and Merryweather traipsed down the front stairs of Merryweather's house and headed into her front garden, their torches zig-zagging a path through the snow. The snow had been falling heavily for hours now and was lying deep. Trees looked as though they had been placed in Merryweather's garden straight from a Christmas card, and it was no longer possible to distinguish clearly where the pathways around the house ended and the lawns and borders of the garden began.

Tom led the way, followed by Jack as they crunched their way through the fresh snow towards the clump of mature bushes in which they had deposited Gus less than an hour previously.

"He should be in here," offered Tom, hopefully, as they reached the mini-thicket.

Merryweather had been meaning to prune back these particular shrubs for ages but had not managed it before the autumn; she was now glad that she hadn't, as she mused that they were indeed the perfect place in which to hide an oversize dragon.

"Gus," hissed Tom. "Gus… are you there?"

There was no reply. Tom peeled back the branches of the bushes and tried to enter the clump, only to be showered with snow from the laden branches for his trouble.

"Urgh, great…" he groaned as some of the snow found its way down the back of his neck.

"Gus... Gus..." Jack was shouting more loudly.

Still nothing.

"Are you quite sure you left him in here?" asked Merryweather.

"Yep," said Tom, "totally sure. We didn't have any other option."

His torch alighted on a large heap in the centre of the bushes, semi-covered in snow. Tom bent down and scraped off some of the snow before he picked up the edge of the now discarded tarpaulin.

"We used this to disguise him on the way here," he said.

"Well, wherever he is now, he's not in here," replied Merryweather.

"Do you think he's flown away?" asked Jack. He looked at Tom, willing him to say no.

"I dunno." said Tom. "He seemed too weak to fly, but maybe he regained some of his strength."

Tom paused. "I mean, he was *really* confused by the time we reached here."

"Well, so would you be if you'd just been woken up," said Jack.

"What do you mean, 'just been woken up', Jack?" asked Merryweather.

"Well, he told us – among a load of other things – that he'd just woken up and was still feeling drowsy. Oh, and hungry, too. He was ravenous. Kept eating all sorts: wood, coal, stones - you name it, he was trying to munch it."

Merryweather had stopped searching the bushes with her torch and turned it towards Jack as she asked her next question.

"What else did he tell you? What other things?"

"Well, as well as being hungry, he seemed to be looking for something – in a hurry..."

A cry from Tom interrupted Jack's recollection of Gus's earlier, disorientated rummaging around in the old church.

"Look!"

Tom was pointing his torch towards the snow on the far side of the clump of bushes.

"Footprints! He must have moved. Come on."

There, in a random pattern and half-covered already by the falling snow, were several very large footprints, each one over a foot and a half in length and each with the same distinctive pattern: three large toe-prints at the front and one even larger toe-print to the rear. Merryweather and Jack both shone their torches at the mass of footprints as they joined Tom.

"Well, I never…" Merryweather's voice trailed away as her torch picked out the messy patterns the footprints had made in the snow.

"See," said Jack, "told you he was confused."

"Yes, quite," replied Merryweather, "though I was focusing more on the fact that these could not have been made by any animal found in these islands."

"That's 'cos he's a dragon," said Jack, with a nod of his head conveying the certainty of his statement.

"Jack Wanless, your ability to state the obvious is, in equal parts, endearing, annoying and commendable, in its own way," said Merryweather.

"Thanks," said Jack, taking what he was sure was another compliment.

"It looks as though your friend may still have been a little confused," mused Merryweather as her torch continued trying to find order in the snow chaos that surrounded the bushes.

"We need to establish where he went to next."

Tom let out a cry.

"Auntieprof, Jack, come and look at this."

Tom had wandered several yards from the bushes, following a trail of footprints which had sizeable gaps between them. Next to where the footprints stopped and started again, at irregular intervals, were what appeared to be the remains of what had until recently been living branches of evergreen trees.

Tom pointed his torch at this trail of footprints and mangled, discarded branches and leaves that stretched into the night – and towards the side of the house.

Merryweather and Jack caught up with him.

"I think he was still hungry – and maybe trying to fly?" said Tom.

"Yes, but with little success, judging by the state of the snow here," replied Merryweather. She tutted as she inspected the trees surrounding the route taken by the footprints.

"Oh, look at the state of these: my poor holly trees will never be the same."

"Come on," said Tom and he was off, following the trail of footprints and discarded bits of tree that led down the side of the house.

There was a regularity to the pattern in the snow as it recurred all the way towards the back garden of Merryweather's house: the large, distinctive shapes of several footprints, one after another for a few yards, then a gap and then a messy area of disturbed snow, followed by another batch of the very large, unmistakable footprints for several more yards.

As the three of them made their way along the side of the house, Merryweather observed, "This dragon of yours seems to have been determined to fly away."

"He must have been scared," replied Tom.

As they reached the back garden, Tom saw for the first time that it sloped downwards and was long, extremely long, in fact. The trail continued down the hill, with ever larger distances between the clumps of prints which were clustered together before each of the gaps, each of which was then followed by a splodgy mess of snow; and all of which were now being filled in by the falling flakes.

Tom, Jack and Merryweather inched their way down the hill by torchlight, trying not to slither and slide all the way down until they reached the bottom of the garden. There, in front of the back fence, was a large wooden hut, with glass windows and doors, which had been transformed by the snowfall to look like an urban ski chalet.

"Look," cried Jack, pointing at the wooden fence.

There was a hole in it, large enough for a child to squeeze through, but not sufficiently big enough for a dragon.

"Well, he was certainly hungry," said Merryweather, "but I doubt he managed to fit his way through that gap."

Tom interjected, "He didn't have to. Look at this."

Tom was shining his torch towards the rear of the hut, or rather, what was left of it. Some of the upright timbers of the frame remained, but most of the back panels were gone and those few which remained were fractured and ragged.

"He's eaten my lovely summer house!" exclaimed Merryweather. "Why couldn't he have used the door?"

Tom was already pointing the beam from his torch at the hole in the building. As the light zig-zagged its way around the interior's darkness, it alighted upon a very large, partially snow-covered dark olive-green heap, which took up most of the space inside and which appeared not to be moving much.

"Gus! He's in here," shouted Tom as he made his way through the remnants of the back wall of the summerhouse.

Merryweather poked her head through the gap and immediately froze to the spot. Her mouth fell open as her eyes took in the scene in front of her. The bundled-up heap was rising and falling ever so slightly, and it was snoring.

"Well, I never," she said for the second time this evening. "There's an actual dragon asleep in my summerhouse…"

"See, told you," said Jack, triumphantly.

"The poor thing must be frozen solid; he wasn't designed for a night such as this – and nor were we," said Merryweather, with a shiver.

Her eyes flitted between the sleeping Gus and the hole in the wall, which exposed the summerhouse to the elements.

"Jack, go back up the hill to the front garden and fetch that tarpaulin. We need to block this hole."

"Okay," said Jack, and he scuttled off out of the building and back up the hill.

"Do you think he'll be okay?" asked Tom anxiously.

"I don't know," said Merryweather, bending down to take a closer look at her unexpected houseguest.

"I doubt the cold agrees with him – not that it agrees with anyone, really. Not this amount of cold." She paused and shone her torch at Gus's comatose body.

"What on earth are you doing here, in this time and place?" she mused.

Merryweather went down onto her haunches next to the sleeping Gus. She took off her left glove and tentatively reached out her hand to touch his skin. It felt cold and slightly clammy, too. Instinctively, Merryweather withdrew the tips of her fingers from the surface and stood up abruptly.

"What does this mean?" she wondered aloud.

"Do you think he's meant to be here, Auntieprof?" asked Tom.

"I have no idea, Tom. I am genuinely lost for words. In all my years researching the world's antiquities, this is quite the most astonishing sight I've ever seen – and I've seen a fair few. Dragons are supposed to be the stuff of legends, of fairytales; and yet... and yet, here he is, fast asleep in my summerhouse - having eaten half of it, I might add."

"He kept saying he had to find something and that he'd been asleep for ages," explained Tom.

"It was hard to understand what he was going on about, though; he was all over the place. Said something about protecting Santa, too. It was all we could do to get him out of that old church we found him in before the guys with the guns arrived. We told him there would be more food for him here and that worked, 'cos, oh boy, was he hungry."

"Yes, evidently, he was," said Merryweather, as she ran her fingers up and down the ragged edges of what had once been the back wall of the summerhouse, her face growing ever more puzzled by the second and gradually, contorting into a frown. Tom could see that she was thinking and processing what she was seeing, but also sensed that she couldn't quite believe her own eyes.

"We need to warm him up. Make him comfortable for the night," Merryweather decided.

"You mean just leave him here?" asked Tom.

"Well, given his size, Tom, we can't very well move him."

She flashed her torch around the interior of the summerhouse until it alighted on a switch. Flicking it, she said to Tom, "I'll turn the patio heater on. That should help a bit."

From outside the summerhouse, there came a scrunching and clumping noise as Jack slithered his way down the final few yards of the hill.

"Got it," he announced as he arrived at the hole in the summerhouse's rear, brandishing the tarpaulin.

"Good boy, Jack," said Merryweather. "Now, the pair of you help me cover this almighty hole with it and let's try to warm this poor fellow up a bit."

The three of them set to work, attaching the tarpaulin to the remaining rear timbers so that it covered the gap, blocking out the cold and preventing any more snow from billowing in. Gradually, the temperature within the summerhouse rose as the heater did its job and the tarpaulin helped to keep the cold at bay.

As the heat built a little, so Gus's breathing became shallower and his snoring more erratic.

"I think he might be waking up again," said Tom.

Gus's arms and legs started to twitch and his tail began swishing from side to side, which, given the dimensions of the summerhouse, left little room for Tom, Jack and Merryweather. They occasionally had to jump out of the way as Gus swept the surrounding floor with his jagged, scaly rudder.

And then the sneezing started. With each expulsion of air, the still slumbering dragon created a cloud of smoke, which filled the interior of the summerhouse. Tom, Jack and Merryweather succumbed to coughing fits.

"Jack, quickly, open that window. It'll let the cold in, but at least we'll still be able to breathe," said Merryweather.

Jack quickly released the latch and shunted the window open, letting the smoke escape and the cold air encroach inside again.

"I wonder, does he always create as much mess as this?" Merryweather asked Tom.

"On recent evidence, yes. He was trying to breathe fire when we found him, but was just making a load of smoke instead," said Tom.

"What other surprises does he have in store for us?" wondered Merryweather aloud.

An eye in the middle of the dark olive-green heap opened. Wide. And from somewhere else in the midst of the heap, a very long neck uncoiled and stretched. The head at the end of the very long neck was framed by a large yawning mouth, a darker green in colour and displaying its rows of jagged, very white and very sharp, gleaming teeth and its large variegated dark green and pink forked tongue.

Gus was now properly waking up.

The yawning noises stopped abruptly; he gave several large sniffs and then pivoted his large, scaly face downwards until it met Merryweather's slightly nervous gaze.

"Hello…" she offered uncertainly.

Gus sniffed her.

"Surprises? Who mentioned surprises? I *love* surprises."

He sniffed her again and his eyes narrowed, his face taking on more of a scowl.

"Are you a knight?"

"Me? Oh no, I'm not anything like that."

"Hmmm, what are you then?"

"I'm… I'm a professor of physics and antiquity. At the university. I teach people about the universe and ancient things and times."

"Aha!" exclaimed Gus. "Someone wise!"

"Well, I don't know about that," demurred Merryweather.

Gus then noticed Tom and Jack.

"Ah, you two again. Did we make it here okay? It's all still a bit… hazy…"

"Hi," said Tom. "We left you in the bushes, Gus. To hide you? Whilst we spoke with my aunt? Remember?"

Gus looked at Tom blankly.

Tom persevered, and turning towards Merryweather, he introduced her to the dragon, "Gus, this is my aunt. Professor Octavia Merryweather. Auntieprof, meet Gus."

"Very pleased to meet you, wise woman," exclaimed Gus.

"And I, you, Gus," replied Merryweather. "Now, are you still hungry?"

Gus paused for a second to consider this question and then his enormous head veered back down towards Merryweather.

"Yes. Yes, I am! See, I knew you were a wise woman: you even knew I was still hungry."

Merryweather glanced at the temporary tarpaulinated back wall of her summerhouse and replied with a wry smile, "Lucky guess."

She motioned to Jack and Tom to come and help her with the next task: to bring in some semi-frozen logs and kindling from the log store next to the summerhouse.

"Come on, we'll soon have you fed, Gus, don't you worry."

The three of them bundled themselves up against the snow and gathered as many pieces of wood as they could carry before returning to the relative warmth of the summerhouse to feed them to one very grateful dragon.

"Oh, thank you, this is brilliant," said Gus as he chomped his way through yet more small logs, twigs, and pieces of bark.

"Mmmmm, a tasty wee bit of oak there, my favourite."

Merryweather was looking at Gus as he ate, as though she was inspecting something or looking for clues. Eventually, the question that was bothering her formed, and she addressed him directly.

"Gus, where did you come from?"

Gus paused mid-crunch and thought for a second or two.

"That's a bit of a tricky one. Do you mean tonight? I just followed these two to your house all the way through the snow."

"No, that's not what I meant. Where did you come from originally? And why are you here? Here now, I mean. Do you know?"

Gus's prior demeanour of contentment was now giving way to one of confusion as he considered Merryweather's questions.

"Well, it's all a bit of a blur." He shrugged and paused, thinking about whatever it was he either could or could not remember.

"See, I'm still waking up and everything that happened before is all hazy."

Then, his face broke into a huge toothy grin – which, given the size of his teeth, was actually terrifying.

"I do remember parts of it," he announced with a flourish. "I've lost something and I need to find it."

There was a pause as Gus cocked his head to one side, thinking about what else he could remember.

"And I have to protect him… what did you two call him again?" Gus turned to Tom and Jack.

"Santa?" offered Jack.

"Yeah, that was the name you used, although he's St Nicholas to me."

Another pause.

"And I was being chased. I remember now! I was being chased somewhere far from here, in the countryside."

Gus frowned his face into an angry frown.

"Bad men. Not knights. Wicked men chased me all the way to here."

"And where was here?" asked Merryweather gently.

Gus's expression brightened again.

"The church these two laddies found me in. The Church of St. Nicholas, of course."

"Of course," agreed Merryweather, "and what else can you recall?"

Gus's face now looked worried again.

"They were evil men. They were going to kill me, so I had to fly away. Fly for my life. All the way from the borderlands to that church. Long time ago now. In your years, sixteen hundred and something or other."

"The 'borderlands'?" said Merryweather, "I see…" even though she didn't. "Go on."

"I had something... something with me... something important. I definitely brought it with me, but now I can't find it."

"What was it?" asked Tom. "What did you have?"

"The box," whispered Gus, now staring into the middle distance. "It was the box."

Jack chimed in, "Was that what you were looking for earlier on in the church?"

"Yes, laddie, it was." Gus's voice was now so quiet it was barely audible. He also sounded scared. "And I need to find it."

Gus was trying to pace around the summerhouse, which, given his size compared to that of the interior of the summerhouse, was an impossible task and simply made him more agitated.

"Gus," said Merryweather, resting her hand on one of his winged arms, "it's all right. We can help you."

Gus stopped trying to pace temporarily and looked at her.

"You're the wise woman."

Then he veered towards Tom. "And you, laddie, are brave."

"What about me?" piped up Jack.

Gus paused again, looked down at Jack, and gave a big grin.

"You are a good and cheerful wee fellow."

Jack puffed out his chest and stood tall, looking very pleased with himself.

Merryweather continued, "What is it that is so important about this box of yours?"

"That's the thing," the dragon replied, as he unleashed a massive yawn. "It wasn't mine."

He lowered himself back down onto the floor again and gave another yawn, a stretch of his be-winged arms and a flick of his tail. His wings folded away as he settled onto the floor and his eyelids drooped.

"Sleepy… still so sleepy… must just have another wee nap…"

"Gus… Gus…" Merryweather shook his winged arm as Gus's eyelids fell shut. One eyelid popped back open as she jolted his arm back and forward.

"What was so important about the box?"

Gus gave another enormous yawn.

"I was protecting St Nicholas… guarding him…"

"Protecting him? From what?" persisted Merryweather.

Gus gave her a big, sleepy grin, before pronouncing, "Nighty night." With which, his head fell downwards, draping itself across his outstretched arms on the floor, and he promptly conked out.

"Gus," Merryweather shook the now sleeping dragon. "Gus," she shouted his name once more, louder this time. It was no use: Gus was snoring again.

Merryweather stood up and turned to both boys.

"I need to speak to Nicky," she said, sounding half-distracted. "Ancient lore has always been his deep specialism. He may be able to figure out what all of this means and why Gus is here at all."

"*And*," she reminded herself, "I need to find out what he's been up to with Gris Corp."

"Gris Corp?" asked Tom. "Do you know someone who's been working there?"

"Yes, in a manner of speaking," replied Merryweather. "My colleague, Dr Auld – remember, you saw him at my office. Well, he's apparently been working with them on some sort of secret project – that's what those men at the door earlier on were here about – and now, we need to find out what he's been doing – and quickly."

"We'll leave Gus be. He'll be fine here overnight now the heater's on.

Merryweather ushered Tom and Jack out of the door of the summerhouse and back into the snow, pausing as she closed the door to gaze at the sleeping dragon. She turned out the light, closed the door and instructed Tom and Jack, "Come on, you two. With me. We've got work to do."

CHAPTER TWENTY-FOUR

Back indoors, Tom and Jack had barely had time to dry themselves off a bit and sweep the melting snow from their jackets before Merryweather was ushering them out of the house again and towards her large double garage.

"Come on, let's get out of the cold and into the car," she urged.

Neither Tom nor Jack was for arguing.

With some effort, the three of them cleared the snow away from the base of the garage door and it gradually opened. There, pristine in the relative warmth of the garage, was Merryweather's car: an ancient, beaten up, deep blue coloured Land Rover Defender.

"Woah," exclaimed Jack, admiring the vehicle, "you've got an actual Defender. This'll be like off-roading."

Surveying the snowy scene as she opened the car doors, Merryweather agreed, "Yes, I rather think it might."

The car started first time and Merryweather slowly nursed it out into the snow.

As the garage door shuddered its way closed again, Merryweather turned to both boys.

"We should be okay; she's running on winter tyres. Are you both buckled in?"

Tom and Jack nodded their assent.

"Good. Here goes."

And with that, they were off, with Merryweather explaining their route home.

"I'm going to quickly swing by Nicky's place. I really need to talk to him about all of this and it's en route, anyway. You two can come with me; Nicky won't mind. Actually, he'll probably be glad of the company."

As the Defender slithered its way down the hill – slowly – Tom instinctively held onto both his seat and the door handle, his face set into a frown of concentration. Jack, meanwhile, was loving it.

"This is *actually* better than off-roading," he piped up gleefully.

The car continued to crawl its way through the deserted city streets, slithering and sliding its way through the night. After some twenty minutes, they turned into a crescent of houses, in one of the city's quieter outlying areas, with most of the snow undisturbed as yet, but not quite all of it. Merryweather drew the Defender to a halt outside a nondescript, newish bungalow, number fifty-two on the street.

"This is it – Nicky's house," she announced to the boys. "Come on, let's go and talk to him."

The house, like every other one in the crescent – and indeed the crescent itself – was in darkness. Tom and Jack jumped down from the Defender and landed with a satisfying whumph as their boots sank into the deep, freshly fallen snow. The pair of them and Merryweather made their way up the path towards the front door. Though the snow had been falling steadily for hours, the snow covering the road and the pathway to the front door of the house was uneven and lumpy. Tom peered at it and saw that there had been tyre tracks and footprints in the snow, although these had by now largely been filled in.

Seeing Tom inspecting the lumpy and bumpy snow, Merryweather sounded a warning, "Be careful, we may have company here."

As Merryweather spoke, Tom noticed another sign that not all was as it should be.

"Look, it isn't closed," he said, pointing at the front door of the house; it was open ever so slightly, no more than a crack.

"Okay, that's weird," said Jack. "No one leaves their door open on a night like this."

"Nicky didn't - look." Merryweather pointed towards the door, specifically to the handle and the lock. Tom and Jack could see that the lock and handle looked slightly wonky and were hanging half-out of their usual location and not quite in alignment with the rest of the door.

"It's been forced," said Merryweather.

She motioned the two boys to get behind her and whispered, "Follow me – slowly – let's proceed with caution - just in case there's anyone else in here who shouldn't be."

Tom could feel his mouth drying up, and the only sound he could hear was his heart pounding in his chest as Merryweather gradually eased the door open, just far enough for them to edge their way past it and go inside.

The three of them inched their way into the corridor of Nick Auld's house and as their eyes adjusted further to the darkness, Merryweather sensed that there was something odd about the whole situation. Tom, too, was feeling uneasy.

"Do you think there's someone else still in here?" he whispered to Merryweather. Before she could answer, there was a tremendous crash immediately behind the pair of them. Tom instinctively turned his torch on. There, buried underneath a pile of books and boxes, lay Jack, grinning apologetically.

"Sorry... I sort of tripped over them; they were all over the place, anyway." He shrugged as he excavated himself from underneath the mess.

Merryweather spoke first.

"Are you all right?"

Then, almost as an afterthought, "Tom, you should switch your torch off, though I don't suppose it matters now... if there was anyone here they would have fled or attacked us by now after that commotion."

Tom kept his torch on and was slowly sweeping it across the rest of the hall and into what he supposed had been the living room.

"Auntieprof, I think you'd better come and look at this…"

Merryweather was about to be short with Tom about his continuing torch use when she saw what Tom was picking out with his torch's beam. The inner part of the hall that led further into the house and into the living room was strewn with upside down furniture, half-emptied boxes and books, ornaments and other trinkets. There was a television face down beneath one of the side windows in the living room. Nothing was where it should be and rather a lot of it had been smashed or broken.

"Good grief, the whole place has been ransacked," said Merryweather, as though she were talking to herself.

"Wow, this looks even worse than my bedroom," was Jack's contribution.

"Who do you think did this?" asked Tom.

"I don't know, Tom, but on a night like this, they must have been pretty determined and in a hurry to find something. They've upended everything. It's as though… as though…"

"As though they were looking for something?" Tom offered.

"Yes," replied Merryweather, "and I doubt whether they've found it."

She scanned the room once more, then whirled around and did a quick sweep of the rest of the house. Every room looked the same: as though a tiny bungalow-sized tornado had swept through it, trashing everything in its wake.

Merryweather turned to the two boys.

"Come on, we should get out of here. Back to the car. Close the door behind you, Jack."

"Are we going home now?" asked Jack, as they scrunched their way back to the Defender.

"Yes – eventually," said Merryweather, sounding as though her mind was already somewhere else, "but first we have one more place to check on our way."

"Where are we going now?" asked Tom, as they climbed in. Jack was still buckling up as Merryweather started the engine.

"To Nicky's office at the university. I need to check something – and to find him."

Merryweather drove slowly once again, this time towards the university in the west end of the city. The streets were deserted, save for the very odd car, puncturing the darkness with its headlights and slithering about all over the road. The journey was mostly in silence after Jack had asked another of his 'daft laddie' questions.

"Do you think Dr Auld will be okay, Prof?"

Tom shot Jack a look and rolled his eyes skywards. Jack replied with a silent look, his palms outstretched and a mouthed, "what?"

Merryweather sighed a long sigh in response to Jack before she began replying.

"Jack, I honestly don't know. Something is seriously remiss – that much I do know. Nicky should be in his house – and he isn't. And his house has been torn apart by somebody – someone who was clearly looking for something – and I don't know who, though I have my suspicions that it may be something to do with those people who were at my door earlier on."

Upon arrival at the signs announcing the university campus, Merryweather turned off the main road and down a narrow, tree-lined side street, composed of several large, elegant, Victorian red and gold sandstone townhouses. She guided the Defender as best she could into a space at the far end of the street, in a spot that was usually quieter than the end that was closer to the main road. Of course, this evening, everywhere was eerily quiet and dimly lit. As the Defender finally slithered and jolted its way to a halt, Merryweather turned off the engine and motioned for the two boys to get out.

"Come on," said Merryweather. "With me. We're going to check Nicky's office."

The three silhouettes made their way in the darkness, along the quiet, tree-lined street, until Merryweather drew them to a halt outside one of the golden-coloured Victorian townhouses which was so draped in the evening's snowfall that it looked for all the world like a scene from a Christmas card.

Merryweather signalled to the two boys that they had arrived at their next destination and they began picking their way through the snow, up the pathway to the front door of the converted townhouse, being guided by the jerky zig-zags of their torch beams.

Once again, Tom noticed the general lumpiness of the snow all around the front areas of the building, from the road right up to the front door. True, they were in the middle of the city now – which could have explained some of the disturbance on the road and the pavements, but perhaps not the covered-in footprints all the way up and down the pathway.

Tom's mind daydreamed as he pondered what the inner quadrangle of the university – his route to Merryweather's own office - would look like in all this snow. Doubtless, it would be silently beautiful. He then wondered what it would look like in the daylight when Merryweather snapped him out of his reverie.

"Here we are," she said, pausing in front of a tall set of solid-looking wooden double doors.

Surveying the recently disturbed snow on the pathway and then the double outer doors of the building, Merryweather observed, "Well, If Nicky's visitors have been here, they've at least closed the door after themselves this time."

She took off her gloves and fished around in her coat pocket for a few seconds, producing a chunky bunch of keys. She then inserted the largest one into the lock and turned it. The lock made a heavy clunk-clack noise, and the door fell open slightly.

"Right, we're in. Come along, it's just along the corridor."

The three of them set off along the interior corridor until Merryweather stopped outside a nondescript wooden door, numbered E-458.2. Tom's torch picked out a small sign below it which simply said Dr N. Auld.

Merryweather reached into her coat pocket again for the bunch of keys, when Tom noticed the door wasn't completely closed.

"Look," he said, pressing on the door. It swung open. "It was on the latch."

"Maybe he's here already?" Jack offered, trying to be helpful.

Merryweather's face was now looking very serious.

"I hope so – but I doubt it. Be careful – let me go in first."

The scene, as they edged into the office of Nicholas Auld, Reader in Physics and Antiquity, was a very different one to that which they had found in his house less than an hour earlier: the entire office was very much as one would have expected the working environment of an academic to look, though on closer inspection, Merryweather pointed out certain anomalies to the two boys.

"That's odd," she began, pointing to a half-drunk cup of tea, sitting on the desk in the middle of the room. "Nicky is always fastidious about cleaning up mugs and plates from his workspace every day."

She lifted the cup. "Still smells fresh; I doubt he's been gone very long." She paused. Next to the cup was a side plate with a half-eaten digestive biscuit on it.

"Nicky's usual biscuit of choice, but he was never one for not finishing a cup of tea and a biscuit unless…"

"Unless what?" asked Tom.

"Unless he was interrupted," replied Merryweather. "Whatever happened here took him away in a hurry from whatever it was he was working on."

She began rifling through the papers on his desk, picking the occasional one up to peer at it more closely.

"Hmmm, this looks like his standard day-to-day university work," she mused. "I wonder…"

Tom and Jack watched as Merryweather walked over the office's built-in bookshelves and began looking along the rows and rows of books.

"It must be here somewhere…"

She ran her finger along the spines of the books on the shelves, before pausing on an old, rather large and battered hardback book.

"Ah, here we are," she said, easing it out of its place on the shelf, before putting it down on the desk before the two boys.

Tom looked at the ancient dark green cover with its faded gold lettering.

"Ancient Scottish Folklore: Myths and Legends by A.R.W. Mulberry. I don't understand. What's so special about this book?"

Merryweather looked at Tom and Jack and grinned.

"Nothing particularly special about it to the untrained eye, though it was written by my father."

She began opening the book slowly and fiddling around with the back cover.

"But I know this book means a lot to Nicky. It's what sparked his interest in all matters of antiquity when he was about your age."

She continued, "I also know that, inside this book's back cover, there is a little surprise."

She ran her fingers down the inside of the back cover of the ancient tome and pressed against the join to the very back page. At which point, the back cover popped open to reveal a shallow compartment.

"Oh good, it's still here."

Merryweather shone her torch on the interior of the compartment and started picking at the edge of some sticky tape within it, before peeling it back and producing a small, iron key, which she held up in front of the two boys as though it were a trophy.

Merryweather was now smiling for the first time in what seemed like ages to Tom. He wasn't used to seeing his aunt looking as stern and serious as she had been for so long this particular evening.

Merryweather turned to Tom and Jack and explained.

"Well, whoever it was who was here with Nicky this evening, they haven't found this – and that could be very important."

"I don't understand," said Jack. "Why is it important?"

"Because, young Jack Wanless, this isn't just any old key," replied Merryweather, as she bent down and began crawling under the large, oak desk, shining her torch on its underside as she did so.

"It is…" began Merryweather as she levered herself into position, "the key…" she was fiddling with the key on the underside of the desk, "which, if one knows exactly how to use it…" there was a metallic rattling and jiggling coming from underneath the desk now as Merryweather tried to insert the key into its lock, "can open up a part of this desk…", more fiddling around and rattling – and then a clack and a clunk, "to reveal the secrets therein."

There was a whirring noise followed by a snap and a thud as part of the desk, next to the drawers on its right-hand side, appeared to fall down vertically onto the floor and then fell off.

"Voila!" exclaimed Merryweather. "We're in."

Tom and Jack both turned their torches onto the now open part of the desk. Inside it, there was a brown paper folder, tied together with a string fastener, its paper contents bulging as though trying to escape their shackles.

"Well, look at this. What have we here?" mused Merryweather as she picked up the folder whilst extricating herself from underneath the desk.

She laid the folder down on the top of the desk and began opening the string fastener.

"What do you think it is?" asked Tom.

"I've no idea," replied Merryweather. "But whatever it is, Nicky clearly didn't want anyone else to know about it."

"But how did you know about the key in the book?" asked Jack.

"Well, because I gave him the book a very long time ago," said Merryweather.

"But what about the key? How did you know about the key – and the desk?" asked Tom.

"I gave him the desk, too," grinned Merryweather. "Teachers should always know how their students tick, boys, and no one knows Nicky and how his mind works quite like I do."

Merryweather sat down in the chair behind the desk, and slowly began leafing through the large, higglety-pigglety bundle of papers contained in the brown card covered folder. Tom and Jack peered over her shoulder as she did so. She flicked through many of the papers quickly, but would occasionally pause on one sheet for a few seconds, reading it in more detail.

After a couple of minutes of this, Merryweather looked up, took off her glasses, and placed them down on the desk. She stared into the middle distance and murmured, "Oh my…"

"Are you okay, Auntieprof?" asked Tom.

"I'm not really sure, Tom," she replied. "Here, the pair of you, take a bundle of these papers each and start reading through them as quickly as you can. We shouldn't hang around here for too long."

With this, she divided the bundle of papers up into three portions and handed a bundle each to Tom and Jack. The two boys took their respective bundles and pored over them, using their torches to aid their scrutiny. Tom stood on the opposite side of the desk to where Merryweather was sitting and slightly to the side as he ploughed through his pile. Jack, meanwhile, was sprawled on the floor and rummaging through his sheaf of papers in his usual chaotic fashion.

It was Jack who punctured the silence – bar the turning of pages and rustling of papers – first of all.

"Woah, no way!"

"What have you found, Jack?" asked Merryweather.

Jack got up off his haunches and was brandishing some sheets in his right hand.

"There's a load of stuff here about old churches – and a dragon!" he exclaimed.

"Go on," said Merryweather.

"Well, it all sounds a bit old-fashioned, but there are stories about all these ancient churches scattered all over Europe and stuff and then there's a bit about what links the churches and it's got something to do with St. Nicholas and then there's some legends about how a dragon was seen occasionally throughout history across Europe, often near some of these churches and then there's one page that says that the dragon hasn't been seen since 16-something and was last seen *in Scotland* and it says that it was so long ago that all the stories are now legends and…"

Jack had poured out his own unique summary of the papers he had been consuming but was halted by Merryweather raising her right hand.

"And relax," she said, with a kindly smile. "What else does it say?"

Jack paused and thought for a moment.

"Well, that's the main stuff, but there's one thing that keeps repeating over and over: the dragon. Some of the descriptions sound an awful lot like Gus."

Merryweather motioned for Jack to hand her his bundle of papers. Jack rummaged around on the ground for a few seconds and then thrust the papers into her arms. She began sorting through them and reading them for herself.

"But that's impossible," said Tom. "If it was Gus, he'd be hundreds – maybe even thousands - of years old. Nothing lives that long."

"No, Tom, not nothing. No creature that we know of in the modern world. There is a difference," said Merryweather.

"But… but… how could he have survived all these years? And where has he been since the 1600s? It's not like he could have hidden away. He's not exactly small, is he?"

"Those aren't the questions, Tom, good as they are. The questions are: who was Nicky doing all this work for – and why? This must have taken him months to collate – and then he hid it all away, as though he wanted to keep it a secret."

"So, you knew nothing about any of this then, Auntieprof?"

"No, I had no idea. And now we have a problem. Well, two problems – no, actually, we have several problems."

Merryweather was speed-reading the papers as she spoke.

She looked up and at Tom.

"Anything in your bundle that is of interest?"

"Same as Jack's. More stuff about churches and relics – whatever they are – and the legends about how these relics all got scattered around all over the place. Seems like a lot of people were fighting all the time back in the Middle Ages."

"Give them here," motioned Merryweather again, and she began poring over Tom's bundle this time.

"So, if those weren't the questions, well, I have one more: Gus said he had been asleep, right? Do you think he meant hibernating?" asked Tom.

"Possibly," murmured Merryweather.

Tom continued, "And why's he suddenly reappeared right now? Do you think he really is on some sort of mission? He kept going on about guarding St. Nicholas, but that makes no sense, does it?"

Merryweather stood up.

"I said we had several problems – but we could equally think of them as mysteries to be solved or questions to be answered: why was Nicky doing this research, and for whom? I suspect it's something to do with my other visitors from earlier on this evening, but we need to find out what all of this means."

She swept her hand across the sheaves of papers scattered on the desk and continued addressing Tom and Jack.

"We also have the small matter of a sleeping dragon in my summerhouse. We need to figure out what to do with him. Also, that rules out going to the police. They'd flip and likely shoot the poor beast.

"Oh, and we're in the middle of a global power outage caused by the largest solar storm the world has seen in well over a century - and there's a snowstorm. Either of these would be sub-optimal, taken individually. In combination, well, they're *extremely* sub-optimal. Gus is clearly important according to these legends, so we have to protect him, and keep him safe from harm until we figure out what is going on and what he has to do with all these churches – and St Nicholas – *if*, indeed, it was him all down the ages.

"It is likely that Nicky doesn't fully understand what it is he has unearthed here. He would have – quite reasonably, given the lack of any recent incontrovertible evidence to the contrary - dismissed the stories about a dragon as mere legends, but we have living proof that they aren't mere legends – and that proof is currently fast asleep in my summerhouse. Indeed, he has eaten half my summerhouse; we'll need to repair that, too!"

She flashed them a wry grin.

"Come on, I need to take you two home to Jack's. We can compost this little lot overnight and figure out what to do after a good night's sleep."

Merryweather bundled all the papers together and began searching around the office.

"What are you looking for?" asked Tom.

"Some paper. I'm taking this little lot with me," replied Merryweather. She pointed to the bundle. "We don't want it falling into the wrong hands, but we shouldn't leave the compartment empty – just in case."

Merryweather rooted around in one of the office's filing cabinets.

"Here we are," she said, pulling out some loose-leaf paper and a couple of notepads. "Quickly, help me tear this lot out."

She threw an A4 sized pad each to Tom and Jack, who began ripping out the pages, Once Merryweather decided they had a suitable amount of paper to form a new, dummy bundle, she gathered the fresh bundle of blank sheets together and placed it back into the folder, then carefully reinserted it back into the desk's secret compartment, before resetting the spring mechanism which had unveiled the compartment's existence and finally replacing the key back into the ancient tome that was its hiding place and carefully positioning it back as she had found it.

"Job done. Come on, let's go," said Merryweather, ushering Tom and Jack back out of the office and then the building. She locked the office door and the main outer door carefully and they headed back towards the car. The snow was still billowing down and had, in the time they had been in Nick Auld's office, deposited a fresh layer several centimetres thick on the Defender.

The three of them swept the snow from the windscreens and the windows before going inside the car. Tom was shivering. Merryweather apologised to both boys for the lack of heating.

"It's an old car; sometimes, the heating can be somewhat wonky."

She drove to Jack's house, with Jack providing directions along the way. The streets were, if anything, even quieter now. This did not feel like the Friday before Christmas. Usually, the streets would have been packed with revellers and partygoers, the restaurants and bars would, to use the vernacular, have been heaving with people. Tonight, though, the streets were silent, with only the odd snowplough or occasional car inching their way through the snow. Given how dark it was, it was easy to spot them, their headlights acting like shifting antennae of light, picking their way through this dark yet white alien world.

The journey to Jack's house only took around half an hour and, other than Jack's occasional directions, it passed in silence. As they neared Jack's house, Merryweather spoke.

"So, we're nearly there. Can you two find your way around to mine again later on tomorrow morning? That should give us all time to have a good night's sleep, including Gus."

Tom shifted around uncomfortably in his seat.

"I'm not sure, Auntieprof. I should really go back home, given the weather and everything."

As Merryweather nursed the car into Jack's street, she kept her gaze firmly on the road, but addressed Tom.

"Thomas Brightly, what are you saying?"

Tom grew red in the face and ever more awkward.

"Well, it's just... well, I want to help, but it sounds like it could be dangerous, and Mum and Nan will be worrying about me."

"But they know you're at mine," piped up Jack.

"Yeah, but... I *really* should go home," said Tom firmly.

Merryweather drew the car to a halt outside Jack's house and turned around to face Tom.

"Tom," she began gently, "Gus specifically asked for our help. He asked you first out of all of us. We have a duty to help him and to do the right thing. There are strange deeds afoot here and we need to be brave and figure out what is going on."

She paused, letting her words sink in.

"I know it's been a very peculiar day, but we have a duty of care to that creature. He's out of sorts, lost and confused, and we can help him. We owe him that. And besides," she flashed a grin at Tom, "the pair of you brought him to my house and he's chomped his way through my summerhouse! So, the pair of you can jolly well help me repair it. Understood?"

Tom nodded, sheepishly.

"Good, now get inside out of the cold and make sure you have a good night's sleep. We've work to do tomorrow."

"Okay," said Tom. "Sorry, Auntieprof."

"Don't be sorry," Merryweather said gently. "Be brave and proceed with good heart."

Tom nodded.

The boys opened the car doors and got out, saying their goodnights to Merryweather.

"I'll see you at mine tomorrow. Come to the back door. Late morning. Don't forget," she reminded them.

And with that, Octavia Merryweather, Professor of Physics and Antiquity, and her ancient car trundled off into the snowy night, leaving Jack and Tom standing on the path which led to the front door of Jack's house.

"Quite a day," said Tom, with deliberate understatement.

"Totally!" replied Jack. His excitement faded as they reached the front door.

"And now for the hardest part yet: dealing with my sister," he grimaced as he opened the front door.

CHAPTER TWENTY-FIVE

Nicholas Auld was having a bad evening. Much and all as he loved his work, to the extent that he had, of his own free will, been working on the Friday evening before Christmas, in a snowstorm – and a global power outage, this was because it was work (in this case research on the propensity of ancient Egyptian tombs to hold clues to recognisable cycles in the heavens) he both enjoyed and in which he was deeply immersed.

The same could not be said of the work he was currently being forced to do under armed guard. At least Auld thought his guards were armed – and the two of them were sufficiently huge and carried a whiff of danger about them so that he didn't want to put his theory to the test.

Following his brief yet singularly unpleasant encounter with Max Gris and then, with Slymington, the two Gris Corp security guards had forcibly removed Auld from his meeting and had once again frogmarched him along corridors; this time, to a clinically designed meeting room, buried deep within the sprawling maze of the headquarters building.

Like most of the rest of the building that he had seen, this space had been designed to maximise interior light and was mostly frosted glass once again. Auld felt as though he was being marched around the interior of a giant vase before being deposited in a different, slightly smaller vase.

The two guards, Simmons and his identikit sidekick, indicated to Auld that he should go inside the room and it was to be his 'office' to undertake the work on the scrolls for Gris.

"In here please, sir," ordered Simmons. "You'll find you have everything you need to complete your work." Despite the veneer of manners, the meaning was clear to Auld. Simmons placed the wooden box containing the scrolls on the glass table which, like most of the meeting rooms in the building, dominated the room.

Auld blinked and looked inside the room. It was the same sterile, corporate design as every other space he had seen in his journey around the building. The walls were mainly glass, mostly frosted, and it was dazzling in the interior. Far too bright for his liking.

He scrunched his eyes slightly and turned to Simmons.

"What if I need anything?"

"Everything you need is right in there, sir," replied Simmons as he looked over Auld's head.

"Really? What if I need to go to the bathroom?"

"There are facilities attached to this room, right over there," said Simmons, with a nod of his head. "Now, if you need anything else, we'll be right outside."

With this, Simmons and his sidekick had left the room, closed the door, and had taken up their positions directly outside it. It was clear to Auld that no one was entering or leaving the room unless the two security guards allowed it.

This had been several hours ago. For a long time, after they had left him in the room on his own, Auld sat slumped in a chair, staring at the wooden box in front of him. He felt as though he was a child again, one who had been given an especially unpleasant task to complete for homework. A task he resented yet which he knew would have to be completed, else there would be consequences. That Auld only knew in part what those consequences could be only fuelled his resentment further.

He remained in this fugue state of growing irritation for ages, arguing with himself: his stubborn side did not want to lift even one scroll, nor to do anything that might assist that ghastly woman. His other, more pragmatic side kept pointing out that the sooner he began re-deciphering the scrolls, the sooner he would be out of his temporary prison. He hoped.

Eventually, his pragmatic side won the argument, and he sat upright in the chair, slowly putting on the special gloves that had also been provided, so as not to damage the delicate scrolls. Once he had adjusted the gloves, so they fitted snugly, he lifted the first scroll out of its container, placing it gently down on the table in front of him and teased it open.

His memories of working on the scrolls flooded back. It had involved many hours of working late into the evenings, after he had completed his usual university work, over the course of many months earlier in the year. Then, it hadn't seemed such a chore: there had been a novelty to investigating each of the ancient pieces of parchment and his interest and excitement had grown as he built up his knowledge through deciphering each successive scroll, with the pieces of a larger picture becoming clearer and more connected.

He had been instructed that Max Gris was taking a keen interest in this particular area of antiquity. In Auld's experience, this was not altogether uncommon amongst those he considered to be super wealthy. Usually, they ended up following some passion or other and often this extended into his world if their interests aligned with the areas of antiquity with which he was familiar.

So, he hadn't considered Gris's original request to be anything too out of the ordinary. She had a deep interest in Christmas, partly borne out of her role in business over many years, and this had extended to wanting to understand more about the origins of one of the key people in the Christmas tradition: Santa Claus himself. Also known as St. Nicholas.

Auld had never had a satisfactory explanation as to where, when, or how Gris had acquired the ancient scrolls. He had learned from experience that it was seldom a good idea to interrogate the owners of such objects of antiquity as to their provenance. Besides, even if one asked, one rarely, if ever, received the full facts about how the object or objects had come to be in an individual's possession.

And so it had been with Gris. He had tentatively asked her about their immediate history, but other than hinting that they had been – somehow – acquired by her father and therefore had been in her family for years and years, he had been given scant further details; rather, he had been given clear and specific instructions: Gris had explained at the outset that the scrolls could be connected to St. Nicholas and she wished to understand what they said and what this meant, down to every last detail.

Eventually, after many months, Auld had presented her with his findings: all six of the scrolls appeared to form a whole. Each one mentioned a specific location, in which some relics of St. Nicholas were said to be located. Because of the age of the scrolls, which he had estimated to be many, many centuries old, it had initially been rather difficult to pinpoint the exact correlation between the ancient territories described and their modern equivalents, but through persistence and determination, Auld had given this his best shot, right down to the precise details of the buildings or locations in which the relics were said to be interred; indeed, there were even specific details about the locations of the relics within the buildings and areas, together with very precise instructions as to how to locate these once inside the building or area in question. Auld had, of course, presented these to Gris with a health warning that, given the age of the scrolls, it was entirely possible that the buildings would have been altered or even destroyed and even if they were still – broadly – in their original form, there was no guarantee that the relics themselves would not have been moved. Ancient and important objects had a habit of disappearing over the centuries, usually as a result of human intervention. Or ransacking, as he preferred to call it.

Nonetheless, he had been satisfied that, insofar as he had been able to, he had deciphered the scrolls, though there had been two aspects to their detail which had left him somewhat baffled. Firstly, there was a running strand throughout all six rolls of parchment that suggested that all the various relics should remain apart and that this was important, though, frustratingly, it was never made clear as to why this should be so.

He had tried to ask Gris about this, but she had ignored the question and changed the subject to his payment terms, which had had the desired effect of distracting him at the time.

Secondly, on one scroll, there had been a section missing towards the bottom. Auld had asked if there was any knowledge of where the missing section could be, but there was none. He had been told by Slymington that it had been procured in that state and that he would simply have to use what he had in front of him in order to decipher its meaning.

This Auld had done to a point where he had been satisfied that he was ninety-five per cent sure that the location he had found was correctly identified. And he had also been ninety-five per cent certain that the building in which this cache of relics was said to be located was no longer there, or a ruin at best.

He had tried to make this point when he had been paraded in front of Gris to summarise and deliver his findings, but it had been downplayed due to her insistence on certainty. Foolishly, he had been rather more bullish about this particular scroll than had been entirely sensible, given that which had now transpired.

Because his deciphering of that one scroll, as he had now been forcibly told, had not been correct in its conclusion: i.e., that the location was an old, now ruined monastery in Ireland; Auld now realised, with a heavy heart, that his five per cent of doubt had not only been prudent, but indeed had been an understatement.

As he picked his way through the scroll in question once more, with these memories flooding back into his mind, he questioned his previous conclusions. If not in Ireland, then where could this location be? Had he misread any of the words in front of him? Even though his knowledge of Latin, the language of all the scrolls, was second to none, Auld knew that the sense of what he had translated and the subsequent meaning which he had deciphered could be altered by those words which were unseen, namely the words contained in the elusive missing piece of the scroll.

And so, over many hours, he tried once more to make sense of the ancient, cryptic words and clues, this time discounting his original conclusions and reaching deep into his own knowledge for alternative theories and conclusions. He read the incomplete scroll once more in conjunction with the fully intact other five pieces of parchment, to see if, upon a re-reading, they, too, might yield further – and different – clues.

If not Ireland, then where? Read this way, the clues suggested another area on the periphery of northern Europe, with a pre-history of paganism yet linked to Irish Celticism.

As the evening went beyond midnight and into the wee small hours, Auld became almost manic in his work, determined to find the answers. He grew more and more convinced that he had alighted on the wrong Celtic nation in his previous conclusion and that the correct location was far closer to home. Indeed, it was home. It was Scotland. But whereabouts? He narrowed down the search. Mention was made of a place that, he reasoned, was the location – at least centuries ago – of this particular batch of relics and of a church at a cross – which could also be a monastery of some sort.

Auld was sure that if the scroll had been complete, he would have been able to narrow down his search definitively, but as it was, he was having to – literally – fill in the blanks. Upon his closer reading, he had noticed for the first time that the very last section appeared to be different in its sentence construction. It was subtle, but noticeable. He wondered why. Perhaps it had been written at a different time, as an afterthought. Or a postscript.

Or, because something had happened – or had been happening at the time of writing. He scrutinised the words even more carefully. After the reference to the building that was no longer there – or ruin, as he had taken the words to mean - there was a mention of an escape to *viridi cavas*, a green hollow. These few words were almost a throwaway line and appeared to be secondary to the principal focus of the scroll.

Auld was now being overtaken by fatigue and sat back in his chair as he pondered what they meant. A green hollow could be anywhere, and what did the escape mean? Further on, there was also another fragment which spoke of *falsum cor est:* the heart is false. He wondered if this meant that there had been some sort of betrayal and whether this had led to the escape. His eyes were stinging with tiredness by now, after hour upon hour of poring over the scrolls, and he dearly wanted to go home, but he needed to give Gris and her cronies some other credible location.

Auld swung on his chair, a habit that had endured since childhood whenever he was stuck on an especially difficult problem that he needed to solve. He swung on his chair for several minutes, trying to connect the fragments of phrases from the past contained within this problematic scroll, which hinted at something bigger.

And then, mid-swing, he stopped. He stood up in such a hurry that the chair clattered over to the ground as he made for the door.

Opening it, he was met by Simmons, looking the same as he done hours previously: stony-faced and threatening.

"Go fetch your boss. I've got it," said Auld.

Simmons raised an eyebrow.

"Well, if you're sure, sir," he replied.

"Oh, I'm sure all right," said Auld.

"Very well, sir. If you'd be good enough to resume your seat, we'll be with you in a few minutes."

Auld stepped back into the room and retook his seat. He was exhausted, but also elated at his deduction. This time, he had cracked it – and he would soon be going home. He allowed himself a wide grin of satisfaction and sat, staring into the middle distance, marvelling at his discovery.

Within minutes, his reverie was fractured, as the door to the room clicked open and Max Gris herself, accompanied by Slymington, entered.

Gris was at her condescending best, "Well, Nicky boy. Simmons here tells me you have a bit of news for us."

"Yes, I have."

Gris stared at Auld. "Well, out with it. Come on, we haven't got all night."

As he spoke, Auld wondered if Gris ever slept or whether she was always both manic and unpleasant.

"The last batch of relics isn't in Ireland. It's in Scotland."

"Scotland? *Okay...* and?"

Auld could see that Gris was looking at him expectantly, and for a brief flash, he felt as though he held some power over her. Slymington soon disabused him of any notion on that score.

"Mr Auld, we have so little time. As does your pet." Slymington's tone may have been as flat as ever, but Auld recognised the threat.

Auld continued, "I had thought it was almost certain they were in Ireland, at the ruined monastery, because the scroll described this – or seemed to – but there was always a sliver of doubt because of the missing section."

Auld paused, as much to gather his thoughts as for effect. He could see that both Gris and Slymington were now hanging on his every word.

"Upon close and careful rereading, in conjunction with the rest of the scrolls, I have reached a different conclusion. There is talk of a land on the northern periphery of Europe with a strong pre-historic pagan tradition. That could mean Scotland as well.

"Also, the main part of the scroll appears to have been amended at a later date. It mentions an escape to a green hollow. Now, at first, this didn't appear to help much – that could be anywhere - but a green hollow is also the English translation from the Brittonic *glas cau*, which over time we have come to know as 'green place' or *Dear Green Place*."

Auld paused to let that detail marinate. He didn't have long to wait.

"*Glasgow?*" exclaimed Gris. Her eyebrows had shot upwards.

"Are you *absolutely sure* this time?" She was staring directly at Auld, who felt as though her cold, dark eyes were boring into his very soul, but he was too tired to debate the point with her, too tired even to think anymore. He raised his head, straightened himself up in his seat, his eyes met those of Max Gris and he simply said, "Yes."

Gris stalked over to the corner of the room and stood, staring at its glass wall. After a moment or two, she spoke again.

"This sounds like a breakthrough, Dr Auld."

Auld immediately wondered why she was calling him by his professional name once again.

He noticed Gris reaching into her pocket. She brought out a small, thin wooden box and placed in on the table directly in front of Auld.

"Well," said Gris expectantly, "open it."

Auld did as he was told, carefully prising open the old, battered lid. Inside was some ancient, yellowing paper. Auld's eyes were stinging with tiredness by now and it took him a couple of seconds to realise what he was looking at.

"Is this… the missing piece?" he asked, looking first at Gris, then Slymington.

"Bingo!" exclaimed Gris. "That's precisely what it is, so now you've deciphered the major piece… again – and let's hope you've got it right this time – you can crack on with this bit."

Auld didn't to know whether to laugh or cry. Gris was at her hyperactive zenith right now and unlikely to listen to any kind of reason. He sighed.

"Ms Gris, why did you not give this piece of the scroll before?"

Gris leant over the table and stuck her face right up to Auld's once more. She spoke in a low, faintly patronising tone.

"Because, Nicky boy, I am giving it to you *now*." She drew herself up. "Now, get on with translating it. We don't have all day. Or all night."

"No."

Gris whirled on the spot.

"What did you say?" she asked.

Auld gulped and repeated himself, "I said no. I'm not translating anything else tonight. I want to go home."

Auld could see Gris was staring at him, a look of disbelief on her face. He supposed she wasn't used to people telling her no.

And he was right.

But she didn't erupt. She walked to the end of the table, pressed something in her ear and coldly said, "Bring it in."

And then stared at Auld. There was a long silence. Auld grew more and more uncomfortable. He started to speak.

"Ms Gris, it's not that this work isn't interesting, it's just that I am exhausted…"

Gris put her finger to her lips, indicating to Auld that he should stop talking.

The door clicked and Simmons entered, with a black Labrador in tow

"Dakers!" Auld exclaimed. The Lab started wagging his tail at the sight of his master, but Simmons kept him on a short lead. Dakers whimpered at this constriction.

Auld realised why. Simmons had brought out a gun and was pointing it at the confused animal.

"No!" cried Auld.

"Translation?" said Gris.

"Yes, I'll do anything. Just don't hurt him."

"Now." Said Gris. "Take the animal away."

Auld glared at Gris, at Slymington and at the two heavies, before he slumped back down into his chair and began reading the fragment of scroll. He realised he needed to do this in a hurry.

"Er… erm… It mentions the false heart again – *falsum corde* – and it's next to a sentence that says something about *de aliorum Cathedrali*, the Cathedral of the Others… I've no idea what…"

Gris banged the table, which gave Auld a start.

"You said Glasgow, didn't you?" She was grinning. Wildly, thought Auld.

"Yes," replied Auld, unsure of where this particular line of enquiry was going.

"And the heart thing?" asked Gris.

"What about it?" replied Auld.

"Well, it's mentioned twice, isn't it?"

"Yes…" Auld was hesitant in his reply this time.

"Well, Nicky boy, you've cracked it at last. Only took nine months in the end."

Auld looked at Gris blankly. He was both too tired to care about the scrolls and secrets anymore, as well as having no idea where Gris was going with this outburst.

"If you say so," he offered.

"Glasgow Cathedral. Main church in good old Glasvegas and it's been around *forevs*!"

Auld could see that Gris was now off on one of her more manic episodes, and figured it was best to stay quiet. Trouble was, she was staring directly at him, as though she wanted confirmation of her theory.

"I *do* say so. Do you not see the giveaway?" she asked Auld.

Auld shook his head, "You've lost me, I'm afraid."

"A cathedral in Glasgow. Well, there aren't many to begin with and only one ancient one – and in it, lie the relics of one St. Valentine. He of the heart and romance fame."

Auld looked puzzled. There might be something in this, but it seemed to him as though Gris was grasping at anything and everything in order to construct her theory. He sighed.

"I don't follow."

Auld could see Gris was now adopting the look of someone who was about to lecture a small child. With the tone to match.

"A cathedral. In Glasgow. Containing relics. Which everyone has always believed are those of St Valentine, but the clue is right there, staring you in the face, Nicky boy: a *false* heart. They're not St Valentine's relics. False heart…"

Auld was befuddled by this and could sense that Gris was growing impatient.

She continued, "Oh, do I have to do *all* the thinking around here, as usual? Anyone?"

Gris whirled around to Slymington, who impassively stated, "You have deciphered the answer, ma'am."

Gris whirled back around to face Auld.

"Got it in one, Slimey. The scroll tells us the answer: it's an ancient cover story. Those relics aren't St Valentine's; they're the relics of St. Nicholas!

And they've been here, right here," she gave a sweep of her arms, "all along."

Auld didn't know whether to laugh or to cry at this revelation.

"Well, Nicky boy, whaddya think?" she exclaimed.

Auld could see she was waiting, expectantly, for his response.

"Well, it is possible."

"Precisely! Moreover, it is not just possible, it is happening – and it is happening *now*!"

Auld watched Gris zoom over to the comms panel at the end of the table and begin punching in a phone number. He picked his moment.

"Can I go home now?"

Gris didn't even look up.

"You're going nowhere, Nicky boy. Not until we've tested my theory and proved it right. We'll make sure you have suitable board and lodgings."

She glanced up at him and smiled her most patronising smile.

"Don't worry, you'll be home in time for Christmas. I can assure you of that."

Auld no longer had the energy nor the fight left in him to argue, and he slumped back down in his chair.

After several seconds of static-charged silence, the speakerphone rang out. After several seconds more, a gruff, digitally-fragmented voice answered.

"Yes?"

"Grunk, it's me."

"Hello ma'am."

"Is he still with you?"

"Yes, he is."

"Good. Bring him back here quickly. The relics are here in Glasgow, right under our noses. Use the boat and be quick about it."

"Very good ma'am."

"And Grunk?"

"Yes, ma'am?"

"Stay in touch."

"Understood."

As the line returned to electro-static silence, Gris turned to Slymington.

"The back-up mobile service is hanging by a thread, Slimey. Make sure you get people on it immediately and boost the power. We need to keep something in this whole organisation semi-functional."

"Very good, ma'am," replied her faithful assistant.

With tired eyes, Auld watched Gris switch off the speakerphone console, wearing the look of someone who had just become Queen of the World. Through his tiredness and brainfog, he had one recurring thought: he hoped that, however lunatic her theory was, it would prove to be correct.

CHAPTER TWENTY-SIX

Tom wasn't entirely sure what woke him up. He thought it might have been a loud noise but was still too drowsy to be certain. He looked around the room. It was dark, with a chink of daylight peeking through the long, thick curtains that covered the tall windows. It took him a moment to figure out where he was, and then he remembered he was in Jack's house, in the spare bedroom. He lay in the bed for a few moments, trying to remember everything that had happened the previous evening. Had any of it been real? After a night's sleep, it all seemed very surreal and distant to him. He wondered if he was still asleep and dreaming when the sound of a door being slammed snapped him out of his reverie. This was followed by the sound of raised voices.

Tom prised himself out from underneath the bedclothes and started shivering. He could see his own breath. Of course, still no heating because of the power cuts. Maybe last night had been real, after all.

He threw on his clothes and was glad of them, rubbed his hands together, blew into them and headed downstairs to see what all the commotion was about.

Upon entering the living room, he found Jack poking around at the woodburner.

"Morning!" said Jack as he caught sight of Tom.

"Morning, what's all the noise?"

"Katie. She's grumpy 'cos there's still no Wi-Fi. And that it's freezing –
no heating or leccy. Still, this ought to help a bit."

Tom could see that Jack had built an impressive inferno in the
woodburner already and headed towards it for a heat. He had always
assumed that, unlike in the countryside, woodburners in the city were
largely decorative, but to Jack's credit, he knew how to use it – and use it
properly.

"It is Baltic in here," said Tom.

"Yeah, the whole house is freezing, but give it a few minutes and this will
heat us up," Jack replied.

"So, what was all that shouting about?"

"Katie. Cold, tired, hacked off, having a go at me for us coming in so late
last night – and then nipping at me to get the fire started."

Tom paused, and then his face scrunched into a look of panic.

"You didn't... you didn't tell her anything about what happened last
night, did you?"

"What, you mean about breaking into a ruin in the Gris Corp grounds,
finding a dragon and then escaping from gun-toting goons, before
hiding the aforesaid dragon at your aunt's?" said Jack with an innocent
face.

"Seriously?" asked Tom.

Jack grinned. "Nah, don't be daft. She would have gone loopy. Or she
wouldn't have believed me. Or both. She was just going on and on and
on about how she'd been worried sick about us, didn't know where we
were, had no way of contacting us, what if something had happened to
us, to her, blah blah blah..."

He continued, "Pretty funny when you think about what actually *did*
happen last night."

There was a bang as Katie burst through the door.

"Have you got that thing going yet?" she asked – or more accurately, shouted at – Jack.

"Yes, dearest sister, I have." Jack thrust his hands towards the woodburner in an exaggerated fashion and pretended to heat them.

"Now, all you have to do is to keep it lit today," he continued, with more than a little sarcasm.

Katie shot him a look.

"Why do *I* have to keep it lit?"

"Because *we* are going out," replied Jack.

Tom had paid little attention to what it was like outside until now (other than there being daylight) but since Katie's next question was likely to be directed at him, he wandered over to the window to have a peek at the world beyond it. Everything was white. There had been a whumphing of snow for sure, and it looked as though it had continued throughout the night. It was several feet deep. Tom had never seen such snow in the city before – or in the countryside, for that matter – and the streets were empty. It was the type of snowfall that muffled the world and shrouded it in beautiful silence for a while. He looked up: clear, pristine arctic skies of blue as far as he could see, with cold late December sunshine dappling the snowy city. Glasgow had never looked more beautiful.

"Tom… *Tom…*"

Tom snapped out of his wintry reverie. It was Katie. She was standing right next to him, looking at him expectantly, as though he was supposed to do something.

"Well?" she asked.

Tom looked at her blankly.

"Well, what?"

"Are you going to tell me?"

"Tell you what?"

Tom noticed Jack sniggering as he poked around at the woodburner.

"Honestly, Tom, you're not even awake yet. Did you even hear the question I just asked you?" Katie was looking directly at him. Tom thought for a moment and decided that honesty was the best policy in this situation.

"Er, nope. I was looking out the window at all the snow. Look, it's really lovely out there now."

"I asked you where the pair of you were all yesterday evening and since my droid of a brother isn't giving me any answers, perhaps you might," said Katie. Tom could now see she was cross.

"Oi," shouted Jack, "I am *not* a droid."

"You might as well be for all the answers you've given me about where you both were last night, little brother."

Jack stood up from his woodburner poking and prodding duties and replied, "Well, at least I would be a useful droid, darling sister, because I can make a fire and heat this place up."

He gave a nod to the door. "Come on, Tom, let's get going. We've got some serious sledging to do."

Tom was now rooted to the spot. He didn't want to annoy Katie anymore (albeit that seemed like an impossible task given her existing bad mood levels), but very much wanted to leave her and her bad attitude as quickly as possible; however, nor did he want to be rude.

Katie whirled round to her brother as Jack made his way to the living room door.

"You are *not* going anywhere today. It's not safe out there. Anything could happen," she shouted at Jack.

"Oh yes, we are. *We* are going sledging. It's a perfect day for it. A log or two on the burner every hour and you'll be grand. Don't let it go out. Come on, Tom, let's get some snackables and hit the park."

Tom sidled towards the door.

"Jack. Jaaaack. JACK! Get back here NOW!" Katie was now shouting at the door, as Jack had already exited through it.

"Gotta go," spluttered Tom, as he dived through the living room doorway after Jack.

"The pair of you are NOT going anywhere!" shouted Katie.

Tom popped his head back around the door.

"Last night... we were out, playing in the snow... amongst other things. Just lost track of time, that's all. Byeeeee!"

Tom galloped out of the living room and back down the stairs towards the hallway on the ground floor of the house.

"Here," said Jack as he threw Tom his hat, scarf and gloves. His instruction was half-incoherent, mainly as he had a huge chocolate cookie hanging out of his mouth.

"Thanks," said Tom as he made a grab for the airborne items of outdoor winter clothing.

Behind them, Katie was still shouting from the living room at them not to leave the house or else unspeakably bad things would happen to them, including the wrath of Jack's parents when they found out about what the boys had done.

"Ignore her. She won't want to leave the living room now it's the only non-Baltic place in the entire house," said Jack. He sounded very sure of this, thought Tom.

"Do you have the snackables?" asked Tom.

Jack produced several packets of crisps, biscuits and a couple of cartons of juice from his pockets and grinned.

"We are golden, my friend. Let's go fetch the sledges from the garage."

"Are we actually going sledging?" asked Tom.

Jack paused from stuffing his feet into his boots, turned and looked at his friend.

"Don't be daft. This is our cover story for Katiepoops, that's all. We, my friend, have a dragon to go visit."

"So, last night really happened then? I was starting to wonder if I had dreamt it," mused Tom.

"Oh yeah, last night *really* did happen – and today we should find out all about Gus. Assuming he's awake. And can remember. And hasn't flown off somewhere by now," said Jack. "Come on, let's go."

The two boys bundled out of the front door of the house and set off into the brilliant white wonderland of the wintry city, scrunching through the snow to fetch their sledges and begin their trek to Merryweather's house for their morning appointment with a dragon.

CHAPTER TWENTY-SEVEN

The Shadow yawned. He was sitting in the back seat of a large, black SUV, accompanied by two of Max Gris's fabled security detail, one of whom actually had a name: Grunk. He was the one who was driving. The Shadow could feel his eyes drooping. It had been a long night and the warm, stuffy atmosphere was befuddling his brain and causing him to crave sleep. He considered asking Grunk to turn off the heating, but he doubted he would do so. Besides, it was preferable to be warm than to experience more of the cold and the snow outside. A coffee or two and I'll be fine, the Shadow thought to himself and he counted his blessings: at least they were now on dry land and the snow had stopped falling a couple of hours ago. He did not want to repeat the experience of being on a high-speed boat in rough seas with zero visibility due to a blizzard ever again.

Through his fuzziness, the Shadow considered again what little he knew of the sixth and final location in which he was to look for the relics. He was convinced that the original intelligence about their whereabouts being in Ireland had been completely wrong. Not only were they not in the location in which he had searched for them, but his gut instinct was that he had been looking in the wrong place – and by that he meant the wrong country. Something about what Gris and her acolyte, Slymington, told him about the batch's location hadn't rung true. Maybe it was the half-a-story he had been told to explain their original supposed location; maybe it was the way Gris and Slymington had made leaps of logic to justify their conclusion; or maybe the facts as presented simply didn't sit well with him. The Shadow couldn't be sure exactly why, but his years of experience had taught him two things: firstly, never to ignore his gut instinct; and secondly, when he did, invariably, bad things happened.

So, this morning, as daylight broke on the last leg of his snowy journey to Gris Corp HQ, the very last thing the Shadow was going to do was to take anything Max Gris, Slymington or Grunk would tell him at face value. They needed him to complete Gris's obsessive quest to recover all the relics of St. Nicholas and, more to the point, the Shadow wanted paying, including his very large bonus for delivering all the relics. Besides which, this mission was now a matter of personal pride to him: he had never previously failed in obtaining that which was asked of him, and he wasn't about to start now. He had a reputation to maintain.

The SUV shuddered to a halt outside the entrance to Gris Corp HQ.

"Time to meet the boss," grunted Grunk.

The Shadow sighed and prised himself out of the warm seat, before opening the door to the cold, snowy morning outside. He was jolted awake as the cold air hit his face and filled his lungs. His eyes scrunched up in reaction to the bright, wintry sunshine that was streaming into them.

"Let us go then," he said to Grunk.

Grunk and his associate took the Shadow through the labyrinth of glass corridors to the main boardroom. As they entered, all the Shadow could think about was his need for coffee. Urgently. First, however, there was the not inconsiderable matter of Max Gris herself to negotiate.

"Ah, monsieur, delighted you could join us. What a pleasure it is to meet you in person," Gris exclaimed.

"Bonjour, madame. And you," the Shadow replied. He wondered how on earth it was possible for anyone to be as effervescent as Gris appeared to be on such a morning as this. Then, he noticed Slymington, standing in the corner like a miserable coat stand.

"Good morning, monsieur," Slymington monotoned.

The Shadow replied in kind, observing to himself that interacting with Slymington in the flesh was an even less appealing proposition than doing so by phone.

Gris poured a large mug of coffee and placed it on the table in front of him.

"I expect you'll be needing this. Please, take a seat," she said, indicating towards a chair.

"Merci. Yes, more than one. It has been a long night," replied the Shadow.

He watched Gris readying herself to talk. To him or at him? He would soon find out.

"To business," she began. "We have made a breakthrough as to the location of the last batch of relics."

The Shadow sat up in his chair, sipping his coffee and listening intently as Gris relayed the insights – and possibly, he surmised, some degree of supposition – which had been gleaned via Nick Auld mere hours ago about the final relics. As she finished her explanation (and the Shadow had determined very early in this process that she would, as he had half-expected, be talking at him), he realised he could now ask questions.

"Madame, this all sounds perfectly plausible, but I have one question, something that has been bothering me since we began this piece of work. Why the urgency? Why do you need these last relics before Christmas Eve? Surely a collector as sophisticated as yourself could wait a few more days in the interests of ensuring the location is correct this time?"

The Shadow knew that Gris had a reputation of disliking being contradicted or questioned. Or sometimes, even interrupted. But even he wasn't prepared for what came next. The smile vanished from Gris's face and the enthusiasm for her guest evaporated.

"I *need* those relics before Christmas Eve because I *do* – and that is the beginning and the end of it. We have a contract, monsieur, for *you* to deliver those relics to *me*, intact and by Christmas Eve; otherwise, you can forget about your *very* generous bonus," she hissed at the Shadow, before completing her threat, "and your reputation."

Gris, pausing for effect, stared directly at the Shadow and asked, "Now, do we have a renewed understanding?"

The Shadow shifted around in his seat. He had met some deeply unsavoury characters down the years whilst pursuing his chosen profession, but he had now formed the view that Gris was up there – or down there – with the worst of them. Perhaps, given the demonstrable volatility of her moods, she was *the* very worst of all. But on that cold and snowy December morning, what the Shadow wanted most of all was to be paid for his work and never to have to work with Gris ever again.

He took a deep breath, sucking in his cheeks, gave a semi-shrug, and replied, "Yes, of course, madame."

"Good!" exclaimed Gris. The Shadow observed that she had switched her manic grin back on as though flicking a light-switch. However, he still had questions.

"You are certain the final batch is in the cathedral?" he asked.

"As certain as we can be based on the information available," replied Gris. "We're narrowing down the precise location within the cathedral, but it appears that St. Valentine has been a cover story for St Nicholas down the years."

"I'm not following you, madame."

The Shadow could see a look of impatience flickering back across Gris's face once more. It was as though she was operating at a different speed from that of the rest of the world and occasionally – well, actually, frequently – her tolerance for the tardiness of thought by everyone else simply evaporated.

"It's very simple: the relics are in Glasgow. In a cathedral. An ancient cathedral. There aren't many to choose from – i.e., there is one. Which happens to house the relics of St. Valentine, patron saint of romance. You know, hearts and flowers and all that schmaltz," lectured Gris as she paced the room. The Shadow felt as though he was back in school, given her tone towards him.

"However," she continued, "the materials we have deciphered speak of certain... clues which indicate that St. Valentine is a cover story and that the relics located in Glasgow Cathedral are actually those of St Nicholas.

"Which is where you come in," she finished with a flourish. The Shadow noticed the grin had returned. It was hard to miss it.

The Shadow leaned forward on the table. It had been a long night. Indeed, he felt as though he had been working on this engagement for a long time now, too long, in fact. His bones and muscles ached with weariness, his mind was fuzzy, and his eyelids were drooping once more.

He asked one final question, "You are sure of this?"

"As sure as we can be," Gris shot back.

The Shadow half-shrugged. "Okay, I shall complete the assignment this evening, under cover of darkness, but first, I must sleep for a few hours."

"Of course," replied Gris. "Grunk will show you to your quarters and whilst you rest, we shall prepare our best team who will assist you with…"

"No," said the Shadow, standing up to leave. "I work on this alone. Understood?"

He could see the turmoil in Gris's brain becoming etched on her face before a grin broke out and she replied with false politeness, "Of course, monsieur."

The Shadow seized his moment. "The only two things I shall need are sleep and then a suitable car in which to drive to and from the cathedral. Something fast, but inconspicuous."

He stood up and made ready to leave. This was no longer a negotiation.

"We shall have it for you," said Gris.

"Merci, madame. And now I sleep."

The Shadow hoped he would sleep and that when he awoke, Gris's explanation as to the ultimate stage of his contract would seem more plausible to him than it did right now. However, come what may, this evening, under the cover of darkness, he would break into Glasgow Cathedral, to search for the final batch of the relics of St. Nicholas, and though he was not a religious man, en route he would offer a short prayer that he was not on another fool's errand.

CHAPTER TWENTY-EIGHT

Tom and Jack arrived at the front gate of Octavia Merryweather's house, dragging their sledges behind him. So much snow had fallen that it had long since covered in all their footprints from the previous evening. With a grunt, Tom shoved the gate to move it against the snow and the boys trudged up the path (or where the path would have been had they been able to see it) which bisected the front garden and towards the front of the house. They followed the path around the side of the house until they reached the rear of the property, propped their sledges against its back wall and climbed the stairs up to the back door. There was no doorbell nor a doorknocker, so Tom rapped out a knock on the wooden door.

Rat-a-tat-tat. Silence. Then, the sound of footsteps, before the key turned in the lock and Merryweather threw open the door.

"Well, top of the morning to you both. Come away in, you must be freezing. Take your boots off and come and have a cup of hot chocolate," said Merryweather.

This sounded like an excellent idea to Tom. He could see Jack was grinning at the prospect, too.

"Morning, Auntieprof," said Tom, as he started extricating himself from his wellingtons.

"Morning," said Jack. Followed by, "Where's Gus?"

Tom looked at Jack and then at Merryweather, who gave a wry smile.

"Straight to the point with you, young Jack," said Merryweather. Her smile had turned into a grin, and Tom could have sworn that her eyes were twinkling.

"Follow me," she continued.

The two boys followed her through the small back corridor and into the house's kitchen. The first thing that struck Tom, as the three of them entered the kitchen, was how large it was. It had a lot more space than the kitchen in his own house. Which was just as well, as there, in the middle of it, munching on what looked like half a tree stump, was Gus. In the daylight, Tom thought Gus looked even more imposing than he had the previous evening and far more awake, too. Clearly, he was still hungry as well.

Gus's ears pricked up as they entered.

"Aha, the wee mini-heroes are here at last," he said. To Tom, it looked as though Gus was beaming, and his voice had a warm tone to it. He could certainly see a lot of very large teeth as the dragon resumed his snack.

Both Tom and Jack stopped dead in their tracks. Tom could see that Jack's mouth was hanging open as though he was trying to form a sentence, but no words were forthcoming.

Tom himself could only blurt out, "Hello." He stared in wonder at the surreal sight of an enormous dragon munching on what Tom presumed was his breakfast whilst standing in the middle of a normal, domestic kitchen.

Gus was merrily chomping away on the remains of the tree as though it were the most normal thing in the world. Which, for him, of course, it was.

"We've been talking," said Merryweather, pointing towards the dragon with her thumb and raising both her eyebrows.

"Aye, that we have," replied the dragon, before turning towards Tom and adding, "and your aunt is a wise woman."

"Yes, I know," said Tom.

"I need to thank you both for what you did for me last night. You were very brave, the pair of you," said Gus.

"No problem," replied Jack, as though it was something that he did every day of the week. "How are you feeling? And have you remembered what it was you were looking for yet?"

"I'm feeling brand new and very wide awake, laddie," said the dragon, fully opening his eyes as though to emphasise the point and bending his neck down so that his face was directly opposite Jack's.

Then, as though to further prove the point, Gus took a deep breath as he bent his neck into a more upright position. Tom knew what was coming next – and so did Merryweather.

"No, no, no, Gus. Not indoors," she cried. But it was too late.

Gus was exhaling, half-snorting and half-sneezing, and unleashing even more copious amounts of sparks and smoke than he had managed the previous evening, but this time with a few more flashes of flame thrown in for good measure.

Tom marvelled at the sheer amount of smoke that Gus could produce in the matter of a few seconds and then began coughing. As did Jack and Merryweather. And then the smoke alarm in the kitchen ceiling went off.

"Oh, for goodness' sake," said Merryweather as she rushed to open the kitchen windows. This done, she stood in front of Gus and looked stern.

"Gus, for the last time, you are not to do that in the house. Do you understand? One of these times, you're actually going to produce proper flames and I do not want my house to be burnt to a cinder as a result," Merryweather scolded the dragon.

Gus bowed his head slightly and looked sheepish. Tom couldn't help but grin at his aunt giving the massive beast a ticking off.

"Aye, okay. Sorry about that. I'll save my practising for outside," said Gus.

Merryweather was wafting away the clouds of smoke.

"As I said, we've been talking. Lots," she said to the boys, "and the situation is more serious than we thought. Gus, do you want to explain it all to Tom and Jack?"

"Aye," said the dragon. "Thing is, my wee heroic friends, I've remembered what it was that I had forgotten last night, if you see what I mean."

Tom and Jack were hanging on Gus's every word by now.

"You see, on this occasion, I'd been asleep for a long time, a very long time indeed. Hundreds of years, in fact. Sometimes, it takes the old brain a while to waken up fully after a big sleep like that one," Gus continued. At this, he paused and, to Tom's eyes, appeared to be staring at a spot on the wall.

"Hundreds of years," murmured Gus again, before he stopped staring at the wall and fixed his gaze back on Tom and Jack.

"Since the last time someone tried to destroy Christmas," continued the dragon. "Back then, they banned it, so I had to hide in a different place. I'd been down in the borderlands – a place you folk call Peebles from what I remember - for a good few hundred years, minding my own business, but when they banned Christmas, it wasn't safe to stay there any longer, guarding St. Nicholas's relics, so I upped and flew to the next safest place I could find, which happened to be Glasgow, and I hid the relics again and then settled down to guard them once more."

"Wait, what do you mean, you were in Peebles for a few hundred years? How old are you, Gus?" asked Tom.

"And what do you mean you were guarding St. Nicholas's relics? What's a relic and how come you even know Santa, anyway?" Jack butted in.

Gus grinned. "You two ask a lot of questions. Almost as many as the wise woman."

He paced around the kitchen.

"I'm ancient by human measures – must be getting on for 1,800 years of age by now and I first met St Nicholas – or Santa, as you humans now seem to call him – when I was just a whelp. That's what we call baby dragons, by the way.

"It was a long time ago, in ancient Greece – or perhaps it was ancient Rome – it's so long ago I forget now; anyway, Nicholas had recently become a bishop for the town of Myra. Humans were terrified of dragons, even though they were the ones who had been hunting us down for centuries and had done this so successfully that there were only a few of us left. My parents had been hiding for years in the mountains, staying as far away as they could from the humans who were always after them and trying to kill them. They just wanted to live quietly and be left alone, but eventually the hunters found them and they killed them both – but not before they hid me away in a safe place, to save my life."

"I'm sorry, Gus," said Tom.

"Thank you, laddie. I know you're not all like that. Now, what was I saying? Oh yes. Well, I was still very young and all alone and I didn't really know how to fend for myself properly yet, but I was lucky. I was wandering about one night, very weak from hunger and trying to find something to eat, when Nicholas chanced upon me and rather that calling on the hunters to come and kill me, he took me back to his own home, gave me shelter and protected me. He was the first kind human I had ever come across. We had to be careful, because there were still lots of men who wanted only to kill any dragons on sight, but Nicholas looked after me and in time, I grew bigger and stronger and then I became his protector. He became my best friend, a good and kind man to everyone and I looked out for him any time he might be in danger."

Gus stopped his story for a moment to take another bite out of the remnants of the large piece of wood that had once been a tree stump. Tom was transfixed by the dragon's tale. Both he and Jack were listening intently, hanging on Gus's every word. Once he had chewed and swallowed this latest tasty morsel of wood, Gus continued.

"Eventually, as with all things, Nicholas grew very old and had to leave this world, but he had done so much good that he passed on into another realm and continued his good deeds there, unseen by humans. Before he left, he gave me strict instructions as to what to do with all his earthly remains and important objects – and these are what became known by humans as his relics. I was to take them and separate them into six different batches, to be placed in six different places, carefully hidden away from any humans who might come looking for them. Nicholas knew he would become even more powerful in the other realm and he asked me to make sure that no human could ever gather these relics together again in case they used this power for selfish reasons or to do evil deeds. And, as for the sixth and final batch, this was the most powerful one of all. His final words to me were to make me swear that these particular relics would never, ever leave my sight and that I would guard them with my life for all time – and if I agreed to this, it would mean that I was their guardian for eternity.

"So, of course, I agreed to my friend's dying request, and I did as he asked. I scattered his relics far and wide and placed five different batches of them in safe places, all over Europe. The sixth and final batch I kept with me and placed in a church in Peebles, in the borderlands, which was far enough away from anywhere and anyone else back in those days to be safe from harm. Or so I thought.

"That was until some bad folk called the Puritans came along several centuries ago who wanted to end Christmas forever – which is when I had to move them, and myself, again, to somewhere else. Somewhere that they would never be found. Which is how I ended up here. In Glasgow."

At this, Gus unfolded his winged arms and knocked over a couple of saucepans, which had been hanging on a rack on the kitchen wall, with a clatter.

"Oops," said the dragon, "sorry about that. Still not used to these wee spaces you folk live in."

Tom had been itching to ask more questions and seized his moment.

"Gus, how did you hide away for hundreds of years? I mean, no offence, but you're not exactly inconspicuous."

"Ah laddie, good question. You're a bright lad. Very inquisitive. Well, there was a wee piece of magic that Nicholas left behind with his final batch of relics. Remember, I told you that they were the most powerful ones. Well, once I had safely placed them in their secret location, a church, I stood guard over them as I had promised and then the power of the relics camouflaged me into the fabric of the building and made me go to sleep – like hibernating – for a very long time, so I would be safe – and so would the last and most important batch of relics. It's a bit like being hypnotised but then having a fantastic night's sleep, but one that lasts for hundreds of years.

"To any inquisitive humans, I would merely have looked like a gargoyle on a wall. But there was a problem: were I to awaken, then it would mean that someone or something had discovered the relics – or they were about to come to great harm – and that darkness would be coming to Christmas. The same power that can put me to sleep for centuries can also waken me up in an instant if there is that kind of threat."

At this, Gus sighed and shook his head, half closing his eyes and continuing.

"And, it has now woken me up once more, so that I can protect the relics from evil once again.

"So, you see, now I've woken up, I must fulfil my promise to Nicholas and return to that old church to retrieve the box of relics and make them safe before whoever or whatever is looking for them finds them. And I'm going to need some help – your help – to do this, wee mini-heroes."

"You mean, you want to go back to Gris Corp and to that old ruin?" asked Tom.

"Aye laddie, that's exactly what I mean. I must go back there and fetch the box of relics, to keep them safe."

"Woah…" said Tom, shaking his head, "woah, woah, woah."

"Tom, what is it?" asked Merryweather.

Tom could see both his aunt and Jack – and Gus – all looking at him.

"Well… it's just… I mean… well, it sounds really dangerous. I mean, last night, we saw a load of security guys there and they had guns and dogs and everything. We'll get nowhere near the place," Tom blurted out.

Gus drew himself up to his full height.

"Laddie, St. Nicholas, Santa, as you call him, and Christmas are in peril. That's the only reason I'm wide awake and here. And right now, we're the only thing that stands between Santa, Christmas and goodness knows whatever it is that means to do them great harm. Are you not prepared to help me prevent whatever this evil is that's afoot?"

Tom blushed and looked downwards.

"It's not that, Gus, it's just… it's just… well, it's gonna be really dangerous. Those guys last night were really scary."

Tom turned to Merryweather.

"Auntieprof, shouldn't we go to the police instead? They'd be able to sort all this out, wouldn't they?"

Merryweather looked at Tom and smiled benignly.

"Thomas Brightly, you're a wise and sensible boy, and usually, you would be right. That's exactly to whom we should speak to about this. But... we have a somewhat unusual set of circumstances here," said Merryweather, pointing towards Gus.

"We cannot very well report all of this to the police with Gus in tow, now can we? I mean, can you imagine their reaction?" she asked.

Tom nodded and shifted uncomfortably from one foot to the other.

"Couldn't we leave Gus here instead and just tell the police what we know and let them investigate it all?" piped up Jack.

"Again, Jack, another good idea," replied Merryweather, "and ordinarily, I would agree, but have a think about what Gus has just told you. How would we explain all of that to the police so they would believe us? They would think we were wasting their time.

"Also," she continued, "we would be reporting something that, by the sounds of it, isn't actually yet a crime – at least not insofar as the sixth batch of relics is concerned. So, what could they actually investigate?" she asked.

"Oh," said Jack.

Merryweather turned to both boys.

"Gus is convinced that the relics are still in that old, ruined church somewhere. If we can return to it, we can help him retrieve the relics and stop any foul deeds from occurring," she said.

Tom was still shuffling from one foot to the other before he looked up at his aunt.

"But how do you actually know that anyone is even looking for them? Or that they'll do bad things with them even if they find them?" he asked.

Gus bent his long neck down towards Tom and spoke quietly.

"Laddie, trust me: the only reason I would have been woken up is because darkness is afoot and someone bad is looking for these sacred objects. The last time this happened was when those bad folk I told you about before tried to end Christmas forever back in the Seventeenth Century. It is as serious as that. It could not be any more serious, in fact. Do you understand now?"

Tom looked into the dragon's kindly golden-flecked eyes. He could see that Gus was being sincere in what he said and also that his eyes and face were etched with concern.

Tom nodded that he understood.

Jack stood, looking dumbfounded, mustering up the courage to ask the questions that were bothering him. Intensely.

"So, what happens if we don't find the relics? Does that mean no more Christmas? Forever?" he asked.

"Aye, laddie. That's what could be at stake here."

This was enough for Jack. He turned towards Tom.

"Mate, we have got to do this. No more Christmas ever again? Can you even imagine?"

Tom's eyebrows frowned and his face grimaced.

"Don't," he said to Jack. "This is going to be really dangerous."

Jack was still looking at him. As, too, were Merryweather and Gus.

"I have to go back home at some point," said Tom, throwing his hands up in exasperation and rolling his eyes towards the ceiling.

None of the three others said a word. Tom sighed a long and deep sigh and closed his eyes.

"Okay, okay," he said at last, "what do we have to do?"

Merryweather, Gus and Jack were all grinning.

"Excellent," exclaimed Merryweather. "I knew you'd come round. Just like your father – you always get there in the end." She gave Tom a hug, and Jack thumped him on his back.

"We'll need to go back to the ruined church under cover of darkness. Tonight. There's no time to lose," Merryweather began. "I would suggest we go immediately, but Gus would draw too much attention and there's no way we can disguise him again."

"So, we'll drive over there later on, once it's dark and Gus can follow us, by flying," she continued.

"Oh, can you fly again now?" asked Jack.

"Aye, laddie, had a wee practice this morning," replied the dragon, and he began unfurling his wings.

"Don't!" commanded Merryweather. "You'll wreck the kitchen. Outside only, remember?"

"Ah. Oops. Aye, of course," replied Gus.

Merryweather resumed, "As I was saying, we'll head over there under cover of darkness tonight. Once we're there, we can get inside the building with Gus, and he'll go to the relics and retrieve them."

"And what do we do then?" asked Tom.

"We'll figure out that part once we have the relics," said Merryweather. "One step at a time."

"I could always fly away again to somewhere else," said Gus.

"A lovely thought, Gus, but the world is a much smaller place these days. I doubt you'd find it as simple as that," replied Merryweather.

"Och, I don't know," said Gus, "there are always places to hide away, quiet places."

"Well, we can sort all of that out once we're safely back here with the relics," said Merryweather. "Now, let's plan precisely what we're going to do later on."

"Yeah," said Tom, turning to Gus, "and we need to start with what you can remember about where the box of relics is."

Gus sat on his haunches in the middle of the kitchen with a puzzled look on his face. He scratched his head and pondered.

"I think I might need another snack for this bit," he said with a grin.

CHAPTER TWENTY-NINE

Max Gris was in the boardroom at Gris Corp HQ and she was pacing. Up and down. Continually. She hated waiting. For anything. And right now, she was waiting for something big to happen. Something that had been her heart's desire since she had been a little girl, from the very day on which her father had explained to her what he had found out about St Nicholas and Christmas, the truth about St Nicholas and Santa and what could be achieved if the right person could gather all the lost relics of St Nicholas and undertake the sacred ritual of bringing him back: possessing Santa and Christmas itself. She had been mesmerised by this and by her father's plan to achieve that very objective.

"And then, you see, my dear Maxine, he who possesses the spirit of Santa himself will have full control over Christmas itself. Think of the power you would wield, think about all that you could do with such power and control over the entire world. And think of all the money you could make! This is my life's work now. All the rest of it is just a sideshow, a means to an end," her father had explained to her.

And for several years, he had put his plan into action. The business continued to grow, ably guided by the ever-loyal Slymington, under her father's direction; in his every spare moment, her father had dedicated himself to continuing his quest to locate all the missing relics. That was, until the fates whisked him away forever and with no hint of a warning, and Maxine's young life – and her destiny - was altered forever.

"And now, Father, it is up to me to complete your work – and I shall. It will be a she who possesses the spirit of Santa and who controls Christmas, and that she will be me," Gris said aloud to herself. "It is within touching distance now."

The door to the boardroom slid open and there, framed by the weak December sunlight, bursting through the glass, stood Slymington, with a short, fat, bald man by his side; unlike Slymington, the other man was grinning, Gris noted, like an idiot. She would soon put a stop to that.

"Ah, Slimey and... Rudderts, come in. What news do you have for me?"

Rudderts gulped nervously and began, "Well, ma'am, we have spent the night narrowing down the location of the potential winner. Or should I say, the prospective winner."

Gris frowned. "Well, which is it? Has someone won Apotheosis or not?"

Rudderts was now perspiring slightly and was shifting around uncomfortably as he stood in front of Gris. She was enjoying this. Torturing Rudderts was one of her simple daily pleasures in life, and she was about to do it yet again. She even noticed that Slymington might have the hint of a smile on his face. This was tantamount to egging her on.

"Ma'am, we've had some difficulty in *re-acquiring* last night's data," said Rudderts, before half-closing his eyes and waiting for the inevitable onslaught.

Gris sighed, frowned, and then let rip.

"Rudderts, what do you mean '*difficulty*'?" she asked, boring into Rudderts with her dark eyes.

She could see that Rudderts was now apparently terrified at the way the current conversation was going and this gave her an inner satisfaction. Almost a warm, fuzzy glow inside.

"The solar storm, er, appears to have caused more damage than we at first thought, ma'am and we may not have immediate access to the back-up servers which could tell us who the winner is... erm, if of course, anyone has actually won yet..." croaked Rudderts.

Gris observed that even Rudderts didn't appear to be convinced by his own pathetic attempt at an explanation. Time to make herself very clear. Again. She stepped towards Rudderts and grabbed his lapels. Given Gris was taller than Rudderts and considerably more imposing, this, she observed, had the effect of reducing him to even more of a human jelly than he usually was.

"Rudderts," she began, "I'm going to spell this out to you for the last time: I *need* the name of the winner and I need it NOW."

Rudderts had scrunched up his eyes and if he could have done so, he would have retracted his head into his body. As it was, he was going to have to take the full force of the Max Gris 'hairdryer special'.

"No more excuses! No more delays! Fix the IT and get me that name! DO YOU UNDERSTAND?"

"Yes," squeaked Rudderts.

"Good," said Gris, as she released Rudderts from her grip. "Today is Saturday, the 22nd of December. We were supposed to have a winner by yesterday evening at the latest. We are on the clock here, Rudderts. It will be Christmas in less than three days, and *we need our winner*. Now, GO AND FIX IT!"

"Yes, ma'am," squeaked Rudderts. "I'll get the name for you as soon as possible." He scuttled towards the door.

"SOONER!" shouted Gris after him as he disappeared at speed.

She turned to Slymington.

"How's our French guest, Slimey?"

"Sleeping like a hibernating dormouse, ma'am," replied Slymington, in his monotone.

"Good. Give him a few more hours and then shake him awake as soon as it's sunset. He has work to do – and so have we," Gris instructed.

"Very good, ma'am."

Gris bit her lower lip. The clock was ticking on, but there was still time – just – to pull this off.

"I won't fail you, Father," she said out loud and clenched her fists. Tighter than she had ever clenched them before.

CHAPTER THIRTY

As he crept out of the darkness, the Shadow shook his head once, then twice. He was awake, but he did not feel fully alert yet. Too little sleep after too long a want. He wet his lips with his tongue and then stopped himself midway. I am nervous, he thought to himself. He knew why: not enough time to plan this stage of his current engagement with his usual meticulous detail. A total reliance on a series of additional facts - or more accurately theories – from his current employer, about which he had had no time to undertake any level of due diligence. However, what was bothering him most of all was Max Gris's unerring faith in her own abilities, which were now apparently honed sufficiently to distil a several centuries old text into a precise geographical location. In which, the Shadow was now standing, daring not to breathe.

He was always wary of anyone who spoke in absolutes and certainties, having found that matters were rarely as straightforward as that in reality, but when coupled with the type of megalomania that Ms Gris displayed, such attributes were often dangerous. And in this instance, the risk was they could become dangerous to him. If there was one thing that the Shadow valued above money, it was his liberty and his freedom to operate in the world, however he liked, wherever he chose to and whenever it suited him to do so.

His current situation was as far removed from his preferred operating mode as it was possible to be. Virtually no time to prepare, a set of black and white instructions to follow and, worst of all, a mini-squadron of Gris Corp security operatives parked discreetly in the streets surrounding the Shadow's current site of operations, waiting for him to re-emerge successfully with the spoils – the final batch of relics – so they could whisk him back to Gris Corp HQ at top speed.

It was all the Shadow had been able to do to insist that he should undertake the final piece of this mission alone. The eventual compromise of the 'ring of security' around the cathedral was, he suspected, as much to keep tabs on him as it was to assist him should any unlikely interlopers happen upon his evening's work. He had already felt out of sorts due to a paucity of sleep; this further imposition on his usual working practices had discombobulated him ever more.

He shook his head again, to clear his mind of the swirl of thoughts from the recent hours. You must concentrate on the here and now, he told himself. And the setting for the here and now was the vast interior of Glasgow Cathedral, in darkness and silence for the evening. Just the way the Shadow liked it.

This time, it had been straightforward to break into the building: the CCTV cameras dotted around the cathedral were still non-functional, courtesy of the solar storm, he supposed. Nevertheless, the Shadow took no chances: he was wearing his trusty balaclava, as was customary on such occasions. The cathedral had already been in darkness by the time he had found a way in, through one of the side doors. There had been little time to gain much of an understanding of the layout, but Gris had assured him he did not need this. Rather, he needed to find one location only: the place in the cathedral where the supposed relics of St. Valentine were displayed. This was his sole target, for as Gris had reminded him, these were not the relics of St. Valentine, but rather those of St. Nicholas himself.

The Shadow had his doubts about her reasoning, but he was in no mood to argue. He wanted to complete this job, deliver the relics to Gris, receive his very large bonus payment, and then never set eyes on Max Gris, Slymington or any of her other henchmen ever again. The completion of this engagement could not happen quickly enough now.

In the silence, the Shadow pressed the button on his torch. It clicked and gave a slight echo. He looked again at the piece of paper he held in his other gloved hand: the floor plan to the cathedral. The location was clear: the relics were on display in a glass case in the nave of the cathedral. He moved on his tiptoes towards the target. Truth be told, this was about as straightforward a set of circumstances as he could have wished for: no power, no CCTV, no security, no alarms – assuming there was no back-up power supply. And there wasn't. Slymington had provided that information to the Shadow before he had left to begin his evening's work. Nevertheless, he had still undertaken a quick sweep of the building's perimeter, if only to satisfy himself that the information was accurate. It had been – at least insofar as he had been able to establish the matter.

He reached the nave. The glass case, complete with the information board detailing the history of the relics, was there, directly in front of him. Could he prise the glass case open? Always preferable to do so, rather than to have to resort to the cutters. Quieter, too. He looked for the weak spot in the casing with the torch and, upon finding the seal, prised a short, stubby knife into the seal between the two edges. Ever so slowly, he jiggled the knife backwards and forwards to gain some purchase, and the seal came apart. After around a minute, he had loosened the seal sufficiently to prise open the side of the glass casing.

Carefully, he removed the panel, laying it against the exhibit's stand. He reached into the large (overly large, in the Shadow's opinion) display case and grabbed the box of relics. It wasn't even locked. He flipped open the lid and… nothing. The box was empty. He checked its exterior to see if there could be a hidden compartment or some other clue which could reveal the relics, but there was nothing. The exterior dimensions of the box matched those of its interior. And its interior was most definitely, resolutely and completely empty. He tapped his watch and took a date and time-stamped picture of the scene. He wanted there to be no debate about what he had – or rather hadn't – found inside the cathedral.

With this done, he quickly began reversing his previous steps, replacing the box in the display case precisely as he had found it and then fitting the case's glass panel back into place so that it was whole once more.

It was time to leave, as he had arrived: quickly, quietly and empty-handed.

Once he had replaced the side door of the cathedral back in situ, the Shadow walked out of its grounds and straight along the adjoining street until he reached another street which ran perpendicular to it. He walked halfway down its length to the agreed rendezvous point. The black SUV which was waiting for him started its engine.

The Shadow opened the door and got into the front of the vehicle. Grunk was sitting in the driver's seat.

The Shadow spoke first.

"Go, quickly. Back to HQ."

"Success?" asked Grunk, as the vehicle moved off.

"No," replied the Shadow. "The box was empty. Another wild goose chase."

"You'd better radio the boss," said Grunk.

The Shadow pressed the comms link button on the SUV's dashboard. There was some static and then a tone. He was connected.

"You have completed the engagement?" asked a monotonic voice. It could only be Slymington. The Shadow was in no mood to deal with him.

"Negative. Let me speak to her," he replied.

"One moment," replied Slymington. A pause, more static and then…

"Yes?" It was the unmistakable sound of Max Gris. Her tone was curt.

"Madame, your information was wrong again, unfortunately. There was nothing there. Just an empty box," the Shadow explained.

Silence and faint static.

"Are you absolutely sure?" asked Gris.

"Yes," replied the Shadow. "You need to interrogate your sources once again. I shall return immediately."

"See that you do," said Gris.

The line went dead.

"Well, that went about as well as expected," said the Shadow.

Grunk grunted something that sounded like his assent to the statement and hit the accelerator, speeding the pair of them back to Gris Corp.

The Shadow leaned his head back in the seat and closed his eyes. He wanted this to be over and for it to be over soon.

CHAPTER THIRTY-ONE

Nick Auld was lying on a bed, staring at the ceiling. In a room that looked very much like a hotel room. Except this room was at the heart of the Gris Corp empire HQ and wasn't so much hospitable as it was a luxurious prison cell. He had everything he could want – except any means of communication or escape. Outside the room's locked door, there was a deployment of two of Gris Crop's most enormous security guards. Armed security guards. He had considered the window, but had worked out that not only were these all electronically locked firmly shut, but there were also no ledges outside any of them, and he was at least five storeys up. In short, he was trapped here, a guest at Max Gris's pleasure until she deemed he could leave.

Auld picked up the remote control to the television and was considering whether it was worthwhile trying again to see if any of the normal programming had returned yet when he heard the now semi-familiar click-buzz of the door to his room being unlocked. He stood up and dropped the remote on the table. The door burst open and Gris launched herself into the room, followed by Slymington and Simmons.

"Nicky," oozed Gris, fake smile caked all over her face. "Well, here we are again, so you can guess what this means."

"I can go home now?" asked Auld, more in hope than expectation.

Gris laughed a fake laugh.

"Oh, very good," she said as her laughter abruptly stopped and the smile vanished. "But not quite correct. Brief update: checked the cathedral.

Bad news: no relics. So, back to the drawing board for you, Nicky boy."

She flashed the smile again.

"I hope you've had a good rest, because we need you back, hard at work, looking at those scrolls again until we find another location to try. So, come on, get your things together and follow me." Gris turned on her heel and was heading back to the door.

"No," said Auld quietly, "I want to go home.

"What?" said Gris, as though she couldn't believe what she had just heard.

"I said, I want to go home," repeated Auld.

Gris took a few slow, deliberate steps towards him.

"Nicky boy, I don't think you quite understand your situation right now," she began. Her tone of voice had changed. There was no longer the pretence of any bonhomie, even of the fake variety.

Auld felt a lump in his throat and swallowed hard.

Gris continued, "There's bad news and good news. The bad news – from your point of view – is that you are going nowhere until we have located and acquired the final batch of relics. The good news is that we need to do this by Christmas Eve, so you will be back home for Christmas. As will your pet. If you co-operate."

"Dakers? You'd better not have hurt him," said Auld.

Gris smiled her most condescending smile.

"Your little pet is fine – and will remain so *if* you co-operate with us, so come on, back to work. Hurry it up, we don't have forever!" Gris clapped her hands to emphasise the urgency of her statement.

Auld did not move.

"I'm not doing it anymore. I've read and reread those scrolls a dozen times or more. There's nothing more I can give you. I want to go home," he said impassively.

Gris stared at him for a moment, then the wide, fake smile was back.

"Oh Nicky, Nicky, Nicky, you need to have more faith in your abilities. You're the very best there is. That's the only reason you're still here and that your little pet is still alive," said Gris. She paused and tilted her head slightly.

"You're tired. I see that. You know, they work you far too hard at that university. I understand. You've been working all the hours on your own research and now there's all of this, too. You need a break. So, here's my proposition: find the location and I'll treble your fee. No questions asked. Now, from memory, your original fee was pretty handy, so I reckon that trebling it should be about enough for you to set yourself up solo. Become a consultant. To the university, if you like," proposed Gris.

Auld stood, quiet and listening, before he replied.

"It's not about the money," he began.

"Nonsense," roared Gris. "It's *always* about the money, Nicky boy. Anyone who says it isn't still has his or her price, so tell me, *what* is yours?"

Auld swept his hands back over his face and through his hair, and his shoulders slumped.

"I just want to go home to my own house, to my own bed," he sighed, "and I don't think there's anything else left to decipher from the scrolls. I've given you everything I could."

Gris approached him and put her index finger to her lips.

"Except, you said that before, Nicky boy, and then came up with a treasure trove of new information. So, no more negative thoughts, there's a poppet. Back to your scrolls and give it one last heave. There's a good fellow," said Gris.

Auld looked at Gris, then Slymington and finally Simmons, who was, he noticed, still armed, and realised that he really had no choice. He would not be allowed to leave, and there was no obvious means of escape. He was about to acquiesce when there was a buzz on Simmons' walkie-talkie.

Auld saw Simmons glance at the flashing light on the device and the text on its screen.

"Ma'am, you'll want to take this," said Simmons.

Gris stopped staring at Auld and walked over to Simmons, grabbing the device he was proffering to her. She glanced at the screen and pressed the comms button.

"Bring him to the boardroom. I'll be right there," she spoke into the receiver, before handing it back to Simmons.

"Right Nicky, lots to do, people to see. Simmons here will show you back to your 'office'. We'll speak again in, say, two hours. Good luck – and get me that location."

And with this, Auld watched Gris stride out of the door and head out into one of the many corridors of her labyrinthine HQ, with Symington following in her wake.

"Right sir, come with me," grunted Simmons.

Auld picked up his coat and did as he was told.

The Shadow was about to help himself to a cup of coffee when Max Gris swept in through the door to the Boardroom.

"Ah, monsieur, you have returned. Making yourself at home, I see. Well, don't mind me," she said.

The Shadow kept filling the cup.

"It has been another fruitless adventure, madame," he said.

"Yes, sorry about that. Turns out, our intel wasn't quite spot on," said Gris.

"Again," interjected the Shadow.

"Quite," said Gris.

The Shadow could tell from the tone in her voice that it was not a good idea to pursue the error in the information with which he had been provided any further. He took the coffee and sat down at the Boardroom table.

"What is the 'plan' now?" he asked.

"Ah, the plan. Simple. Our expert is back at it, hard at work deciphering the ancient intel and we should have a new location for you to have a crack at in a couple of hours," said Gris, before adding, "maybe a little longer."

The Shadow raised his left eyebrow.

"Really?" he asked.

"Really," stated Gris firmly. She was staring right at him, something which the Shadow always found unnerving. So certain, always so sure of herself, even when she had recently been so manifestly wrong.

"We will have new info for you later this evening. Believe me, we're on a tight schedule here. I need that final batch of relics before Christmas Eve. Will you stay? Have one final crack at it?" said Gris.

The Shadow decided he was going to have a little sport.

"You never did explain why the Christmas deadline, Madame..." he left the end of the statement floating in mid-air like a lure, whilst he waited to see if Gris would take a bite.

She smiled back at him.

"No, I didn't, did I?" Gris fired back. "And guess what."

The Shadow tilted his head slightly and raised his left eyebrow once again.

Gris continued, "That piece of information is strictly on a need-to-know basis and you do not need to know anything, other than I need that those final relics. By Christmas Eve. Understood?"

"Of course, Madame," replied the Shadow. He realised Gris would not provide any further information to him about the deadline for the acquisition of the relics and he did not wish to push the point any further. He did, after all, ultimately want to collect his bonus.

"I understand the position," he continued, "and I shall stay to complete the engagement." He stood up and stretched.

"However, it has been a long couple of days," he said as he grabbed the cup and gulped down a mouthful of coffee. "I need to take some air. Clear my head. May I go for a walk in the grounds?"

"Of course," said Gris. "Grunk can show you around."

"Alone," emphasised the Shadow. He stared straight at Gris.

She grinned.

"Of course, monsieur. Please, take as long as you need – the grounds are extensive. Just don't be *too* long: we'll have that new intel for you soon," replied Gris, holding her arm outstretched towards the door of the boardroom.

"Very good, Madame, I shall look forward to that," said the Shadow, buttoning his coat.

"Now, if you'll excuse me, I need to check on the progress regarding that new location we're going to get for you," said Gris, and she headed for the door. "Slimey, will take you downstairs."

"If you'll come with me, monsieur," said Slymington.

One thing was for sure, thought the Shadow, no matter how cold it was outside, in the snow, under clear skies, he doubted he would shiver as much out there as he did whenever Slymington spoke to him. He wrapped his scarf around his neck, pulled it tight and followed Max Gris's faithful sidekick towards the lift, which would take them to the main lobby, glad that his time with her human robot would be brief.

CHAPTER THIRTY-TWO

Tom was crouching behind a tree and peering into the darkness. He was experiencing a distinct sense of déjà vu: he was in exactly the same spot in the Gris Corp HQ grounds as he had been the previous evening, albeit this time with a few key differences. For one thing, it wasn't snowing heavily. It was still dark, but there was more light being given off by the reflections on the snow-covered grounds than there had been the previous evening, even in the continuing absence of any streetlights. He could feel the cold seeping into his cheeks, through the woollen balaclava he was wearing to fend off both the cold and any risk of being recognised by anyone working for Gris Corp. The stars were twinkling and sparking in the winter sky overhead and the night was one of those rare winter nights where the cold penetrated everything and everywhere, no matter how many layers one wore, and everything was snow-covered and frozen solid.

A further difference from the previous evening was that this time, he was there, hiding in the darkness, not just with Jack but also with Merryweather, and all three of them were waiting in the shadows for the arrival of the fourth and final member of their quartet, whilst silently praying that he would do so with the minimal amount of noise.

Which, given that the fourth member was an eight-foot-tall dragon not hitherto noted for his stealth, was going to be a bit of an ask.

Tom was trying not to breathe at all; it sounded as though every breath he took was louder than the last and that each one of them was all he could hear. Well, that, and the thumping of his heart in his chest.

"Where is he?" whispered Jack, for the third time in as many minutes.

"He'll be here," replied Tom.

"Shush," chipped in Merryweather, followed by, "Be patient. He shouldn't be too much longer. It's not an evening to hang around."

It had been Merryweather who had suggested that they wait until it had been fully dark for a couple of hours so that they could minimise any chance of Gus being seen en route to the rendezvous at Gris Corp HQ. There was no way, however much they had wanted to, that he had ever been going to fit in her Defender, so that part of their plan was finessed to give Gus instructions on the aerial route he was to take to the meeting place.

Tom was running through the rest of the plan in his head, over and over. Stage one was to gather in the same place as last evening: in the trees beyond the old, ruined church – and this included Gus.

The next few stages had sounded simple. Or at least they had when they had all discussed them through the course of the afternoon in his aunt's kitchen. Retrace their steps from the previous evening in finding the side entrance into the church. Then, make their way into it quietly and quickly – including Gus. At which point, they were relying on Gus being able to remember the precise location of the precious box of relics. Once those were acquired, they were to exit the building swiftly and head back out of the grounds. Tom, Jack and Merryweather on foot; Gus by air. The four of them had discussed the timings over and over. Tom had been clear to the others that the one thing they had to avoid was attracting any kind of attention from any Gris Corp security personnel who might be patrolling the grounds.

They had had no idea how many – if any – of them would be around this evening. Hence, as Merryweather had suggested, the need for both speed and stealth – and also balaclavas.

Tom rubbed his gloved hands together as quietly as he could. They had only been fully out in the cold for around ten minutes, but he could already feel the tips of his fingers tingling. On the upside, so far, they had not seen a single security guard.

"Must be too cold for them tonight," Jack had commented.

"Or they've got better things to do than be out on patrol on a night like this," countered Tom.

Tom was wondering how long it would be before his fingers went completely numb when there was a WHOOSH WHOOSH THUMP. Followed by a couple of crunching noises.

Gus had landed – practically on top of the three of them. They turned to look at him and Tom could see the dragon's massive toothy grin, even in the permagloom.

"Even though I say so myself, that was a perfect landing," said Gus, puffing out his vast chest with pride.

"Gus, shush. Get down," hissed Merryweather.

Gus looked confused for a moment and then remembered precisely where they were and immediately dropped down onto his haunches.

"We cannot make any noise," Merryweather whispered. "Understood?"

Gus nodded.

"Okay, let's go," said Merryweather, and they set off, Tom leading the way, with the three of them trying not to make too much noise as they scrunched their way through the crusted layer of snow.

The short walk to the derelict building could only have taken around a minute, maybe less, but each step had seemed to take a minute in itself to Tom. They arrived at the old and now somewhat wrecked side door to the ruin.

"Looks the same as last night," said Tom. "They haven't repaired it."

Merryweather stared at the ragged outline of what had once been a complete door and asked, "What on earth happened to it?"

"Gus," replied Tom and Jack in unison.

"To be fair, we were in a bit of a hurry," chimed in the dragon.

"No matter, makes it easier to gain access. Right, in we go," said Merryweather.

Tom went in first and turned on his headtorch. Merryweather followed him, then Jack, with Gus finally squeezing himself in and bringing up the rear. Tom swept the interior of the church with his headtorch.

"Coast is clear," he said after a few sweeping motions.

"Okay, Gus, last night, when we found you, you were over there in that far corner. Is that where we should start looking?" asked Tom, shining his headtorch towards the corner of the building which was strewn with rubble and stray bits and pieces of wood.

"Let me think for a moment," said Gus, stroking his chin.

Tom, Merryweather and Jack stood, waiting, hoping that he would remember something, anything. All three were holding their breath, staring intently at the dragon.

Gus's face brightened and he snapped his claws together.

"Aha! Got it. Follow me," he exclaimed and began clumping over to an entirely different area of the church, stopping at a nook in the back wall. He pointed his wing towards the general area of the wall.

"It's here. I remember now. I hid it in this wall and then settled down to sleep right above it. Right up there. See all those missing bits of ceiling up there?"

"I think so," said Tom, flashing his torch towards the ceiling, though he wasn't entirely sure that he saw anything.

"That was me. That's what I did when I woke up," said Gus, with pride once more.

"What, you wrecked the ceiling?" asked Jack.

"Naw, laddie, I fell out of it. Collateral damage, you might say," said Gus.

Tom noticed the dragon was now wearing a look of both pride and satisfaction, as though falling out of a ceiling and causing significant masonry damage was a badge of achievement.

"Gus, this is a good start. Now, whereabouts in the wall did you put the relics? Can you remember?" asked Merryweather.

Tom could see that his aunt had her serious face on, which he had figured out meant she was not her usual calm self. This had always been the part of the plan which she had considered could take the longest time and thus, was its riskiest stage. He knew they had to seek, locate and obtain the box as quickly as possible. It was time to accelerate the process.

"Gus, if you can remember which stone it was, we can make a start on chiselling it out," said Tom. He could see that the dragon was staring at the wall, pondering behind which of the higgledy-piggledy stones the box lay.

"I think it was this one," Gus began, pointing at a random stone. "Or maybe it was this one," he continued, poking a second stone. "Och no, daft old dragon, it must be this one." He extended his wing towards a third, seemingly random stone.

"Gus, do you have *any* idea which particular stone it was?" asked Merryweather. Tom sensed from his aunt's tone that her patience was fraying regarding Gus's guessing game over the stones.

Tom was shining his headtorch all over the wall, trying to help Gus find the stone in question, when something about one stone caught his eye. He turned the headtorch up to full power and moved closer. There were indentations in one particular stone located about four feet from the ground.

"What's this?" he asked, running his fingers over the indentations. "They look a bit like letters."

"Could be some sort of inscription," said Merryweather, and she bent forward to inspect it. "That looks like it could be an 'a', no hang on, 'ax' and then there's a gap and, oh dear, these are rather instinct, but it looks like a part of a word, ob... obis... obiscum. Seems to be missing some letters..."

"Pax vobiscum!" exclaimed Gus. "Here, let me see." He bent his neck down and then jumped back upright. "That's it. That's the one."

"Latin... peace be with you," murmured Merryweather, "Hmmm, how appropriate."

"This is the one we have to take out," said Gus.

Tom whipped off his rucksack and took out two of the three items it contained: a hammer and a chisel. "Okay, stand back," he said. He placed the chisel on the centre of the stone and walloped it with the hammer.

The clang it made rattled around the church for an age. The strike had made a small dent on the stone, but not much more. Tom drew his arm back and thumped the chisel again. Another massive clang echoed around the interior of the old ruin for ages. The dent had grown a little bigger, but not by much.

"Do you think you could make some more noise with that thing?" deadpanned Jack.

Tom gave his friend a look.

"Listen, Einstein, I'm doing it as quietly as I can," he replied.

"Tom, Jack's got a point. That option isn't making much progress, but it is making a load of noise," said Merryweather.

Gus cleared his throat.

"If I might be so bold. Young Tom, stand out of the way. You two, stand back," said the dragon as he took several steps backwards, paused, took a deep breath and proceeded to charge directly at the stone before thumping it with his left forelimb, gouging at the stone with his claws and shattering it into dozens of smaller fragments.

The noise this act generated was considerably louder and its echo more prolonged than either of Tom's initial efforts, and it reverberated around the church for several more seconds before hush descended once again.

Tom and Jack stared at Gus in disbelief. Merryweather simply shook her head.

"What?" asked the dragon, wearing a semi-hurt expression on his scaly face. "It worked, didn't it?"

Tom stepped forward and starting picking the remaining fragments of the stone out of the way. He peered into the void behind where the intact stone had been with his torch, and spotted a dark, oblong shape nestled at the very back of the space. Even with the headtorch, it was dark, but he thought it looked like some sort of box or container. Taking off his gloves, he reached into the gap, towards the object and nudged it from its resting place with the tips of his fingers. It felt like stone at first, then wood, then he realised it was both: stone with a wooden lid and ice cold to the touch. Gradually, he eased the container towards him, before he could eventually get a proper grip of it and extract it from its hiding place of several centuries.

"I've got it!" he exclaimed triumphantly and thrust the box towards Gus. "Gus, is this it? Is this box of relics?"

"Aye, laddie, that it is. Well done!" beamed the dragon.

"Well in," said Jack.

Merryweather smiled and simply said, "Excellent. Now, everyone, we really should leave this place asap – by which I mean now."

"Ah, there's just one more thing I want to check before we go," said Gus, and he shuffled off into the darkness at the far end of the church.

"Gus," whispered Jack, "where are you going?"

"Just off to nab a special piece of wood," said the dragon, as he disappeared from view.

"Gus," called Merryweather after him, in a low voice. "Gus…"

"Seriously?" said Tom. "He's thinking of his stomach at a time like this?"

"What's wrong with that?" asked Jack, wearing an innocent face. "Snacks are always very important."

"Yeah, but maybe not quite so much when we're in the middle of a burglary, doofus," replied Tom.

"Now, now, you two, this isn't helping. And it's not a burglary. We're reuniting Gus with something that belongs to him anyway," Merryweather reminded them. "Where *has* he gone?"

She peered into the darkness, but none of them could see the dragon.

"Quickly, Tom, get the box into your rucksack. We need to get out of here pronto," said Merryweather.

"Should we not check the box or something? Open it up before we go? Just to make sure all the relics are in it?" asked Tom.

"What an excellent idea," said a voice from the shadows. Tom, Jack and Merryweather froze in the darkness as the powerful beam from a torch turned on the three of them, semi-blinding them instantaneously. There was a series of quiet steps on the stone paving stones underfoot, mixed with the scrunching of the fragments scattered all over them as a tall, thin man, dressed all in black, stepped towards them.

Tom, Jack and Merryweather were all trying to shield their eyes from the piercing beam of the torch, trying to see who it was who was speaking to them. He addressed Tom first.

"I believe, young sir, that you have something which does not belong to you. Now, if you would be so kind as to hand it over to me, I'm sure I could be persuaded to forget about this little incursion of yours this evening and you can go on your way."

"Who are you?" asked Tom. He thought the man sounded French.

"It is of no concern of yours who I am," replied the man. "Nor any concern of mine as to who you might be."

There was a click as Tom managed to squint and finally get a proper look at the man. He was tall and slim for sure and was dressed completely in black from head to toe. His short, dark hair was receding slightly, and he had a moustache, which added to his dapper appearance. Lines etched his face and he wasn't smiling. He was also pointing a gun at Tom. It took Tom a fraction of a second to process that the noise of the click had been the gun being cocked.

"Ah yes," the man continued, "as you can see, you do not hold a strong negotiating position here. The box. Now." The man gestured with his free hand, motioning to Tom to give him the box.

Tom was rooted to the spot, clutching the box.

"Tom," said Merryweather quietly, "do as he says. Give him the box."

"But, but Auntieprof, it isn't..." stuttered Tom.

"Tom, just do it," insisted Merryweather.

"Ah, madame, you are a wise and pragmatic woman," said the man. "Now, if you would please, young sir, place the box on the ground in front of you and then all three of you take ten steps backwards. And then, we can discuss…"

Quite what the Shadow intended to discuss with his three captives would never be known because, at that precise moment, Tom looked over the Shadow's shoulder into the darkness, then his eyebrows shot up and he threw the box upwards with all his might, as high as he could in an arc directly over the Shadow's head.

"Idiot boy, what are you doing?" shouted the Shadow.

"Tom!" cried Merryweather.

As the box crashed to the floor and split open, spilling the hidden relics inside it all over the stone paving stones of the church, there was an almighty roar and from behind the Shadow an incoming cloud of sparks, smoke and the odd lick of flame billowed with fury.

The fog of Gus's biggest exhalation in several centuries completely engulfed all four humans in front of him with near immediate effect, but it enveloped the Shadow first – and most of all. There was the crack of a gunshot, followed by the noise of a ricochet as the bullet unleashed by the flailing Shadow careered off the stone wall above Tom's head.

Tom could barely see anything and all of them were coughing and spluttering, but he wiped his eyes in time to see Gus drawing back his head, shouting, "Well, it doesnae belong to you either, pal!" and proceeding to headbutt the Shadow square in the face, knocking him to the ground and rendering him semi-conscious with one blow. The Shadow let out a primeval scream unlike anything Tom had ever heard before in his life. Gus's intervention had left the elegant Frenchman flattened on the ground, clutching his face and moaning.

In the midst of the melee, Tom spied a gun on the floor of the church and kicked it away as far as he could with his left foot. Gus loomed over the Shadow.

"Ya cheeky sod," said the dragon, "making out that that box was yours. Well, you won't do that again in a hurry."

"Owwwwww," yelped the Shadow, "my dose". Tom could see him curl up into a ball on the ground, his hands over his head, trying to protect himself from Gus.

Through the fog, the coughing and spluttering, Merryweather shouted, "Come on, all of you! We have to go. Now."

The four of them ran, leaving the Shadow rolling around, groaning and whimpering, "please don't hurt me, please don't hurt me…" in the darkness. They reached the door.

As Merryweather and Jack bundled through it, Tom stopped dead at the entrance.

"The box!" He glanced at the pair of them for an instant and ran past Gus, back towards the still flailing Shadow. In an instant, Tom swept the flagstones with his headtorch. There were bits of the box's exterior scattered all over the floor, along with what Tom hoped were some of its contents. In one move, he skidded to a halt, swept down towards the debris and grabbed pieces of it, stuffing it in his pockets.

"Tom, come on!" shouted Merryweather. "There are people coming!"

Tom scooped up another handful of the box's detritus and ran for the door. He shoved through it in time to see Gus taking off into the night, and then he and Merryweather ran into the cover of the woods. Tom just had time to see the zig-zag of Jack's headtorch about a hundred yards of ahead of him before Merryweather grabbed his arm and dragged him along the path behind her.

From some distance beyond the church, he could hear the distant sounds of angry, barking dogs growing louder and louder.

"This way," said Merryweather as they fled deeper into the trees, towards the entrance to the Gris Corp grounds.

After a few more seconds of running and stumbling through the snow, Merryweather grabbed Tom's arm again. "Wait. Stop," she said. "Listen."

The pair of them held their breath. There were now two distinct groups of barking dog noises, one coming from behind them, near the old ruin and one which sounded as though it was now in front of them.

"Headtorch off," said Merryweather.

Tom switched off his headtorch.

"We cannot go back to the main gate. There must be guards and dogs swarming all over the place."

"Where's Jack?" asked Tom.

There was a scrunch.

"Helloooo," whispered Jack, waving at the pair of them.

Tom nearly leapt out of his skin.

"You dingbat," he chided his friend. "You nearly put me into orbit."

"Ah, sorry about that," said Jack.

"Right, you two, how are we getting out of here?" asked Merryweather.

"That's easy," said Jack. "Follow me."

He led them down a sideways path for another few hundred yards and then pointed towards an old, gnarled oak tree. One of the many perimeter trees that Max Gris had been forbidden from cutting down when her HQ was being constructed, complete with its manicured, futuristic grounds. Left unchecked for several centuries, the oak had grown wild and its branches went everywhere, including one which had eluded the perimeter wall of the Gris Corp HQ grounds.

"Jack Wanless, sometimes you amaze me," said Merryweather. "Well done. Let's go."

The three of them shinned their way up the tree, the sounds of the barking dogs in both directions ebbing and flowing through the frigid night air. By now, Tom was panting and the cold was hurting his lungs; they were already stinging from Gus's dragonbreath and the sprint through the snow and the bitterly cold air had exacerbated this. He paused for a second to catch his breath as Jack and Merryweather continued to edge their way along the branch overhanging the wall.

As Tom sat, nestled in the branches and trunk of the ancient oak, he saw some brighter lights in the distance, some way apart from the main HQ building, but they were too far away to make anything out distinctly. He reached into his rucksack for the other item he had brought with him this evening, a pair of ancient binoculars his aunt had given to him "in case they came in handy" and peered through them.

In the far distance, he could see several of Max Gris's security detail busily moving items into what looked like some sort of big tent, of the kind in which you went to see the circus. The main doors to the tent were open and inside, it looked like the interior of some sort of very ornate church, with lots of gold and red decorations and lighting – and not just lighting, mini-floodlighting.

"What on earth?" he murmured to himself.

Tom was transfixed by this spectacle, but then the sounds of the barking dogs growing louder snapped him out of trying to figure out what it was he was looking at. He stuffed the bins back into the rucksack and shimmied his way after the others onto the escape branch.

One by one, the three of them draped themselves down onto the street below it: Jack first, to show the other two the way; Merryweather next, and finally, some moments later, Tom followed.

He landed with a soft thump on the snow.

"What kept you?" asked Jack.

"Tell you both later," said Tom.

The three of them took off down the snowy street, heading back towards the side street where they had left Merryweather's trusty Defender.

As they rounded the corner of the street in which the ancient vehicle was parked, Tom fist-pumped at the sight of it.

The three of them piled into the car. Merryweather started the engine, which spluttered into life at the first time of asking.

As the car moved off, Jack let out a whoop.

"Yes! We did it!"

Merryweather grinned and replied, "Yes, Jack, we certainly did."

Tom didn't join in this immediate celebration. Instead, he sat, silently looking out of the window at the snowy streets and pavements, wondering about what he had just seen.

CHAPTER THIRTY-THREE

Max Gris was pacing and thinking. It was taking her mind off the intense cold that was gnawing away at her – and everyone else around her – in the centre of the ruined old church which sat, hidden like the ancient eyesore it was, on the periphery of the beautifully sculptured grounds which surrounded the epicentre of her global empire. She wished she was back in the warmth and comfort of her boardroom, or that she was striding around her beloved HQ building's corridors, or its atrium, barking orders at all and sundry, but no. Tonight, she had been called to this dingy old dump of a building because there had been an 'incident'.

At first, Gris had considered sending Grunk – solo - to deal with whatever had happened, but then she found out who had reported the incident and in an instant, had assumed total and sole charge of the developing situation, ordering Grunk to bring himself and a squad of his best personnel to accompany her. Slymington had, of course, automatically followed her as she burst out of the HQ building and stormed her way through the snow to the old, ruined church.

Mid–pace, as she scrunched on the debris littering the flagstones of the ruin, Gris stopped, and turned to the person who had sounded the alarm, gave him a look half of faux pity and half of suspicion. She was trying to block out the background noise of half of Grunk's security detail rigging up floodlights throughout what was left of the church's interior, which the other half had already been tearing apart for several minutes.

"Tell me again exactly what happened," she addressed the Shadow. The Frenchman was sitting in the remnants of what had once been a pew of some sort, head bowed forward and applying a handkerchief to his nose, trying to stem the flow of blood from it.

The Shadow looked up and began retelling the story once more.

"As I already told you, Madame," he began, "I was out walking in the grounds, taking in some air and clearing my head, when I thought I saw some lights coming from the far end of the grounds. I made my way towards them and as I drew closer to the building, I saw that the lights were zig-zagging their way around its interior." The Shadow paused to daub at the bloody mess on his face before he continued.

"I made my way quietly around the perimeter of the building - I could see that it had been some sort of religious building from the exterior – until I found an entrance and then I slipped inside to see what was causing these strange lights." The Shadow paused again.

"And?" said Gris impatiently. "What happened then?"

"I crept inside, to take a closer look, and to find out what was going on. My natural curiosity got the better of me. The place was dark, so it was quite straightforward to hide in the darkness and listen. I felt at home in the shadows." He smiled ruefully.

"Quite," said Gris, "and then what?"

"I realised I had stumbled across a burglary of some sort. There was an older woman, and two children with her – and something else. I thought it was a man at first; it sounded Scottish. I released they were looking for something and then one of the kids mentioned something about a box of relics. Well, Madame, given our conversations of the past several months – and where I was – I decided at that moment to intervene. Fortunately, I had my favourite method of persuasion with me." He brandished his newly reacquainted gun around to emphasise the point.

"Yes, please don't wave that thing around too much. It's already gone off once this evening," said Gris.

"Of course," said the Shadow, as he re-holstered the weapon. "However, my intervention did not go entirely to plan. I made myself known to them, but there were only three people present, after all – the woman and the two children. And I asked for the box of relics that one of the kids was holding, but then he threw it up in the air and it landed behind me and smashed and then..." his voice trailed off.

"And then?" asked Gris, giving the Shadow her best quizzical eyebrow.

"And then, some sort of giant lizard thing attacked me. The detail is fuzzy afterwards. It struck me in the face – as you can see - and there was a lot of smoke and commotion. I eventually managed to grab the box and the remaining relics, but I think that one of the kids may have escaped with a few fragments. Once I had recovered my senses, I radioed into your HQ and the rest, well, you know."

"I see," said Gris, as she thrust the stone box with the wooden lid towards the Shadow.

"And this is the box?" questioned Gris.

"Yes, Madame. That is the box they referred to as the box of relics."

"And... a giant lizard, you say?" asked Gris.

"Yes, Madame, a giant lizard of some sort."

Gris looked at the Shadow with an ongoing mixture of pity and scorn, before sitting down next to him on the pew and smiling.

"How giant? I mean, are we talking six feet tall? Seven? And just how badly did you bang your head?"

"Madame, I know how it sounds, but I swear to you, I know what I saw – and it wasn't human."

"So, an old woman, two kids and a giant lizard break into this dump of a building to do some vandalism or something; you disturb them at gunpoint, the lizard attacks you and they all get away?"

"That's one way of putting it, Madame," said the Shadow, with a shrug of his shoulders.

"Yes," said Gris. "Yes, I suppose it is. Except, it doesn't sound like it was vandalism. It sounds as though they knew what they were looking for – and now we have it."

There was a loud crash behind them, from deep in the recesses of the church building.

"Would you lot be careful down there!" shouted Gris into the now-floodlit back half of the ruin.

"Sorry, ma'am," came a shout back.

"They are wasting their time," said the Shadow. "They won't find anything else in there. That little raiding party knew what they were coming here for, but they didn't achieve their objective. You, madame, are now in possession of the final batch of relics."

"How can you be so sure? On both counts? Hmmm?" asked Gris.

"I saw the box and what spilled out of it. You now have the box and its contents. All that kid took were some bits and pieces of stone and dirt. Now, look around you. Up there – if you look carefully where part of the roof and wall has collapsed, you can make out the fragments of an inscription: *de alio... ...edrali*," said the Shadow, pointing.

"What does that mean?" asked Gris.

"Madame, the complete inscription would read: *de aliorum Cathedrali*," replied the Shadow.

"Cathedral of the Others," murmured Gris. "Well, I never... Hah! Right under my nose all along." She was grinning.

She turned to Slymington, who had been watching impassively, as the Shadow had retold his tale once more.

"Slimey, organise the CCTV footage back at HQ. Let's review it and find out who our visitors were. Very rude of them to break in like that and not even pop by to say hello," said Gris.

"Very good, ma'am," replied Slymington.

"And as for you, my favourite Frenchman, we had better get you cleaned up back at HQ. And a doctor for, well, for what's left of your nose," she said, standing up.

"And this," said Gris as she picked up the ancient stone box with the wooden lid, "is not leaving my sight."

Gris, Slymington, Grunk and the Shadow reconvened in the Gris Corp HQ Boardroom one hour later. This had given the Shadow time to clean himself up and to be examined by the Gris Corp doctor, who had pronounced that his nose may well be broken and that it should be attended to in a local hospital. Gris had deferred this further action on the Shadow's behalf until they had reviewed the CCTV footage.

Slymington had organised the collation of this next aspect and now they were gathered, ready to review the footage.

"Okay, Slimey, what have we got?" asked Gris.

Slymington ran the footage on the large screen that had emerged from the ceiling of the Boardroom. It was massive and though the raw footage wasn't very distinct, Slymington had a few tricks up his sleeve.

"As you can see, ma'am, the back-up generators did their job and we have a complete record of the events of this evening," said Slymington.

He started replaying the footage, pausing when the first images of the three shadowy figures entering the Gris Corp grounds flashed on screen.

"Can you enhance that shot?" asked Gris.

"Of course," replied Slymington, keying in instructions on the control pad.

The images on-screen became magnified as the technology zoomed in on them. It was now clear to all in the room that there was one adult and two children in the party of three.

"Three of them. Just as you said," said Gris to the Shadow.

The Shadow simply nodded.

"Shall I continue, ma'am?" asked Slymington.

"Yes," said Gris.

Slymington ran the footage forward. They all watched as the three figures inched their way further into the grounds until they neared the old ruin, whereupon they stopped and waited for several minutes.

"Slimey, fast forward this bit. They're just sitting there, waiting," said Gris.

Slymington did as he had been instructed, until, after several seconds on fast forward, a larger figure popped into the frame.

"Stop. Go back," instructed Gris.

Slymington reversed the footage to the point a few seconds before the larger figure appeared. He then inched forward, frame by frame, until the three people on-screen were joined by the fourth.

Gris stood, watching the footage, open-mouthed.

"Enhance it, Slimey," she said.

Slymington zoomed in on the fourth and largest figure. There, in plain sight, standing eight feet tall and conversing with the other three people in the shot, was something that was clearly not human.

"What on earth...?" murmured Gris.

"As I told you, ma'am," said the Shadow, "it is a giant lizard."

Max Gris's face was a mixture of incredulity and fury.

"Find out what that thing is. Now! And who the other three are. And how all four of them evaded our security. Grunk, I'm looking at you on this one," she shouted.

"Yes, ma'am," grunted Grunk.

Gris turned to Slymington.

"If I didn't know any better, I'd say that looked like some sort of...*dragon*, Slimey?"

"Indeed, ma'am. It is impossible, yet there it is, on the screen in front of us. I suggest we locate these people immediately. They do, after all, have rather a lot of explaining to do," said Slymington, flatly. "Breaking and entering, vandalism, criminal damage, theft. It's quite a charge sheet."

"How do we find them? We cannot even see their faces clearly," said Gris.

There was a knock at the door.

"Yes?" shouted Gris.

"Hello, ma'am," said Rudderts, popping his head around the door. "Can I come in? I've a little piece of news which might be of interest…"

Gris rolled her eyes. "What is it? Spit it out."

"Well, ma'am, we have restored the back-up servers with the details of last night's updates to Apotheosis."

Gris was interested now.

"Go on," she barked.

"And the thing is, that there were a couple of young lads who turned up at HQ last night, claiming to have 'won' the game," gushed Rudderts.

"What?" snapped Gris.

"Um, yes. Well, I told them not to waste anyone's time, what with us being in the middle of an emergency and everything and there was no way they could have won because the power was down everywhere," he blurted out.

"You did *what*?" shouted Gris.

"And well, um, the thing is, er, now we've restored the back-up servers, it appears that – somehow – by a million to one chance - they may have been, um, ah, *telling the truth…*" Rudderts squeaked out this final sentence and then stood, rigidly, having closed his eyes as though in silent prayer.

The explosion Rudderts was expecting from Gris did not arrive. Instead, she spoke softly and quietly to him, her voice low and almost a whisper.

"Rudderts, what happened to the two of them?"

Rudderts popped open an eye. Gris was staring directly at him.

"Ah well, ma'am, you see the thing is, what with one thing and another, I didn't have time for any of their – as I thought – silly games – and so I... I... um..."

"Yes?" said Gris, curtly.

"I sent them away and told them not to bother us with their nonsense," gabbled Rudderts, scrunching his eyes closed once again, waiting for the onslaught.

"You did what?" said Gris, with ice in her voice.

"Sent them away," repeated Rudderts, "Only, the thing is, the engineers have now confirmed their story..."

If, at this moment, Rudderts had been able to roll himself up into a ball like a frightened hedgehog, then he would have done so. However, unfortunately for him, he was not able to do this.

Gris walked over to Rudderts.

"You," she began and poked him in the chest.

"Sent" (another poke).

"Them" (and another one).

"Away?" (A final poke).

"Yes," whimpered Rudderts.

Max Gris's face turned scarlet, and she threw her hands up in the air as she erupted.

"Why do I even *employ* you people?" she shouted, directly into Rudderts' face.

"Find out who they both are, where they live, and bring them here. Now!" Gris began pacing up and down the boardroom. Mainly to distract herself from her desire to wallop – or fire – Rudderts for his outright stupidity.

Rudderts eventually opened his eyes and cleared his throat.

"Well, ma'am, tiny bit of good news," he croaked. "We have their names from the server."

Gris whirled round.

"Yes? And?"

"They're called Jack Wanless and Tom Brightly. The only registered address is the Wanless one: 50 Killermont Drive, Glasgow."

"Rudderts," said Gris, turning towards her hapless Head of PR.

"Yes, ma'am," replied Rudderts, with a tinge of hope in his voice that he wasn't about to be fired.

"Go with Slymington. I want a review of all the CCTV footage from Friday evening. I want to know everything about these two boys. NOW!" she shouted.

Rudderts scurried away, with Slymington following him in his usual, measured way.

As Slymington was about to leave the room, Gris shouted after him.

"Slimey, a thought. We should move the chamber construction."

Slymington turned around, his face impassive as ever.

"Where were you considering moving it to, ma'am?" he asked.

"Move it to the old ruin. It's apparently our lost 'cathedral', after all – even if it looks like a complete dump. Besides, it'll give the ceremony more atmosphere. Just make sure your men give the interior a good tidy up."

"As you wish, ma'am. It shall be done."

With this, Slymington exited after the hapless Rudderts. Gris turned to her Head of Security.

"Grunk," said Gris.

"Yes ma'am," replied Grunk.

"Get a team of your best men ready. Once we've confirmed the details, I want you to find out where those two boys are now, and to fetch them here immediately," said Gris.

"Yes, ma'am," said Grunk and he exited the Boardroom.

Gris turned to the Shadow and picked up the box of relics from where it had been resting on the Boardroom table.

"Well, monsieur, it appears your work here is now done," she said, waving the box around in front of him, "whereas ours is only just beginning." Max Gris was smiling again, the self-assured smile of someone who was winning, and winning big.

CHAPTER THIRTY-FOUR

Merryweather, Tom and Jack were gathered in Merryweather's kitchen once again. Tom and Jack were grinning and high-fiving as they took off their jackets, scarves and gloves. Gus was sitting in the corner, munching on a stick. Merryweather looked pensive.

"Okay, you two. Get out of those things and then let's think for a minute or two," said Merryweather.

Tom could see his aunt was frowning.

"What's up? he asked his aunt as he draped his jacket over a chair.

His aunt's frown became even more pronounced.

"We need to figure out what we're going to do next," said Merryweather.

"We've got the relics now. Sorted!" said Jack, his grin growing even wider.

Tom was emptying the fragments he had grabbed onto the breakfast bar in the middle of the kitchen.

"Especially with those," said Merryweather.

Jack looked at the small pile.

"Okay, so we've got *some* of the relics," he said.

"We've just been shot at, Jack," cautioned Merryweather, "and we don't even know who that maniac was."

"I took care of him," said Gus, beaming.

"Yes, you did," said Merryweather, "but he also saw you – and that isn't going to lead to anything good."

"I'm ready for anything now. My fire is back," said Gus.

"Yes, Gus; that's not my point," said Merryweather.

She sat down at the breakfast bar in the middle of the kitchen, looking grave. Tom's grin had now disappeared. His aunt wasn't looking happy at all.

"We will need to hide Gus for a while until all of this settles down. Whoever that man was, we have to work on the assumption that he was likely working for Max Gris – which means that she will now know we were there... and that she will now know about Gus. Plus, the whole place is bound to be littered with security cameras."

"But we were wearing balaclavas," said Tom. "How are they going to find us?"

"Aren't you forgetting something?" asked Merryweather, nodding towards Gus.

"What?" said the dragon, mid-munch.

"You're somewhat conspicuous, Gus," said Merryweather. "I rather suspect that Ms Gris will want to know what on earth an eight-foot-tall dragon was doing roaming around all over her property – and why. And where you are now."

"Plus," she continued, "we still don't know where Nicky is."

"But," interrupted Tom, "we *do* have the relics. Or at least some of them."

"Yes, I know, Tom," said Merryweather, "and I'm trying to work out where would be best to hide them again – and who might be able to help us with this."

Tom could see that his aunt was thinking deeply as she wondered what to do next. Her frown was turning into more of a look of worry. He wasn't sure if this was the right time to mention the strange building and activity he had seen from high up in the tree as they had made their escape, but took a deep breath and began.

"There is one more thing," Tom began.

Merryweather turned to look at him.

"What?" she asked.

"Well, I saw something weird when we were up in the tree. In the distance. It was like some sort of big top that you'd see in a circus, and there were loads of lights and people swarming around it, moving stuff. But when I used the bins, I could see the inside of it – well, a bit at least - and it looked like a church or something." Tom half-shrugged his shoulders at this point. He became aware that as well as Merryweather, Jack and Gus were now looking at him, hanging on his every word.

"Like a church?" repeated Merryweather.

"Yep. Looked like some sort of altar thing being set up on a stage and it was all red and gold inside, with ornaments and stuff. And lots of lights. And tons of people, moving stuff into it," said Tom.

"Right," said Merryweather, "that settles it."

She stood up and walked over to Gus.

"Gus, we're going to have to hide you for a few days. You'll need to be out of sight – just in case."

"What, you mean back in that wee wooden building in your garden?" asked the dragon.

"No, I mean downstairs in the cellar. It's rather large, and I can make it warm enough, and we can bring you some logs to chomp on. We need to keep you safe for the time being whilst we seek out someone who might understand all of this," said Merryweather.

"Can't we just go to the police now?" asked Tom. "I mean, someone tried to shoot us – and there's definitely something dodgy going on at Gris

Corp. The police would sort it out."

"No," said Merryweather. "Not an option. Think it through. Even if they believed us, the first thing that would happen would be that they would speak to Max Gris and if they ask to look at the CCTV footage…"

"They'll find out about Gus," said Tom quietly.

"Exactly," replied Merryweather. "And then all hell would break loose."

She turned to Gus.

"I'm sorry, Gus, but we must keep you hidden for now whilst we sort out putting these in a safe place where Max Gris cannot get her hands on them," said Merryweather, pointing to the pile of relics. "And I'm rather of the view that the safest place might be with you."

Gus bowed his head down and nodded slowly and reluctantly. For the first time since they had met him, Tom thought that the giant dragon looked sad.

"We need to work out what Max Gris is up to," continued Merryweather, "because all we have done for now is to stall whatever her plan is – and once she realises that she doesn't in fact have all the relics… well, one can only guess at what she'll do next."

"What *do* you reckon she'll do next?" asked Jack.

"Figure it out, you dingbat," said Tom. "She'll come looking for the relics, won't she?"

"Well, we don't know that for sure," said Jack.

"Tom's right, Jack," said Merryweather. "She needs these relics for whatever it is she's up to and she's clearly up to something big, if she's constructing some sort of church or temple."

Jack went quiet and nodded.

"Tom, gather up the relics and I'll take them down to the cellar," said Merryweather. She turned towards Gus.

"Gus, come with me. I'll show you to your new temporary quarters downstairs. You two, make sure you have some tea and warm yourselves up. Once Gus is settled, I'm taking you back to Jack's house."

"What are you going to do then, Auntieprof?" asked Tom.

"I'm going to see the one man who might be able to assemble all the pieces of this puzzle so that it makes some sort of sense - if he's still talking to me, that is," said Merryweather, as she opened the kitchen door for Gus.

"We'll need to be ready to leave in an hour, so you have some time to warm up, dry your things and have some food," she instructed the two boys as she exited, with Gus plodding along after her, ducking so as not to bang his head on the kitchen doorframe. As he did so, he half-turned around to face Tom and Jack.

"I'll see you two wee legends soon. Listen to the wise woman and be brave," said the dragon.

With this, he gave them a wave and a final flap of his wing and followed Merryweather en route to the safety of her cellar.

CHAPTER THIRTY-FIVE

"Well, what have you got for me?" snapped Max Gris as Slymington pressed the controls to load up yet more CCTV footage on the large screen, which was once again descending into the boardroom. By his side stood Rudderts, beads of sweat trickling down his forehead. Grunk had also been summoned back for this presentation.

"We've reviewed all the footage from Friday evening and this evening, ma'am," monotoned Slymington, "and have enhanced some images, as you can see here."

He flashed up several larger images of the two visitors to Gris Corp's HQ on Friday evening, zeroing in on their faces.

"As Mr Rudderts explained earlier in his story, it does indeed appear that these two boys presented themselves at the front door on Friday evening, whereupon they had a brief conversation with Mr Rudderts, after which they were despatched, into the snow, from whence they came," said Slymington. His tone was slightly more disparaging and less monotonous than usual.

Rudderts was now trembling involuntarily.

Gris turned towards him.

"Rudderts, you really and truly are a complete fool, aren't you?" she said icily.

Rudderts took a massive gulp and croaked out a "yes, ma'am."

"Keep going, Slimey," ordered Gris.

"Yes, ma'am," replied her faithful sidekick.

He pressed some more buttons on the controls and further detailed images of the two boys' faces appeared on the massive screen.

"We were able to significantly enhance the two boys' faces and features in extreme close-up from the Friday evening footage."

Slymington then allowed himself a minor moment of triumph. Had he ever smiled, this would have been one of those vanishingly rare occasions. As it was, he resumed his monotone after a long pause for effect.

"We then undertook the same process using the footage from this evening. In this instance, we were somewhat constrained in our ability to enhance the three humans' facial features due to them all wearing balaclavas."

Slymington paused briefly once again.

"However, the balaclavas did not entirely cover their faces and so we could enhance the area around the eyes with a great deal of precision."

Slymington now zoomed in on these images of the two boys and, after pressing yet more buttons on the control panel, also brought up the images from the Friday evening footage.

"We could thus undertake a comparison using our latest facial recognition software," he continued, as the two sets of images merged into one composite image for each of the two boys.

"And, as you will note, the software has confirmed a one hundred per cent match for each of the two of them."

Slymington wasn't done yet, however.

"We also then used the thermal imaging footage from this evening in order to confirm the facial recognition. It is uninhibited by any facial coverings."

He punched several more buttons on the control panel, and false colour images of the two boys' balaclava covered faces flashed up – and were once again merged with the images from Friday evening.

"Ma'am, this again confirms our initial conclusion: Master Jack Wanless and Master Tom Brightly both came here to report that they had won Apotheosis on Friday evening, and then returned on Saturday evening to the ruin in the grounds, with an as yet unidentified older woman and this… thing."

At this point, Slymington pulled up an enhanced image of Gus.

Max Gris was grinning wildly.

"Superb work, Slimey!" she exclaimed, slapping him on the back. Slymington did not appear to relish this human interaction one iota.

Gris stopped to gaze at the screen in disbelief.

"And what the blazes is that?" she asked, pointing at the large, toothy dragon filling the entirety of the screen.

"We're not sure, ma'am, but our best guess – and I realise how this will sound – is that it may be a *dragon*," replied Slymington.

"A dragon? For real?" asked Gris, her eyebrows nearly taking off from her face.

"Yes, ma'am," said Slymington.

"Well, well, it really is Christmas," said Gris. "And you're absolutely sure about the identity of these two boys?"

"Yes, ma'am," spluttered Rudderts. "Everyone who entered the game had to upload photo ID and we've cross-matched the images above to those held on the database – and they check out."

"Good, Rudderts," said Gris coldly. "You may yet redeem yourself."

"Th-th-thank you, ma'am," said Rudderts, forcing out the words.

"One more thing you should be aware of, ma'am," said Slymington. "Look at this."

He flashed forward to some of the later images captured by the CCTV earlier on in the evening which showed Tom exiting the church and fiddling repeatedly with his jacket pockets as Merryweather led him away.

"What am I looking at?" Gris asked her faithful sidekick.

"We're not completely sure, but this boy – Master Brightly – appears to be most concerned with whatever it is that he has in his jacket pockets," replied Slymington. He paused.

"What is it, Slimey?" asked Gris.

"Ma'am, I do not share our French friend's optimistic view that this boy merely picked up stones and dirt during the melee. He appears very protective of the contents of his pockets – more than might reasonably be expected were those contents to be mere 'dirt and stones'. And if I may, I do not consider that the Frenchman would have been in any fit state to know definitively what the boy had taken."

"So, what are you saying, Slimey?" asked Gris.

"We are checking all of the batches of relics to to confirm my supposition, but I strongly suspect he may have grabbed a few relics from the final batch," came the monotone reply.

Gris thought for a moment or two.

"Well, we have the address of the boy called Jack, yes?" asked Gris.

"We do, ma'am," confirmed Rudderts.

"Well then, it's simple: find that boy and we'll find the relics – and, as a bonus, that thing," said Gris, pointing once more at the picture of Gus that was still on screen.

She turned to her Head of Security.

"Grunk, you know what to do. Get to it."

"Yes, ma'am," replied Grunk and headed out of the room at speed.

"You two, I don't need to remind you we're on a tight deadline now. Slimey, make sure that work is proceeding to schedule for the ceremony and as for you, Rudderts, get the press releases ready to announce we have our winners."

"And hurry up, the pair of you. Christmas is coming – and we've not a minute to waste."

Max Gris was smiling the smile of someone who had got what she had wanted – at last.

CHAPTER THIRTY-SIX

As Merryweather's ancient Defender turned the corner at the junction that led into the top of Jack's street, Tom stared idly out of the window at the snow-covered houses and flats. All things considered, the drive across the city had been reasonably straightforward, if not altogether quick. Whilst some roads had been cleared of snow, most of the side streets had not and remained tricky to drive along. More than once, he had heard his aunt take a sharp intake of breath, which was followed by some indecipherable muttering as the rear of the vehicle decided to go in a different direction from its front - and from that which Merryweather had intended.

The drive had also been made a little easier by the intermittent illumination of some of the city's streetlights. Tom figured that gradually, more of the power networks must be being restored. He fumbled in his pocket and checked his phone again, but it was still showing no signal. He would have to try to call home from the landline once they reached Jack's house. As he glanced up from the phone, out of the corner of his eye, he saw something large, shiny and black flash past on the opposite side of the road and turn down a perpendicular side street.

"Did you see that?" Tom asked Jack.

Jack was mid-yawn.

"See what?"

"Did you see it, Auntieprof?"

"What, Tom?"

"It looked like one of those big Gris Corp cars."

Tom was looking backwards, but the vehicle was already out of sight.

"It looked like it was in a hurry," said Tom.

"Likely, just a coincidence. There are a lot of these SUVs around the city these days. Probably driving too fast for the conditions because the driver thinks he or she is invincible," said Merryweather.

The Defender continued to navigate its way down the long slope towards the midpoint of Killermont Drive and towards the Wanless residence. Tom could see that Jack was now yawning his head off and this, in turn, made him yawn, too. It had been a long day, and he was feeling drowsy due to the cold and his tiredness. He was looking forward to a good night's sleep and hoping against hope that the power had been restored to Jack's house. Given that he could see lights now on in some of the houses along the street, Tom was more optimistic about this the nearer they got to Jack's house.

Merryweather brought the Defender to a halt a few car lengths from Jack's house and parked it into the side of the road after a fashion, piles of cleared snow notwithstanding. The three of them got out of the vehicle and the cold air hitting his face temporarily snapped Tom out of his torpor. Jack led the way towards the house. The first thing that Tom noticed as they neared the front gate was that – to his disappointment – the house was in complete darkness.

"I hope the power's back on," he said to Jack.

"Fingers crossed," replied Jack, "though on the upside, it looks like Katie's not still up to greet us."

Jack opened the gate and strode up the path, but then stopped suddenly as he neared the front door.

"What's up?" asked Tom.

"Look," said Jack, pointing at the door. Barely discernible in the darkness, the door wasn't fully closed; it was lying half an inch ajar.

Merryweather, bustled in through the front gate, closing it behind her, and hurried up the path, bringing up the rear.

"Well, come on, the pair of you. Don't dilly-dally; let's get in out of the cold."

Tom and Jack stood motionless, looking at each other and then back at the door.

"What is it?" asked Merryweather.

"Look," whispered Tom and Jack in unison, pointing at the ever so slightly open front door.

Merryweather peered through the darkness momentarily at the door, then turned to Jack.

"Did you find it like this?" she asked.

Jack nodded.

"Okay," said Merryweather, "let's make our way in, slowly and carefully."

"I'll go first," said Tom, barging past Jack and through the front door.

"Tom!" hissed Merryweather, but it was too late. Tom was already inside the house.

Tom fished around in his pocket for his headtorch as he inched along the downstairs hallway. He found it after a few seconds and switched it on, picking his way through the hall to the large, breakfasting kitchen at the far end of the hallway. Behind him, he could hear the footsteps and the odd creaking floorboard of Jack and Merryweather following him. By now, Tom was hoping that there was no one else in the house who shouldn't have been there, for he suspected that, given the amount of noise the three of them were making, they would not stay undetected for very much longer.

As he crept along, staying close to the wall, he noticed a lamp on its side on the floor, its base and lampshade looked damaged. He neared the kitchen and edged towards the door. It, too, was ajar. Tom prised it open, half expecting someone to leap out at him, but there was nothing other than the sound of the wooden door creaking as it swung its way into the room.

Tom flashed the light from the headtorch around the room. It was quiet and looked very much as it had that morning.

"That's weird – it looks untouched," said Jack. Tom could see Jack's own headtorch picking out various parts of the kitchen.

The room began to illuminate.

Tom spun around to see Merryweather, her index finger on the kitchen light switch.

"I figured it was worth a try," she smiled. Her smile vanished into a look of puzzlement as she, too, surveyed the kitchen in the Wanless household.

"Well, it all looks perfectly normal- apart from the front door being open," said Merryweather.

"You don't think Katie went out or something?" asked Tom.

"I need to find her," said Jack, and rushed out of the room.

Tom ran behind him, and he and Jack began careering around the house, downstairs, then upstairs, galloping through each room, flicking on lights and shouting for Katie at the tops of their voices. In return, they were met with silence. After a couple of minutes of this, Tom heard his aunt's voice calling from the kitchen.

"Boys," shouted Merryweather. "Boys!"

Tom stopped flinging open cupboard doors for a moment.

"What is it?" he shouted back.

"Come back down here. I know where Jack's sister is," shouted Merryweather.

Tom flew back downstairs, with Jack huffing and puffing in his wake. The pair of them re-entered the kitchen to find Merryweather standing, stock still, holding a piece of paper, her reading glasses on.

She passed the note first to Jack, who read it and then passed it silently to Tom.

Tom looked at the A4 sheet. It was Gris Corp headed notepaper. He read the brief message.

'We have your sister. Return the items you have stolen.'

He looked at his aunt and then at Jack. For several moments, none of them said a word, then Jack broke the silence first.

"We have to go to the police now," said Jack. "Katie's in danger."

"But… but… how could they know about the relics? And how did they connect it to here?" asked Tom.

"No idea," said Merryweather, "but figure it out they have. Or, rather, they've figured out something. I must say, though, that whatever it is Max Gris wants these relics for, she's serious about it. We can now add breaking and entering and kidnapping to being shot at whilst in pursuit of these objects."

Tom looked at Jack. The colour had drained from his friend's face and his brow was furrowed. Tom could only imagine what was going through Jack's head right now. He gave him a gentle punch on the arm. Jack's expression was unchanged.

"When the two of you went to report your win in this game thing, who did you speak to?" asked Merryweather.

"You mean at the HQ?" asked Tom.

"Yes, did you give your names or get anyone's name?" asked Merryweather.

"No, we didn't have the chance to," said Tom. "The guy we met didn't believe us and told us to get lost."

"Then how could they have got this address?" asked Merryweather.

"We entered it when we registered for the game," said Jack flatly.

Tom slapped his forehead.

"Of course," he said.

"Go on," encouraged Merryweather.

"We had to give all our details online when we entered Apotheosis," said Jack, "and I put my address down for the pair of us."

"So, the people at Gris Corp could, in theory, be able to connect you to this address?" asked Merryweather.

"Yeah, but how do they know anything else about us?" asked Jack. "I mean, we covered our faces and everything!" He threw his hands up in the air in exasperation.

"But not on Friday evening," said Tom.

"What?" asked Jack.

"We weren't wearing balaclavas on Friday evening," said Tom.

"Yeah. So?" said Jack.

"So, on Friday, they would have got a good look at us when we turned up at the HQ building."

"If the cameras were working," said Jack.

"Well, the lights were on, so they must have had some sort of power. Oh no," said Tom.

"What?" asked Jack and Merryweather together.

"If the cameras were working, they could have seen us on the Friday evening at the ruin, which means…" said Tom.

"Gus!" exclaimed Jack, his face now completely ashen.

The three of them were silent again for a few moments.

Tom finally broke the silence.

"We have to return the relics."

"No," said Merryweather.

"But they've got Katie!" said Jack.

"And they'll know about Gus," added Tom.

"Look, the pair of you, I know that. But if we give them the relics now, there's no telling what Max Gris will do with them. They're our strongest bargaining chip. Our only leverage," said Merryweather.

"We need to go to the police and then return the relics with them," said Tom.

"No," said Merryweather. "Think it through. Then what would happen?"

"I dunno, Max Gris gets arrested?" said Tom.

"Oh boys, you have so much to learn. We'd be the ones being arrested for breaking and entering – and theft – knowing that woman," said Merryweather. "And then there would be the small matter of Gus to contend with."

Tom felt a chill run down his spine at this point. "Gus..." he muttered.

"We should get out of here," said Jack.

"Good plan. To the car, boys. Now," ordered Merryweather, and the three of them made for the front door.

CHAPTER THIRTY-SEVEN

"Can you see anything yet?" whispered Jack.

"No... I don't think so. Wait, there's something," replied Tom. He was in the back of the now rather cold Defender, with its lights out and engine off, peering out its back window through his binoculars, up the hill towards Merryweather's house.

"What? What is it?" asked Jack.

"What can you see, Tom?" chipped in Merryweather.

"I'm not sure. Looks like a bunch of Gris's goons leaving the garden. A couple of them are talking to each other. There's a big guy I've seen before. Huge. Has a thick beard. He seems to be giving out orders."

Tom shuffled around on the back seat, trying to steady his elbows so he could get a better look at what was going on.

"Still talking... more of them milling around and coming out of your garden, Auntieprof," said Tom.

"They'd better not have ruined any of my plants," muttered Merryweather.

"It looks like they're getting into their cars. Man, those things are like tanks," said Tom.

"Uh oh," he continued.

"What?" said Merryweather.

"Looks like they're turning and coming back down the hill."

Merryweather turned the key in the ignition.

"Time to go," she said, as the Defender spluttered into life.

Tom was jolted around in the back seat as the Defender lurched off. His aunt wasn't hanging around. Holding his bins in one hand, he grabbed the seatbelt in the other and, after some fiddling about, he clicked it in.

Merryweather was still accelerating as she turned into first one side street and then another, before slamming on the brakes and bringing the car to a sudden halt.

"We should be okay waiting here until they've gone," she said. "And we can just about see the very back of the house and garden, too."

Tom peered through the window into the darkness. If his aunt could see her garden, he figured she must have better night vision that he had.

"Do you think they found Gus?" asked Jack.

"Well, I didn't see any obvious signs that they had when they were leaving," said Tom. "I mean, there wasn't any smoke or fire coming from the house, so hopefully…"

"We have to presume for the moment that they didn't find Gus," said Merryweather. "Had they done so, as you have rightly pointed out, Tom, I suspect we would have known about it."

"But where is he then? You don't think he could still be somewhere in the house, do you, Auntieprof?" asked Tom.

"I doubt it. Even though the doors to the cellar are fairly well hidden, if those goons had carried out a thorough search, they doubtless would have found one of them," replied Merryweather.

Jack shifted about in the back seat of the car and blew into his hands.

"Wherever he is, I hope he's somewhere warm," he said.

"Another couple of minutes, Jack, and we'll be moving again," said Merryweather.

Tom could see Jack pulling his jacket and scarf around himself even more tightly, to emphasise that he was now officially 'very cold'. He was also rummaging around in his pockets to highlight that he had run out of snacks. Tom knew that, for Jack, this combination was the opposite of good and that the grumbling would begin shortly if at least one of these two states wasn't remedied – and soon.

"As for Gus," Merryweather continued, "I just hope that somehow he escaped and that he's somewhere safe for now. I'm sure he'll be back, but for the moment, he's going to have to fend for himself."

Tom noticed that for the first time this evening, his aunt's tone of voice sounded almost distracted. He was trying to ignore Jack's continuing efforts to keep himself warm and could see that his aunt was staring intently at the place where the very rear of her back garden was. Tom decided he was more hopeful about the likelihood of Gus returning sometime soon than his aunt sounded. After all, the dragon was now equipped with a fully functional inbuilt weapons system. Meantime, there was still the small matter of the rest of the relics to resolve. Before he could raise this latter point, though, Merryweather spoke again.

"Right," said Merryweather, "well, it's pretty obvious that it would not be sensible to return to the house this evening with the possibility of more of those Gris Corp gorillas swarming around, so we had better go somewhere else. Agreed?" She hit the steering wheel to emphasise the question.

"I guess so," said Tom.

"Where are we going to go?" asked Jack.

"Don't worry, boys," said Merryweather as she started the Defender's engine. "There's a place we can go where I know we'll be safe and the man who lives there is the one person who can help us untangle this whole conundrum."

"Where?" asked Jack.

"Who is it?" asked Tom.

"An old friend," said Merryweather, as the Defender spluttered into life and trundled off once more through the snow, and onwards, on into the night.

CHAPTER THIRTY-EIGHT

"Put me down! Get off me! I don't want you carrying me! Get off me! This is kidnapping!"

Erasmus Grunk had had many difficult and awkward assignments working for Max Gris over the years. He had been thumped, beaten up, attacked, thrown about – and worse – more often that he cared to remember. But right now, he would have cheerfully swapped any of these predicaments for his current circumstances and mission, which was all about trying to restrain an irate Katie Wanless as he transported her from the lead SUV to the room in which Max Gris and Slymington would shortly interrogate her. So far, he had made it as far as the lift in the main Gris Corp atrium with his charge, who had by now attracted the attention of the few Gris Corp employees who were still around in the wee small hours with her shouting, kicking and screaming. The mini-crowd, which was more of a huddle, really, stopped in their tracks, one by one, to watch the spectacle.

All in all, the journey was not not going well and Grunk's legendary patience was wearing thin.

"Miss Wanless…" he grunted, as Katie thrashed and kicked with renewed vigour.

An elbow to his ribs. Again.

"… it would be better…"

Scratching down his forearms. The lift doors opened.

"… for all of us…"

A heel to his left kneecap. Grunk bundled himself and Katie into the glass lift, followed by a further two of his men. He had chosen the one with the frosted glass to try to screen what was going on from onlookers. It didn't work. Katie's yelling and screaming was reverberating around the vast Gris Corp atrium as the lift doors closed.

"… if you would stop…" Teeth biting Grunk's left shoulder.

The small huddle of employees watched as the lift sailed its way upwards, with a large, blurred, tall figure, dressed entirely in black, trying to keep a smaller bundle of thrashing arms and legs under some sort of control.

"… behaving like a deranged octopus…"

One of the ground-based security detail grunted at the huddle to disperse and "get back to work", and the employees reluctantly did so, with the sounds of shouting becoming more distant and muffled as the lift headed skywards.

The lift jolted to a halt. Katie, who had paused her shouting and screaming just long enough to land a full-on bite on Grunk, now resumed it with even more vigour.

"Let me out of here, you ape!"

"As you wish," grunted Grunk, as the lift doors opened.

This last comment caused Katie a moment of confusion – which was just long enough for Grunk to tighten his hold on her and bodily carry her along the corridor to the secondary meeting room.

"Where are you taking me? Put me down! Did you hear me? I said PUT ME DOWN!"

One of Grunk's two helpers flashed the card to open the door to the room, and Katie Wanless at last got what she wanted as Grunk deposited her into one of the executive chairs in the room.

"With pleasure," he muttered.

Katie paused for a moment to take in her new surroundings, which were, like most of the building, mainly made of glass and futuristic in their design. But still uber-corporate.

"Where am I? What is this place? I want out of here."

She made to stand up.

Grunk stood in front of her.

"Miss Wanless, that would be most unwise. Sit down," instructed Grunk.

"The hell I will. Get out of my way," shouted Katie as she again began to lever herself upwards.

"SIT. DOWN. NOW," bellowed Grunk.

Katie looked at the Head of Gris Corp's security detail, then went silent and meekly sank back slowly into her chair. Grunk often had that effect on people.

The door to the room opened again and in walked Slymington.

"Ah, Grunk, I see our guest has arrived," he intoned flatly, "though I did hear her from quite some distance away."

If this was Slymington's attempt at humour, Grunk wasn't smiling. Katie stared at the thin, pale-faced, balding, late middle-aged man wearing the dark two-piece suit, complete with white shirt and black tie, who had entered the room and recovered her voice.

"Who the hell are you?"

Slymington paused for a moment to consider his response to this question and opted to open with a measure of sarcasm.

"How charming for one so young. You can call me Mr Slymington," replied her new host.

Katie looked at Slymington and snorted. She wiped her sleeve across her face to remove some of the slavers and snotters from it. And then threw her face into a sulk.

Slymington, unsurprisingly, was unmoved by this attempted display of teenage petulance.

"You are probably wondering why you've been brought here," he stated.

Katie gave him a look of pure sullenness and snorted. Again.

"Well, no matter. I shall tell you anyway. You have a younger brother. Jack, I believe," Slymington left the sentence hanging, as though half-finished, in mid-air.

Katie looked up, despite herself. She sat up slightly in the chair and half-shrugged.

"Yeah, what about him?"

"We are most concerned to find him as soon as we can." Slymington was staring at her, boring into her with his cold, dark eyes. He could see that this had the desired effect as Katie's shoulders involuntarily shuddered.

Katie looked up at him.

"Why?"

"Miss Wanless, we have brought you here for your own protection. So that the media cannot get hold of you or cause you any... *difficulties,*" said Slymington.

Katie stared straight back at Slymington.

"You've lost me, Slimeyman," she spat the words at him.

Slymington ignored the attempted insult.

"You may be aware that your younger brother was playing our global game, Apotheosis."

There was a flinch of recognition from Katie.

"Oh yeah, that stupid thing," she said disdainfully and shrugged her shoulders again.

Slymington continued, "But what you may not be aware of is that he has won the game, along with his young friend." He waited for the words to land on their intended target.

Katie opened her mouth as though she was going to come out with another smart remark, but then closed it again and merely shrugged once more.

Undeterred, Slymington pressed on.

"This makes him very important to us here at Gris Corp."

He stepped towards Katie and bent forwards slightly. As he did so, Grunk also moved one pace closer to the back of Katie's chair.

"Do you know where Jack is?" asked Slymington.

Katie stared at the floor, keeping her gaze fixed on a particular spot in the corner of the room, and said nothing.

"Miss Wanless, it really is for his own good. Now, I shall ask you again. *Where* is your brother?"

Katie continued to stare at the same spot in the corner of the room and remained silent.

"Miss Wanless, we can do this the easy way or the very much more laborious way, but please understand one thing: we shall get an answer out of you before we are done," said Slymington.

With this, Grunk took another step forward and bumped the back of Katie's chair. She jumped and looked round at him.

"Tell Mr Slymington where your brother is," instructed Grunk.

Katie turned back around, returned her gaze to the same place as previously in the corner of the room, before looking up defiantly at Slymington.

"I don't know," she said finally. "He left the house this morning to go sledging with his friend and I haven't seen either of them since."

She turned halfway around to look at Grunk again.

"Happy now?" she said sarcastically.

"Ecstatic," said Grunk, replying in kind.

The door to the room swooshed open and there, framed in the glass doorway, stood Max Gris. She flashed an initial smile in Katie's general direction, which vanished almost as immediately as it had appeared as she addressed Slymington and Grunk.

"So, this is her, is it?" asked Gris, eyeing Katie up and down. "Too old. Pity, she might have come in useful for Project Drake. As it is, we still need someone younger."

"She may have information concerning her brother," offered Slymington.

"Well, what have you got out of her so far?" asked Gris.

"Very little that's of any use," replied Slymington.

"Typical," said Gris. "She looks like just the sort of spoilt brat who…"

Katie stood up from her chair and erupted.

"Would you stop talking as though I'm not even here? I'm not old – I'm only 16," she spluttered. "And who the hell are you, anyway?"

Gris smiled one of her finest fake smiles as Grunk forced Katie back into the chair. The smile then morphed into a derisive laugh.

"Who the hell am I?" repeated Gris. "Look around you, little madam, and you'll understand *exactly* who the hell I am."

"This is Ms Gris to you, young lady," said Slymington.

"Thanks, Slimey," grinned Gris, as she turned on Katie. "Typical overindulged teenage brat. Well, my dear, I have some breaking news for you: you are of utterly no use to us other than for one purpose - as bait, to lure in your baby brother, his little friend and their *pet*."

Katie looked at Max Gris in disbelief. "You're mad. You've kidnapped me and brought me here against my will. I'm going to go to the police, the media and everyone and tell them what you've done."

The smile vanished from Gris's face once again.

"Oh, I don't think so, bratfink. You're not going *anywhere* until we've located your brother and his little friends," said Gris.

"What are you even talking about?" exploded Katie. "Friends? He has one friend with him and I told old Skeletonface over there that they both went sledging this morning and I haven't seen them since! Now, LET. ME. GO!"

Katie screamed the last sentence, though more in hope than in any expectation.

"Pathetic," said Gris with complete disdain. "You, my dear, are going nowhere – and it's high time you calmed down and had a little rest." She nodded at Slymington and Grunk. Slymington walked over to one of the built-in control panels in the wall of the room and punched it. Part of the wall slid back and revealed a small medicine cabinet. He reached in carefully and brought out a small metal device which looked like a cross between a gun and an industrial stapler. He had also picked up a small phial containing some clear fluid and fitted it carefully into the metal device.

"What are you doing? What's that?" shouted Katie.

Grunk held Katie's arms to pin her to the chair as she struggled and lashed out.

"Enjoy your rest, my dear," said Gris as she made to exit the room. "And let us hope that when you wake up, you'll be in a far better mood and much, much more co-operative."

Gris closed the door behind her in time to hear Katie's screams becoming muffled before they suddenly abated. She smiled and walked down the corridor to a room at the far end. Stopping outside it, she pressed a sequence of buttons and the viewing panel in the door slid back. She saw Nick Auld look up from the bunk where he was resting.

"Ah good, Nicky, just checking that you're chillaxing," said Gris. "Excellent idea. I'd definitely get some more sleep if I were you. You've a big couple of days coming up."

Before Auld could reply, Gris hit another button to close the viewing panel. After all, what would be the point of any further conversation, anyway? Unless, of course, it was all about her and her impending glory.

CHAPTER THIRTY-NINE

"Should we try it again?" asked Jack, pointing to the buzzer on the exterior of one of the city's grander Georgian buildings, long since converted into several spacious flats.

"Patience, Jack. He'll answer in a minute or two. It is rather late, after all," replied Merryweather.

Tom looked over at his friend. He could see that the normal cheerfulness that exuded from Jack's face – and most especially whenever there were 'snackables' to hand – had been replaced by a serious look which occasionally morphed into more of a deep frown. His smiles and grins had been temporarily expunged by worrying about his sister. Tom was worried about her, too, and rather more than he cared to admit, even to himself.

He glanced down at his watch. At least it was still working, unlike every other piece of technology he owned. It was nearing 1 o'clock in the morning. No wonder he felt tired. Another few seconds passed and then there was a crackle on the intercom.

"Hello, who is it?" asked an older sounding man's voice.

"Atticus, it's me. Can you let me in, please? I need to speak to you," replied Merryweather.

"Octavia? What on earth are you doing here at this hour?" came the reply.

"It's rather… urgent. I'll explain all to you face to face."

There was a brief pause.

"Well, I suppose you'd better come up then," said the man's voice and there was a buzz and a click of the external door to the house opening.

Merryweather turned to the two boys.

"Now, whatever happens, you let me do all the talking. Understood?"

Tom and Jack nodded their assent as the three of them entered the communal hallway and made their way up the two flights of stairs to the top floor of the building. There, waiting for them at the doorway of the one flat on that level, stood an older man Tom recognised from the evening of his maths lesson earlier that week.

"Atticus," said Merryweather, by way of greeting as they reached his doorway.

"Octavia," replied Atticus Sharp, "and who might these two young gentlemen be?"

"You may remember Tom from the other evening, my courtesy nephew and maths tutee. And this is his friend, Jack," said Merryweather.

"Ah, yes. Well, good evening, Tom and Jack. Or should I say, good morning," said Sharp. "Come in." He motioned the three of them to enter the flat.

After dispensing with their coats and other outer garments, Sharp invited them through to his rather large and ornate living room. Tom noticed a grand piano in one corner, a fire which was now mere embers in the hearth and an enormous Christmas tree, festooned with lights, standing proudly next to one of the many imposingly tall windows. There were random candles burning all around the room, which added to its general atmosphere of being warm yet peaceful, the whole ambience being laced with the quiet of the wee small hours, with only the metronomic ticking of an old grandfather clock interrupting the silence.

"Battery powered," said Sharp as Tom realised that he had seen him gazing at the lights on the tree. "Which is just as well," he continued, "given all the power cuts we've had."

Sharp turned to the three of them and asked, "Now, would any of you care for a drink?"

"Boys?" asked Merryweather.

Tom and Jack both replied, declining the offer, as did Merryweather, at which point Sharp invited the three of them to take a seat and then did so himself, though he sat rather upright in one of the two very large leather upholstered chairs which were on either side of the fire. Tom noticed a half-read hardback book draped over the arm of the chair furthest away from the fireplace and thought this made him look as though he was about to read them a story; as it was, Sharp started asking them questions.

"Well, Octavia, what brings you here of all places on such a night as this? And so close to Christmas, too?"

Tom could see his aunt shifting around a little on the other leather chair, which was opposite Sharp's. She looked ill at ease as she spoke.

"Atticus, we have stumbled across a *situation*," she began, "and we need outside help – which is why we are here."

Tom could see Atticus Sharp raise his left eyebrow and lean forward ever so slightly.

"What sort of *situation?*" he asked.

"That's the thing. It's rather hard to explain – and in many respects, it may be better for you if you know nothing further," replied Merryweather.

"I see," said Sharp, even though to Tom it looked as though his face was conveying precisely the opposite meaning.

"And this *situation*," he continued, "is it serious?"

"Very," shot back Merryweather instantaneously.

"Does it involve all three of you?" asked Sharp. "I had noticed that these two young gentlemen were a little on the young side to be students just yet, even though at my advanced age, all students now look very young to me."

"It does involve all three of us," said Merryweather, "and…"

"Yes?" queried Sharp. The raised eyebrow again.

"And…" Merryweather closed her eyes as she completed the sentence, "Nicky."

"Auld?" asked Sharp. "What on earth has he done now?"

"It's the Gris Corp work," said Merryweather, with a hint of resignation.

Sharp leapt up and out of his chair as though it had suddenly become red hot.

"I knew it!" he exclaimed, as he began pacing around the room. "I warned him – and you – that it wasn't a good idea to work with that organisation. What's happened? What's he done?"

"You may have warned him, but you didn't stop him," said Merryweather ruefully.

"Nor did you, Octavia," snapped Sharp.

Merryweather nodded.

"As it goes, quite a lot has happened," she said, "albeit we don't know the full extent of Nicky's involvement as yet."

Tom could see that Atticus Sharp was looking more and more pensive as he continued to pace up and down the room.

"Go on," said Sharp.

"I think Nicky may be in trouble," said Merryweather.

"What kind of trouble? How serious is it?" asked Sharp.

"I don't know yet," replied Merryweather.

"Where is he now?" asked Sharp.

"I don't know," said Merryweather. "We went to his office and his house and he wasn't there. What's worse," she continued, "they had both been ransacked – burgled – by the looks of things."

"What?" said Sharp. His tone was now cold.

Merryweather nodded.

She leant forward in her chair and looked at Sharp, imploringly.

"Atticus, I need a favour. A huge favour. With no questions asked. I... I mean, *we* need to check on something."

"Go on," said Sharp coolly.

Merryweather took a deep breath.

"I need access to the Hidden Archive at the university," she said. Tom could see she was staring intently at Sharp.

Atticus Sharp stopped mid-pace and then gave a half-laugh, half snort.

"Impossible. There is officially no such place. And even if there was, you know that there is absolutely no way that you could ever legitimately be granted access," he stated flatly.

"Oh, Atticus, please... let's not go through this pretence. We both know it exists and we also both know that I wouldn't be asking for access unless it was in extremis – and I can assure you that we are very much *in extremis* right now, so to whom do I have to speak in order to gain access? If it's not you, then who is it? We have no time to waste. Please..." said Merryweather. Her tone was urgent now.

"Octavia, even if this *archive* existed - which it officially doesn't - and even if I did somehow have access to it, you know how the university works as well as anybody. How on earth would you expect to be granted access at such short notice? And can I also point out that it is gone one in the morning, on a weekend, amidst chaos caused by an unprecedented solar storm that's knocked out most of the globe? Oh yes, and it's two days before Christmas and the university is now closed for the holidays, anyway," said Sharp. Tom thought his tone sounded as though he was drawing the discussion to a close.

There was an awkward silence which persisted for what felt to Tom like minutes, but which was only a few tens of seconds. He hated it when grown-ups argued – he wasn't used to it - but he especially hated it when he only partially understood whatever it was they were arguing about.

Tom could see that Jack was also becoming agitated about the way in which the conversation between Merryweather and Sharp was progressing and was squirming about in his seat. After what seemed like an interminable pause, Tom heard his aunt sigh before she began the next stage of her argument.

"Atticus, we have known each other for how long?" asked Merryweather.

Sharp stood still, considered the question for a moment, then gave a half-shrug and said, "It must be almost thirty years now, I suppose."

"And in all of that time, have I *once* ever asked you about anything like this or requested this level of favour?" asked Merryweather.

The question hung in the air, awaiting a response.

"Well, have I?" asked Merryweather again, with even more urgency.

Tom could see Sharp close his eyes, sigh, slump his shoulders, and shake his head as he replied.

"No. No, you haven't."

"So, what do you deduce from the fact that I am now making such a request of you in the circumstances which you have so accurately described and yes, indeed, two days before Christmas?"

Sharp walked back over to his chair and sat down; this time perched on its edge.

"That this *situation* which you have mentioned must be very serious indeed," he said, "and I appreciate you would not have made such a request of me lightly, but… you must understand that I am not in a position to grant you *safe and legitimate* access to this place which, I might add, even if it were to exist officially, is not what you think it is at all."

Tom could see his aunt's face hardening.

"We don't need *safe or legitimate* access to it; we just need access," she said.

His aunt now had a tone in her voice which was scaring Tom.

"Octavia, I cannot…"

"Atticus, you *must* give us access."

"No," said Sharp firmly. "I cannot and that is final."

Tom saw him bend his head slightly forward and run his fingers through his thick, black hair before he looked up at Merryweather once again.

"It is simply forbidden, Octavia. If I could change that to help you, then I would, but I cannot," said Sharp. He adopted a kindlier look.

"Besides, what could possibly be *so* serious that you would even make such a request in the first place? What is it that you cannot or will not tell me?" he asked.

Tom saw his aunt, sitting there in silence, her face impassive. It was as though she wanted to say something further to Sharp, but that she could not quite bring herself to do so.

Sharp persisted. "Can you not go to the police about any of this?"

"No," said Merryweather, curtly. Tom could see his aunt had gone red in the face. This did not bode well.

He looked towards Jack. For several minutes, Tom had been aware that Jack had been fidgeting on the couch, growing more and more agitated with each exchange between Merryweather and Sharp. He now shot Jack a look. Jack raised his eyebrows back at him. Tom recognised his friend's growing anxiety and shook his head slightly at him. Jack raised his eyebrows even more. He looked as though he was about to burst. Tom mouthed a 'no' at him. Jack was mouthing a complete sentence back at Tom, who was trying to interpret it, when he heard Sharp address the pair of them.

"Are you all right here, lads?" asked Sharp.

Jack was now shifting around uncomfortably in his seat for all he was worth.

"S'pose," he mumbled, then paused before continuing, "it's just… it's just… well, it's my sis…"

Tom stood up and spoke loudly over Jack.

"We have a problem with a dragon," he blurted out.

The entire company fell silent, and only the steady tick-tock of the grandfather clock punctuated the air.

Sharp picked up a glass tumbler that had been resting on a side table by his chair and took a sip from it. He put the glass down slowly and deliberately on the table as he addressed Tom.

"A what?"

"Um, a dragon," mumbled Tom, as he sat back down on the sofa. He saw both Jack and Merryweather staring at him, open-mouthed.

Sharp stared into the middle distance and considered this new information for several moments.

"A dragon?" he asked Tom.

"Yes," replied Tom.

"I see," said Sharp as he rose from his chair and paced around the room once more. "Well, that would certainly constitute a situation of the most serious variety," he mused.

"Atticus, I can explain," began Merryweather.

Sharp held up his right hand as though to halt her words mid-sentence. Merryweather fell silent at the sight of this gesture.

"Do not utter one more word. Any of you," he instructed. He walked over to the fireplace and stood next to it. Tom noticed that Sharp was looking at an extravagantly decorated, ancient wooden box which sat to the right of centre on top of the mantlepiece. He stared at it for several moments.

"It's a strange time, this time in the morning," began Sharp. "One can often see things that aren't really there; the imagination plays tricks on itself; the mind can be so overtired and in need of rest that it ventures down some mental alleyways that are full of dark imaginings. It is so quiet and yet, you can hear sounds that suggest that old buildings are almost alive, or mishear things that were never really said…"

Sharp was standing, staring intently at the box on the mantlepiece now.

"Yes, so silent in the wee small hours, only the steady beat of the old grandfather clock to break the silence now," he said. "Do you know I wind that old clock up once every evening?"

He gently rapped the wooden box in front of him.

"But here's the thing, I never check it from one evening to the next, ergo I would never know if anything occurred to it - or anything that may be within it - from one evening to the next…"

The grandfather clock's ticking now seemed louder than before to Tom.

"Atticus, I swear…" began Merryweather.

Sharp once again held up his right hand to show his preference for silence. He turned to face the three of them.

"Do not, any of you, utter one word more about any of this. Please. For all our sakes," instructed Sharp.

Merryweather looked at him.

"Can we stay here this evening?" she asked.

"Of course," said Sharp. "I'll show you to the spare room and get some bedding sorted for the two boys. Now, the other spare bedroom is out of commission at the moment, so are you two okay sleeping in here this evening?"

Tom and Jack nodded their assent.

"Good," smiled Sharp. He disappeared off into the inner reaches of the flat with Merryweather to grab some bedding, leaving Tom and Jack alone in the living room.

"What on earth was all that about?" asked Jack.

"Dunno, grown-up stuff. They always make it complicated," said Tom. "Are you okay?" he asked Jack.

Jack shrugged.

"I'll take that as a no then," said Tom. He looked at his friend and put his hand on his shoulder. "Don't worry, we'll get her back."

Jack nodded as he pulled away, aiming a "shurrup" in Tom's direction.

Sharp and Merryweather returned with pillows and sleeping bags.

"It's not quite luxury hotel level, but I'm sure you two will manage okay with this lot," said Sharp, nodding to the pile of improvised bedding he had dumped on the sofa. He walked over to the fireplace and placed a fireguard in front of the now darkened hearth.

"Right, I shall bid goodnight to you all and wish you a good night's sleep. Until the morrow," said Sharp as he exited the room.

Merryweather, Tom and Jack wished him a goodnight in return.

Merryweather waited for several moments and then walked over to the mantlepiece and reached into the box.

"Auntieprof, what are you doing?" asked Tom, looking bemused.

Merryweather scrabbled inside the box before producing a key from its innards.

"I, young Thomas, unless I am very much mistaken, am acquiring our access to the Hidden Archive," replied Merryweather.

"I don't understand," said Jack.

"You don't need to, Jack," said Merryweather, "and indeed, in many respects, it is best that you never do."

She walked over to the grandfather clock, still keeping time with its clockwork efficiency at this early hour. Merryweather placed the key in the front panel of the clock and turned it.

"You see, boys, the thing about Atticus – and this is something one learns about him only by having known him for decades – is that he rarely speaks directly about certain topics – or indeed about anything much at all."

Merryweather prised the panel open until it gave a loud clunk.

"But," grinned Merryweather, "he does provide clues, if you are generally alert enough and paying attention to the specifics... Tom, come and help me with this." She motioned Tom over.

"I'm going to hold this door open; it's spring-loaded. I need you to reach in there and scrabble around until you find something. Got that?" asked Merryweather.

"What am I looking for?" asked Tom.

"No idea," said Merryweather, "but you'll know it when you find it. Now, quick as you like, before this door snaps my arm off."

Tom did as he was told and reached into the dark recesses of the clock's innards, fumbling and fishing around to see if he could feel something – anything – that shouldn't be there.

"Any luck yet?" asked Merryweather.

"No, there doesn't seem to be anything in here... wait..." said Tom, "there's something right at the very top here..."

Tom had reached into the very top of the clock's interior with his fingertips and could feel something cold and metal. He tried to pull it at first, but it didn't move much. With more fumbling around, he worked out that it was wedged into the side of the clock somehow and then he tried sliding it first towards the ground, before – successfully – making it move by sliding the object towards the top of the clock.

There was a thump as the metal object fell from its location and into the base of the clock. Tom reached down and fished it out: a long, thin brass box.

He stood in front of Merryweather, holding the box. She let the door go and it snapped shut with another loud clunk.

"What is it?" asked Jack, looking at the box.

"I'm not sure," said Merryweather, "but it appears to have an inscription on it and, unless I'm much mistaken, it also has some sort of mechanism within it."

"*Claustris reclusistis*," said Tom, slowly reading out the inscription.

"Cloisters," translated Merryweather. She spoke the word softly. "That's where it must be within the university."

Tom was fiddling with the box, trying to open it.

"There are numbered dials, four of them. Must be an entrance code or something. How on earth are we supposed to work that out?" he asked, looking at his aunt.

Merryweather thought for a moment.

"Try turning the dials to one, four, five and one," she said to Tom.

Tom spun the dials until the requisite numbers aligned in the centre of each row. As he clicked the final number one into place, there was a short, sharp clicking noise, followed by a whirring as the interior of the long, thin brass box came to life. After a couple of seconds, there was a further click as the top of the box magically separated by a fraction of a millimetre from its body.

Tom looked at his aunt in wonder.

"It worked!"

"The year in which the university was founded," said Merryweather with a big grin. "Lucky guess."

Tom gingerly opened the lid of the box to reveal its hollow interior and there, nestled in its base, lay two keys, one long and rather thin; the other, more solid and squat. Both appeared to be very old and somewhat rusted. Merryweather peered into the box, picked out the keys, and held them up, one in each hand.

"Well then," she said, "we know where we're going tomorrow morning: to find whatever it is that these two keys unlock. Starting at the university cloisters. But for now, we sleep."

CHAPTER FORTY

Max Gris was standing in the middle of what had been to her, until the events of the previous evening, merely an old ruin that she had been prevented from demolishing by the local planning authority several years previously when, as she recalled, she had simultaneously been lavishing millions on building the new Gris Corp HQ, including the creation of the adjoining science park, complete with manicured grounds and futuristic sculptures.

Now, however, the aforesaid ruin had been transformed into a building site, with Gris Corp employees frantically clearing up the more obvious piles of rubble and general detritus which had accumulated after years of neglect, whilst yet more Gris Corp employees began reconstructing the interior of the part-built temporary altar which they had hastily dismantled upon receiving fresh instructions from Slymington a couple of hours previously.

It pleased Gris greatly to see all these people scurrying around like worker ants, wearing their hi-vis jackets and hardhats, as they put her latest plans into effect. Even at this late stage of the night, with it being well past midnight and now into the wee small hours of Sunday morning, she felt the glow of satisfaction growing within her, that at long last, her dream was within touching distance.

Slymington joined her as she walked around the interior of the ancient building (or 'heap', as Gris herself had hitherto referred to it) that she now knew to be the Cathedral of the Others. Gris smiled a satisfied smile, knowing that the building was hers; the work to construct the interior in readiness for the ceremony was on track and that the final minor difficulty which her plans had encountered would soon be dealt with.

"Ah Slimy," she beamed, "good of you to join me. What news do you have of our young friends and their overgrown helpers?"

"I have taken the necessary steps to find them and lure them to us," replied Slymington, "and if that doesn't work, we will flush them out and *procure* them."

Most other human beings hearing the last part of that sentence would have involuntarily shuddered at its content, but Max Gris, as she often reminded others (and herself when no one else was around), was no ordinary human being.

"Good," said Gris in her best matter-of-fact manner. "I expect no more failures. I've waited too long for this moment to allow a couple of kids to jeopardise it."

"I understand, ma'am," said Slymington.

Gris took a couple of steps forward and paused, gazing at the work that was being undertaken in front of her, before she turned to Slymington once more.

"Impressive, isn't it? From a derelict pile of rubble to this," Gris nodded towards the scores of Gris Corp workers, scurrying around all over the ruined church, "and all in a matter of a few hours."

"Slimey, we are so close to this now, my father's dream, the dream he worked for all his life, only never to see it realised. The dream that I am now going to make reality," Gris said as she clenched her teeth together and her whole body tensed.

Slymington was, as ever, unmoved by his boss's display of emotion. It was his job to remain rational at all times, but given his temperament and general demeanour, this wasn't a huge stretch for him. He contrived to make the correct noises in reply.

"I know, ma'am. It was a tragedy that your father did not live to see this moment. He would have been very proud of you, of all you have accomplished, but especially, for nearing the ultimate prize," intoned Slymington.

"I hope so," said Gris. Her smile had gone, to be replaced by a frown as she continued.

"Tell me again what he told you when you first discovered the legend."

"I recall the day clearly, as though it were yesterday," began Slymington. "Ever since I had begun working for him, all those years ago, your father had always had an interest in collecting and especially, in those antiquities connected to what might be supposed by some to be the stuff of myth and legend. As his business grew bigger, on its way to becoming the empire it is now, he pursued this specific interest with ever more assiduousness and vigour. He would attend selective auctions to bid for items that were of note and visit the more circumspect dealers of such collectibles whenever he was on his travels."

Gris was now hanging on Slymington's every word, as though this was the first time she had heard this story, even though, in the several years since her father had passed away, she had heard it at least a dozen times – maybe more.

"Over time, an awareness of his interest in objects of antiquity became more widely known amongst those who dealt in such things, which led to two notable developments. One, that whenever he pursued such items, he would find that their price often became artificially inflated as soon as his name was mentioned; he and I soon worked around that particular problem without too much difficulty. Our interest simply became ever more anonymous and discreet. However, the second development was much more useful: in time, the dealers of such collectibles started approaching your father whenever objects which they believed could be of interest entered their orbit." Slymington paused.

"Go on," said Gris.

"A few years before he passed away, he was approached by an older gentleman with whom he had never previously had any dealings. The initial approach was very tentative, merely enquiring as to whether your father would have any interest in some ancient scrolls which purported to contain within them a legend concerning St Nicholas, or, as he has become better known to us in modern times, Santa Claus."

"And he had never met this person before?" asked Gris.

"Never," replied Slymington, "but your father's interest was piqued. After all, he was, even back then, the world's leading toy manufacturer. How could he resist an ancient story about the most legendary toymaker and gift-giver of all?

"As it transpired, he asked me to make the necessary arrangements to indicate to this dealer that we would indeed be interested in having an initial conversation with him about the objects he had in his possession and thus, I did so. It was unusual for your father to become personally involved in such transactions by that stage of his career, but he took a very keen interest in this particular one from the very outset," said Slymington. "It is as though, somehow, he knew…"

"Tell me once more how you brokered the deal," said Gris.

"With pleasure, ma'am. As your father had asked, I set up an initial meeting with the dealer. He was very clear from the outset that he wanted to meet somewhere private but in the open, somewhere anonymous and where there was next to no likelihood of anyone else seeing or overhearing the details of the meeting. Given your father's general approach to circumspection in such matters, this entirely suited him. He even left the choice of location to the gentleman concerned."

"That was very unlike Daddy," said Gris.

"Indeed," said Slymington, "but the very fact that he was so agreeable to the terms of another does perhaps demonstrate how keen he was for that initial meeting to go ahead. As I said, even from the initial contact, your father's full attention had been captured. In the event, arranging the meeting did not prove to be excessively onerous. The gentleman wished to meet outdoors, somewhere private and local, so we organised to meet him here." Slymington gave a sweep of his arm around their current location.

"Of course, this was long before its transformation into the science park that it is today. Back then, it was merely a piece of waste ground with some old, derelict buildings that your father had recently purchased. Crucially, it was uninteresting enough so as not to catch the attention of any passers-by."

"And what happened when you met him again?" asked Gris.

"There, I can only provide you with a second-hand account, I'm afraid," replied Slymington. "When we arrived, the dealer, whom as I mentioned was an older gentleman, white-haired and dressed all in tweed, including his hat, was very insistent that he and your father should discuss the matter at hand one to one, with no other observers. Naturally, I disagreed with such a suggestion and expressed my opinion to your father, but your father dismissed my concerns and assured me that all would be well, so I had to stand and wait – and watch – as your father and the gentleman dealer went for a long stroll in the afternoon sunshine.

"They must have walked and talked together for at least half an hour, often stopping as one of them made a particular point to the other, and when they had concluded their discussion, your father shook hands with the gentleman, which I took to mean that the transaction had been agreed, and then they both walked off, going their separate ways," said Slymington.

"But you asked him what they discussed, right?" asked Gris.

"Yes, of course," replied Slymington.

"And?" asked Gris, looking at Slymington expectantly. Part of her sensed Slymington was almost enjoying retelling this story to her yet again – though, as ever, it was hard to tell because of the default expression on his face of complete impassivity – but the bigger part of her wanted to hear it once more, as though it was some sort of security blanket, a last connection to her father and a simultaneous link to that which was yet to come.

"It took some time and many conversations with your father in order to establish more details of what had transpired," Slymington continued. "He was most reluctant to divulge much of what he and the gentleman dealer had discussed at first, other than the bare details of the transaction upon which they had both agreed. Namely, the gentleman had agreed to part with the scrolls in exchange for a substantial sum of money, but with one condition…"

"It had to be gold," murmured Gris.

"Precisely, ma'am. Gold. The ancient store of value and of timeless wealth. Portable, untraceable and, given the subject matter of the scrolls, rather appropriate, wouldn't you say?"

"Yes, Slimey. I would," agreed Gris.

"However, we are getting ahead of ourselves here," continued Slymington. "After he had imparted the initial details of the deal, your father gradually, over time, revealed a little more about what he and the dealer had spoken about and what the scrolls contained. He told me that the dealer had refused to tell him where he had first acquired the scrolls, only stating that they had been in his family for many, many generations

– and that they were genuine and his to sell. The gentleman agreed that your father could, under strict conditions, test one scroll to establish the veracity of its age, and it was indeed found to be many hundreds of years old when subjected to carbon dating.

"The dealer said something to your father by way of explanation as to why he was selling the scrolls: he had fallen upon hard times in recent years and now wished to retire from his business. He assured your father that this transaction would be his last, but he also had to make sure that the scrolls would be in safe hands as they had the potential – albeit remote – to unleash 'great power', which in the wrong hands would create more problems than it would ever solve." Slymington paused again.

"Ah yes, the *great power*. Or, as I like to refer to it: the prophecy and the ritual," said Gris.

"Indeed, ma'am. Of course, at the outset, the dealer merely hinted at both, claiming that the scrolls contained a legend about how to effect the *return* of St Nicholas – or Santa Claus - himself. I say *return*, but a more accurate description would be to use the word *summons*," noted Slymington. "This, in turn, would bring complete control over Christmas itself."

He continued, "I'm still not sure that I ever heard the entire story from your father, nor if he was told the complete history by the gentleman himself. However, your father did impart that the gentleman explained that the scrolls, as well as outlining the legend of St Nicholas, and the prophecy of his return to this realm, also provided a sort of map of the whereabouts of those of his artefacts – or *relics* – required in order to undertake the ritual and fulfil the prophecy. However, there were… certain aspects, shall we say, which were not well understood, not even by the dealer himself.

"In part, this was due to the very great age of the scrolls. There was a need both to translate and also to interpret their instructions as to the various locations of the artefacts. Your father soon had people translating them, but the interpretation piece proved somewhat more difficult. And then, there were the other aspects of the prophecy which proved even more puzzling," said Slymington. "Namely, those parts which spoke of immortality upon the return of the saint and also some wording regarding a child of light being required for the ritual successfully to fulfil the prophecy."

"Ah yes, that's the trouble with the ancients," grinned Gris. "They never speak clearly enough down the centuries."

"Quite, ma'am. And well, the rest you know," said Slymington. "Your father brought in many experts to narrow down the locations of the ancient artefacts, but without success. It was always as though something else was missing and then, well..."

"And then, one day, he collapsed in his office and died," stated Gris, matter-of-factly, though her bottom lip was trembling slightly, and her eyes were starting to burn. She turned to face Slymington, her eyes widening and her scary smile returning.

"Daddy died before he could achieve his dream," stated Gris quietly. "The return of Santa Claus himself, total control over Christmas... and immortality."

Her voice grew louder and more determined. "But I shall succeed where he failed. I *shall* control Santa Claus *and* Christmas and I shall never *ever* die."

Slymington nodded at this declaration in a slightly unenthusiastic manner, as though he had heard it all before.

"We are within touching distance of it now, Slimey. Can't you sense it?" asked Gris. She turned away and stared into the middle distance. Around the pair of them, the clamour and hubbub of the ongoing construction continued. Gris walked towards the altar, motioning Slymington to accompany her. She had snapped back to the present moment and to the business at hand.

"They're going to have to work at this through the night and tomorrow if we're going to be ready for dusk on Christmas Eve. We do not have the time to indulge any more mistakes. Do they understand this?" Gris asked Slymington.

"I have made them acutely aware of the proximity of the deadline, ma'am, and that they cannot miss it under *any* circumstances," he replied.

"Good. And what of the other loose ends?" asked Gris. "Did you dispatch our French friend?"

"I gave him his agreed remuneration, ma'am – after we had had him patched up," said Slymington.

"Hmmm, yes, nasty business," said Gris, sounding for a moment as though she might be about to express some sympathy. "Still, he was very well paid for what he did. Do you think we can rely on him to keep his mouth shut?"

"I have every confidence that we can rely entirely on his discretion," replied Slymington. "His name does him justice in that respect."

Gris looked at Slymington. She was frowning. A deep frown.

"And you are quite sure that there have been no indications that any of the churches have realised that their relics are missing?" she asked.

"Nothing at all, ma'am – and if I may, whilst the solar storm has obviously been extremely disruptive in very many respects, this is one instance where it may actually have been a beneficial distraction. The churches will all have had rather more pressing matters to attend to in the short-term, not least the panic of the faithful. Indeed, I doubt if any of them will have had the time to realise that anything is even missing as of yet."

Gris's frown scrunched into a different, more pensive gaze.

"All of which is good," she noted. "However, they will eventually notice, and you can be sure that once the news is out about the first one which figures out its relics are gone, the rest will soon check on theirs, too."

"I realise that, ma'am, which is why we are pressing on apace, both with the preparations for the ceremony," said Slymington, looking towards the beginnings of the chamber that was taking shape in front of the pair of them, "and also hunting down the two young annoyances and their helper."

"And the pet," interjected Gris. "Don't forget that monstrosity that they brought with them."

She turned towards Slymington, grinning and her dark eyes gleaming.

"I want them all found and brought in, Slimey. We need those relics they stole to make the whole ceremony work properly.

"And I want that… *thing…* whatever it is, to be captured and put on display here, once we have control of Santa and Christmas. It can be our new foremost visitor attraction, suitably tranquilised, of course. We don't want any more nasty accidents such as the one which befell our recently departed French friend."

Gris was on a roll now (some people would simply have called it a rant) and Slymington stood, robotic as ever as she expanded on her plans.

"That monster will form part of the centrepiece in our new global empire, the one in which we control Christmas itself. It will be our gift to the world – for a suitable entrance fee obviously – a living fantasy, a relic from fairy tales made real – and that's before we chuck in Santa himself."

"I am sure the entire world will pay attention, ma'am," said Slymington.

"Oh, they will, Slimey, don't you worry. That dragon will be our marker of credibility: once we've proved what it is, no one will doubt us when we produce old Saint Nick to the watching masses."

"And do you wanna know the best bit?" asked Gris.

"Go on, ma'am," replied Slymington.

"I will preside over this – all of this – for all of eternity. Every single child growing up all over the world shall associate the name Gris with Christmas forevermore after tomorrow. There won't be any more letters to Santa, because Santa will work for me!"

Gris paused for breath, her eyes wide open and shining at the thought of the future that was now agonisingly, tantalisingly within reach.

"We have one shot at this, Slimey," she said, lowering her voice to emphasise the point. "All those churches will eventually notice what is missing and what we have of theirs – and doubtless soon. You must find those brats and the relics they grabbed and do whatever it takes to bring them here. Understood?"

"Yes ma'am," replied Slymington. "We have the sister of one of them. That should be bait enough, but even if it isn't, we have everywhere they could go being watched 24/7. We will have them soon enough."

"Good, get to it. The sooner we have them – and their pet – here in our safe custody, the better," said Gris. She turned to look at the altar, threw her cape over her shoulder and gave a derisory snort.

"No two brats are going to stop my plan now," she said in her iciest tone. "Soon, Christmas will be all mine!"

CHAPTER FORTY-ONE

It was still dark as Tom clicked the front door of Atticus Sharp's building shut behind him. Merryweather had woken him and Jack and told the pair of them to get ready to leave, and quickly. The two boys had done as instructed, rolling up their bedding into a heap in Sharp's living room. There had been no time for goodbyes. Nor breakfast.

Tom was still in a half-awake state as he climbed into the back of Merryweather's Defender once more. It was dark and cold (or, as Jack had just pointed out, "utterly Baltic"). The deep snow had a thick crust of ice on it now and was crunching underfoot and Tom, as well as not having had enough sleep, was hungry.

And if he was hungry, this would mean that Jack was ravenous. Which didn't take long to manifest itself.

"Prof, I was wondering," began Jack.

They were driving through the dark, empty city streets.

"Yes, what is it?" asked Merryweather.

Tom knew what was coming next.

"Do you think... I mean, would it be possible... if we saw somewhere convenient en route... to maybe... pause for a few seconds and obtain some snackables?" Jack ended the sentence with an optimistic tone.

"No time to stop, Jack," replied Merryweather, dashing his hopes immediately. Tom could see her reaching into the glove compartment and grabbing something from within it.

"Here," she said, lobbing over a couple of packages into the back seat. "Something I rustled up earlier. Should tide you both over for the next few hours.

Jack grabbed both packages, then looked at Tom and semi-sheepishly and handed one over. Tom grinned at his friend in the darkness.

"Thanks," he said, and the boys opened their respective packages, an unwrapping that revealed peanut butter and banana sandwiches.

"Might be a bit of an unconventional 'brekkers'," said Merryweather, "but it was the best I could manage in the circumstances. You'll need to share this though," she said as she passed back a water bottle.

"Make sure you take a good swig each. You need to stay hydrated, and it could be a long day ahead."

Tom could see Jack looking at him, whilst stuffing the first sandwich into his mouth.

"What's up?" Tom asked.

Jack shrugged. "Well, it's better than nothing."

Tom laughed at his friend. Always thinking about his stomach and making the best of whatever foodstuffs came to hand.

After several minutes of munching, with Merryweather ploughing on through the snowy streets, they drew nearer to the university.

"Right, we're almost there," she began. "I'm going to park a couple of blocks away from the main entrance and we can walk the last bit. We'll need to be discreet regarding why we're there and we may need to talk our way past the security guard on the gate, so once again, let me…"

"Do the talking," replied boy boys in unison.

Merryweather chuckled. "You're learning," she beamed. "We should be all right if it's the usual fellow. He's been working there for years and knows me well."

She drew the Defender to a halt.

"Right, out you get."

The three of them exited the vehicle and began treading through the snow and up the hill to the main gate of the university, beside which, as Merryweather had forewarned them, was a small cabin occupied by an elderly, cold-looking and somewhat disinterested man, dressed in a uniform and bundled up against the cold.

As they approached, he came out to greet them, breaking into a smile as he recognised Merryweather.

"Hello, Professor Merryweather, and what brings you here at this hour on a Sunday?" asked the guard.

"Hello, Donald. Need to pick up a bit of last-minute research before Christmas. Goodness me, you look frozen. I hope you have a heater in there," replied Merryweather, reaching into her pocket for her pass.

"Certainly do, ma'am – and it's on full blast in this weather. Quite a spell we're having."

The guard spied Merryweather fishing around for her pass.

"No need for that, ma'am. In you go. These two young men helping you on this one?"

"Yes, Donald, this is my nephew, Tom, and his friend, Jack. They've kindly agreed to help me collect a few things."

"Good to see such dedication in a couple of young lads. They must be keen," replied Donald.

"Yes, you could say that. Anyway, we'd best crack on. We don't want to be here too long today," said Merryweather.

"In you all go. Quite right, it's too close to Christmas to be working. Even I'm getting off for the holidays soon."

As the three of them made their way past him, Merryweather wished Donald the guard a Merry Christmas, which was echoed by Tom and Jack, and they walked onwards to the main building of the university.

"We made it through," said Tom.

"Yes," said Merryweather. "Helps if one has been working here forever."

"Where are we going now?" asked Jack.

"To the cloisters, Jack. The entrance to what it is we're looking for is in there somewhere; whatever it is that is unlocked or opened by these two keys. Now, we just need to find it," said Merryweather.

"How will we know what it is?" asked Tom.

"Trial and error, Tom. We will have to make our way systematically around the cloisters – and the quadrangle – until we find it, so look for something with a lock. Or maybe two. Let's split up. We can cover the ground more efficiently that way. Ideally, before it turns fully light," said Merryweather.

The three of them headed off in separate directions. Tom to the left, Jack to the right, and Merryweather straight ahead to the faraway end of the cloisters and the quad.

Tom began pacing along the building, looking for anything bearing a lock of the kind which either key could fit. He could feel the ends of his fingers going numb once again, having only been outside for less than half an hour, and hoped that one of them would find whatever it was they were looking for – and quickly.

The old building's sandstone walls were not yielding any clues as Tom inched his way around them. He glanced over to the opposite side of the quad, where Jack was mirroring the same task with, it appeared, an equal lack of success.

There were a couple of heavy, ornate wooden doors at each end of Tom's patch, and he inspected each one in turn, trying to figure out if either could be a candidate for one of the two keys that they had procured in Sharp's flat, but both had locks which were far too large for either key. Fitting either key into these doors would have been like putting a pea into a drum.

After several minutes of considering each door from every conceivable angle, Tom turned around and retraced his steps along the outer walls once more, scrutinising the walls, windows and doors intently, trying to find something that he had missed on his first pass. It was to no avail. There was nothing he could see which came anywhere close to being a candidate for either of the two keys.

He saw Merryweather crunching her way back towards him, through the cloisters, motioning Jack to come and join her as she did so. The three of them reconvened underneath the archways of the cloisters. The half-light of dawn had given way to the bitterly cold sunshine of a late December morning.

"Well, anything?" asked Merryweather.

"Nothing," replied Tom.

Jack shook his head.

"Hmmm, this could take longer than I had anticipated. It's clearly not going to be anything obvious, so what else could it be? What is it we're missing?" asked Merryweather.

"Could it be something up beyond ground level?" asked Jack.

"Possibly," replied Merryweather.

"Or inside the main building?" asked Tom.

Merryweather sighed.

"Again, that is possible, albeit..." Tom saw his aunt hesitate.

"What is it, Auntieprof?" he asked.

"Well, it's just that if it is something inside the main building, it would have to be very well hidden indeed. I've been around that building for years, studying in it, researching in it, lecturing in it, and I've never seen the likes of anything within it which could fit the bill," said Merryweather.

"No," she continued, "I'm convinced that we are looking for something which is located somewhere on the exterior. Trouble is, I have no idea what it is."

"Or where it is," chimed in Jack.

"Yes, quite," replied Merryweather.

"Let's split up again. Take different sections. Second pair of eyes and all that. Off you go."

And so, this time, Tom took the route his aunt had previously taken, scrunching his way through the ice-encrusted snow towards the far end of the quad. The next half hour proved just as fruitless for the three of them as the previous one had been, and they returned once more to their central rendezvous point underneath the cloisters without success.

"This is most vexing," said Merryweather. "I knew it was always referred to as the Hidden Archive in university folklore, but I didn't appreciate that its entrance would be completely invisible!"

"Should we split up again and cover the last bit we each haven't looked at already?" asked Tom.

"Yes, let's give it another go. Fresh eyes once more," replied Merryweather.

"I hope we find it soon," said Jack. "I'm definitely feeling peckish after all this fresh air. I find I do my best work on a full stomach."

"Don't worry, Jack. There will be more 'snackables' soon," Merryweather reassured him.

Tom rolled his eyes at his friend and gave a wry half-grin.

"Come on, Mr Famished, one more heave and then it'll be time for elevenses."

The three of them split up again, and Tom headed off to his left, to pore over the area which Jack had been inspecting on his first stint. As he walked towards the left side of the quad, Jack shouted at him.

"I might be Mr Famished to you, but every living thing needs fuel, you know."

Tom turned around and shouted back.

"Yes, but some living things need more fuel than oth… oooft."

And then landed in a heap on the snow.

"That's what happens when I don't pay attention to where I'm going," he muttered to himself.

"You all right?" shouted Jack.

"Yeah, nothing broken," Tom shouted back. "Just a bit of a sore one…"

He stopped mid-sentence and stared at the sandstone blocks in front of him, near to ground level. Unlike most of the surrounding aged dark honey-coloured stones, Tom's eye alighted on one block which appeared far ruddier in colour, but that wasn't the only thing that had caught his eye. Something in the very bottom left of this particular block of sandstone was glinting in the weak wintry sunlight and he was fairly sure that it wasn't ice. Lifting himself up off his snowy landing zone, he dusted himself down and scrunched his way towards the stone in question.

Upon reaching the wall containing the stone, he lowered himself down on his haunches and peered at the stone more closely. There, in the lower left-hand corner of the stone, semi-obscured by the surrounding snow, was the source of the glinting: a discoloured metal insert wedged securely into the sandstone block and held in place by several bolts. At its centre, an old and very frozen looking lock.

"Auntieprof, Jack, come and have a look at this," shouted Tom, standing up and motioning towards the other two. Merryweather and Jack scrunched their way back towards him, breathing out clouds as they did so.

"What have you found?" asked Merryweather.

Tom pointed at the solid-looking lock embedded in the stone.

"Well, I never," said Merryweather.

"How did we miss that?" asked Jack.

Tom shrugged. "It wasn't at eye-level. The only reason I spotted it was because I slid on my backside and happened to land in the right spot to see the sunlight glinting off it, else I'd likely have missed it, too."

"Have I ever told you that you're a very observant young man, Tom?" asked Merryweather.

Tom shrugged again.

"Because you are," said Merryweather, as she fished around in her pocket for the two keys, eventually producing the larger of the two.

"This looks like it could be a candidate," she said.

"The lock looks frozen," said Jack.

"Never fear, Jack. I came prepared," said Merryweather, producing a spray can from her pocket. "This will open anything. Borrowed it from Professor Sharp. Thought it might come in handy, given the prevailing conditions. Right, let's give this a go."

Merryweather unleashed a blast of the spray directly at the lock, before handing the key to Tom to insert into the lock. Tom took the key and looked puzzled.

"You found it, so you have first dibs on trying to unlock it," she said.

He squatted down and inserted the key and tried to turn it. Without success.

"Could take a couple of minutes for the spray to take effect," said Merryweather.

After a few moments, she tried another blast of the spray. Jack watched as, once again, Tom inserted the key, but still the lock's mechanism refused to budge.

"Okay," said Merryweather, "one big blast of this stuff and then third time lucky. Are you ready, Tom?" Tom nodded.

Merryweather gave a huge blast of the spray towards the lock until it was drenched. All the ice and snow surrounding it had by now melted.

Tom eased the key into the now dripping lock once more and wiggled it around. This time, there was some give.

"I think I've got it this time," he began as the key twisted in the lock.

"Excellent," said Merryweather. "It may take a couple of turns before something happens. Keep turning it."

Tom did precisely that. On the third turn, there was an almighty clunk from deep inside the wall in which the sandstone was situated and a low, grinding sound began. Tom instinctively stood up quickly and retreated from the wall, joining Merryweather and Jack several steps back from it, as it started to move…

The grinding and clunking continued for several more seconds.

Jack had scrunched his face up.

"That is a bad noise," he exclaimed. "I mean, it really doesn't sound very well," he said, pointing at the wall.

"I suspect that's because whatever is making that noise hasn't been activated for a long time," shouted Merryweather over the growing din. "A very long time."

After several moments, the noise stopped as suddenly as it had begun. There was a pause and then a muffled clanking noise began, growing in volume over several more seconds.

And there, in front of the three seekers of the Hidden Archive, the previously solid wall of sandstone broke into its parts, namely the individual blocks of sandstone, some of which shifted individually inwards and outwards, as though some strong invisible forces were moving them into the building from the outside. Over the next half a minute, half a dozen of the blocks, which were stacked above one another and to the right of the block with the lock in it, moved inwards in unison, creating a gap big enough in the wall for a person to squeeze through.

"What on earth?" murmured Tom.

Around a minute later, all the noises stopped, and there was a clear opening in the wall.

"I believe we have found the entrance," said Merryweather. "Shall we?" she asked as she ushered the boys towards the gap in the wall.

The three of them nosed their way through the gap, one at a time, with Tom leading the way, followed by Jack, and then Merryweather bringing up the rear. Grabbing his torch from his pocket, he flicked it on. He was in some sort of corridor; it was very dark, very dank and was sloping downwards. Tom flashed the light around and about himself and saw that he was standing on a tiny landing, leading down from which was a rough, stone staircase which disappeared into the gloom which lay beyond the beam of his torch.

"Stairs," he said, turning round to Jack and Merryweather. "Mind your step."

Gingerly, Tom inched his way down the stairs. As his left foot landed on the twelfth stair, the clunking noise began again and was accompanied by the grinding sounds the three of them had heard earlier.

Tom turned around, flashing his torch. Behind him, he could see Jack, followed by Merryweather. The three of them were all safely through the gap and on the downward descent.

"Would you get that light out of my face? What's happening?" asked Jack.

"Sounds like the mechanism that opened the door may now be closing it again," said Merryweather.

As she spoke, the grinding ratcheted up to make an even bigger din than it had previously, and then there was an almighty final clunk. Followed by silence.

Merryweather flashed her torch towards the place in the wall where the entrance had been.

"It's closed over," said Merryweather. "Onwards we go then."

After several more minutes of inching their way carefully down the stairs, Tom made to take another step down, only to find that his foot hit level ground.

"Think that was the last of the stairs. We're on the flat now," he said to the other two.

He took a few more steps forward, only to be confronted by a solid stone wall.

"And we've reached a dead end," Tom confirmed, as Jack and Merryweather caught up with him.

"Scan the walls. There must be something here," said Merryweather.

The two boys and Merryweather flashed their respective torches all over the stone walls; their collective efforts revealed they were standing in a tiny, slightly dank, room of some sort.

It was Jack who found the dial mechanism.

Running his torch all over the walls in a zigzag, some would say chaotic, manner, he saw the flash of reflected light which had a golden tinge.

"Got something," he shouted, fixing his beam on the source of the reflection.

The three of them approached the spot on which Jack's torch beam had locked.

"Looks like some sort of wooden panel with a lid or something," said Tom.

"Lift the lid," said Merryweather.

There, underneath the wooden lid, was another series of four dials.

"Oh good, another code to crack," said Jack. "This is worse than school."

"I have a hunch this code may not be too difficult," said Merryweather. "Letters or numbers?"

Tom peered at the four dials in front of him.

"Looks like they're all numbers."

"Okay," replied Merryweather, "try a one on the first dial."

Tom duly moved the first dial to the number one. There was a distinct click as he nudged the digit into place.

"Now, for the next one, put in the number four," instructed Merryweather.

Tom spun the second dial until it showed a four. Again, there was another click.

"Try five for the third dial," said Merryweather.

Again, Tom nudged the dial to a five and a further click followed.

Merryweather was grinning.

"I think my hunch is about to pay off. Try one again for the final dial."

Tom inched the final dial around until the number one slid into place. A last click followed, then a pause of a couple of seconds and a mechanical noise grew louder and louder directly in front of the three of them, producing a muffled echo throughout the corridor.

"Lucky guess – again," said Merryweather with a smile.

The whirring of metal sorted itself into a series of more organised clunks and clicks (and bangs and clatters) and once again, the previously solid wall directly in front of them started moving inwards, creating a gap as it did so. A gap which was – again – just sufficiently large for someone to squeeze through.

"Success," cried Merryweather.

Tom already had the beam of his torch fixed on the gap and, as the mechanical whirring and clunking came to a halt, was the first to step through, followed by Merryweather and then Jack. As Tom flashed his torch around the walls, it picked out what looked like a large and deep cavern, constructed from the same sandstone with which the rest of the main university building had been built, but it had been blackened by time. The space smelt somewhat musty, and it looked and felt like a place from a bygone age and also, Tom thought, as though no other living soul had been anywhere near it for a very long time.

Tom heard a click behind him and then a low, buzzing noise, which began overhead and stretched off into the distance. The darkness was replaced by a very low-level light, which was gradually growing stronger. Turning around, he saw Merryweather standing close to the gap where they had come in and next to an ancient-looking switch.

"Found the lights," she said with a smile. "Looks like the uni's back-up generators are still working."

A series of long, fluorescent lights had spluttered into life and were slowly illuminating the space which they lined, revealing it to be a long room, with endless shelves from its midpoint, extending into the gloom. Shelves that were crammed with ancient books, objects and other artefacts.

"Wow," said Jack, staring open-mouthed at the scene that was being lit up in front of the three of them.

"Wow indeed," said Merryweather. "Right, best get started looking through this lot."

"What exactly are we looking for?" asked Tom.

"Not entirely sure," said Merryweather, "but anything to do with that old church at Gris Corp, or dragons or Christmas, would be a good place to start. We should begin with the books, I think. The older, the better."

"Did you know any of this was here?" Jack asked Merryweather.

"Well, there were always rumours, but I never imagined anything as vast as this, Jack. This looks like a treasure trove of antiquities."

As the three of them started inspecting the many books on the shelves, the two boys were full of questions.

"How has this place stayed a secret?" asked Tom.

"I don't know," said Merryweather, "but perhaps it is just as well that it has remained so. Who knows what these books contain?"

She turned to Tom and Jack.

"Sometimes, it is for the greater good that not everything should be known or rather, that certain knowledge which once was known to many is slowly, gently and quietly allowed to fade into the shadows."

"Why?" asked Jack.

"To stop people like Max Gris from abusing such knowledge, Jack. As we have already discovered, not everyone's intentions would be good if such information were to fall into their hands," replied Merryweather.

They continued methodically to search their way along the long, antique wooden bookshelves, which were all stacked with books. The minutes ticked away, with the three of them finding nothing that was immediately useful to their current predicament.

After a couple of hours, Merryweather paused the search to dish out more snacks.

"How much longer will we have to keep looking?" asked Jack in between mouthfuls of the chocolate bars Merryweather had dispensed.

"I have no idea, Jack," said Merryweather, "but I'm sure there must be something in here – somewhere – that will give us further clues as to whatever it is that Max Gris is planning, so we must keep searching."

"What makes you so sure that there's anything here at all?" asked Tom.

"Look around you, Tom," said Merryweather. "This place is packed with ancient tomes and artefacts and goodness knows what else. And it's been hidden away from everyone for decades, maybe centuries, *underneath* the city's premier seat of learning. If there's nothing about Gus or Christmas or that ancient church in here, well, I don't know where else it *would* be stored."

With this, Merryweather ushered them back to the search. After around another hour of carefully poring over books and occasionally inspecting the odd one which might be of interest, only for his aunt to confirm, time after time, that none of them were precisely what they were looking for, Tom sat down on the floor, feeling disconsolate. He gazed up at the shelves holding all the books. They looked endless, extending for many more yards into the further recesses of the underground chamber. The hum of the lights above, creating the artificial light which was illuminating the room, seemed to grow more intrusive with each passing second. Tom looked at his watch. They had now been searching the chamber for over three hours, without success. He rested back on his hands and wondered for a moment how much longer it would be before they found anything – *if* they found anything at all.

Sitting on the cold stone floor, he felt a cold draught hitting his wrists.

"Gee whizz, it's cold enough down here already," he muttered to himself. He was about to get back to his feet when he had a notion to check where the draught was coming from, into the otherwise airless and musty room. He flashed his torch in the general direction of the cold air and saw that one of the wooden panels which lined the wall from floor to ceiling was slightly out of alignment.

Squatting down, he reached for its edge with his fingertips and pulled it. The panel moved a fraction. He gave it more of a yank with his next pull, and a couple of books clattered down off the shelves above, landing with a muffled thump on the floor behind him. Tom gave another pull and the wooden panel came free, revealing a deep compartment behind it, with several old wooden crates stacked up inside it.

"Auntieprof, Jack, come and look at this!" shouted Tom.

The other two came over to the spot where he was by now standing next to the open wooden panel.

"Look what I found," Tom grinned.

"Well now, whatever do we have in here?" asked Merryweather.

The three of them began lifting out the wooden crates.

"I'll wager these have been here for a while," said Merryweather, inspecting the rusting nails which had been used to seal the lids of the crates tightly shut.

"And look," said Tom, pointing to an illustration on the side of the crates. "What's that?"

The three of them looked at the crates. All of them had the same imprint: a drawing of the sun setting behind a hill, but with flames spouting from the top of the sun itself.

"I've never seen it before; looks like some sort of ancient symbol," said Merryweather, "and it's on all of them, which suggests they could be connected in some manner."

She dragged one crate into the centre of the room.

"Here, help me with this one. Let's get it open," she instructed the two boys.

After some prising around the rim of the lid with Tom's Swiss army knife, the lid of the first crate came loose. With some more effort, the three of them eventually pulled it free.

Tom shone his torch into the crate. It was lined with some sort of dark material and full of scrolls, piled higgledy-piggledy on top of each other.

"Well," said Merryweather, "this looks interesting."

Merryweather reached in and began fishing out scrolls, dishing them out to Tom, Jack and herself in roughly equal numbers.

Tom and Jack began sifting through their respective piles of scrolls, with Merryweather joining them once she had completed doling out the pile within.

It was Jack who struck lucky first.

"Dragon!" he shouted, seconds after he had started inspecting the fifth scroll in his batch.

"Let me have a look," said Merryweather, peering over his shoulder at the battered-looking and fragile scroll.

Tom craned his neck to have a look as well. There were indeed several pictures of what was unmistakably a dragon, accompanied by many lines of neatly written text, faded but still legible. Tom didn't recognise the language.

But Merryweather did.

"It's older French," she told the two boys. "Now, let me see what's going on here…"

She started reading the ancient text aloud.

"The endless war that tore the country asunder in the 1600s,

When Old Christmas was declared outlawed,

And people were punished for celebrating,

Drove the Old Christmas from the land,

And its ancient protector, the dragon,

Awoke once more,

As he had oft before, down the many centuries.

But even he could not stop those most evil of men,

Who drove him from his slumber,

By calling up the Great Horned Beast,

And setting it upon the dragon,

Thus, forcing him to flee.

And all who would love and cherish Old Christmas,

And he who would protect St Nicholas,

Were made to hide themselves away,

For many, many years,

Until the danger had passed,

And fear and the Beast,

No longer stalked the land,

And all was once more settled,

And Old Christmas returned.

But of its protector, the dragon,

There was never any sight again,

Nor of St Nicholas, too,

Except, as foretold, on rare occasion,

When, but once a year,

He visited the good and true children of the land,

Who still believed in him,

And the peace and goodwill,

Which he brought to all at Christmastide.

As Merryweather finished reading the text on the scroll in front of her, Tom could see Jack standing stock-still, his eyes nearly popping out of their sockets with amazement.

Tom simply uttered, "Wow... so, Gus really is ancient then. It's all true."

"Well," said Merryweather, "everything Gus said has been written down here by someone a long time ago, and it is just as he told it to us."

"And he returns whenever Christmas is in danger, like he explained," said Tom.

"Yes, it would appear so," said Merryweather.

"So, whatever Max Gris is doing now must be pretty major – in a bad way – for Christmas, right?" Jack had regained the power of speech.

"Yes," said Merryweather, "and she may well be out of her depth by the sounds of things."

"What do you mean?" asked Jack.

"The Great Horned Beast," said Tom.

Merryweather nodded.

"What do you think it is?" asked Tom.

"I don't know," said Merryweather, "but I doubt it is anything good – and especially not if it forced Gus to flee. I mean, he's not exactly the smallest creature ever to walk this earth, is he?"

"And he can breathe fire and everything," piped up Jack.

"Quite," said Merryweather. "Let's keep looking, to see if there's anything else."

The three of them rummaged through several more scrolls each; this time, it was Tom who cried out.

"Woah… woah, woah, woah," he exclaimed, holding up another scroll that was even more tattered than the previous one. "This one's covered in more drawings of dragons and someone who looks like Santa."

"Jackpot!" exclaimed Jack and he high-fived Tom.

"Let me see," said Merryweather, taking the fragile scroll from Tom. "This one has seen better days." She pointed to the bottom of the scroll, which was ragged and torn. Then, once again, she began translating the ancient text.

"Upon the first star of Christmas Eve,

Should the ancient relics of St. Nicholas

Be found and arranged in sequence

In their rightful place,

The key elements,

By the brightest child,

Who be filled with grace,

These sacred words below

Shall bring forth the spirits of Christmas

With all their power to bestow

Reanimation and timelessness itself."

Merryweather paused.

"What does the rest of it say?" interrupted Jack.

Merryweather cleared her throat and continued the translation.

"Take and hold this sacred relic,

borne from the past unto the present,

and now return it to its rightful place

at the zenith of this carapace.

I call upon the ancient powers

of many days and countless hours,

to usher forth down through time

all of Christmas and make it mine."

Merryweather glanced up as she broke off reading. Tom could see that the colour had drained from his aunt's face.

"What's wrong? What does the last part say?" he asked.

Merryweather cleared her throat and took a moment to collect her thoughts.

"Some of the text is missing, but it talks about some sort of 'swap of souls' to achieve timelessness and then... oh, my... it says that if the dragon ever appears again, Christmas – and the world as we know it - will be in very great danger and that if he appears close to Christmas Day itself, it will be the final Christmas of all."

"What? Ever?" said Jack.

"Yes, ever. That's what the scroll says. It purports to be a prophecy, and the wording of that ritual is clear. This must be what Max Gris has been planning," said Merryweather.

"Well, we have to stop her somehow," said Tom. "She can't just end Christmas forever – and mess up the world as well. No one can do that."

"We have little time," said Merryweather. "Not if these words are true. You heard them: we only have until the first star is sighted on Christmas Eve."

"She's got Katie as a prisoner, too," Jack reminded them.

"Yes," said Merryweather. "And Nicky... goodness alone knows what that woman is planning, but I doubt she fully understands what she is messing around with or what she may be about to unleash on the world."

"We must stop her," said Tom.

"Well, we do still have some key items she needs in order to carry out the ritual: namely, the last of the relics," said Merryweather.

"But we need to get Katie and Nicky back safely," said Jack. "Couldn't we do a trade?"

"We could, but then Ms Gris could do whatever she wanted to Christmas – and the world – and we would be partly responsible. Besides, I wouldn't trust her to keep her side of the bargain, anyway. Assuming we could even agree on a bargain with her in the first place," said Merryweather.

"Well, in that case, we need to go to the police," said Jack. "They'll stop her."

"Oh Jack, I wish we could, but right now, the police will be dealing with hundreds of other matters in the aftermath of the solar storm, and we also have the not so trivial matter of Gus to contend with – and I am *quite* sure that Max Gris would quickly use that against us. Plus, she practically owns half the city already – including the police – with all the money she's thrown around."

"Well, what *are* we going to do then?" said Jack, throwing up his hands in the air.

"I wish my dad were here right now," said Tom. "He would know what to do. He always knew the right thing to do." He was staring into the middle distance.

Merryweather walked over to him and gave him a hug.

"Now, young Thomas Brightly, you listen to me," began Merryweather. "Your father would be proud of you for all you have done so far, but now is not the time to lose your nerve. Your father, were he here right now, most of all would want you to be brave and to think for yourself, and not to be relying on him, but rather to be relying on yourself. You, too, will always do the right thing. So, my question to you is: what would you do now, Tom? Right now?"

Tom's eyes were stinging as he bit his lip and thought for several moments.

"We need to stop Max Gris. However we can. And rescue Katie and Nicky. She's got all her goons, but we've got Gus – if we can find him again – and he's here to protect Christmas and he asked for our help. So, we must do whatever we can to help him. Help him and save Christmas – and the world – from whatever it is Max Gris is planning to do to it," he said.

"So?" asked Merryweather.

"First of all, we find Gus."

"Huh, easier said than done," said Jack. "He could be anywhere by now."

Tom carried on, undeterred, "Then we go to Gris Corp with Gus. We have what Max Gris wants – what she needs – to carry out the ritual: the final few relics. We can do a swap, but a clever one. Give her some fake relics. Gus can create enough of a diversion for the three of us to split up, nab some of the genuine relics and free Katie and Nicky.

"We only have to keep the last batch of relics safe from Max Gris until dusk on Christmas Eve, and we'll have wrecked her plan. Well, for at least another year. That should give us enough time to figure out what to do about her – and also about Gus as well. But for now, we need to go to Gris Corp tonight. With Gus. And some fake relics." Tom looked at Merryweather and Jack and grinned.

"I like your thinking," said Merryweather. She flashed her torch around the lines of shelves.

"I'm sure that we could *borrow* a few objects from here and use them as stand-in relics," she said, as she fished around in her pocket. She produced the shorter, squatter key from within it and held it aloft.

"I wonder what this one's for?" Merryweather mused aloud.

"Might've been a red herring," suggested Tom.

"Possibly," replied Merryweather as she examined the key once more.

Jack stood bolt upright.

"Right then, time to get started," he said, and began piling the scrolls back into their crates. "What was it you said again, Prof? We should leave a place as we found it?"

"You're learning, Jack," replied Merryweather with a wry grin, as she and Tom began putting more scrolls back into the crates.

"Best get a move on then," said Jack, "'coz we have a dragon to find – for starters."

CHAPTER FORTY-TWO

Max Gris swept into the formerly derelict Cathedral of the Others, her cape flowing and wearing an extravagant fake fur hat atop her head to ward off the cold. It was another frigid day, the weak December sunlight making no impact whatsoever on the deep blanket of snow that covered the entirety of Gris Corp's HQ and its surrounding park, aside from the access roads which Gris had instructed Slymington to have cleared. He had duly organised this and the angular lines of their black tarmac surfaces now stood out against the white backdrop like a series of arteries designed by a computer that only understood straight lines and right angles.

As it was, Gris barely noticed the contrast of the roads with the deep snow, so intent was she on "getting to the church on time", as she had quipped earlier that morning to Slymington. It was now noon, and she was preparing for the final stages leading up to the most important event of her life, the details of which she announced to the assembled group of people who were waiting for her in the now converted interior of the old church.

"Good afternoon to you all," she began. "And what an afternoon it promises to be. Welcome to the first rehearsal for the most important event of your pathetic, miserable, insignificant little lives."

She had specifically addressed the last sentence towards two of the assembled company who had not yet even formally been introduced to each other. Doctor Nicholas Auld was in handcuffs, which were chained to the inside of one of the newly installed metal cages within the interior of the church. In the cage immediately to his left, also handcuffed and chained to its steel bars, was Katie Wanless.

Gris gazed at the pair of them with a look which was comprised partly of scorn and partly of pity.

"Such a shame that the pair of you will be mere footnotes – if you even make it to those giddy heights – to one of the greatest triumphs in all of human history," she snorted derisively.

Neither of the two prisoners said anything in reply. In fact, as far as Gris was concerned, they may both as well have been statues. She turned to Slymington, who was, as ever, by her side and muttered to him, sotto voice.

"Slimey, how much of the sleeping drugs did you administer to this pair?"

"The usual doses, ma'am," replied her faithful assistant, in his normal, robotic voice.

Gris gave another derisive snort.

"Humph, they must be particularly susceptible specimens. They look like a pair of propped-up zombies. Still, good work on the handcuffs and the chains. Can't be too careful," she pronounced, raising an eyebrow as the rest of her face formed a smirk.

Gris strode over first to the cage containing Auld, and sidled up to its bars, as though she was going to have a furtive one-to-one chat with him.

"So, Nicky boy, aren't you wondering what all of this opulence is for? Hmmm? I mean, cast your eyes around the place: gold and red velvet everywhere, right down to the nooks and crannies. Even though I do say so myself, my team has done a magnificent job on this wreck, especially given the time constraints. Still a few details to be ironed out, but we have until tomorrow afternoon. Well, until the first star is sighted, actually, but one likes to err on the side of caution with timescales." Gris ended her mini-monologue and waited expectantly for a response, but none was forthcoming.

"What's the matter, Nicky? Nothing to say? I would have thought you would at least have had a passing interest in the good use to which all your terribly diligent academic work has been put…"

Auld had been staring at the floor throughout this one-sided exchange, but now looked up, and directly at Gris.

"If I had known what you wanted my research for, I would never have agreed to undertake any of it." He spat the words out, as though trying to rid himself of an unpleasant taste in his mouth.

"Oh, Nicky, Nicky, Nicky, no need to be so full of regret. You have achieved a great thing here. You," at this, Gris pointed directly towards Auld, "and all your hard work are the very foundation to all of this magnificence." She swept her arm around, as though showcasing the entire interior of the church.

"All of it." The raised eyebrows.

"Because of clever old you." The fake grin.

"You should be proud." The instruction.

Auld looked tired. "You're quite mad," was all he could manage.

Gris adopted a look of mock incredulity. "Mad? Mad? Hahahahahahahaha."

Her laugh switched off as quickly as it had begun.

"No, Nicky. Not mad. Determined. Shrewd. Resilient. Visionary. Clever. And extremely, fabulously, ostentatiously rich. There, fixed it for you." Gris threw another self-satisfied smile in Auld's direction.

"We need to keep you around in case there any last-minute hiccups, so you aren't going anywhere until tomorrow evening, but don't worry, you'll be home in time for Christmas. Well, to what's left of your home…" Gris's voice trailed off.

"And just think, you'll have a ringside seat to watch the return of Santa Claus himself, summoned at will, by me, to grant me immortality and ownership of Christmas and everything associated with him – and it – forever. History in the making, wouldn't you say?" asked Gris.

"I'd say that you are completely and utterly unhinged," replied Auld.

Gris let rip another maniacal laugh for several seconds before she halted it once again and drew a line under her chat with Auld.

"No, Nicky. I'm right. And by tomorrow evening, I'll be the most powerful woman in the world. I'll be the woman who's going to live forever and who's showing off Santa Claus himself to the entire world. Me and Santa: besties forevs. And he'll be doing everything I tell him to – which will just be A-MAZ-ING!"

At this, Gris span around to face Katie. And uttered the first thing that came into her head.

"Oh, my dear, look at the absolute *state* of you…"

Katie Wanless was staring directly at Gris but remained silent. Even Gris could tell that she looked furious.

"You see, this is what happens when you indulge in all those teenage temper tantrums of yours: you wear yourself out," oozed Gris, in mock sympathy.

"It's as though you haven't even slept for a week, you poor thing. Except, I know you must have slept last night, courtesy of Mr Slymington's magic medicine."

As this, Katie threw herself against the bars of the cage and tried to grab Gris, who deftly stepped back a couple of paces and chided her.

"Now, now, that is no way to repay our very generous overnight hospitality, is it?" said Gris. "And besides, my dear, you aren't going anywhere anyway, so if I were you, I'd simmer down as Auntie Max tells you about your very important role for the next hour or thereabouts."

Katie was glaring at Gris now, her eyes red with fury.

"You, my dear, are about to have the central role in the first rehearsal for tomorrow's ceremony, standing in for your little brother – for now," announced Gris.

Katie continued to glare at her.

"What? Not even a flicker of excitement? Oh, very well, suit yourself, but you know I'd expected a little more enthusiasm," said Gris.

She walked around the interior of the church as she began explaining what Katie was about to do next.

"So, the thing is, once Nicky boy eventually completed all his *endless* research for me, we had all the deets required to rustle up the return of old Santy Claus. Deciphered all the ancient scrolls my father had acquired years and years ago, then gathered all the relics from right across Europe – and let me tell you, *that* cost a small fortune – scouted out a suitable location – which is where your bro and his chums helped us no end – and then just had to find a bright child.

"Because, you see, my dear, both the prophecy and the ritual were crystal clear on one part of the whole shebang. In fact, it was practically the first part of the puzzle that we deciphered. I say we; I mean the bold Nicky here. Albeit, paid by me. So, really, it's all down to me in the end, anyway.

"Now, the thing is, we needed a child to complete the ultimate act of the ritual to summon Santa. Made sense in a way. Patron saint of children, brings them all presents once a year, loves them all dearly, blah, blah, blah. Really never understood why though. I hate children. They're annoying and they never spend enough of their pocket money on all my toys.

"Anyway, we needed to find a child – but not just any old child. The instructions for the ritual were unambiguous: it needed to be a clever child. A brilliant child indeed. So, do you know what I did?"

There was no response to Gris's question from either Katie, nor from Auld.

"Oh well, gonna tell you anyway: we created Apotheosis, the first truly global virtual reality gaming sensation. Swept the world. Nabbed us loads of publicity. Made me a fortune. Loads of noble reasons fed to the public, especially parents, about why we created it: mainly some nonsense about educational attainment. As if… But, most important of all, we created it specifically so we could find the smartest all-rounder kid on the planet, and it worked. We found the aforesaid child who just happens to be your little baby bro. I mean, what are the chances? Actually, I know the odds, so I can answer that question. But you can't. I mean, you *do* have the advantage of being related to him by birth, but that's about it."

Gris plastered on a fake smile as she continued to stride around the church. Katie watched Gris throughout this display, her gaze unbroken.

"But for the next hour, you get to play his part in our little rehearsal for the big event on Christmas Eve. So, you see, that's actually two purposes you'll be fulfilling: as your brother's understudy and also as the bait to lure him to us. Multi-tasking, you might say. Just by being *you*."

Gris paused at the altar of the church to admire her surroundings.

"Pretty neat stage set-up we have going on here now, wouldn't you say?"

Still no response. The Gris Corp security personnel, who were posted in each of the four corners of the church and its newly repaired doorways, with Grunk on the main door, stood like statues. Armed statues, but still as the night.

After drinking in the spectacle for a few seconds, Gris turned back towards the cages again.

"You know, you two simply do not appreciate all the effort and hard work that went into making this place look so wonderful. You should have seen it yesterday. Total dump," said Gris.

She strolled back towards the cage holding Katie.

"There is one bright spot for you, my dear. You, too, will be returning home for Christmas," said Gris.

A pause.

"Though probably without your little brother," she finished casually.

Katie finally took the bait.

"What do you mean I'll be going home for Christmas without Jack? What are you going to do to him?" she shouted.

"Ah, finally, the ice maiden cracks. Weeeellll, there is a teeny-tiny point of note regarding Jack's part in all of this," began Gris. She continued sauntering towards Katie, almost tip-toeing her way across the church.

"You see, Jack does have a *very* important role to play in the ceremony. Indeed, it's an especially crucial one at the culmination of the whole ritual, the apotheosis, you might say."

Gris laughed at her own pun before continuing. "He has to put the first relic in its correct place in order to start to summon up the big guy himself. It's just that..." Gris let her voice trail away for effect.

Katie's face was now pressed up directly against the bars of the cage.

"It's just that WHAT?" she shouted at Gris.

Gris took a final step towards her, close enough so she could feel Katie's breath in the cold air of the church, but far enough away to be slightly beyond her grasp.

"It's just that the very last part of the ritual also requires a *transference* of the soul, or it might be the life force – hard to tell from the translation – from the child (that's Jack) to the person who will gain immortality (that's me)... and it's a transference of the 'we're-not-entirely-sure-if-it will-be-survivable' variety, it appears. That's if we've understood the translation and the interpretation of it all correctly," said Gris matter-of-factly.

"You're a MONSTER!" shouted Katie. "You're totally EVIL!"

"No, no, no, my dear, I'm neither, but I am about to become the most powerful person the world has ever seen," schmoozed Gris right back at her.

"You'll never get away with any of this!" ranted Katie. Auld had, by now, gone grey in the face.

"Oh really, such histrionics. Do we have to medicate you yet again?" asked Gris, with a hint of condescension in her voice. "Slimey, would you?"

Katie began screaming in rage at this point. Gris took another step back from her cell, as Slymington walked towards the cage holding a loaded tranquilliser gun.

"One way or another, my dear, the show must go on – and that includes your part in the rehearsal - whether you like it or not," smiled Gris, as Slymington fired a dart into Katie's left leg.

Katie let out one last shriek of rage and then fell silently into a crumpled heap on the floor of her cell.

"Slimey," said Gris, with a hint of exasperation in her voice, "I told you to medicate her, not knock her out. Honestly…"

"Sorry, ma'am," said Slymington.

"You'd better give her another shot of something that will waken her up. We've a rehearsal to complete," instructed Gris.

Slymington impassively reached into the left pocket of his suit jacket and brought out another phial which he inserted into the tranquilliser gun, as though this was the most mundane act of his daily life. He aimed the gun once more at Katie and fired a second dart at her in as many minutes, this time into her right leg.

There was a pause of several seconds before Katie began murmuring to herself and then she sat bolt upright as though she had been shocked back to life. She clutched at her throat and was shaking.

Gris looked on approvingly. "That's better. Now, where were we? Oh yes. Rehearsal time. Now, pull yourself together, dear, and get ready. Simmons here will chaperone you through it all, step by step."

Gris turned on her heel and walked towards the altar, before turning around to face Katie and dish out one further instruction.

"Oh, and don't get any ideas into that messed-up little teenage head of yours about trying to run. You'll find Simmons is *very* effective at stopping people from doing that."

"Right, Slimey, let's do this!" With this, Max Gris strode onto the stage that had been erected in the centre of the newly decorated church in all its ornate glory. She threw her head back and raised her arms up to the lights, beaming down on the stage, before shouting at the top of her voice.

"Let the ceremony begin!"

CHAPTER FORTY-THREE

"Well? Can you see anything?"

Jack was craning his neck as though he was going to stick it through the rearmost side window of the Defender, trying to peer through the gathering darkness up the hill towards Merryweather's back garden.

In the front seat of the vehicle, Merryweather was peering intently through a pair of binoculars at precisely the same spot.

"Nothing," she said. "No sign of movement either in or around the house – and the house is in darkness."

Tom was biting his lip. The three of them were back, in the Defender, in the same spot as they had been the previous evening, parked in the cul-de-sac which lay at the foot of the hill which ran all the way down to it from the rear of Merryweather's long back garden.

Merryweather removed the bins from her eyes and turned to the boys.

"I can't be completely sure, but the house looks like it's empty. It'll be completely dark in another few minutes and then…"

"Then what?" asked Tom.

"And then, we have a choice," said Merryweather. "Either we can go in the front door by driving up towards the house." She paused. "Perhaps walking the last part – just in case. Or…"

"Or?" asked Jack.

"Or we leave the car here and go up the hill. On foot. Into the back garden and in through the back door. Less chance of being seen in case anyone is still hanging around the front of the house."

"The hill," said Tom immediately.

Merryweather gave a slight sigh. "I had a feeling you'd pick that option. Come on then. Hills aren't climbed magically."

The three of them emptied out of the car and into the freezing winter air and began walking along a path through all the new build houses on the estate and towards the base of the hill that led up to the back edge of the garden which lay to the rear of Merryweather's house. The hill was covered in snow, with a thick crust of ice atop it.

Tom strode forward, through the gate at the end of the path and began leading the way on the long trudge up the hill. With his first step into the snow-covered field beyond the gate, his left leg plunged through the icy crust and down into the deep snow, up to above his knee.

Jack began grumbling.

"This... is... going... to... take... ages..."

In between huffing and puffing.

Silence fell after that outburst. Tom figured that even Jack had realised it was better to conserve his energy for the climb. The three of them trudged onwards up the hill, one foot in front of another – and sinking, often knee-deep, into the snow. More than once, Tom let his mind wander and imagined what it would be like to sledge all the way down the hill. The speed would be incredible, and it would be a long ride down. He would just have to figure out a way of dealing with the large wooden fence which formed the border between the flatter part of the field at the bottom and the new housing estate. In Tom's experience, such immoveable objects were best dealt with by tumbling off the sledge in use at the time, thus leaving it to take its chances with the wall or fence or ditch or occasionally, burn [1].

After around ten minutes of non-stop trudging, the three of them arrived at the rear of Merryweather's long back garden. They took a few moments to get their breath back, and then Merryweather spoke.

"Looks like the coast is clear. No sign of lights or any movement in the house. Come on, let's go."

She opened a gate in the old, rickety wooden fence that bordered the back garden and ushered Tom and Jack through.

They made their way back up the garden and towards the house, before stopping once more at the foot of the stairs leading up to the back door.

"Okay, one at a time, follow me... but be ready to run if any of these goons are still here."

Merryweather put the key into the lock of the back door and turned it; the door creaked open. Tom watched her inching her way into the kitchen, all the while scanning the surrounding area as though he were a sentry meerkat.

But there was nothing.

Merryweather turned, smiled, and said, "All clear. No one else here except us, it seems." She pulled open a drawer and fetched out a few candles. Once they were lit, there was enough light for the three of them to see, but not so much that it would be immediately noticeable to anyone watching the house.

"Doesn't look like there's been too much damage, either," said Merryweather.

The three of them gathered in the kitchen. Tom noticed it was a little less tidy than it had been when they had last been in it, but there had been no major breakages. He felt a tingling in his fingers and toes as the residual heat in the house started to thaw them out. Whoever had been rooting around in Merryweather's house hadn't interfered with the old solid fuel boiler, which was, he noted with grateful thanks, still chugging away full blast.

Tom began taking off his jacket and was about to run through the plan for their visit to Gris Corp in a few hours when there was a very large – if muffled – thump from the general direction of the back garden. A series of smaller thumps followed in quick succession – and then stopped.

Tom stood bolt upright and ran to the kitchen window, to keek² out of it. As he did so, Merryweather quickly moved to extinguish the candles.

"What is it? Can you see?" she asked Tom.

Tom was staring out into the wintry gloom of the back garden. As his eyes adjusted, he could make out a rather large, ungainly shape rolling around in the snow. Tom sprang towards the back door.

"What is it?" asked Merryweather.

"Gus!" Tom replied with excitement, both in answer to his aunt and as a greeting to the dragon, who was now struggling to his feet in the snow and generally huffing and puffing as he did so.

"Och, this is total nonsense, all this snow. Makes trying to land a total game of chance, so and it does."

Tom grinned at Gus's harrumphing and ran down the stairs towards him.

"Gus! Where have you been? We've been worried stupid about you!" he shouted, as he ran up to the dragon to give him an enormous hug. Well, tried to. His arms barely made it halfway across Gus's not inconsiderable stomach.

"I've been flying around, laddie. Found some trees to have a wee rest in whilst I waited for all of you to come back. More of those bad knights turned up last night - I smelt them – so I flew off before they had the chance to find me with those noisy swords of theirs. Too many of them to take on all at once – and my stomach was still sort of half-asleep."

"Noisy swords? You mean guns, Gus," said Tom.

"Aye, that's the ones," replied the dragon.

"Come on, let's get out of the snow," said Tom. "You must be freezing."

"It's a wee bit nippy," replied the dragon.

Tom led Gus up the stairs, where he was welcomed by Merryweather and Jack. Merryweather ushered him into the kitchen – after telling him there was to be no practice fire-breathing. As he thawed out, the three of them explained to Gus what they had found in the Hidden Archive.

"So, anyway, Tom slipped over on the ice and snow and then he found the lock. And then we had to check which of the keys…" Jack was hyper. Gus was looking at him, puzzled, and trying to ingest all the information Jack was spewing out.

"And pause for a mo', Jack," said Merryweather. "Gus, what he's trying to say is that we found some ancient writings and scrolls in the archive that explained – well, all about you."

"Some of them even had pictures of you from long ago," chimed in Tom.

"Yes, that was a big clue," said Merryweather.

The dragon now wore a serious face.

"What did these scrolls say?" he asked.

"They described your last adventure, back in the 17th century, in great detail and about how Christmas was banned and you were chased and had to flee," explained Merryweather. "Gus, you really have been in hibernation for centuries."

"I knew it was a long sleep this time," mused the dragon.

"Hundreds of years, Gus. Do you know how this happened? Is there anything else you can remember?" asked Merryweather.

Gus shook his head. "No, just what I told you before: that I was protecting Santa, as you call him, from the evil men who hated Christmas, and I had to hide the relics and then… I was asleep. In the church. For ages. Until I wasn't."

"This is puzzling," said Merryweather.

"Not to me," said Gus. "I told you, the relics are very powerful – and if I'm awake here and now, then it's because Santa is in danger."

"It's not just Santa," said Tom. He looked at Merryweather. "Go on, tell him."

"Tell me what?" asked Gus.

"We also found a prediction, a prophecy, if you like, about your return and what it means," said Merryweather.

Gus looked at her expectantly. "And?"

Merryweather took a deep breath and gave a long sigh. "It's about as bad as it could be. The prophecy specifically states that you will return when Santa, Christmas and the world itself are in very great danger."

"Oh…" said Gus, sitting down on his haunches.

"That's not all," added Tom. "We also found a scroll which described a ritual which is undertaken to summon Santa in order to possess him and take control of Christmas and the entire world and… this needs to happen at the sighting of the first star on Christmas Eve in order for it to work."

"And that's tomorrow," piped up Jack.

"Oh…" said Gus, his eyes widening, "but that means…"

"Yes," said Merryweather, "we have less than twenty-four hours to stop Max Gris – but fortunately, we have a plan." She smiled.

"Are we going to attack the knights with the noisy swords?" asked Gus.

"Not if I can help it," said Merryweather. "We're going to swap something we have which Gris wants in return for some people she has who we want back."

"People?" asked Gus.

"She's kidnapped Katie," began Tom.

"She's my sister," interrupted Jack.

"And Dr Auld," continued Tom.

"He's my assistant at the university," said Merryweather.

"Why's she done that?" asked Gus.

"Well, Nicky – Dr Auld – was helping her with the research into Christmas and as for Katie, Gris and her goons have taken her as blackmail, so that we'll bring the last of the relics to her," replied Merryweather.

"Which we're going to do," she continued.

Gus's eyes opened even wider.

"But, if you do that, the evil woman will be able to perform the ritual and destroy everything," said Gus.

"Which is why we will not take the genuine relics," said Merryweather, "but rather, some fake ones which we happen to have *borrowed* from the Hidden Archive."

"So, they look ancient – and by the time Max Gris has figured it out that they're not the real deal…"

"It'll be too late!" pronounced Jack in triumph. "And we'll be long gone."

Gus rubbed his long chin with one of his claws as he pondered the plan.

"And what about the bad knights that this evil woman has?" he asked.

"Well, that's where you come in," said Merryweather. "Jack and I will go to the main building with the fake relics in order to create a diversion – and hopefully, do a deal to get Katie and Nicky back. Meanwhile, you and Tom will be searching for the genuine relics. It's worth checking the old, ruined church first, just in case we missed any of the relics on our last recce there. Also, Gris was setting up some sort of big marquee for the ceremony. There's a good chance the bulk of the relics are in it or somewhere nearby. Once we've met Gris, Jack and I will swap the fake relics for Katie and Nicky. Everyone will be happy. Gris will think she has all the relics, so she should have no more need of Katie and Nicky and, as Jack said, by the time she realises the relics are fake, it will be too late."

"And what do you want me to do in all of this?" asked Gus.

"Back-up. For Tom," said Merryweather. "If anything goes wrong, that's where you come in. How's your fire-breathing coming on?"

At this, Gus perked up. "Think it's almost back to normal. Do you want to see?"

"NO!" cried the three others in unison.

Gus gave an embarrassed smile. "Aw yeah. Inside. Forgot about that."

"What about the real relics we have?" asked Tom.

"They'll be safe, secreted away downstairs in the cellar. That place down there dates back to the last war, a hidey-hole which also doubles as a secret way out of the house. No one will ever find it – or them - even if they were to tear the rest of the house apart," said Merryweather.

"Aren't we forgetting something?" said Jack. "Gris also needs some sort of special one to perform the ceremony. What if she keeps one of us there to do that?"

"Yeah, and what if she catches all of us?" said Tom.

"That, unfortunately, is a risk we'll have to take," said Merryweather. "However, even if she does capture all of us, she still won't have the real relics and as I said, by the time she realises this, it will be too late – for at least another year. All we have to do is to run down the clock until dusk on Christmas Eve and then we'll have scuppered her plan, which buys us more time, if nothing else."

"And if that doesn't work?" asked Jack.

Merryweather peered over her glasses at Jack.

"Well, then we'll just have to improvise." Then she grinned. "Come on, we need to get prepared for our visit to Gris Corp.

In a quiet, deserted, snowy street, Grunk sat in the driver's seat of an anonymous four by four vehicle, parked at the top of the hill. His face was impassive as he picked up the binoculars lying on the passenger seat and held them up to his eyes, scanning a house halfway down the hill. He viewed the house for a few seconds, before lowering the binoculars and placing them back on the passenger seat.

Grunk was beyond bored now but remained stoic. He was wearing extra layers to ward off the cold and was waiting patiently, a hunter in his urban camouflage, waiting for his quarry to reveal itself.

There was a brief snap of static from the other object that lay on the passenger seat. Grunk reached over and picked up the walkie-talkie that had crackled into life after sitting dormant for hours. He pressed the talk button on it.

"Grunk to HQ. Are you receiving? Over?"

There was a further crackle of static as Grunk waited for another human voice to interrupt the dead air. Nothing.

"This is Grunk, calling HQ. Are you…"

"Grunk, I thought I told you we were using codenames from hereon in?" Max Gris's voice, though tinny and rattling, was as unmistakably harsh as ever.

"Oh yeah, sorry. I meant Francis to Golden Hind," said Grunk, correcting himself.

"Bit late now, isn't it?" shrilled Gris.

"Yes boss. I mean, ma'am."

There was several seconds of static-infused dead air before the next question came.

"Well, what have you got for me?" asked Gris.

"Activity in the house. The two boys, the older woman and also…"

"Yes, and?" barked Gris.

"And that *thing*," said Grunk.

"The dragon?"

"Yeah, if that's what it is," replied Grunk.

"Excellent!" The excitement had returned to Gris's voice. "Do not, under any circumstances, interfere. Just keep watching, and if they leave, follow them. As we discussed. Understood?"

"Yes, ma'am," said Grunk.

Another pause of static and crackling dead air.

"And whatever you do, do not lose sight of them. If you need any more men, make the call. I want all four of them, and I want them intact and unscathed. Got that?" instructed Gris.

"Yes, ma'am." Grunk paused, his finger hovering over the talk button of the walkie-talkie as he grabbed the binoculars once more and held them up to his eyes.

"Bingo," he muttered to himself as he pressed the talk button.

"Looks like we've hit gold, ma'am. They're on the move. Over and out."

---

1. Scots: stream.

2. Scots: to peer

CHAPTER FORTY-FOUR

Merryweather's trusty Defender rattled to a halt at the end of a street, a couple of blocks away from the Mackintosh Innovation Park (a.k.a. the Gris Corp grounds – at least in Max Gris's mind. After all, as she never tired of reminding all and sundry, she had paid for the whole park). Merryweather had parked the vehicle next to a piece of waste ground, beyond the houses that lined the upper end of the street, though it was hard to tell precisely what was road and what was pavement anymore, such was the depth of the snow which lay everywhere. The sporadic snow-clearing efforts had, as yet, evidently not reached the outer reaches of some of the urban streets.

"Come on, we'll have to walk the last part. Best chance of not being noticed," said Merryweather, as she, Jack and Tom tipped themselves out of the relative warmth of the car and into the penetrating cold of the December evening once again.

Tom looked upwards. There, set against the backdrop of the clear sky, complete with stars all twinkling and a wafer-thin crescent moon, was a strange dark shape, circling overhead and occasionally swooping upwards and downwards.

Tom grinned: Gus was enjoying stretching his wings once again. He also gave a small sigh of relief. The sight of the dragon, even several hundred feet above him, gave him a feeling of reassurance. Gus had been through similarly difficult situations before – albeit a very long time ago. He would know what to do if they ran into trouble, which, in Tom's head, was one potential outcome. He shivered as he recalled the sight of Gris's goons, swarming towards the ruined church, with their guns and the dogs, and then had to remind himself that this had only been a couple of nights ago, when his and Jack's biggest concern had been that they needed to report their Apotheosis win. He shook his head when he recalled everything that had happened since, including making a new friend – who happened to be an ancient dragon.

He could feel his stomach churning as he, Jack and Merryweather trudged through the snow en route to the entrance to the park. He tried to put the images of Gris's security operatives out of his mind and focused on the two aspects of their plan that were in their favour. For one thing, they had surprise on their side, though how long that would be the case remained to be seen. The other thing was that they had Gus with them once more and this gave Tom some hope, if only because of the extra firepower Gus brought. He mused for a second about what Gus in full-on fire-breathing mode would look like, half wanting to see this, but half wanting not to, because if Gus had to resort to this tactic, well, it would likely mean that their plan had gone awry in some way.

But still he wondered what his friend would look like breathing fire…

Merryweather snapped him out of his wonderings by announcing that they had reached their destination.

"Brrrrr, we're here," she whispered. "You both okay? Ready for this?"

Tom and Jack both nodded.

"Okay, time to split up. Jack, with me. Let's go negotiate with that awful woman, and free Katie and Nicky," said Merryweather. "Tom, give Gus the signal and then head to the old church. Try to see what you can find and if you should locate any more relics, then grab as many of them as you can. If you have no luck there, try that marquee thing you saw, but be careful with it: it's likely to be guarded. Okay?"

"Yes, Auntieprof."

"Oh, and Tom… good luck," said Merryweather.

"Good luck to you, too. Do well, dingbat," said Tom, giving Jack a playful punch on the arm.

"We'll be back here before you know it," grinned Jack. Irrepressible as ever, thought Tom to himself.

The three of them split up, with Merryweather and Jack heading towards Gris Corp HQ, whilst Tom edged his way along the park's perimeter towards the old church, sticking as close to the trees that lined the park's outer rim as he could. Even with the relative lack of moonlight this evening, Tom didn't want to risk being out in the open for any longer than he had to be. As he nipped from tree to tree, for some moments more, he could just about still make out Jack and Merryweather receding into the distance as they as they headed towards the HQ complex, before the clumps of trees grew thicker and obscured his view.

After a few minutes, he reached the edge of the final thicket of trees, the one in which he and Jack had been hiding when Jack first spied Gus the night before last. Tom looked towards the old, ruined church. It lay in darkness. A good start, he thought to himself.

It was time to give the signal to Gus. Tom let out a long, low whistle and waited… and waited… and waited. He looked skywards, trying to spot the flying, swooping silhouette against the canvas of twinkling stars, but of Gus, there was no sign.

"Where is he?" muttered Tom to himself. "This is not the time to go AWOL." He pursed his lips and gave another low whistle, even longer than the first one, wondering if – somehow – Gus had become so carried away with his aerial acrobatics that he had flown out of range, though he recalled the dragon assuring him earlier that evening that his hearing was so hypersensitive that he could hear a footstep from over a mile away. So, in theory, a long, low whistle from several hundred feet away should not present very much of a challenge.

Tom held his breath, straining to hear anything beyond the usual muffled sounds of a wintry December evening in the eerily quiet city.

And then, as he was about to exhale (quietly), there was a snapping noise from overhead. Followed by further cracking and snapping noises. Tom peered upwards: it looked as though the tree directly above him was collapsing – from the top of its canopy downwards and through its branches towards the ground.

Instinctively, Tom sprang away from the base of the tree and dived into a snowy clearing, rolling himself into a human snowball, before he came to a stop.

He picked himself up and looked at the pile of debris that had collected at the base of the tree: a mixture of branches, twigs, some leaves, a load of snow and – sitting up in the middle of it – one rather dazed looking dragon…

"Gus," Tom hissed at the dragon, "nice of you to drop in." He brushed some of the snow off himself. "Next time, do you think you could give me a little more warning before you fall out of the sky and almost onto my head?"

Gus gave himself a shake and stood up.

"Aye, sorry about that, laddie," he said in a quiet voice. "Misjudged the landing a wee bittie. No harm done though, eh?"

"Misjudged the landing? You took out most of a tree on your way down!" said Tom, before adding, "Are you okay?"

Gus was banging one side of his head with his long, scaley hand, trying to shake the snow out of his ears.

"I think so. The snow cushioned my fall."

"Thank goodness for that," said Tom. "Come on, we need to get a move on and check out the ruined church – and Gus, remember, we need to be quiet."

"Aye, laddie. Got that. Not a peep," said Gus as one of his enormous feet cracked a frozen branch in two.

"Oops, sorry," said the dragon, smiling sheepishly.

Tom rolled his eyes. He realised Gus was trying to be as quiet as he could be, but at eight feet tall and weighing goodness knows how much, it was always going to be a challenge to expect the dragon to tiptoe around.

Tom stood, half-hidden by an outermost tree, and held up his hand, indicating that they should stop and stay still. He lifted the binoculars out of his rucksack and scanned the old church. Nothing. It was dark and quiet.

Then, he looked through them, over to the HQ building itself, lit up like a Christmas tree, and he could just make out the odd person moving around inside it.

Finally, he scanned towards the marquee structure he had first seen from up in the tree the previous evening. It, too, was also in darkness. Tom wondered again what it was for, as he quickly replaced the binoculars back into the rucksack, reasoning that he and Gus would shortly find out once they finished searching the old church.

He motioned with his hand that it was time to move forward and traverse the last few hundred yards towards the old church and promptly set off at a swift jog, with Gus following him, clumping his way through the snow. Tom could hear every one of Gus's footprints as though it was a mini earthquake going off behind him and was fervently hoping that everyone else in Gris Corp HQ would be too busy and distracted to notice the two of them zipping across the snowy clearing.

They neared the old building and Tom headed for where he and Jack had found the entrance previously.

In the main boardroom of Gris Corp HQ, a walkie-talkie lying on the boardroom table crackled into life. Max Gris picked it up.

"Golden Hind to Francis. What have you got? Over."

"Francis to Golden Hind. One adult and one child en route to HQ. One child and one *thing* heading to the old ruin," replied Grunk.

Max Gris sighed. "It's a dragon, Grunk… anyway, good. We have visual on both. Do nothing with the two at the old church until they are inside, then grab them. We'll deal with the other two. Understood?"

"Roger that. Francis out."

Max Gris replaced the walkie-talkie on the table and turned towards Slymington.

"Not much longer now, Slimey. The plan is working."

Tom and Gus had reached the entrance on the side of the old building, but it looked different.

"That's weird. It looks like this has been repaired. Remember, you charged through it on Friday night and left the door in bits?" said Tom.

Gus gave a frown and scrunched his face up.

"That first night's a bit hazy, laddie," he replied. "I was still waking up. Might take a few more days for my memory to return, but if you say so..."

"Trust me, Gus, there was hardly anything left of this door after you careered through it."

"Are you sure I wasn't trying to eat it? Looks pretty tasty," said the dragon, eyeing up the door.

"Not now, Gus, we've got a job to do," said Tom. "Look, I'm certain this door has been fixed, so... just be careful, okay?"

Tom went to move the door and this time, it shifted much more easily that it had before. He flicked on his torch as he entered the gloomy interior of the old church, with Gus clumping behind him, but its beam was stuttering on and off.

"Oh, not now," said Tom, as he rattled the torch, trying to bring its light to life as the pair of them edged their way further into the gloom and into the central part of the ruin.

With one hefty bang, the torch finally provided a steady beam and Tom flashed it around the inside of the church. As he did so, the light reflected back at him, shining and dazzling as it bounced off metal surfaces.

"That's weird, I don't remember any of this being here last..."

Tom never completed the sentence as a voice began booming out, echoing all around the inside of the ruin.

"Ah, Master Thomas Brightly, good of you to drop in with your... *friend.*"

Tom and Gus stood, immobilised in the darkness. The familiar voice of Max Gris was ricocheting all around them.

Tom tapped Gus on one of his wings and muttered, "Run." The pair of them crept away slowly at first, then broke into a jog (in Gus's case it was more of a shamble) to make their way back to the side entrance.

As they did so, the voice boomed again.

"Leaving so soon? Such a pity. I was so looking forward to meeting you both."

A pause.

"Indeed, I still am."

Tom and Gus reached the door through which they had both entered. Tom grabbed its handle and rattled it, but the door refused to budge. He yanked at it again, but still it remained firmly shut.

"It won't move," said Tom to Gus. "It's locked."

Gris's voice boomed out again. "Oh yes, I should have said. We replaced the door that you and your friend here smashed to pieces the other night. In fact, we've made a few updates since your last visit. Would you like to see them?"

Tom let go of the door handle and turned to Gus.

"Gus, I think we're in trouble here..."

"Don't worry, laddie. I'm ready for it," Gus replied.

As the last echoes of Max Gris's booming voice faded, several powerful lights started buzzing and flashing into life above his and Gus's heads, illuminating the interior of the formerly ruined church.

Tom gasped at the scene that was revealed. The entire inside space of the former ruin had been transformed. The place was awash with gold decoration and ornamentation, including what looked like some sort of raised stage, towards the far end of the church, where previously there had just been a few old, broken pews and other assorted debris. Every wall was festooned with red velvet, which was draped over all the old stonework, giving the whole place an almost regal look.

Gris spoke again, "What do you think? Not bad for a long day's work, is it? Pity you won't have too much longer to admire the craftsmanship and sheer attention to detail that has been lavished on this, the Cathedral of the Others. Indeed, young Thomas, I doubt your pet here will even recognise the place.

"Now, these nice gentlemen are going to bring you to HQ. Do be a pair of dears and come along quietly. I really don't want any trouble and nor do I want anything to be damaged. See you soon."

Her voice stopped once more and as it did so, Gris Corp security personnel began swarming into the church, each one with a raised gun, all of them pointing at the pair of them. Grunk led the way, his face, beneath his exorbitant beard, set like stone.

"Do not move," he bellowed. "Put any weapons you have down on the floor in front of you. Slowly."

"We don't have any weapons," shouted Tom.

"Yeah? Then, what's that thing?" shouted Grunk, pointing at Gus with his gun.

"He's my friend," shouted Tom. "Don't hurt him. He won't harm you. Right, Gus?" He glanced at Gus. He could see the dragon's face turning into a scowl as he began taking a huge intake of breath and stared at all the assembled Gris Corp security.

"Oh no," murmured Tom.

"Bad knights, laddie…" muttered Gus. He let out an almighty roar and started to exhale. At first, sparks flew towards the Gris Corp goons. These were followed almost immediately by licks of flame which grew larger and longer as Gus started to move towards the gun-toting Gris Corp goons.

Two steps closer was as far as he reached though, as the entire battery of Gris Corp security assembled in the old church began firing their guns and a hail of darts began raining down on Gus. The Gris Corp security personnel had trained all of their weapons on Gus and were strafing him. Tom dived to his right and landed in a heap on the floor as the miniature missiles struck their target. He could see the ceiling above him being lit up by Gus's bursts of flame and the heat began prickling his neck. He scrambled under a table to escape it and crouched there for a second, scanning for a way out – any means of escape at all. And then, the hood of his jacket was yanked backwards, and he felt the whole garment tighten around his neck.

"Gotcha, you little troublemaker," said Grunk, with a note of satisfaction in his voice. Gasping, and trying to loosen the zip on his jacket, Tom lashed out, his arms and legs flailing around in mid-air, as he tried to wriggle free from Grunk's hold.

In the middle of this, Gus let out another roar that turned into a howl and the nascent flames sputtered out as his gigantic eight-foot-tall frame tensed from the top of his huge, scaly head to the tip of his long, pointed tail, and he toppled over, like an ancient oak being felled.

"Gus! GUS!" yelled Tom. "What have you done to him? GUUUSSS!"

Tom was punching and kicking at any bit of Grunk he could reach as he screamed his friend's name out, over and over again, but mostly, his punches and kicks missed. He was fighting with the air. Grunk remained impervious to the youngster's protests – Tom may as well have been an ant biting an elephant – and had him held fast in his vice-like grip. He tolerated Tom's wriggling and squirming and generally making a nuisance of himself for a few more seconds after Gus's collapse, before placing him in a tight headlock, and uttering one solitary threat.

"Stop struggling or you'll meet the same fate as your friend here."

Tom's whole body tensed as he continued to struggle and writhe, using all his strength to try to make one last desperate attempt to escape Grunk's grasp, before he realised it was futile. His body relaxed and his head dropped as Grunk bodily carried him out of the church in a fireman's lift.

Grunk bellowed one further instruction, "Bring that thing up to HQ as quickly as you can. Meet me there."

He turned his attention back to Tom.

"You're coming with me, like it or not. You've caused enough mayhem for one night."

And with this, they were outside, the cold air slamming into Tom's face like an icy punch. He fell silent, with tears burning in his eyes as he tried to process what he had just seen: Gus's giant body lay flat out and still on the floor of the church. As Grunk transported him through the darkness and the night air towards the Gris Corp HQ building, all Tom could think about was whether his new friend was still alive.

After a couple of minutes of being carried through the grounds in the darkness, Tom was aware he had reached Gris Corp HQ as the light from the main atrium pierced his blurry eyes and a wave of warm air replaced the biting cold. He managed to half-wipe his eyes and face with his sleeve, but still couldn't properly see where he was going as Grunk had him wedged over his shoulder, facing backwards. He spotted the odd Gris Corp employee scurrying around as his journey continued through the HQ, but the place was eerily deserted.

After several more minutes, they arrived in a large room. Tom could see Grunk punching a code to open the door, and then they were inside a large, brightly lit room that was very bare, save for a stage at one end and a few chairs. The walls, as with most of the HQ building, were made entirely of glass, in this instance, frosted glass.

"Sit down," instructed Grunk, pointing at a chair. Tom silently did as he was told. He looked at the security man, who was standing, staring at nothing in particular and waiting, but for what?

As it turned out, Tom didn't have to wait long to find out. A door opened at the far end of the room and through it strode Max Gris herself.

"Ah, Master Brightly, you've joined us. Welcome," she began, before adding a short, "Good work, Grunk."

Grunk gave a nod.

"I expect you're missing your friends, aren't you?" said Gris. Tom stared at her and said nothing. "Well, I have a surprise for you."

At this, through the door at the far end of the room, a phalanx of Gris Corp security came marching in, bringing with them, Merryweather, Jack and Katie, walking in a line in their midst.

"Thought it was time for a reunion," smirked Gris. Tom looked at the three other prisoners. His aunt's face was stern. Jack looked terrified, and Katie could barely keep her head up.

"Please, sit down," said Gris. "Tea? Coffee? Juice? Actually, forget that, this isn't a social occasion."

The three of them sat down in the seats next to Tom. He looked at his aunt and mouthed "what happened?", but her face remained tight set, giving nothing away. He tried to catch Jack's eye, but he was looking down at the ground and, as for Katie, she seemed to be half-asleep.

Gris continued, "Well, your little plan – whatever it was – has failed. And you still have something that I want – and I want it, or should I say them – very badly indeed. So, now I only have one question for all of you: where are my relics?"

There was silence.

Gris sighed.

"Well, don't all rush me. Listen, you merry little band of adventurers, your plan - if one can give it such a lofty name as that – is over. I have captured you, neutralised your *pet* and you're going nowhere until one of you tells me where those relics are, so you may as well get it over with now and then we can all move on with our lives."

Still, there was only silence. Tom looked at his aunt, but Merryweather kept staring straight at Gris. Then she spoke.

"Whatever you're planning, Ms Gris, it won't work."

Gris turned to Merryweather.

"What? What did you say? It won't work?" She began laughing hysterically, right in Merryweather's face.

"Oh dear, oh dear, ancient Professor Merryweather, you really have no idea what on earth you're talking about. Now, be a dear and tell me where you've stashed those last relics, won't you?" Gris raised her eyebrows into an arch that a suspension bridge would have been proud of.

There was silence again in the room, and only the clack, clack, clack of Gris's shoes as she stalked her way around the four of them. She let out a huge theatrical sigh.

"Oh, very well. It's going to be like this, is it? Why do they *always* choose the hard way? Grunk, turn on the screen."

Grunk strode over to a control panel on the wall and pressed a combination of buttons. A large, thin screen lowered from the roof. As it came to a stop and clicked into place, Gris spoke at the four captives.

"One of you is about to tell me where those relics are. Don't care who it is. Just give me the info."

She turned to the screen as it flashed on. There, in its centre, was a giant, grey green heap, with flashes of purple. Immobile and on some sort of platform – and tied down with bulky chains.

"Gus!" blurted out Tom, half-wondering if their friend was still alive.

Standing around the platform were yet more Gris Corp security, holding guns, all of which were trained at the dragon.

"Simmons, can you hear me?" barked Gris.

"Yes, ma'am," replied Grunk's deputy.

"You can begin the process now," said Gris.

"What process?" shouted Tom. "What are you going to do to him?"

Gris flashed a smile of pure evil.

"Oh, you'll see, and very soon, you're going to give me what I want. Because, young Master Brightly, I *always* get what I want."

Tom, Merryweather and Jack all had their eyes glued to the screen, waiting to see what would happen. Out of the corner of his eye, Tom could see that Katie's head was doing its best impersonation of a nodding dog. He couldn't understand how she could be so sleepy at a time like this. Tom could see that Simmons was carrying some sort of long, metal stick. He shouted at one of the other security goons to "switch it on" and approached Gus, pointing the metal stick directly at the centre of his body.

"Ready, ma'am," said Simmons down the videolink.

"Do it," instructed Gris, the smile now vanished from her face.

Tom watched as Simmons poked the stick directly into Gus's side and from it blue flashes and sparks appeared to fly everywhere. Gus's entire body tensed up and went completely rigid, and from the speakers of the screen came a sound unlike anything Tom had ever heard in his entire life: a muffled bloodcurdling roar and scream combined. Muffled, because as Gus tried to raise his head, the vast weight of the chains held him down, pinning him to the platform. Tom could see that his mouth had also been wrapped up and chained – and padlocked – firmly shut.

Tom sprang out of his chair and made to run towards Gris, shouting.

"Noooooo! What are you doing to him? Stop it! Stop doing that!"

Grunk intercepted Tom and felled him. Then he lifted him up and threw him back into his chair.

"SIT. DOWN."

Tom felt as though his guts had been knocked out of him as he fought to catch a breath.

Merryweather stood up, her face stern as she looked at Gris.

"Stop it! He's a child, you brute of a man. This whole thing is evil. Gus is a defenceless creature and you're torturing him. You're going to kill him if you keep going! Stop it now."

"That's enough for now, Simmons," said Gris as she raised her right hand in the air, indicating he should stop.

She looked at Merryweather and snorted.

"Defenceless? I think not, Professor. Why do you think we have him trussed up like a Christmas turkey? One wrong move and he would roast us all to a cinder," sneered Gris.

Merryweather kept on staring at Gris.

"I pity you, Ms Gris. You clearly revel in wickedness and cruelty. If you had any humanity in you, you would let that creature go, along with the rest of us. Goodness knows, you've already committed many enough crimes as it is these past few days. Why not quit while you're ahead?" Merryweather threw the question like an accusation at Gris.

Gris strode over to her, security goons hovering by both her side and Merryweather's. As Tom watched, Gris put her face right next to Merryweather's and spoke sotto voce.

"Nice speech. Always remember that virtue is only ever an option. You could make all of this stop right now, your ancient professorship. Just tell me where those relics are, and you can all go home. It's up to you…" Gris was grinning right in Merryweather's face.

Tom watched as his aunt could restrain herself no longer and drew her hand back to strike Gris. She never made it past the backswing., Grunk grabbed her wrist and fired out another instruction.

"You need to SIT DOWN, lady."

With which, he shoved Merryweather back into her chair.

"Temper, temper, professori!" grinned Gris. Then, she turned back to the screen and issued another instruction as casually as though she were ordering her favourite coffee. "Right, Simmons, give it another blast."

The hulking, black-clad goon that was Simmons did exactly as he was told, shoving the long, metal rod straight into Gus's tail this time, producing sparks and bolts of electricity which flashed around it and spread all over Gus's body. He then stood laughing as the dragon's entire body tensed from head to toe once more, at the same time as the same spine-chilling howl of pain as before spilled out of the speakers. After several seconds of this, Simmons withdrew the electrical prod, which was still flashing and sparking, and Gus's body relaxed slightly, albeit this time, with random twitches and spasms all over it.

Tears were burning Tom's eyes again. Jack was sitting, his head in his hands, and as Tom looked at his aunt, he could see her eyes were misty as well.

Merryweather spoke. "I beg of you, Ms Gris, before you kill that innocent creature, please stop this."

Gris strode over to Merryweather and once more bent down, sticking her face directly in front of the professor's tearful eyes.

"Give. Me. The. Relics."

Tom could stand it no longer. "All right, all right!" he shouted. "Stop it. You can have your stupid relics." He reached deep into the pocket of his jacket and brought out a bag, holding it out to Gris.

Tom looked at his aunt, who shot him a look. Tom couldn't tell what this meant, but right now, he had only one concern.

"Just stop hurting Gus. Please…" Tom wiped his eyes. And nose.

Grunk grabbed the bag of relics from him and handed it to Gris, who smiled thinly.

"A wise decision, Master Brightly. Wait here," she said.

Gris walked across the room and disappeared through another one of its many doors.

"Where's she going now?" whispered Tom to Merryweather.

"No idea," replied his aunt.

They soon had their answer.

A panel of cloudy glass on the far side of the room slid its way downwards, revealing a further tinted pane of glass directly behind it and immediately beyond, a room with a table, next to which Max Gris was standing, holding some sort of remote control. Tom saw a tall, thin, bearded man sitting at the table with his head bowed. He didn't recognise him, but the man's hair and clothes were a mess and his face, whilst bearded, was also bestubbled, as though he hadn't shaved in a while. His face looked strained, and he had huge dark circles under his eyes.

"Who's that?" Tom whispered to Merryweather.

"Nicky…" murmured Merryweather.

"He looks awful," whispered Tom again.

"I know," replied his aunt.

The speakers next to the giant screen buzzed back into life. Gris walked over to the table and placed the bag of relics on it. Carefully.

"Open it," she said to Auld. "Go on, open it and take them out."

Auld raised his head, though he looked defeated. He opened the bag and reached into it, fishing the relics out one at a time and placing them on the table.

"Well?" asked Gris once Auld had laid all the relics out on the table in front of them. He picked up one of the ancient artefacts and turned it over right in front of his face, peering at it intently as he did so.

"It's hard to tell… I mean, they look old, but also different from the other batches," said Auld.

Gris turned to face the screen as she addressed Auld, as though she were a barrister summing up in a trial.

"Doctor Auld, do these relics, in your expert opinion, match those contained in the other batches you have recently inspected?" she asked.

Auld hesitated, turning the relic in his hands over and over in front of him before he delivered his conclusion.

"I would need to run some carbon dating to be absolutely sure, but no, upon first inspection, they don't appear to be the same as the rest of the batches of relics."

He paused.

"Where did you say you found them again?" he asked.

"I didn't," snapped Gris. "Thank you, Doctor Auld. That will be all. You've been most helpful."

Tom looked at Merryweather and raised his eyebrows. If Merryweather was worried in any way about what had just happened, her face was betraying none of her inner fears. She kept staring forwards, impassive and projecting an exterior visage of calm.

The screen speakers clicked off as the frosted glass wall inched its way upwards again, gradually sealing off the scene in the room beyond.

A door slid open, and Gris burst through it.

"Grunk, get Simmons back on screen. I've had enough of being messed around. Our guests *will* now tell me where the genuine relics are – or their pet will die."

Tom looked at his aunt. She was still staring impassively straight ahead of her, her face not giving anything away.

Simmons reappeared on the screen in front of them all and Gris began shouting orders at him.

"Simmons, double the strength and fry that thing again. Now!"

There was a low buzzing sound coming from the screen as Simmons adjusted a series of dials and buttons before taking the long metal rod, now fizzing and crackling even more than previously with blue sparks and flashes, and prodded it straight into Gus's rump. Immediately, the sparks and flashes intensified and the dragon's whole body went rigid once more. The bloodcurdling, howling roar, muffled by his jaws being locked shut, began again, too. Sparks were bouncing around all over the trussed-up dragon's body and blue-grey smoke fogged up the camera providing the pictures. This carried on for several seconds longer than the previous bursts before Gris raised her hand and called for Simmons to stop. Gus's body tensed up completely once more and then jerked three times before becoming still.

Gris turned to the row of captives.

"I would say we could keep doing this all night, but frankly, a couple more bursts at that strength and your friend will be too far gone to save."

She paced in front of the four of them.

"Last chance: tell me where my relics are. Now."

Tom looked at Merryweather and then at Jack. Jack was wiping his eyes and silently weeping. He saw a tear trickle down his aunt's face and her top lip was quivering – but she remained silent.

Gris let out an enormous theatrical sigh.

"Very well then. Your choice. Simmons, go to the maximum and don't stop this time," she instructed.

"Yes, ma'am," came Simmons' reply.

He fiddled around with the controls for a few seconds. The electrical rod was now popping, crackling, and fizzing violently with blue sparks and mini-lightning bolts. Simmons raised the rod once more, ready to plunge it into Gus when Tom leapt up.

"Stop! Stop it now! I'll tell you where they are!"

Gris looked at Tom.

"Excellent, some common sense at last. Hold it there, Simmons," she said.

Tom looked at Merryweather, who was staring directly at him.

"Well," asked Gris, "where are they then?"

Tom gulped.

"They're at the professor's house, hidden away," he said.

"Impossible," said Gris. "My men have already searched the entire house."

"They're in a secret hiding place in the cellar of the house," blurted Tom. "Your men wouldn't have found it. No one would unless they knew exactly where to look."

Gris walked backwards and forwards in front of the screen. On it, Simmons was waiting in anticipation of the instruction to carry on.

Gris paced over to Tom.

"You'd better not be lying or else your pet will die," she snarled.

"I promise, I'm telling you the truth. I'll take you there myself," pleaded Tom.

Gris strode over to face Merryweather.

"Well? Is this true?" she snapped.

Merryweather, glanced at Tom, before she turned her focus back to her tormentor and gave a single nod of her head.

"Excellent. At last!" said Gris, grinning. "Simmons, you can stand down – for now."

She turned to Grunk and pointed at Merryweather and Katie.

"Grunk, have these two taken to the cells."

"What?" shouted Merryweather. "This is outrageous. You can't keep us prisoners."

"I can do whatever I like," replied Gris coolly, "and you're not going anywhere until I have those relics."

She turned back to Grunk.

"Take them away. They're annoying me now. Once you're done, take this one," she said, pointing at Tom, "and retrieve the relics. ASAP."

Tom saw Jack looking confused as Merryweather and Katie were led away.

"What about me?" blurted out Jack.

Gris turned towards him and flashed an evil smile of satisfaction.

"You, young Master Wanless, are our winner. I have *big* plans for you. *Very* big plans indeed."

As Grunk grabbed Tom once again by the collar of his jacket and dragged him away, Tom saw his friend's eyes widening as his face contorted in fear.

"Don't worry, Jack. It'll be okay. I'll come back for you…" shouted Tom, before Grunk clamped his plate-sized hand over his mouth as he hauled Tom from the room.

CHAPTER FORTY-FIVE

Tom was sitting in the back of a very large SUV, wedged between Grunk and one of his henchmen. He could still feel the faint trails of the heater that had originally been on full blast as they left Gris Corp HQ. He was sitting bolt upright, his whole body tense, and he was sweating slightly, but not because of the relative warmth of the car. Other than a perfunctory instruction from Grunk to "get in and shut up", there had been no further communication throughout the journey.

It was pitch black outside. Tom noticed that the streetlights, which had been blinking on and off occasionally earlier on, now appeared to be out again. He wondered if this meant that the intermittent power cuts were still happening. It made it hard to figure out precisely where they were – but he knew where they were going. Max Gris's orders had been clear: go to Merryweather's house, retrieve the last of the relics and bring them to Gris Corp HQ as quickly as possible.

Tom's mind raced as he tried to figure out what would happen next, what he could do – if anything – and what would happen to him once he had handed over the relics. He didn't imagine that it would be anything good. He now realised just how desperate Gris was to obtain the relics. Three of his friends held as prisoners until the relics were delivered and a fourth held in captivity under threat of further torture, plus his aunt's colleague, who looked as though he hadn't slept for about a week, also detained. Tom realised Gris would stop at nothing to get the relics, all of which made whatever he chose to do next an impossible decision.

In the front of the car, another of the Gris Corp security detail was driving steadily and efficiently through the snowy city. Slymington was sitting in the passenger seat; Tom recognised he was Gris's deputy. His being here underscored the importance of this stage of her plan. As Tom was being escorted to the SUV, Slymington had already made it clear that the clock was ticking down to an immoveable deadline and that there would be no further chances either for him - or especially for Gus - if he wasted any more of their time.

Tom was turning this over and over in his mind as he tried to figure out how to solve an insoluble dilemma: give Gris the relics and she would unleash hell on Christmas as the entire world knew it and become even more powerful than she already was – perhaps even the most powerful person in the entire world. Tom involuntarily shuddered at this thought.

However, not to give her the relics would lead to an awful fate for Gus, Jack, Merryweather, Katie and Nick Auld, too. Tom shivered again to himself as he mulled over his options and the likely consequences. There must be some other way, he thought to himself, as he racked his brains once again, trying desperately to come up with another plan that didn't lead to either of the two afore-mentioned outcomes.

But try as he might, no other plan was forthcoming.

The car slowing up jolted him out of his thoughts. It came to a halt outside Merryweather's house.

"Get out," said Grunk, as he unplugged Tom's seatbelt. "And don't try anything smart, or your friends are toast. Understood?"

Tom nodded as he shuffled his way out of the car behind the other security guard. He could feel an air of resignation creeping over himself.

Slymington approached him.

"Now, young Master Brightly, this is what is going to happen next. Grunk here is going to open the door to the professor's house. You will follow him in and show him where the relics are. I shall follow you. These other two gentlemen will stand guard at the front door to ensure we are not disturbed during the retrieval. Do nothing untoward or else you and your friends will regret it. Do I make myself clear?"

Tom looked hard at the tall, thin man's unsmiling face and nodded slowly.

"Good. Grunk, lead the way."

The five of them made their way up the pathway to the front door. Leaving the two security operatives at the foot of the stairs leading to the front door, Grunk strode up them and chivvied away at the front door lock. After a couple of seconds, it clicked open, and he went inside.

"Come on," he instructed Tom.

Tom did as he was told. Grunk had switched on a torch to illuminate the pitch darkness in the house.

"Right, where are they?" he growled menacingly at Tom.

"In the cellar," said Tom quietly.

"Well, lead the way then, Master Brightly," said Slymington.

Tom inched his way forward, with Grunk keeping step with him, and shining the torch to light their way.

Halfway along the hallway, they reached a small door.

"This is it here. The entrance to the cellar, I mean," said Tom.

"Open it," said Grunk.

Tom did as he was told. Grunk poked his head inside and flashed the torch.

"Stairs. Narrow. Low ceiling. Single file. You first," he said as he shoved Tom towards the top of the stairs. "I'll shine the torch to light your way and I'll be right behind you, so don't try anything, right?"

"Yes," nodded Tom, as he edged his way down the narrow staircase, one slow step at a time.

"I'll wait here. Don't be long," said Slymington to Grunk as the man mountain prised himself through the narrow opening and stooped so as not to bash his head on the ceiling. The very sound of Slymington's voice gave Tom the creeps, and he was relieved he would not be joining them in the cellar.

As he descended the stairs down into the cellar, the light from Grunk's torch zig-zagging slightly ahead of him, Tom could feel his heart racing.

This was it. The end. He would need to give Grunk the relics and then what? Tom reached the bottom of the stairs and paused, closing his eyes and trying to breathe. The air in the cellar felt cold and smelt of mustiness with a faint tinge of burnt wood. Tom wondered if Gus had been secretly enjoying some snacks in his brief time in his new home. He closed his eyes and tried to figure out what Merryweather would do if she were here.

A grunt and a shove in his back from Grunk snapped him back to the present.

"Right, you. Where are they?" barked Grunk.

"They're over there, in a box hidden in an alcove," said Tom, pointing to a faraway dark recess.

"Well, you're going to go and fetch them then," growled Grunk, "and I'll be right behind you."

Grunk shone the torch towards the general area where Tom had pointed. Tom walked towards it, taking his steps slowly, like a condemned man. He knew he had to do something, but what? He reached the alcove and bent down to uncover the box from its hiding place.

"Slowly now," instructed Grunk. "No sudden movements."

Tom reached down and into the darkness, his fingers feeling for the box. He felt the knobbles of a wooden stick and tugged it towards him before throwing it onto the floor behind.

"What are you doing?" asked Grunk.

"The box is hidden under a bunch of sticks and branches in there. I'm going to have to pull them all off it before I can get to it.

"Do it carefully," said Grunk.

Tom nodded and reached deep inside the alcove, feeling for the next stick to dismantle the box's hiding place. He grabbed it and dragged it out, once again throwing it behind him. This process went on for a few minutes. He could sense Grunk was becoming impatient and growing more agitated with each passing second.

"Have you found it yet?" asked the henchman.

"Almost," said Tom, as his fingertip alighted on the exterior of the ornate metal box itself.

He grasped at the edge of the box until he had inched it towards himself and then dragged it out of its hiding place.

He drew it out towards the musty cellar and shuffled backwards towards Grunk. Standing up, Tom handed the box to Grunk, who furrowed his brow and tried to prise open the box with both hands whilst still clutching the torch between the fingers of his right hand so he could see what he was doing. Which he could – just. As Tom stood there in the darkness, shaking, he realised it was now or never.

With Grunk still absorbed in trying to open the box whilst balancing the torch to give himself some light, Tom slowly bent down and scooped up a handful of the dirt and muck on the cellar floor. He seized his chance and hurled the mucky mixture straight into Grunk's face.

Grunk let out a roar and dropped both box and torch, which promptly went out. Tom leapt towards a small door by the alcove and yanked it open, diving into the claustrophobic passageway that lay beyond it. He started scrambling his way along it, but as he was drawing his left foot in, he felt his ankle being grabbed.

"Oh no you don't, you little sod," shouted Grunk.

With all his might, Tom aimed his right foot back towards Grunk and smashed it in the general direction of the human manacle that was clutching onto his left ankle. And then again. And again.

"Get out of there," shouted Grunk. "I'm going to massacre you for this!"

"I…" Tom thumped Grunk's arm with his foot.

"DON'T," and again…

"THINK…" and again, though he was now being dragged back towards the door.

"SO!" With all the determination he could muster, Tom drew back his right foot once more and propelled it towards his assailant with full force.

This time, he got lucky: Grunk had dragged him out of the passageway sufficiently to expose his face to Tom's incoming boot. Which connected directly with Grunk's nose, causing it to explode instantly in a bloody mess which, in turn, made the man mountain recoil and instinctively clutch it.

With the iron grip on his ankle released, Tom squirmed his way back into the passageway and scrabbled his way along it as quickly as he could, panting with fear.

From behind him came a snarl and then a shout of, "I'm gonna kill you, you little runt!"

Tom kept moving along the passageway as quickly as he could. He had one chance here, and this was it. Grunk's threats were receding into the distance, and then, finally, they stopped.

Tom's brain was racing now. Why had Grunk gone quiet? He wondered whether he had returned to the others. One chance. One chance…

He reached the door at the end of the passageway and shoved it open, pulling himself out headfirst and landing in a heap on the snow below, knocking the wind clean out of him. He was at the very bottom of the rear of the house. He sat upright and listened for a moment. Faint shouting. He had seconds. Getting up, he sprinted towards the rear of the house behind the kitchen and raced towards his quarry, propped up against the back wall in the darkness: his sledge was still there. Tom lunged towards it and grabbed it, before throwing it down on the ground in front of him, diving headfirst onto it and racing off down Merryweather's back garden towards the field beyond.

He could hear the shouts getting louder now.

All Tom was thinking was, aim for the gap… aim for the gap…

With all his strength and skill, he steered the sledge towards the gap in the fence that Gus had made when he had careered around Merryweather's back garden on that first night they had found him. The sledge had picked up speed as it raced down the icy crust of the deep snow covering the back garden.

Tom and the sledge hurtled towards the fence. The sledge hit a bump as it neared the gap and flew through it, almost causing Tom to part company with it. As it was, his arm scraped the side panel of the fence and he let out a shout, more in fright than in pain and then, he was free and streaking down the hill beyond Merryweather's house, across the hard-packed snow and onwards, into the night.

As he picked his way carefully through the snow and towards the rear of the house, Slymington, impassive as ever, was examining the contents of the small, ornate metal box that Grunk had handed him a few moments earlier.

One of the two other Gris Crop henchmen crunched his way up the back garden towards him.

"Well?" asked Slymington.

"He got away. He's down that hill somewhere. Couldn't see him," said the goon.

"No matter," said Slymington. "We have what we came for. The boy can wait – for now."

By this side, a bloodied Grunk was clutching a handkerchief to his nose to staunch the blood still seeping from it.

"When I find the little git, I'll separate him from his breath," he growled.

"You'll have your chance soon enough, Grunk. He won't have gone far," said Slymington. "We'll deal with him once we've delivered the relics to Ms Gris. Come on. To the car. We need to return to HQ."

CHAPTER FORTY-SIX

Tom opened his eyes. Everything was white. He turned his head. Everything he could see was white. He was confused. And cold. He looked around. All white. He sat upright and as he wakened up, he started to remember. He reached his arm out to touch the whiteness. It was real. This wasn't a dream. This was real, hard-packed snow all around him. Walls and a roof. This was an igloo, small enough to be cosy, but big enough for a child to fit inside – and he was in it.

He didn't know how long he had been asleep for, but it was still dark outside from what he could see through the entrance of his temporary accommodation. He had stuffed his rucksack into the gap last night, not completely blocking it, but enough to keep most of the frigid night air from entering. Fairly successfully, as it had turned out. The igloo, whilst not anyone's first choice on such a bitter night, had worked, just as he had read about: it had been warmer on its inside once he had crawled in and sealed the front of it with his rucksack. Not exactly toasty, but warm enough to stop him from shivering (eventually) – and freezing to death.

As he grew more alert, Tom recalled the events of the previous evening. The desperate escape from the Gris Corp squad and especially the awful Grunk; relocating, then diving onto his sledge and finally, racing down the hill to freedom. It had all been rather a blur that had lasted only a matter of minutes, but by the time he had reached the bottom of the long slope behind his aunt's house, Tom had been shaking, his heart pumping so loudly he could hear the blood racing through his ears as he listened intently into the night for any sounds that might indicate that his tormentors were following him.

But there had been nothing. Nothing other than the usual, faint sounds of a wintry evening: the faint crunching and revving of a solitary car off in the distance somewhere as it tried to navigate the hard-packed snowy roads, accompanied by the occasional hooting of an owl somewhat nearer by.

Tom had crunched his way towards the fence that bounded the base of the field and had thrown his sledge over it, before hauling himself over, too, and landing on a snow-covered footpath on its other side. He picked himself up and grabbed the sledge, moving towards the wooded area that lay behind the path, between it and the estate full of houses beyond. He found a tree he would remember – an old oak – and placed the sledge at its base, hurriedly covering it over as best he could with snow.

That done, he reached into his pocket for his mobile phone, hitting the power button to turn it on.

"Come on," he urged as the screen blinked into life. For a few seconds, he was hopeful as he willed there to be a phone signal once more, but as the seconds ticked on, the signal indicator on his phone remained at zero. He tried calling home anyway, but there was nothing other than the faint hiss of electrostatic. Not even a connection – and his battery was now low, which didn't help matters, either.

"Rats," muttered Tom, pressing on the power button to turn the phone off, before stuffing it back into his jacket pocket once more.

"Now what do I do?" he asked himself. As he gazed upwards into the night, his only reply had been silence, followed by a further solitary hoot in the distance. Tom knew he had to get out of the cold and find some sort of shelter somewhere. But where? He couldn't contact anyone. He ran through his options: he could wander up to a random house, but what would he say? What *could* he say that wouldn't immediately lead to a phone call being made to the police? Of course, he could go directly to the police, but he knew that this would lead to more problems for his friends and would likely spell the end for Gus. There was no way to return home, given the ongoing power cuts and the state of the roads. And again, even if he could, what would he do then? What would he tell his mum and nan?

All routes that he could think of led to a well-meaning grown-up calling the police if he so much as told any of them even a fraction of the story of the past few days. Deep down, he knew that such a response from any adult would not, on the face of it, be unreasonable, but each time he nearly gave in to this option, his mind returned to Gus and the peril he was in. Max Gris was so twisted she would just as surely give the order to kill Gus as to let him live, were there be any threat to her evil plan. And that was if she didn't already have connections with the police, thought Tom. He didn't know what to believe anymore, given so much of what he had previously understood about the world had been upended in the past forty-eight hours.

His mind had been spinning in circles as he scrunched around in the snow. Tom knew he had to find somewhere to hunker down in for the night – and soon. He looked up at the night sky, seeking some sort of inspiration, and noticed that, for the first time in several nights, there were no stars to be seen: clouds had rolled in. This was good news: now it might only be slightly Baltic instead of mega-Baltic overnight. His mind was mulling over the options before him when he stopped. Of course. He did have one final option: Atticus Sharp. He might listen to him without resorting to calling the police straight away. The trouble was, his flat was on the other side of the city – and there was no way Tom would make it there tonight. He had to find somewhere to hole up in for the evening – and overnight…

He had trudged his way towards the housing estate beyond the woods. Fortunately, the edge of the trees bounded the back gardens of the houses beyond. Doubly fortunately, the houses themselves dated from before the Second World War and as a result – and in contrast to many modern houses – had rather large back gardens.

He walked along the perimeter of the trees, sticking close to the edge, in order to keep out of sight as much as he could. Most of the houses now had some sort of lighting in them, albeit its dimness suggested it was temporary rather than being powered by the mains electricity, and he could also see a number which had their Christmas trees relit again. Tom shook his head once more. How on earth had he ended up in such a mess mere days before Christmas? And more importantly, how on earth was he going to extricate himself and all his friends from it before Max Gris started on her full-on evil plan tomorrow?

He plodded onwards, looking for something, anything, anywhere, he could hide out for the night. He peered in garden after garden, some with their snow cover untouched, some with footprints and animal prints and a few with various types of snowmen standing sentry-like in the darkness.

He was shivering near uncontrollably by now. He didn't know precisely how long it had been since he had escaped from Grunk, but it had been too long to be out in the cold on a night such as this one. He had to find somewhere to shelter soon, else he was going to have to knock on a random front door. And then, as he sidled up to the back fence of yet another garden to peer into it, he saw it: next to a particularly impressive snowman halfway down the garden, there was another snow creation. Could it be what it looked like?

Tom hauled himself over the back fence and crunched his way as quietly as he could towards the snowy structure. As he drew nearer, his heart soared. His guess had been right - he had found his shelter for the evening: a decent-sized and solid looking igloo.

And now, the following morning, he was wide awake in said igloo, his stomach rumbling and his cheeks feeling the keenness of the cold as it pinched his face once more. He could see his breath forming its familiar cloud of the past few days as he considered his overall situation and let out a long sigh. The first fronds of daylight were starting to show in the sky. Time to move before whoever had built the igloo popped outside to check up on it.

He grabbed his rucksack from the front entrance and the colder air outside the igloo began flooding into it. Tom crawled on his front, levering himself out of the entrance on his elbows. He gave a quick glance towards the rear of the house and then, as quietly as he could, stole away out of the garden, draping himself over the back fence once more.

He quickly found his way out of the woods by following the footpath and then tried to recall the quickest way out of the housing estate. The day was moving beyond the morning twilight, and Tom could see the odd person venturing out into the cold, snowy Christmas Eve morning. Walking as quickly as he could so as not to slip on the icy pavements, Tom made his way out of the street of houses in which he had spent the night and headed back towards the city centre.

His first clue that things had changed came as he walked past several houses: their lights were on. These were not the dim lights of the previous evening. They looked like proper lights. He passed a middle-aged woman out walking her dog on the pavement.

"Morning," said Tom as he passed her.

"Morning…" she replied. Tom sensed an odd tone in her voice as she replied and he half-glanced behind him. The woman had stopped walking and was fumbling in her pocket. Tom kept walking and after a few more steps, he turned around again. The woman had taken her phone out of her pocket and was aiming its camera at him. He registered its flash going off in the morning twilight.

Okay, that was weird, he thought, as he put his head down and walked on. He wrapped his scarf tighter around his neck to keep out the cold. He could now see the odd row of streetlamps on and blazing away in the lifting gloom. There was definitely some mains power back on again now. All Tom could immediately think of was his stomach and its incessant rumbling. He needed to find some breakfast – and soon. He took off his left glove and thrust his hand into his pocket on the off chance that there might still be a random snackable in it. Rummaging around to no effect, he felt a bobble beyond the pocket in the lining of his jacket.

Of course, you doofus, he thought. The hole was still there. A sweet or something must have fallen through it into the lining. He prised the hole open with his fingers and reached into the lining of his jacket, just managing to reach the bump-causing item. He drew it back out carefully from the lining, through the hole and out into the open air.

It was not, however, the much hoped for morsel. Indeed, as he extricated the item, Tom wondered what exactly it was. It looked like a very ancient, small, carved piece of wood…

He stopped dead in his tracks, inspecting the small object in the dull, grey winter light of the morning, his jaw dropping open.

That was no snackable or foodstuff. This was the pocket in which he had initially stuffed all the relics from the first recce to Gris Corp HQ. It couldn't be, could it? Tom pored over the small object. The size of a broad bean, it had some sort of inscription along its edge, in symbols he couldn't understand.

A flash went off in his face.

"What the..?" exclaimed Tom. A few feet away, a young- looking man was holding his phone up and pointing it directly at Tom's face. The flash went off again.

"What are you doing?" Tom asked the man.

"It's you, isn't it?" asked the young man. "It's okay; they said you were shy. But it's okay, I've found you now. If you come with me, it'll be okay."

"What on earth are you talking about?" asked Tom.

"You're that boy who won the game, but you don't want the prize," said the man. "It's all over the internet and tv this morning. There's a massive reward for anyone who spots you and an even bigger one if you get brought into Max Gris's place."

The man was grinning at Tom, but it wasn't a friendly grin.

"So, come on then… come with me and we can split the prize." The man edged towards Tom.

"I don't think so…" said Tom and backed away from the man.

"What are you worried about? Max Gris has been on tv herself this morning. She explained it all. About how you had solved it all brilliantly but were too shy to claim victory. She just wants to give you your prize, so come on…"

The man was still inching towards Tom.

"She really doesn't, you know," said Tom.

"Ah, come on," said the man, his smile now vanished. "She said you might be reluctant. Just come with me and it will all be fine."

The man lunged towards Tom.

Tom took off like a startled hare along the pavement, his mind now racing. Clutching the precious relic in his clenched left hand, he ran and ran.

The man started to chase him but gave up at the first corner that Tom dived around.

Tom kept running and running. Once he was sure he was no longer being followed, he slowed to a brisk walk before ducking behind a snow-covered hedge at the end of a long driveway. He carefully put the relic into his trouser pocket and took his rucksack off his back, opening it to bring out his mobile phone.

"Come on," he urged as the phone flickered into life.

This time, it picked up a signal. He hit the search engine to look for his own name in the news. A string of results popped up, filling the whole page.

'Gris searches for Christmas winner.'

'Mystery boy scoops global prize.'

'Max Gris appeals for public to help track down shy genius.'

Tom scrolled down the page, his eyes widening with each new line he took in. His photo was everywhere, as was his name. Max Gris had cleverly enlisted the help of the entire population to track him down.

At which point, his phone died. The battery had finally succumbed to the cold.

Tom looked up from his phone, rolled his eyes, and let out another long sigh. Now what? He pulled his scarf up around his nose and mouth and his hat down as far as it would go, to try to hide as much of his face as he could.

This settled it: there was only one place he could go now...

CHAPTER FORTY-SEVEN

It was cold in the so-called Cathedral of the Others, thought Octavia Merryweather as she sat, bound to a chair within a metal cage and tried, once again, to loosen the ropes fastening her wrists together – and to the chair itself. Yet again, this proved to be a pointless task. She was tied fast and going nowhere. A phalanx of Gris Corp's security personnel had ushered her, Jack and Katie out of their overnight accommodation at Gris Corp HQ at dawn to bring them here. In answer to her questions, all they would tell her was that Max Gris herself had ordered that they be taken there at first light and they were then to await further instruction.

Merryweather couldn't be sure, but occasionally, she thought she could feel a faint wisp of heat wafting towards her. She hoped that someone, somewhere had turned on the heating in the now ornately decorated ruin. Once more, she looked around at the transformed interior of the old church and wondered to herself what the next few minutes would bring.

She had been kept separately from Katie, Jack and Nick Auld since they had been escorted out of their 'meeting' with Max Gris the previous evening, having been placed on her own in a room deep in the interior of the HQ in a bizarre, almost luxury, form of solitary confinement. She had then been brought separately – as had the others – to the church, each of them placed in an individual cage within the church's now ornate interior.

Merryweather had tried to converse with both Katie and Jack when they had first arrived in the church, but they had not been making much sense. Both sister and brother now appeared to be suffering from the same type of nodding dog syndrome – a lolling and drooping of their heads as though they could barely keep their eyes open.

She had asked them if they were all right, to which only Jack had responded, barely managing to slur out a one-word answer.

"Placer."

Merryweather wasn't entirely sure what Jack meant by this but suspected it was another aspect of Max Gris's sinister plan.

When Nick Auld had been brought in, he appeared to be in more of an alert state than the two children, albeit his face wore the same haunted look as it had the previous evening. If anything, thought Merryweather to herself, he looked even worse than he had the night before.

The guards had trussed the four of them up to old wooden chairs within each of their separate cages, and the chairs themselves appeared to be secured on the stone floor of the church itself. Annoyingly, the cages were far enough apart to make any firm of communication difficult, if not impossible. Nevertheless, Merryweather was determined to try.

"Nicky," she hissed after the Gris Corp security operatives who had tied him to his chair had closed and locked his cell door and lined up with their other colleagues along the wall of the church next to the main entrance.

Auld looked up at her briefly, before his head fell back down and he resumed staring at the floor.

Merryweather tried again.

"Nicky, are you okay? What is going on? What is she up to now?"

Auld briefly lifted his eyes from the stone floor of the church, stared straight at Merryweather, and shook his head slightly before letting it fall once more.

"What does that mean?" asked Merryweather in a whisper.

This time, Auld didn't even lift his head. He simply shook it slightly once more, and as he did so, he looked even more miserable than he had previously.

Merryweather tried again.

"Nicky, look at me. I could swing for you for being so stupid as to work with this woman, but right now, we need to figure out how we can stop this – and her. What else do you know?"

Auld lifted his head once more, shook it, and his shoulders slumped even further. At last, he spoke.

"I didn't know," he uttered with a heavy sigh.

"Didn't know what?" whispered Merryweather.

Auld nodded his head around at the interior of the church and then specifically, towards the gilded altar at its centre.

"That it would lead to all of this. I didn't realise this was what she wanted the research for."

"What do you mean, 'all of this'? What else do you know?" asked Merryweather.

"Nothing of any use anymore. She's won," replied Auld. His voice was flat, and he shrugged once more before continuing, "She has the scrolls, the translations, and now, she has the relics, too. Whatever she's going to do with them all, we cannot stop her." He gave a half-hearted yank at the ropes binding his wrists together and to the chair. "It's too late."

"Nicky, now listen to me. Do not give up. It's never too late. Look around you. Why do you think she has brought us all here, then? Hmmph? There must be some specific reason," said Merryweather, the urgency in her voice imploring Auld not to give in.

By way of reply, Auld simply shrugged his shoulders once more and resumed staring at the floor, muttering, "Showing off…" to himself as he did so.

"Nicky," hissed Merryweather, but it was no use. For now, he was lost to her. To everyone. Alone with his thoughts. As she was considering her next move and whether there was any means at all by which her chair could be moved, the main door to the church opened and yet another cluster of Gris Corp security appeared in the entrance, escorting some sort of large, covered box-like structure on wheels. Merryweather watched as they duly wheeled the entire ensemble into its position, which was further along the line of prisoners, and then applied a braking mechanism to its wheels, before most of them withdrew to add themselves to the security personnel peppering the interior wall of the church.

Merryweather stared at the whole covered structure for several seconds and wondered if it could be what she suspected.

She also noticed that Auld had barely looked up when the contraption had been wheeled in. This was not the Nicholas Auld that she knew, and she wondered whether he, too, had been given some sort of medication to render him as subdued as he was.

The entrance door to the church clunked open again and this time, the security décor all snapped itself to attention as in strode Max Gris, followed, a few steps behind, by Slymington.

"Good morning, my merry little band of adventurers!" exclaimed Gris, as though she were the charming host of a luxury hotel addressing her guests. "And how are we all feeling on this fine Christmas Eve morning?"

The fake smile. The raised eyebrows. The fake smile dropping into a face of supposed mock concern.

"Oh, not in the festive mood yet, eh? Well, we'll soon fix that."

Gris turned to address her Head of Security.

"Grunk, remove the sheets," she commanded as she clapped her hands together.

Erasmus Grunk, sporting a large bandage over his nose as well as a spectacularly swollen black eye, was assisted by three of his top men as they began removing the covers from the contraption which they had wheeled in several moments earlier. As the sheets fell, one by one, it revealed a large cage, with thick, tightly spaced bars and in its centre, a comatose heap of grey and green, with flashes of purple up and down it – all covered in heavy-set chains, the ends of which were welded to the exterior of the cage.

"Gus!" exclaimed Merryweather.

"Indeed, your professorship, it is your favourite pet," smirked Gris.

"What have you done to him?" asked Merryweather, her face contorting in horror.

"Oh, don't worry, he's still alive. He's simply...*resting*," replied Gris, her words oozing with self-satisfaction. "And he shan't be troubling us for quite a while. My team has made sure of that. Look, I'll even prove it to you. Simmons, give him a blast."

The walking hulk that was Simmons reached for a familiar-looking metal rod and flicked a switch next to the oversize cage. The odious blue sparks and flashes began crackling at the end of the metal prod. Satisfied that it was fully charged up, Simmons stuck the prod into Gus's side, wearing a malevolent grin as he did so.

The flashes and sparks ran up and down Gus's body and once again his entire framed tensed up. This time, he managed to lift his head and the yowl of pain he emitted was more of a snarl before Simmons withdrew the electric prod and Gus's head clattered back onto the floor of the cage.

Merryweather closed her mouth and held her breath, trying not to wretch as the burning smell from Simmons' ghastly display floated towards her nostrils. She glared at Gris.

"You've made your point – yet again – Ms Gris," snapped Merryweather. "Why have you brought us here? And where is Tom?" she shouted at their captor-in-chief.

"Well, since you asked so nicely, Professor," replied Gris as she wafted around the interior of the church. "It's time for a little fine tuning – the final dress rehearsal, if you like - before the main event this afternoon and I thought you should all be here to watch. Including your beloved pet. Although he does still seem to be a little on the drowsy side. Still, no matter. His loss."

She strode towards Merryweather.

"And after all, Muddywater, it's your protégé here who is responsible for much of what you are about to witness later on today. You must be so proud," said Gris sardonically as she burst into a cackle.

"It's *Merryweather*," came the reply – through gritted teeth.

411

"Whatever," said Gris airily, dismissing Merryweather with a flick of her hand as she strode towards the altar. Ascending its stairs, she walked towards its centre and addressed the assembled group.

"Right, everyone. It's almost time for the most important event in all your lives to begin. Thanks to the excellent work of Slymington and Grunk, we now have everything we need for the ceremony this afternoon. There is the minor detail of one of the merry little band here still being at large," – with this she pointed at the captives in their cages – "but we shall find him and bring him in soon enough.

"A reminder to you all about the running order of today's events: we shall begin at 3pm, with the placing of the final relics occurring no earlier than the sighting of the first star of Christmas Eve – or, if it's cloudy, the official time of sunset, which today will be 3.46pm. At which point, the ritual will then summon Santa Claus – St. Nicholas himself – to this very place and time.

"We begin the ceremony in readiness to place the various relics in their respective stations, one by one, until all but the very last relic is in situ. Our little helper, Jack, the winner of Apotheosis and therefore officially the cleverest child in the world, will *place* the first relic into its designated location to start the process; I shall place the final relic into its appropriate location and thus fulfil the ritual and guarantee that old Saint Nick himself will be brought back among us – and will be completely under my control and command."

Merryweather stared at Max Gris as she was barking her commands from the altar, her face set in a frown.

Gris continued to pace the stage, bellowing at the top of her voice.

"Once Santa is doing my bidding, he shall grant me total ownership of Christmas forever and, to ensure that only *I* can possess all that is connected with Christmas, he shall make me immortal to do so."

Gris paused for a moment and closed her eyes, throwing her head backwards towards the ceiling. She snapped out of her micro-reverie to address the next part directly towards the captives.

"You have all been helpful in the end, but none more so that young Jack, who, as well as placing the first relic, will also transfer his soul or life force – or whatever it is - *to me* as the very final act of the whole ritual, thus ensuring my immortality."

She paused.

"All of which is written in the scrolls detailing the prophecy and the ritual which have been so ably translated by Dr Nicholas Auld here," blared Gris, pointing towards a sorry-looking Auld in his cage.

And then, an aside.

"We shall, of course, have the finest medical team on standby in case anything should happen to go awry at any stage."

Gris drew herself to her full height for the culmination of her address to the gathered company.

"And so, by this evening, I shall be the most powerful woman in the world, I shall own Christmas, and everything associated with it, Santa Claus shall be at my beck and call and I shall be enjoying the first evening of the rest of my life, which will be very, very long indeed."

"Once we're done in this place," she waved her hand around the church airily, "your pet here will go on display to the world, as a proof of concept, you might say, before we unveil Santa himself to the globe on Christmas Day. Any questions?"

Merryweather began a question. "How do you think you'll get away with this, you evil...", but Gris shouted over her, cutting her off.

"Good. Let's crack on with the final run-through then. Slimey, give the kids another shot to waken them up. We need them conscious for the next part."

CHAPTER FORTY-EIGHT

Tom trudged his way to the front of the grand Georgian building and hesitated. He banged the clumps of snow from his boots on the steps leading to the front door and took in a huge gulp of air to settle his nerves. He could feel his heart pounding as he took off his gloves to press the entrance buzzer and knew that once he took this step, there would be no turning back – and he did not know where it would lead.

His finger hovered over the buzzer for a few moments before he closed his eyes and plunged it onto it. He held it on the button for several seconds as it scratched out its weak electrical crackly noise, before releasing it and waiting. He could hear the scratching and clunking as someone lifted the intercom handset at the other end.

"Yes, hello?" asked a tinny male voice.

Tom spluttered out a "Hi…"

"Who is this?" asked the voice.

"Tom… Tom Brightly. Can you let me in, please?"

There was no reply, merely the sound of the intercom being hung up and a buzz and click as the door directly in front of Tom was unlocked. He entered the building's communal hallway and took another deep breath. This was it. He was committed now. He was steeling himself for the next conversation, trying to figure out how he would explain everything and whether he would be taken seriously.

He galloped up the two flights of stairs and arrived on the top floor of the building. The front door of the sole flat on this uppermost floor was already open.

Tom drew himself up and readied himself to begin his speech about the events that had led up to this point, when the same – non-tinny - male voice echoed from somewhere along the hallway beyond the door.

"I expect you're rather chilly, aren't you? Best take off your coat and scarf and get something warm into you. Mug of hot chocolate okay?"

The voice was that of Atticus Sharp, who emerged from around the corner at the far end of his hallway bearing a large, steaming mug of hot chocolate and... smiling.

Tom stopped and stood, frozen to the spot, staring at Sharp and wondering what to say next.

"Others not with you? Let me guess: whatever it was that Octavia was up to hasn't worked out and now, you've come to tell me all of this and perhaps to ask for help, hmmph?" asked Sharp.

Tom looked at the older man's face. His eyes were almost twinkling. He still looked like a man of a certain age, but there was something about him, some sort of energy, that was different this morning from that which Tom had witnessed previously.

"Yes... I-I-I didn't know where else to go," replied Tom.

"But you came here instead of going to the police, right?" asked Sharp.

"Yes," said Tom, "I couldn't go to the police because of Gus..."

"Gus?" asked Sharp.

"The dragon," replied Tom.

"Ah yes, the dragon," said Sharp as he smiled knowingly. "Well, it makes sense. You'd better come in, sit down, get yourself thawed out and tell me all then."

He ushered Tom into the large, high-ceilinged living room, in which the fire was crackling away in the hearth.

"Power's coming back now – at last – but I'm taking no chances," said Sharp, smiling at Tom. "One cannot be too careful with a solar storm as big as this one. Makes one realise how fragile all our much-vaunted interconnectedness truly is."

As the pair of them sat down on the large seats placed next to the fire in the vast living room, Tom noticed that Sharp's eyes were now, if anything, twinkling even more.

"Okay, tell me everything that's happened since you left here," said Sharp as Tom sipped at his hot chocolate, "and I do mean *everything*."

Tom recounted the trip to the Hidden Archive, the new information they had found within it – and the alternative relics – before explaining Merryweather's plan to return to Gris Corp HQ – with Gus - to swap the fake relics and recover the real ones to stop Max Gris from carrying out her masterplan to resurrect Santa Claus and take possession of Christmas.

Sharp was listening intently, nodding occasionally, and would ask the odd question.

"So, what went wrong with Octavia's plan?" he asked.

"Pretty much all of it," sighed Tom. "We were all discovered and captured, including Gus, and then brought into a room in the HQ building with Gris and all her security goons."

He looked downwards at the floor.

"They took Gus somewhere else and put him in a cage and… began torturing him."

Sharp frowned at this new information.

"Go on," he said gently.

"It was horrible," said Tom, looking up at Sharp. "He was howling in pain. Gris showed us it all on some sort of video feed."

Tom's head fell once again. He could sense Sharp looking at him, waiting for the next part of the story.

Tom sighed. "I couldn't stand to see Gus being hurt like that, so I gave them the fake relics, hoping it would stop it." He paused.

"But it didn't."

"Why?" asked Sharp.

"Gris has Dr Auld held prisoner, too. He was in a different room, separated from the rest of us. She took the fake relics to him and he said they weren't the same as all the rest of the batches they already had."

"Ah… I see," said Sharp. "I can imagine that Ms Gris would not have been happy at this revelation?"

Tom nodded. "Yeah… she was furious. She ordered her security guys to start torturing Gus again. I thought they were going to kill him."

"So, what did you do?" asked Sharp.

"I shouted for them to stop and told her I'd take them to the real relics," said Tom.

"Which were where exactly?" asked Sharp.

"We had stashed them away in Auntieprof's cellar, where Gus had been hiding," said Tom. "Gris ordered her security guys to take me there to fetch them and then, she took the others away – I don't know where."

"Her goons took me to Auntieprof's house and once we were inside, her Head of Security frog-marched me down to the cellar."

"So, how did you get out of that one?" asked Sharp.

"I waited until it was just the two of us down there and he was inspecting the box of relics after I'd fetched them out of their hiding place, and then I chucked some sand and dirt in his face and used the old wartime tunnel out of the cellar to escape into the back garden. Then, I grabbed my sledge and ran for it. Sledged down the hill behind the back garden and…"

"And?" asked Sharp.

"They didn't follow me," said Tom. "Then I tried to figure out what to do next. I found an igloo someone had built in a back garden and spent the night in it."

Sharp raised his eyebrows. "Very resourceful, young man."

"I didn't sleep very well, but it kept me warm. But then, the next morning, after I'd made my way out into the street, I could see people staring at me. It was weird. I checked my phone on the off chance it was working again and then… I saw the stories that Gris Corp had put out about me all over the internet. Which is why I headed here. Oh, and then my phone died."

Sharp blew out his cheeks.

"You're quite the laddie, aren't you, young Tom," he said. "The question is: what do we do now?"

"We don't have much time," said Tom.

"No, indeed we don't," said Sharp, "and especially not if Max Gris has everything she needs for the ritual. We've only a few hours at most."

He stood up and paced the room.

"Not quite everything," said Tom, as he fished around in his trouser pocket, before extracting the small wooden relic and placing it on the coffee table in front of Sharp.

Sharp bent down and picked up the object, scrutinising it.

"And what is this?" he asked.

"It's a tiny piece of one of the original relics that fell through a hole in my jacket pocket into the lining. I found it when I was checking my pockets to see if I had any snacks left. So, you see, Max Gris doesn't quite have *all* of the relics yet," said Tom, grinning.

Sharp gave a wry smile.

"Well now, this changes everything. I was about to say that our only recourse here was to go to the police, but now we have a bargaining chip. And looking at these inscriptions, a not insignificant one at that," said Sharp.

He placed the wooden relic back on the coffee table, walked towards the fire, and gave a long sigh.

"You know, I always suspected this day would come," Sharp began.

Tom frowned. "What do you mean?" he asked.

"A very long time ago, Tom, I knew Hugh Gris, Max's father. When we were both students. Always meddling with things that he shouldn't have been. Lost touch with him eventually as our paths diverged. He went off into industry and I stayed in academia, but occasionally, I would hear tales that suggested that Hugh hadn't completely lost his interest in the antiquities. Usually concerning him buying up ancient objects at auction for his private collection."

"And from what I've heard, Max Gris appears to be very much her father's daughter – and with all that power and money at her disposal, she's trouble incarnate. As the Poles say, 'the apple does not fall far from the tree'."

Sharp bent down to pick up the relic once more and held it up to the light, inspecting it once more.

"I need to make a phone call, young man. And then, we must leave for Gris Corp HQ. Immediately," said Sharp.

"Are you going to call the police?" asked Tom.

"I should, shouldn't I? But no, it's far too late for that," replied Sharp. "No, now, it's up to us: we must stop that woman before she commits any more idiocy."

Sharp waved the relic in front of himself and Tom with a flourish as he made his final pronouncement.

"And it seems we may have the very means to do precisely that."

CHAPTER FORTY-NINE

It was, by now, early afternoon as Tom and Sharp arrived at Gris Corp HQ. Sharp had insisted that Tom thaw himself out and had made sure he had had a hot meal before they set off across the city in Sharp's car. Tom had asked Sharp what his plan was. It was simple, Sharp had assured him. Tom would show Max Gris the relic at the same time as Sharp informed her of the true consequences which would befall her if she were to proceed with the ritual. If that approach failed, he assured Tom that there were others who would intervene to prevent the ritual from being completed, albeit when Tom had asked further questions about who these people were and how they would stop Gris, he noticed that Sharp had become noticeably more vague, almost evasive, finally telling Tom not to worry and that matters were all in hand. The last part of their journey across the snowy city had taken place in near silence.

However, now, as they stepped out of Sharp's car and began walking towards the imposing glass doors that guarded the main entrance of the Gris Corp HQ building, Tom was worried. Worried about his friends - specifically, whether Gus was even still alive - worried about what Gris was about to do next and worried that – whatever Atticus Sharp thought he had planned to stop Gris – it might not be enough, given how desperately she wanted to possess Christmas.

Tom asked Sharp whether it was a good idea simply to walk brazenly up to the main entrance of the HQ.

Sharp smiled as he replied. "It is the best possible idea, young man. I want Ms Gris to know that we are here, that we have the final piece of the puzzle which she needs and also that what is going to happen next is not that which she has planned."

He turned to Tom as they reached the doors.

"Now, when I say so, hold up the bag containing the relic. And – if we are asked – show her the relic. But only if we are asked to do so – and only when I give you the nod, okay?"

Tom nodded and clutched the clear, polythene bag, in which Sharp had placed the relic prior to leaving his flat, ever more tightly.

A member of Gris Crop's security team appeared at the door, dressed (as usual) from head to toe in black.

"Yes, what do you want?" asked the operative.

Sharp drew himself up to his full height as he replied.

"We would like to speak to Ms Max Gris. Urgently."

"And who might you be?" the goon asked.

"I am Professor Atticus Sharp, a friend of her late father, and this is Master Thomas Brightly. I believe Ms Gris will be most interested in meeting us and hearing what we have to say."

At the mention of Tom's name, the security man bristled and stood more alert, like a sentry meerkat.

"One moment," he snapped as he walked a few paces away and clicked on the radio on his lapel.

A buzzer went off in the Boardroom deep in the heart of Gris Corp HQ.

Max Gris stopped pacing up and down the room and muttering to herself to bark an order.

"Slimey, would you answer that? It's putting me off and I'm *trying* to memorise my lines for later this afternoon."

"Of course," replied her ever faithful assistant in his signature monotone. He reached towards the intercom switch and spoke into its microphone.

"Yes, what is it?"

"Sir, I have two visitors here. A Professor Sharp and... one Thomas Brightly," replied the disembodied voice of the security man.

Gris dived towards the panel of switches.

"Put them on visual!" she shouted.

The video feed sparked into life before the screen flicked to a different camera feed, which showed Sharp and Tom standing by the main doors at the entrance. Tom lifted up the bag containing the relic towards the camera.

"Well, what have we here? It appears our quarry has turned himself in," said Slymington.

"Yes, and what's he showing us now?"

"Another trick?" offered Slymington.

"Perhaps, but we need to be sure," replied Gris.

She switched on the microphone channel before barking a further command to the security operative, who was waiting patiently for his next instruction.

"Radio for back-up and bring the pair of them to the church. Immediately. And they are *not,* under any circumstances, to be harmed. Understood?"

"Yes, ma'am," replied the guard.

Gris and Slymington continued to stare at the screen, watching as the guard radioed for the additional help. Both Tom and Sharp were staring directly into the camera, which was trained on them, with Tom continuing to hold up the bag containing the relic.

"Who's the friend he's brought with him? Recognise him?" asked Gris.

Slymington peered at the picture on the screen.

"His face seems vaguely familiar," he replied.

"Well, we'll know who he is soon enough," muttered Gris in an aside. She stood upright and walked away from the bank of switches and monitors.

"Slimey, we need to leave for the church. Now. It's showtime."

CHAPTER FIFTY

In the cold of Christmas Eve afternoon, standing by the entrance to Gris Corp HQ, Tom was wishing he was somewhere – anywhere – else. After his brief conversation on the radio, the guard had instructed them not to move – and had then radioed someone else. Tom looked at Atticus Sharp, who merely raised an eyebrow.

"I hope you're not going to keep us standing here all afternoon," said Sharp to the guard. "It is a little chilly, after all." He patted himself theatrically on the arms to emphasise the depth of the cold.

"You'll be indoors soon enough," grunted the guard by way of a reply.

At this, several more security guards appeared in the main atrium of the HQ and marched stiffly towards the entrance, brandishing guns as they did so. Tom was about to stuff the bag into his pocket, when he saw Sharp motion towards him, indicating Tom should pass him the bag. Tom did so and Sharp stuffed it into his trouser pocket, underneath his overcoat.

"We're going to the old church. Follow me," instructed the original guard as the clutch of goons behind him raised and pointed their guns at Sharp and Tom.

"Well now, quite the welcoming committee," said Sharp. "Should we raise our arms in surrender?"

"Enough chat. Move," instructed the lead guard.

Tom and Sharp did as they were told and followed the guard as he led the way across the grounds.

"The old church is where we discovered Gus," whispered Tom to Sharp as they marched along.

"Don't worry, this is what I was hoping for," muttered Sharp in reply.

"No talking," barked one of the guards behind them. At this, Sharp again raised an eyebrow.

As they reached the old church, the lead guard instructed them to stop and to wait. He walked to the main door of the old church, opened it, and peered inside, before turning and barking another order.

"Hold them here." The group stopped, waiting outside the church in the weakening afternoon daylight. Tom could see Sharp looking at the exterior of the church, as though his eyes were trying to record its every detail. After several more minutes, a buzzer went off on the lead guard's lapel radio.

"Right, you two, follow me inside."

At this, the guards frogmarched Tom and Sharp into the ruined church, which Tom now knew to be far more than merely an old ruin. The guards directed them towards the centre of the church and ordered them to halt. Tom looked around at the interior of the church. It was now even more decorated than when he had seen it previously. Sweeping red drapes were hanging from the rafters all around them, screening extensive areas of the church's interior; there were gold and jewel-encrusted religious objects adorning the area around the altar and tall, ornate candlesticks, in which were burning candles the size of small logs. Besides the candlelight, bright arc lights had been rigged up in every nook and cranny of the church, most of which were shining towards the altar itself.

As Tom and Sharp, stood in the middle of this decorative scene, the guards surrounding them suddenly snapped to attention and from behind the drapes surrounding the altar came Max Gris herself, dressed from head to toe in flowing red and gold robes and wearing a flamboyant headpiece atop her head.

"Ah, our two visitors," she began as she strode to the centre of the altar. "Delighted you could join us this afternoon for our ceremony. And as for you, young Master Brightly, well, you led us a right merry dance, didn't you?"

Gris was smiling but glaring at Tom. He shuffled around on the spot and dearly wished he were somewhere else.

"Ms Gris," began Sharp, "you don't know me, but I have some very important information for you."

Gris removed her focus from Tom to Sharp.

"And who, pray tell, are you?" she asked.

"Atticus Sharp. Head of the Faculty of Antiquity at the university."

Sharp waved his hand around to highlight the entire interior scene within the old church.

"This – all of this – is not going to go as you think it is," he warned.

Gris, from her place on the altar, literally looked down her nose at Sharp, like an imperious eagle surveying its prey.

"Reaaally," she replied with mock seriousness.

"Yes, really," stated Sharp flatly. "Ms Gris, you are meddling with forces far greater than you could possibly understand and I'm here to ask you to stop before it's too late."

He reached into his pocket.

"Are you now?" said Gris sarcastically. "And what if I don't?"

"Then, I'm here to make you stop," replied Sharp, drawing the bag containing the relic from his pocket and holding it up in front of him.

Gris stopped and stared at the bag.

"This is something I believe you need," said Sharp.

"What is it?" snorted Gris.

"It's the final relic you need to carry out your plan, Miss Gris. Get your men to back off now," Sharp shouted back, swirling around in a circle at the security guards surrounding him and Tom, "or I'll destroy it."

"You're bluffing," shouted Gris. "It's another fake. I'm not falling for that one again."

"This ends now, Ms Gris. You need to stop this ceremony, release those you have taken captive and to understand precisely what you're messing around with. And whom," snapped Sharp.

Tom's gaze was flitting between Sharp, Gris, and around the encroaching pack of security goons. There was a pause as Gris considered what Sharp had said, before she gave the subtlest of nods towards her lead security detail. As Tom looked on, the goon aimed the butt of his gun squarely at the base of Sharp's neck and struck him. Hard. Sharp lurched forward, collapsing in a heap directly in front of Tom, and the bag flew out of his hands. Tom dived for it, scooped it up and did a forward roll between two of the goons, breaking through their circle. He skipped a few paces away from them, backing towards the door.

"I don't think so," said Gris from the altar, addressing the crumpled heap that was Sharp. Tom could see out of the corner of his eye that Sharp was prostrate on the ground and motionless. Gris's smile was long gone.

"Well, young Master Brightly, it's only you left now. So, are *you* going to try to stop me as well?" She started pacing around the altar.

Several guards raised theirs guns and pointed them at Tom.

"Do as he said," shouted Tom. "Stop this now and let everyone go – or this relic gets smashed to smithereens."

Gris laughed her most condescending laugh once more. "You wouldn't dare."

"Wouldn't I?" Tom shouted back.

"It's a fake," shouted Gris dismissively.

"Is it now?" shouted Tom. "Or is it one of the relics that we took from this church two nights ago? How would you even know, eh?"

Gris stopped her pacing, turned towards Tom, and smiled her best fake smile.

"All right, I'll play along. Assuming this stone or whatever it is in that bag is actually real, what is it that you want?"

"We told you: stop the ceremony and release all of my friends. *All* of them," Tom shouted.

"Your friends, eh?" smirked Gris. "Even the dragon?"

"*Especially* the dragon!" yelled Tom.

"I see," she replied. "Well, why don't you ask them yourself how they're getting on – and whether they want to be released?"

She strode towards the front of the raised altar and snapped her fingers. At this, several of the tall, red drapes peeled slowly back, revealing the cages containing the prisoners, with the arc lights in the ceiling fixed on them.

Tom looked on, temporarily dumbfounded at the sight which was being revealed. As the red velvet curtains receded, he saw Merryweather in the nearest cage, pressed up against its bars, peering out of it, with the others each in a separate cage, one by one, all the way along the line to a larger cage at the end, in which lay Gus, either asleep – or worse. All the others except his aunt looked awful and were staring out of their cages in silence, as though they weren't fully aware of where they were or what was going on.

"Auntieprof!" shouted Tom upon sighting Merryweather.

From the nearest cage came Merryweather's voice.

"Tom, is that you?" asked his aunt. She was squinting into the harsh light blazing into her cell.

"It's me, Auntieprof," shouted Tom.

"Tom, get out, it's a trap…" cried Merryweather.

At this, the lights snapped off, and the church fell into silence once more. The drapes trundled back together and then resumed their previous position.

Gris had dissolved into manic laughter from her perch on the altar.

"You're really rather stupid, aren't you, Master Thomas Brightly," she cackled. "Imagine escaping all my security men only to rock up here voluntarily and give yourself up. What an idiot."

Tom was shaking now, half in fear and half in anger at Gris's mockery.

"I warned you, you evil witch. Let my friends go or this gets smashed." He brandished the bag containing the relic at her, then dropped it to the floor and raised his foot, letting it hover over the relic.

"Now, LET MY FRIENDS GO!" bawled Tom.

Gris stared down at him.

"They can go soon enough," she replied. "I shan't have any further need of them shortly, anyway."

That smile again.

Tom looked at her and wondered why she looked so sure of herself. He was tense, his body rigid, as his foot paused in the air at full stretch above the bag with the relic. He felt the hairs on the back of his neck pricking up... at the very last moment...

The blow knocked Tom forward, and he staggered, off balance and careering into a chair, before bouncing off it and sprawling across the floor. The bag containing the relic lay on the stone floor several feet away from him. Tom raised himself up on his elbows, his head reeling. He tried to stand, but as he did so, his legs refused to do as he wanted them to, and he crashed back down into the chair.

From the stage, he heard Gris's cackling laughter as she shouted at him.

"There's no point in trying to run, young Thomas. Grunk has made sure you're going nowhere."

Tom fell backwards onto his side and then his back, grasping for the bag. It lay on the cold stone floor, now mere inches from the end of his fingertips, the relic still inside it. He tried again to lift himself upright, but as he did so, he saw a black be-gloved hand reaching downwards towards the bag.

"Nooooo…" mumbled Tom with a groan. His eyes were woozy, and his head was spinning. This must be what people meant when they said they were seeing stars. With all his effort, he tried to focus his eyes for a moment and the blurry image resolved itself into that of a large, bearded face, complete with nose bandage and a heavily swollen black eye, which belonged to the black be-gloved hand (and arm). As he collected the bag from the floor, the face's owner was laughing. At him.

"Nooooo, not you…." moaned Tom.

Grunk bent down over Tom and waved the bag directly in Tom's face.

"Yeah, squirt. Me. I win," he said.

And with the image of Grunk's smug, bearded face directly in his own, the world blurred again. Tom fought the oncoming darkness, as he had sometimes been able to do when younger and overtired, fighting against sleep. He raised his head and tried to resolve the blurring images once more, but he couldn't. His head fell backwards onto the floor. He exhaled and then everything went black.

Tom came to with a start. He sat bolt upright, disorientated, and not even sure if he was fully awake. He looked around. Metal bars. A cage.

"Hello," said a familiar voice.

"Auntieprof," he replied. He was in the cell next to Merryweather's.

"How are you?" she asked.

Tom rubbed the back of his neck and then found the massive lump on the back of his head. He winced as he touched it.

"Bit of a sore head," he said ruefully.

"Well, the good news is, you're awake," replied his aunt, "and I don't see any blood. I take it one of those apes clunked you?"

Tom nodded.

"The evil brutes. They did the same to Atticus." She pointed towards another adjoining cell, where, in the corner, lay a comatose Atticus Sharp.

"He's still not come round," said Merryweather. "Whoever thumped him gave him a proper wallop."

Tom looked concerned.

"Doesn't he need a doctor?" he asked.

"I hope not," replied Merryweather grimly, "because there isn't one coming anytime soon."

"What do you mean? What's happening?" asked Tom.

"It's showtime," whispered Merryweather, nodding towards the stage. "That awful woman is about to start the ceremony."

"Oh," said Tom as he peered out of the cell. "How long was I out for?"

"About half an hour or so, I think, judging by the loss of daylight outside," said Merryweather. "Enough time for her ladyship and her goons to make everything ready to begin. It must be very close now."

"At least we *tried* to stop her..." said Tom, disconsolately.

"I know," said Merryweather. "You did your best, but I wish we had gone to the police now. As it is, I suppose we're about to find out just what all this is leading to."

"What do you think?" asked Tom.

"I don't know," said Merryweather. "I truly don't know what to expect. All we can try to do is get out of here when – or if – we have a chance."

As she spoke, the red velvet drapes glided their way apart and the low rumble of droning music started filling the surrounding air, reverberating off the walls of the church.

"Here we go," whispered Merryweather as the drapes rolled their way back to reveal the sight of the interior of the church in darkness, other than the flickering from several flaming torches positioned all around the altar.

The music grew louder, with the drone now being accompanied by the hypnotic pulse of chanting.

As Tom watched, several Gris Corp security personnel walked towards the altar area and positioned themselves around it in carefully spaced-out intervals, standing silently and to attention, as though they were ready for action. The chanting increased in both volume and intensity. Tom peered more intently at the altar and in the half-light, he could see that at its centre, there was some sort of large framework structure, about the height of an adult man, adorned – as was the rest of the altar (and the building) - with ornate decoration, which was mostly deep red and gold in colour.

The chanting and droning music built to a crescendo as further becloaked figures emerged from the shadows and positioned themselves directly around the decorative skeleton-like centrepiece on the raised dais of the altar, as though they were forming a guard of honour.

The flaming torches flickered and burned, casting the odd shadows of this growing coterie of guards onto the walls of the old building as the droning and chanting reached its zenith – and then, it stopped. All that remained now was silence.

From the darkness beyond the far end of the altar, swept a further entourage of cloaked figures. This cohort was also wearing golden masks which obscured the top halves of their faces, making them look like strange golden mannequins, all dressed up in the same odd form of fancy dress, and each one of them carrying an ornamental staff of sorts. This group went to places at equidistant intervals around the central skeleton structure and once more stood to attention.

The droning music began again and was accompanied by the chanting, which seemed to emanate from the walls. Tom looked around for speakers placed on the walls, but in the semi-darkness, he could not see any. The pre-recorded chanting and drone music was now being augmented by chanting from those assembled on the stage. The whole cacophony was growing louder and louder and increasing in tempo, with the most recent group of arrivals onto the stage now banging their staffs on the dais in an ever-quickening rhythm.

"They look as though they've all arrived from a pantomime," said Tom in a stage whisper.

"Yes…" said Merryweather, "a terrible one."

As the sound from the altar grew louder and louder, Tom glanced around in the half-light flickering from the flaming torches. He couldn't make anything out distinctly that was more than a few feet away. He could see Merryweather all right, but none of the others in their respective cells. The altar was, by default, the most illuminated part of the old church, mainly because the rest of the building was in almost complete darkness.

As the frenzy of son et lumière on and around the altar increased, so did the banging of the staffs upon the dais. Added to which, the inner circle of figures around the centrepiece were now stamping their feet to mark a steady beat. This stamping grew quicker and quicker, the music raged into a tornado of sound and then, the lights all flared up, as though someone had switched on daylight in the darkest interior recesses of the old church, before the whole spectacle ceased.

Silence.

And darkness.

From beyond the altar, Tom heard a new noise, faint at first, but gradually growing in volume.

Clack.

Then a pause.

Clack.

Then another pause.

Clack.

Louder this time.

Clack.

Louder again.

Tom peered into the darkness. There, on the very far right-hand side of the altar, he could make out a shape, moving slowly, deliberately, towards the altar's centrepiece. And each time the figure moved, there was another in the sequence of noises.

Clack.

It drew closer to the centre.

Clack.

And louder.

Clack. Thump.

Something new.

Clack. Thump.

Tom's eyes were straining in the darkness. He thought he could make out more details in the shape – the figure - moving its way across the dais. It looked tall – no, not tall. There was some sort of headwear, the shape of a semicircle raised up beyond the head, and spikey, too.

The figure was moving steadily towards the centrepiece and the little remaining light that there was in the building. Tom gave a start as he was able finally to distinguish more details as the figure moved towards the dim light shining from the centre of the dais. There, in an elaborate costume draped over her from head to toe, stood Max Gris. She was wearing the largest and most ornate of all the head garments, which looked like a cross between an oversized collar and a giant crown. It was a headpiece that had gone out of control.

Gris stepped her way to the very centre of the dais, stood in front of the altar and raised her arms upwards to the sky. Tom looked over at Merryweather, but she was staring directly towards Gris.

From the centre of the stage, Gris addressed the entire building.

"It is almost time. Time to initiate a ceremony unseen for many, many hundreds of years. A ceremony so ancient and secret that the components for its central ritual lay buried and forgotten across half of Europe for over a millennium.

"Until *I* brought them all back together once more."

Gris turned towards one of her inner entourage and took the flaming torch he was holding before walking around the dais, setting light to several more torches surrounding the strange wooden scaffold in the centre atop the altar. Once she had completed this circuit, she resumed her place at the front and centre of the dais and spoke once more.

"I completed the work – the journey – which was begun by my late, dear father, to gather all the relics required for the ceremony and to decipher the instructions required for the essence of the ceremony, its interior ritual of reanimation and eternal life."

Tom could see Gris's face more clearly now. She looked as though she was in a near-trancelike state. Her face was heavily made up, particularly around her eyes, which appeared so black that they reminded Tom of those of a panda. It was as though she had deliberately chosen to turn into a more extreme version of herself.

"I devised the plan to deliver the key human element of the whole ritual: a clever child. But not just any old clever child – the all-round cleverest child in the entire world."

Tom raised his eyebrows at this statement. If she meant Jack, Gris was being a little overgenerous. Jack may be many things, thought Tom. Decent, kind, a good and steady friend, bit of a shambles sometimes, excellent at procuring snackables, questionable dress sense on occasion, and indeed, he was smart - but even Jack would admit that he wasn't *the* cleverest child on the entire planet.

Gris pressed on with her monologue.

"And now, through Apotheosis, I have found that child: Jack Wanless. The boy who will begin the ritual to bring St Nicholas to our world – under my control. Permanently!"

With this, the lights flared up, and the chanting began once more.

"It is time!" shouted Gris. "The first star of this Christmas Eve has been sighted!"

She turned to face the right-hand side of the dais.

"Bring the child to me!" she shouted at the top of her voice.

As Tom stared at the whole spectacle, with the lights now blazing all around the dais and the chanting and droning growing more and more intense, there, emerging from the shadows at the far end of the dais, was a small figure, also dressed ornately in robes and wearing similar headgear to the rest of the assembled company. Jack was being marched towards the centre of the dais, sandwiched between two very much larger, similarly attired gentlemen, who appeared to be half-prodding and half-dragging their charge across the platform.

"Look, it's Jack, all dressed up," hissed Tom to Merryweather, as his friend's face hove into view.

"I know," said Merryweather. "Goodness knows what Gris has in store for him…" Her voice trailed away.

His two guards had marched Jack into the centre of the dais; he was now standing next to Gris, who spoke once more.

"The first star of Christmas Eve having been sighted, it is time to begin the sacred and ancient ritual to summon St Nicholas – Santa Claus – to come amongst us and to be forever under my power," shouted Gris. She turned to Jack and addressed him.

"Upon my instruction, you shall place the very first relic in situ in the carapace here. You shall then withdraw and stand as you are until I call upon you once more. Do you understand?"

Tom looked on as his friend, cutting a small and forlorn figure amidst all the gaudiness of the ceremony, nodded.

"Good," said Gris. "We shall begin!"

One of the interior entourage paced towards Gris and Jack, holding out a red velvet cushion, adorned with gold braid. Lying in its centre was one of the larger relics. Gris took the cushion from its bearer and held it down towards Jack.

"Take this sacred relic and place it *carefully* in the very centre of the Carapace of Christmas."

Jack stretched his hands out. He was wearing white gloves. With the delicacy of a referee replacing a snooker ball, he picked up the relic and positioned it in the very centre of the wooden structure atop the altar. This action complete, Jack stepped back towards his two minders.

"You will now wait there as I place the remaining relics," instructed Gris.

The chanting and incantations continued for several minutes more, as a series of the guardians surrounding the altar brought forth further relics on similar red velvet cushions edged with golden braid to Gris and she placed each one herself into the carapace, until its gaps slowly filled, one by one.

Eventually, after several more minutes, Gris stepped back from the structure and raised her arms. The chanting, drone music and incantations all instantly stopped.

"And now, it is time. Time to place the very final relic – at the very top of the staff space within the Carapace of Christmas."

At this, a further berobed guard stepped forward, bearing the very last relic on yet another of the decorative cushions. With exorbitant ceremony, Gris picked up the relic and held it towards the ceiling before she began her final incantation.

"I take and hold this sacred relic,

borne from the past unto the present,

I now return it to its rightful place

at the zenith of this carapace.

I call upon the ancient powers

of many days and countless hours,

to usher forth down through time

all of Christmas and make it mine!"

The chanting and droning restarted. With a flourish, Gris swept her arms down towards the carapace and carefully placed the final relic into the last remaining space available in the 3-D jigsaw that was the Carapace of Christmas. She took three steps back from the carapace, closed her eyes and raised her hands towards the ceiling once more and then…

Nothing.

The chanting and droning kept on going – but that was all.

After several moments more, Max Gris opened her eyes and upon being confronted by exactly the same scene as she had witnessed immediately prior to closing her eyes, her face turned to thunder.

"SHURRRUP!" she commanded her impromptu choir.

The chanting and droning of the music abruptly ceased.

"Why hasn't it worked?" she addressed the question to no one in particular. And then she turned to Slymington, who emerged from the shadows, also cloaked from head to toes in the same vibrant robes as the rest of the attendees. It would be hard to say that the robes suited many of the participants in the ancient ceremony, but they suited Slymington least of all. However, as ever, his face was impassive.

"That is unclear, ma'am," he replied, in the usual monotone.

Gris was now storming around the stage, inspecting everything.

"We have the relics, we found the location, we found this child, we deciphered the ritual, made the setting as instructed, created all these robes… so WHY HASN'T IT WORKED?"

Silence.

Gris lifted her robes and strode across the dais and down its stairs. Tom had a start as he realised she was making a beeline directly towards the line of cages.

He had time enough to utter an "uh oh" before she arrived – and her face looked as though she had eaten something unpleasant.

"You two geniuses, you know everything. Why hasn't it worked?" she spat at Merryweather and Auld.

"Perhaps you're the wrong person for the prophecy," said Merryweather coldly. Tom noticed that there was the faint trace of a smile on his aunt's face.

"Very droll," snapped Gris. She turned on Nick.

"What's gone wrong, Dr Auld? Where is St Nicholas?"

Auld approached the side of his cell and looked straight at Gris.

"I don't know," he said, flatly.

"Well, one of you two geniuses had better figure it out, otherwise your pet is going to suffer. Again. And he'll keep on suffering until one of you gets it right!"

Gris turned on her heel and began stomping her way back to the dais when Merryweather shouted after her.

"Wait!"

The stomping ceased and Gris whirled around in a 180 – before stomping back towards Merryweather's cell.

"This had better be good," she said. The threat hung in the air.

"The ancient ceremony calls for a child to place the key *elements*, doesn't it?" said Merryweather.

"Yes…" snapped Gris. "First relic, key relics, something like that, then a sacrifice."

"Key relics?" asked Merryweather.

"Yes, key, first, what does it matter?" said Gris.

"Perhaps try the first relic and the very last relic," Merryweather suggested.

Gris opened her mouth as though to speak, but her face morphed into her best fake smile and she turned on her heel and strode back towards the dais.

"We go again," she bellowed at the top of her voice. "Reset the Carapace of Christmas and get that child ready!"

Tom looked at his aunt.

"Sacrifice?" he asked.

Merryweather kept staring towards the dais and slowly nodded her head.

"That's what Gris thinks…" murmured Merryweather.

"B–b–but that means they're going to kill Jack?!" spluttered Tom.

He looked towards the dais and at Jack, surrounded by robe-glad goons. He couldn't see his friend's face clearly, but the pile of robes which drenched Jack appeared to be shaking.

"Hey, you," shouted Tom at Gris's rapidly receding becloaked shape. "Hey, Max Gris, you've got the wrong kid up there!"

Gris stopped stomping towards the stage.

"What did you say?" she bellowed at Tom.

"You heard me. You've got the wrong kid on that stage. Jack didn't win your stupid game. I did."

"Tom, what are you doing?" asked his aunt, with a tone of exasperation in her voice. Tom gave her a brief look.

Gris stomped her way back towards the cage.

"What do you mean, 'you won'?"

"You heard me. I was the one who completed the final task in the final level in that game, not Jack. So, I'm the one you need to place those relics." said Tom.

Gris turned towards the stage.

"IS THIS TRUE?" she raged in Jack's general direction.

"Yes," squeaked Jack from the dais, nodding.

"GET HIM OFF THERE!" screamed Gris.

She turned to Tom.

"And *you* are coming with me! Get him out of that cage," she snapped at the nearest member of security.

The guard approached Tom's cell, unlocked the door, and grabbed him by the arm, dragging him towards the altar.

"Don't worry," he shouted to Merryweather before the guard told him to shut up and increased his vice-like grip on his arm. The guard speed-walked his way towards the dais, so much so that Tom had to break into a semi-trot to keep pace with him. As they approached the dais, Tom could see all the people lined up for the ceremony more closely. Jack wasn't there – but his robes were, lying in a heap on the floor.

"Put these on," instructed the guard, as he picked up the gaudy bundle and shoved them in Tom's face. Tom did as he was told.

"And these," said the guard, holding out a pair of white gloves towards Tom, who took them from him and put them on. Tom could feel the weight of the robes on his slight frame; he felt swamped in them, but given he was slightly taller than Jack, he noticed that they were not dragging along the ground as he was marched into position by the altar in the centre of the dais. His original minder had been joined by a second member of the guardians of the altar, presumably to ensure he didn't try anything – like escaping, thought Tom.

There, by the altar, Gris now stood waiting for him; Tom thought he could make out her foot tapping away underneath her robes as her patience (what little there was of it) ran out.

"Right, you annoying child, you've already seen this and what your friend had to do. You need to do exactly the same things he did, but also place the final relic into the carapace. Got that?" barked Gris.

Tom nodded.

Gris addressed the room.

"Right, everyone, to your positions again. Let's go!"

The chanting and the droning restarted. Looking around, Tom noticed the guards were extinguishing the flaming torches, all bar the few on the dais. The light in the old church steadily dimmed once more until Tom could barely make out anything or anyone beyond his immediate surroundings on the dais, far less his friends in their cells towards the far end of the church. He glanced around to see how many people surrounded him. Too many. Even if he could find a gap to run at and dive through, he couldn't see into the gloom beyond the dais to figure out what or who could block any potential escape route. His mind was whirling now. What if he could somehow break out and raise the alarm? How far could he get? Would there be time to do so before Gris and her goons set upon his friends? And what would they do to Gus?

"Silence!"

The droning and the chanting ended abruptly. Tom looked at Gris and saw her, in her element next to the altar, arms aloft to the towards the ceiling once more. Tom took a deep breath and tried to breathe out slowly to calm himself as he realised there was no way out of this now: he would have to go through with the ceremony and whatever lay beyond. He could feel his breathing quickening as Gris once more bellowed into the darkness.

"The first star of this Christmas Eve has been sighted. Once more, we undertake this sacred and ancient ritual to summon St. Nicholas – Santa Claus – to come amongst us and to be *forever* under my power!"

"Begin the music of the ancients once more!" shouted Gris with manic glee in her voice.

Tom knew what was coming next.

Gris turned towards him.

"Once I give you the instruction, you shall put the very first relic in its rightful place in this carapace, whereupon you shall then withdraw and stand at peace until I call upon you once to position the final relic in situ at the top of the staff space within the carapace. Do you understand your instructions?"

Tom nodded, slowly and deliberately.

"We begin now!" shouted Gris, clapping her hands together above her head.

Once more, a guardian, dressed head to toe in the trademark red and gold, slowly stepped towards Gris and Tom, bearing the first of the relics – the same larger one as previously – upon the decorative cushion. Holding the cushion out at arm's length, he proffered it directly to Tom.

"You will now take this most sacred relic and carefully place it directly into the very centre of the Carapace of Christmas."

Tom reached for the relic and gently lifted it from the velvet cushion. He walked towards the carapace and positioned the first relic into its designated location at the very centre of the wooden carapace on top of the altar. Having done so, Tom stepped backwards towards his double security detail, just as Jack had done several minutes ago.

"You will now wait there until I have placed all the relics bar the final one," said Gris.

The drone music and chanting now intensified once more, as one by one, the various guardians, in sequence, brought forward the individual relics on identical velvet cushions, with each one once again being placed into position into the Carapace of Christmas by Gris.

Tom felt a bead of sweat trickling down his forehead as, after several minutes, Gris reached the point of placing the penultimate relic into the carapace. As before, Gris retreated from the wooden structure and again raised her arms towards the ceiling. The music and incantations ceased instantly as she bellowed out the next stage in the ceremony.

"And so, once more, it is time. Time for Tom Brightly, the cleverest child in the entire world to *face his destiny* and to place the last relic in the very top of the staff space within the most sacred Carapace of Christmas."

A red and gold cloaked guardian came forward towards Tom this time, offering the final relic, the one which he had found burrowed away in the lining of his jacket pocket, but which was now resting on a luxurious red velvet cushion.

Once more, Tom gently picked up the relic and held it in front of himself.

"Hold the relic towards the ceiling," snapped Gris.

Tom raised the relic upwards.

"Now, don't move as I say the final incantation," she hissed at him.

Tom could feel his head swimming now as Gris began her final chant.

"We take and hold this sacred relic,

borne from the past unto the present,

we now return it to its rightful place,

at the zenith of this carapace.

I call upon the ancient powers

of many days and countless hours,

to usher forth down through time

all of Christmas and make it mine!"

The droning music and the chanting began once again. Gris looked at Tom and motioned with her head and eyes for him to put the relic into the carapace.

Tom stepped forward and delicately positioned the last fragment from so very long ago into the last space within the carapace: the very top of the reconstructed staff. Just as he had been instructed. He paused for a moment and closed his eyes and whispered under his breath.

"Santa, please help my friends this Christmas…"

"Step back. NOW!" hissed Gris.

Tom opened his eyes and took three steps back towards his twin minders. He could see Gris looking upwards towards the ceiling of the old church, waiting expectantly for something – anything – to happen.

Tom felt a draught on the back of his neck. He twitched at this. The old ruin of a church wasn't the warmest place – though it was positively tropical compared to the weather outside the building – but the air within it, whilst on the chilly side, was very dank and still.

The draught he could feel became more pronounced, as though someone was blowing on his neck. He shrugged and twitched his shoulders again, as though trying to throw it off himself. This time, a guard noticed his fidgeting.

"Stand still," he muttered menacingly.

Tom looked at Gris. She was still staring upwards, as though in a reverie, watching the ceiling of the church.

The draught intensified into more of a breeze. Tom shivered this time and as he did so, the guard sandwich he was in the middle of also shuddered, as though they, too, were trying to rid themselves of something cold and annoying.

The breeze was now being felt and noticed by guardians further around the circle surrounding the altar. They all began to shiver and shudder underneath their robes. Gris caught one of them twitching and shuffling out of the corner of her eye.

"You there. Stand still," she instructed.

At this, the breeze whipped up and started swirling around the altar, picking up dust from the floor and random bits of dirt and debris. The dust and muck formed a massing, swelling, thickening circle around the altar and a faint, eerie whistling noise began. As the noise increased, a solitary rumble from somewhere deep beneath the floor of the old church accompanied it, and the entire building shook for a couple of seconds.

Gris steadied herself on the dais as the shaking stopped. Her head spun around nearly as quickly as the gathering vortex of debris. Her eyes darted about all over the dais as her security men, the berobed guardians of the Carapace of Christmas, began, ever so slowly, to back away from the accreting whirlwind forming directly around the carapace.

A huge grin flashed across Gris's face, and Tom could have sworn that her eyes were positively sparkling. She cackled gleefully at the gathering maelstrom, which was intensifying all around her, growing ever more violent, thicker and taller. It stretched upwards, as though in a hurry to reach the ceiling and within a few seconds was over double Tom's height and towering over Gris.

From the foundations of the building came another lower-pitched rumbling. This time, it persisted and the entire building shook and swayed as it continued. Tom was struggling to keep his balance as small pieces of masonry became dislodged from the walls and fell to the floor of the church.

Along the periphery of the accreting maelstrom, anything that was not bolted down or secured in some manner was now being pulled into its screaming, barrelling form. Some of the smaller objects were sucked directly into its accelerating spiral, whilst others were hoovered up, only to be spat out at high-speed moments later. Tom ducked and almost fell over as one of the red velvet cushions whizzed past his head and into the gloom beyond. A table further along the dais moved along its length, picking up speed as it did so. It was as though it was being powered along like some sort of hoverboard. Tom saw it heading directly for him and seized his chance: he grabbed it as it started to topple over and propped it up in front of himself, crouching down behind it.

The rumbling grew louder and louder as the windstorm on the dais intensified and the building was now shaking continually. Larger pieces of stone and masonry fell from the walls and the odd smaller piece fell from the roof. Tom covered his head with his arms as one piece of stone from the roof crashed onto the dais a few feet away from him.

Along with the rest of the guardians, Tom's guards were now backing away from the whistling, spinning vortex, too, leaving him alone and closer to the gathering storm than he would have ever wished to be.

And then, the flashes of lightning began. Tom raised his arms up over his head at the first flash and the crack that accompanied it. When the flashes turned from yellow to blue and grew stronger and more prolonged, he instinctively crouched down as far under the top of the upturned table as he could and tightened his arms over his head whilst trying to hang onto his impromptu wooden shield. His last sight of the guards was of them scattering from the dais and running from the storm in the centre of the church as quickly as they could in their robes.

The spinning, whirling, crackling, flashing vortex was, by now, the size of a miniature tornado and its perimeter had expanded sufficiently to engulf the carapace, the centre of the altar – and Max Gris herself. That which it had not yet engulfed was being gradually dismantled and wrecked as the power of the whirlwind increased. Larger pieces of debris were now flying around all over the church and smashing into its walls and ceiling, before crashing to earth on its old stone floor. Meanwhile, the same walls and ceiling were losing chunks of masonry as the entire building shook itself to pieces.

Hunched up on the dais, head down behind the half-wrecked table which was serving as his shield and barely a step or two from the edge of this burgeoning fury, Tom poked his head briefly above his temporary shelter and held his left arm in front of his eyes to protect himself. He managed to sneak a peek at the unworldly sight unfolding in the midst of the old, ruined church and did so in time to see the whole, destructive spectacle of the tornado in all its fury turn from a pallid grey tone to the deepest, darkest shade of scarlet...

CHAPTER FIFTY-ONE

Tom closed his eyes and gripped the table that was acting as his shield with such force that his knuckles turned white. All around him, debris and pieces of wood and stone were flying through the air, smashing into the old church and whatever else lay in their path. The rumbling of whatever was shaking the building was now a deafening roar, and the eerie, chilling howl of the massive tornado in the very centre of the dais accompanied it; the maelstrom now engulfed the entire altar.

Tom was shaking as he waited for the inevitable: if one of the aerial chunks of masonry did not hit him soon, the expanding vortex of chaos mere yards from him would surely swallow him up.

"Please, Santa…" he whispered, scrunching his eyes even more tightly shut.

The roar reached a crescendo, and then there was an enormous bang, which ended it. All of it. The building stopped its incessant shaking; Tom jumped with fright and opened his eyes. The deep scarlet colour had brightened, and it filled the entire church with a brilliant, deep red light. He peered over the edge of the table: the whole tornado was now awash with sparkling scarlet, as though its outermost surface was alive. It still swirling around and around, but almost peacefully. No longer was it hoovering up everything in range of it and nor was it making the howling sound of a banshee. Gradually, it lost its ferocity and intensity.

As the vortex faded, Tom could see Gris standing in its centre, unmoving and transfixed by the glowing and sparkling scarlet light all around her. The whole church was now lit up by the deep red light as though it were a midsummer day at sunset, but a wonky sunset, where the strength of the sun was as though it was at its zenith at noon. As Tom's eyes adjusted to the brilliant light, he began to make out another, dark shape beyond Max Gris. Taller than her by several feet.

The church shook once more as the tall, dark figure moved towards Gris, making a clanking sound with each step it took. As it stepped into the light, Tom got his first look at that which had hypnotised Gris.

Towering over her was some sort of truly unworldly creature. It looked like a demon, with two long, dark horns sprouting from the top of its forehead and curling back over its head. Its eyes were greenish yellow in colour and its pupils reminded Tom of a goat's, with their anvil shapes. Many lines etched its face, and its colour was that of decaying flesh: pallid, as though no blood had circulated in it for a long time. Two smaller horns – almost like stumps - protruded from above its eyes, and those eyes: piercing, fiery and with rims of a sullied red colour around them. Its nose was long, wrinkled with age and extended and curved over its mouth – which was open, displaying a savage set of long, sharp, and uneven fangs, as though ready to rip flesh from a bone. It had two large, pointed ears, the same deathly colour as the rest of its face and a long, dirty black and grey beard – if one could call it that - which extended over a foot downwards. These long, straggling hairs also covered its cheeks, and on its head, all wrapped and matted around the horns, was further long, straggly hair which extended downwards over its shoulders. From head to toe, it was draped in chains and it wore clothes that were no more than dirty, soiled rags. What Tom could see of its body was covered in thick, dark, matted, and straggly fur of some sort. It had long, elongated fingers and a thumb on each hand, with sharpened, pointed fingernails extending beyond the ends of its fingers by at least an inch and maybe two. Its legs resembled those of a muscular goat, hairy and with cloven feet.

It looked like the devil incarnate.

As his eyes adjusted, Tom could see that what he had thought was a state of hypnosis in Gris was, in reality, pure, unadulterated fear. She stood rooted to the spot, her robes quivering as the horned beast clanked its way closer to her until it was towering directly over the very top of her headpiece.

"Who has awakened me?" it boomed in a voice that was more of a growl than a voice.

"It was I," squeaked Gris. "Wh-wh-who are you?"

"Krampus," growled the creature. "*Lord* Krampus," it added for emphasis.

From far behind him, Tom heard a familiar voice.

"Aw no… it's him… run, laddie!" came the shout in a familiar Scots accent. Followed by a blast of flame and the clanging of the bars of a cell. Tom swung his head round, his heart racing, frozen to the spot and wondering what to do, in time to see Gus – newly awake - and in the middle of trying to destroy the cage to end his incarceration. There was further clanking from the creature mere yards from him.

"Why have you awakened me?" asked Krampus.

"I want to possess the spirit of Christmas and live forever. I searched everywhere for many years to gather the relics and the details of the ritual needed to bring St. Nicholas here on this Christmas Ever… b-b-but you're not St Nicholas…" Gris squeezed the words out to the giant demon bending down over her.

"No," came the reply. "I am not."

It clanked its way around the shaking Gris, circling her and not once removing its eerie yellow-green eyes from her.

"Are you sure?" asked the beast.

"S-s-sure of what?" squeaked Gris.

The beast bent down and placed its face directly in front of Gris. Tom could see slobbers drooling from its putrid looking mouth and running down its straggly beard and long chin.

"That you wish to become immortal," it growled in her face.

"Y-y-yes…" stammered Gris.

"Hmmmm," growled the beast and stepped around her again before it turned and thrust its face straight back next to Gris's trembling features once more.

"Completely sure?"

"Y-y-yes... c-c-completely sure," said Gris, barely squeezing out the words.

"Very well," came the reply.

Krampus took a further few paces backwards from Gris and towards the altar, then turned and snarled, lifting both his arms and pointing them at Gris.

"Immortality be yours!" he shouted, and a river of red sparks flew from the ends of his talon-like fingers towards Gris. Upon reaching her, they wove themselves into a pattern around her, growing thicker and thicker and semi-obscuring her from view. From what Tom could see of Max Gris, her previously terrified features were now those of someone who was in rapture.

The red sparks continued flowing from Krampus towards Gris, forming a glowing red cocoon around her. After several seconds, this levitated off the ground, with Gris in its centre, almost imperceptibly at first and then, with greater steadiness, it lifted her high into the roof space of the church.

Krampus was by now laughing loudly at his handiwork. It was the type of laughter that sounded entirely malevolent, and it sent chills running up and down Tom's spine. He was shivering uncontrollably. From behind him, he could still hear the clanking coming from the direction of the cages, but he could not remove his eyes from the sight of Max Gris, high above him, wrapped in a sparkling red cocoon with a thick ribbon of deep red sparking energy flowing towards it from the demon on the altar mere yards away from him.

As Tom watched, the cocoon edged its way towards the top of a wall in the oldest part of the church – the most decorative one. The one that was covered in carvings and gargoyles. As the cocoon reached the edge of the wall, Krampus spoke once more.

"Eternity is a long time," he growled and then resumed his evil laughter.

Tom was transfixed by the sight high above him. As he stared at it, he could see Max Gris's face lose its countenance of rapture and regain the one that was pure terror. Her eyes rolled up and backwards and she let out a bloodcurdling scream as the cocoon with her trapped inside it started to merge with the wall, glowing an even more fiery red, as though it were melting into it. The light grew brighter and brighter, and Gris's screams grew louder and more desperate as Krampus released one final massive bolt of energy towards the merging cocoon, making it blaze so brightly that Tom had to avert his eyes. From above his head, he heard the sound of an explosion, and then there was only stillness and the background glow of the scarlet light around the church.

Tom peered upwards towards the area of the wall where the cocoon of magical energy had been, with Gris trapped inside. It was gone; in its stead, there was a new gargoyle in the wall, still glowing red, its eyes frantically darting left and right. As Tom watched in horror, the red glow faded and cooled, and the gargoyle turned the same shade of stone as the rest of the church wall. Its eyes stopped moving and were fixed wide open in fear, with its mouth frozen mid-scream.

Max Gris now had her immortality.

Tom's mouth was agape at what he had witnessed, then the hairs on the back of his neck stood bolt upright as he realised what had happened to Gus in the past. He had no time to dwell on this though, as the evil demon, having despatched Gris, was now turning its attention to the rest of the church, and Tom was mere yards from him.

"And now, I shall deal with all of you inferior beings!" shouted Krampus.

Fortunately for Tom, some of the Gris Corp security goons – the ones who had not been cowering in the shadows of the old church - had seen what had happened to their boss and now, having recovered at least some of their wits, and under Grunk's shouted direction, they began shooting their guns at the demon on the stage. Tom hunched down behind his temporary shield once more. He heard the guns being fired, but the bullets never came.

Tom peeked over the edge of the table and not for the first time this Christmas Eve, could not believe what he was seeing: scattered all around the church were the various Gris Corp henchmen, all of them still in their robes for the ceremony, all of them rooted to the spot like gaudy statues, and all in the midst of firing their weapons. The bullets from the guns were stopped, hanging in mid-air all around the dais. As Tom watched, the bullets crumbled to dust and fell harmlessly to the ground. The long talons of one of Krampus's demonic hands were raised in their general direction and was he snarling at them. Loudly.

"Pathetic little humans," spat the dark lord of Christmas at his would-be attackers.

He raised his hand and blasted a ball of energy at one of the security goons nearest to the dais. It smashed into the frozen goon and there was a blinding flash. The self-same bright red cocoon, sparking and fizzing with energy as before, had formed around him and was ascending towards the wall – this time, much more quickly than the previous one. It slammed into the wall, glowing white hot and then cooling. Max Gris's gargoyle now had its own security gargoyle to keep her company in eternity.

Krampus raised his fist again and blasted another hapless guard. As this next cocooned unfortunate zoomed his way towards the wall of gargoyles, something else drew Krampus's attention.

"Stop it, Krampus! Stop it now!" came the loud Scottish voice than Tom knew only too well. He whirled around to see Gus, free from his chains and his cage, the ruptured bars of which were still glowing behind him. Gus took a deep breath and unleashed a ball of flames towards the horned demon.

Krampus raised his both of his bony hands together to deflect them. In doing so, the cocooned security guard who was halfway towards the wall, plummeted to the floor of the church, where he lay, flat out and still immobilised.

"Don't harm anyone else!" shouted Gus, as his flaming breath was cleaved in two and dissipated into the musty air of the church.

Krampus laughed his evil laugh once more.

"And what will you do about it, puny creature?" he taunted Gus. "Have you forgotten what I did to you when last we met, all those centuries ago? It seems you need to relearn your lesson, reptile…"

Krampus raised both his hands together and another red ball of energy started forming between them, fizzing and crackling with red, molten sparks. Gus took a huge intake of breath and launched another salvo at Krampus, but this time, there were crackling blue bolts of lightning mixed in with the flames. The ball of flame and lightning careered into the demon, momentarily knocking him off-balance. He growled in fury at this point and unleashed a fizzing, sparking ball of furious red energy directly at Gus.

Gus strained every muscle in his body to keep the flames shooting towards Krampus as the demon's energy bolt slammed into him, winding him and immediately knocking him off his feet and bundling him backwards into the wall.

"You are no match for me, dragon," boomed the demon. He raised his hands again and another fizzing ball of blood-red energy formed. Gus roused himself, shook down his entire body from the top of his head to the end of his long, scaly tail, and sprang upwards into the air, unleashing another blast of fire and electricity aimed squarely at Krampus's head. The blast unsteadied the demon once more, and he gave a loud roar, which reverberated off every corner of the church.

As Tom watched the two ancient beings doing battle, a glowing stone slightly smaller than a tennis ball landed inches from him. Gus paused his flaming breath and shouted.

"Grab the coalstone, laddie. Put it into the top of the staff!"

Tom lurched forwards and grabbed the stone, immediately singeing his glove. He raced towards the staff in the carapace and rammed the stone into the very top of it. The ground beneath the church started shaking. Krampus turned around and looked square at him. As he stood directly in front of the demon, Tom had never felt smaller. Nor more terrified.

With his left hand, Krampus launched another bolt of energy at Gus, blasting him clean out of the air. The dragon landed with a loud thump in a heap on the stone floor of the church. He raised his right hand, ready to strike Tom down. As the demon did so, another tornado of light formed, this time a brilliant golden colour and started spinning around the carapace, enveloping both Krampus and Tom. At this, the demon raised both his hands to his head, clutching it tightly, and let out a primal roar.

"NOOOOOOOOOOOOOOOOOOO!!!"

As Tom stood amidst this second ferocious tornado, with its brilliant golden light swirling all around him and the entire church shaking all around him, his fear left him, to be replaced by a calmness and stillness he could not explain. Krampus staggered and flailed around the dais within the confines of the rapidly expanding tornado, roaring and howling at the top of his voice.

As Tom looked at the carapace, it started to change and solidify, at first into a dark shapeless form with no features and then the shape lightened and details emerged as they would on an old instant photograph. It was as though the carapace was coming to life. As the details of the shape surrounding the carapace became more distinct, Tom could see it transform into a familiar sight: a man, slightly rotund, wearing a bright red suit, lined with white, with a bold, round face, with ruddy cheeks and a big, bushy beard, and a red hat – with a white bobble on its end - atop his head.

Tom's jaw dropped open and his eyes were wide with wonder. He could only say one thing.

"Santa!"

As he emerged from within the tornado of light, Santa Claus gave a smile towards Tom, then as he saw Krampus, this changed to a frown and he shook his head. The demon was roaring with rage and lifted his bony arm, pointing his talons straight towards Tom. The sparking redness of his demonic energy began to flow down his arm and coalesce at his fingertips. Tom braced himself for what was coming next.

Santa reached back into what remained of the carapace and lifted out his now fully formed staff, pointed it straight and Krampus and blasted a golden ribbon of the tornado's energy at the demon. As it hit him, it wrapped itself around him, winding around his body over and over, until it trussed him up from head to toe. The ball of energy at his fingertips fell harmlessly towards the ground at his feet. Krampus howled in fury at this.

"Oh no you don't, Krampus," said Santa, smiling again. He stepped towards the paralysed demon.

"So, we meet again, eh?" said Santa. Krampus roared his reply directly into the old man's face, but it was muffled behind the golden shell that had formed all around him.

"You still haven't learned, have you?" said Santa. "The world is a beautiful place, full of light and hope, and not as you would make it – a place of shade and anger."

"You are old and weak, old man. This world is mine now!" boomed Krampus.

At this, Santa chuckled.

"Oh no, no, no, Krampus. That is where you are wrong. This world is not yours and nor will it ever be."

He paced around the demon, looked around the church, and raised his staff once more.

"You have caused more than enough suffering here for several lifetimes. It is time for you to return to sleep for a very long time."

He raised his staff and pure white light streamed out of it, puncturing the golden cocoon around Krampus and hitting him square in the chest.

"Back to the void, Krampus! Back to sleep and perhaps next time you waken, you shall be kindlier and more benevolent."

The white light intensified and bathed the demon's whole body from head to toe. As the light intensified, the whole spectacle levitated from the dais and up towards the roof of the church.

Tom watched as the golden white cocoon, with Krampus roaring and raging within it, and trying to burst out of it, floated up towards the same place to which Krampus had despatched Max Gris moments earlier: the wall of the church that was decorated with many carvings and gargoyles. The cocoon nudged towards a space in the wall, next to the newest gargoyle and, as before, began gradually to merge into the wall. Krampus let fly within the cocoon with all his fury, so that its interior glowed with a flaming redness as he tried to blast his way out of it – but it was to no avail. His howls of anger and rage turned into the same chilling, bloodcurdling screams that Gris had made as the cocoon fused with the stonework and the whole spectacle grew so bright that once again, Tom had to shield his eyes from the brilliant light. As Krampus unleashed one final bellowing half roar, half scream, an explosion enveloped the wall and the cocoon; the noise from it rattled the entire church as the sound bounced around its interior, and another new gargoyle took its place on the wall next to the evening's other recent creations.

And then, once more, the lighting in the church fell back to normal levels, but this time it was russet and golden in colour, as though the sun really were streaming into the church through its windows at sunset. Stillness returned to the church's interior once again.

Santa stepped down from the dais and towards where Gus lay on the floor, sprawled in an ungainly heap.

"Hello, old friend," he said, gently stroking the top of the dragon's enormous head. Gus half-opened an eye and Tom thought he saw him try to smile.

"I should have known you would be here. I would ask how you are, but that seems a redundant question right now."

Gus let out a long, low groan. Tom jumped down from the dais to help tend his injured friend.

Mustering all his remaining strength, Gus lifted his head slightly off the floor.

"It is good to see you once more, Papa Nicholas," whispered the dragon.

Santa bent down over his friend and smiled.

"I'm known by all as Santa now," he said.

Santa pulled his staff closer towards him, closed his eyes and muttered something to himself that Tom couldn't quite make out. Then, he pointed the staff at Gus and magical sparks, green in colour this time, flew out of the head of the staff and floated all over the dragon's prostrate body, landing all over his scaly skin from head to tail. As each spark landed, it did so with a small golden flash; Gus's entire body looked as though it was covered in miniature fireworks. After several moments, the sparks and flashes ceased, and Santa replaced his staff into its upright position by his side.

Gus gave a shake of his head, as though ridding himself of the last of the evil magic Krampus had directed at him and raised himself to his feet. He lowered his head in front of Santa, who reached forward and patted it gently.

"Thank you," said the dragon.

"Not at all," replied Santa. "It is I who should thank you for stopping Krampus and bringing me here in time."

Santa turned towards Gus and then nodded towards Tom.

"Now, who might you be, young man? And does one of you want to tell me what has been going on here – because I certainly shouldn't be here and especially not on this evening of all evenings," he said, giving a wry smile. And raising an eyebrow, he continued, "And nor should you be, Gus…"

"This, St. Nicholas, er, I mean, *Santa*, is young Tom, the bravest boy I have ever met and the person who brought you here. He was ready to give up his life to save that of his friend," said Gus.

"Hello Santa, I'm Tom. Tom Brightly," said Tom and he stepped forward to shake Santa's hand.

"Hello, young Tom. Thank you for what you have done. You have been truly brave and good here tonight and on Christmas Eve, too. Brightly, you say, eh? Well now, I suppose it all makes sense: I needed to be summoned by the *brightest* child… not merely the cleverest one," said Santa.

"I don't understand," said Tom, looking puzzled.

"The brightest child *full of grace* is the child who is pure of heart, soul and deed, who shows bravery and goodness in his or her acts, young Tom. You were the only person who could summon me with the coalstone, rather than bringing forth Krampus," said Santa.

"The coalstone!" exclaimed Tom, and raised the palm of his hand to his forehead. He turned to Gus.

"Of course, that's what you were looking for the first night we found you, wasn't it?"

The dragon nodded.

"Once I had been awakened, I knew there was only one reason: the relics had been disturbed. And given that the last thing I could remember before I went to sleep was hiding the coalstone, I had to find it again. Took me a while to recall everything – I was a wee bittie discombobulated – but I found it in the nick of time."

Tom had never seen Gus looking so serious – but it didn't last for long.

"Of course, once I found it, the easiest thing to do was to eat it and let it marinate for a while in here," said Gus, pointing towards his hefty stomach.

"You see, laddie, that's just one of the things that Max Gris got wrong with the prophecy – a bit like her wild goose chase to find the cleverest child in the world, when she needed to find the child of light..." said Gus. "Of course, if she'd asked me, I could have told her," said Gus, smiling.

"But she tortured you... and you still said nothing," said Tom.

"Aye, laddie, it's remarkable how forgetful I can be sometimes," said Gus, giving Tom a wink.

"And who might Max Gris be?" asked Santa.

"She was the bad human who was behind all of this. She was the one who had people gather all the relics and decipher the prophecy so she could undertake the ceremony to try to bring you back here and now, and to control Christmas for her own evil ends," said Gus.

"And where is she now?" asked Santa.

Gus nodded his head towards the upper corner of the wall of gargoyles and carvings.

"Krampus dealt with her..." he said.

"Ah, I see," said Santa, peering up at the wall.

"Can you release them?" asked Tom.

"I'm afraid not, young man. They're all time-locked up there now for at least a hundred years, perhaps longer. There's nothing even I can do to unravel that kind of magic and physics once Krampus has unleashed it. Only time itself can heal that sort of thing – and perhaps their hearts as well," said Santa gravely, as Gus nodded by his side.

"Speaking of folk who are trapped, we'd better release everyone from these cages," said Gus, pointing towards, Jack, Merryweather et al. in their cells. "These people were all taken prisoner by that wicked woman and were trying to help me and to prevent this evil from happening here tonight," said Gus.

"Could you?" the dragon asked Santa.

"Of course," said Santa, as he once more lifted his staff and pointed it towards the metal cages. A ribbon of golden light flickered its way towards the cells, wrapping itself around the locks in the doors of each of the cages and springing each one open in turn.

Jack, Merryweather and Auld inched their way out of their respective cells and slowly walked towards Tom, Gus and Santa. Katie had passed out in her cell and Sharp was still out cold, too.

"What about the other two – Katie and Professor Sharp?" asked Tom.

"Oh, don't worry, they'll be fine," replied Santa, wafting his staff again so further ribbons of green sparks encircled the cells containing Katie and Sharp.

"It may take a few minutes yet for them to come round – and they won't remember any of this," said Santa.

He turned to Tom.

"So then, young Tom, what would you like for Christmas?"

Tom stood stock still. He had almost forgotten it was Christmas Eve. He thought for a moment before replying.

"A new sledge."

"Really," said Santa, looking surprised, "is that all?"

Tom nodded. "I love sledging."

Santa stroked his beard and bent down towards Tom.

"I sense there is something else in your heart that you desire."

Tom looked down at his feet, then at the floor, and shuffled from side to side. Eventually, he looked up and, feeling awkward, began to speak.

"Well, there is another thing…" Tom began.

"Yes, what is it?" asked Santa kindly.

Tom gave a heave of his shoulders and a big sigh.

"I miss my dad," he said. "Every day..."

Santa reached out and placed his hand on Tom's shoulder.

"I know you do – I can see into your heart. You have the heart of a lion, Tom, but it is that of a young lion. You have much to learn yet, but I see you have found excellent teachers." At this, he nodded towards Gus and also to Merryweather, who had stepped forward to join the group. Jack was alternating between gawping and then grinning at the sight of Santa Claus himself, and Auld was rubbing his eyes in disbelief, but unsmiling. He looked as though he needed a lie down and a good night's sleep.

Santa called Merryweather forward.

"Hello, and what is your name?" he asked.

"Octavia... Octavia Merryweather," she replied.

Santa paused and stroked his beard once more.

"Hmmm, you're a professor now, Octavia, aren't you? A truly wise woman."

At this, Tom could have sworn he saw his aunt's face redden ever so slightly as she replied.

"Well, I try," she smiled.

Santa turned to Gus.

"It seems the moment is upon us now... at last."

Gus nodded.

Santa turned back towards Tom and Merryweather. He picked out the coalstone from his staff and broke it into two pieces. As they watched, the appearance of both parts of the stone changed. Their colour transformed from black to purple to blue to white and then finally, both halves of the stone turned clear as glass.

"One of these is for you, young Tom," said Santa, holding up one of the two coalstone pieces. "The other must be placed with its relevant relics and all of the relics need to be returned to their respective resting places across the world. I shall need all of you to help Gus to do this so that no one else can use them for nefarious ends."

Tom, Merryweather and Jack nodded.

Santa continued, "The piece I am about to give to you is very special. You are still young, so Octavia here is to act as its guardian and your guide until you are old enough to use it by yourself.

"I'm giving you this for a very specific reason. Gus and I have been waiting for you to come along now for a very long time indeed. We always knew you would, but we couldn't be sure precisely when. Time... it's a strange old thing and sometimes, despite our best efforts, parts of it can become... *leaky*..."

"I don't understand," said Tom. "You're saying that time can leak?"

"Yes, in a manner of speaking," replied Santa. "You see, I exist mainly in the other realm now, the one beyond time and space. How else do you suppose I can travel around the entire world giving out presents to all its children in a single night, eh?"

Santa beamed his warmest smile as he continued.

"However, despite this, I cannot be everywhere all the time. That would be impossible, even for me. So, I'm giving you this transformed coalstone, so you can help deal with the leaky time I mentioned."

Tom nodded hesitantly. He didn't completely understand what Santa Claus meant, albeit he grasped it must be a matter of the utmost importance, given how seriously Gus was looking at him.

Santa held the clear stone up towards the light.

"This stone has now been transformed into a revenium crystal. It will change colour whenever it detects a leak in time. You may have read of stories of such events; they're often referred to as 'timeslips'. One part of time leaks into another part – it can be a messy business sometimes."

"Now, as I said, I cannot be everywhere, so I need your help."

Santa paused and rested on his staff for a moment, tapping it on the ground, as though to emphasise what he was saying.

"Something has been lost in time which must never, ever be discovered… by the wrong people. It must stay lost to them forever, but… still, they seek it. The clues to its whereabouts are scattered throughout time. The revenium will alert you when a timeslip is forming nearby and if you use the stone wisely, you will find the clues and the trail that they lead to in order to make this object secure forever.

"Used carefully and in the right way, the revenium has the power to guide someone to their heart's desire, so make sure you always use it wisely. Do you understand?"

"I think so," said Tom, nodding. "Just one thing: how exactly will we know when we have found one of these timeslips?"

Santa smiled enigmatically. "Have no fear. You will know it when you find one."

He stood up to his full height.

"I know you shall make matters right once more, young Tom," said Santa, patting Tom on the shoulder.

"For now," Santa continued, "I shall entrust the revenium to your… aunt, I believe?" He held the crystal out towards Merryweather.

"Thank you. How did you know?" she asked, upon taking it.

"I'm Santa Claus," replied Santa. "Also known as St. Nicholas. Special powers!" He gave Merryweather a wink.

Somewhere beyond the silence of the old church, the faint sound of sleigh-bells could be heard jingling in the distance.

"Aha! It sounds as though it is nearly time for me to go. Busy night ahead!" exclaimed Santa.

He turned towards Gus.

"Gus, after you have returned all the relics to their rightful resting places, you will need to hide once more. The world has changed while you were asleep and it isn't safe for you to you be seen," said Santa.

Gus nodded slowly and sadly.

"Does this mean I'll need to be time-locked again?" he asked.

"Well, it is the safest way," mused Santa, as he stroked his beard.

"I can look after Gus," said Merryweather, stepping forward. "There's plenty of space in my house – maybe with a few modifications – and he can live there, in safety."

Gus lifted his head and immediately looked brighter.

"I promise I'll be careful," said the dragon.

"And we'll need Gus's help to find the timeslips," added Tom.

"Plus, he's superb at beating baddies," piped up Jack.

"Please, Santa, let us look after Gus. We'll keep him safe, I promise. There's no need to lock him away again for hundreds of years," pleaded Merryweather.

"Hmmmm," said Santa, as he considered their interjections. He walked around for a few paces and then stopped and beamed.

"Very well," he boomed, "Gus, you can try staying here for a while, but… if it all becomes too much, you will need to return to hibernation for your own protection. Understood?"

Gus grinned his toothiest grin.

"Yes, Papa Nicholas," he said.

"Good," said Santa.

The sleigh-bells grew louder and then there was a crash, bang and a wallop on the roof of the church.

"Sounds like my transport has arrived," said Santa. "It's time for me to leave."

"What are we going to with this lot?" asked Merryweather.

Santa looked up at the Gris Corp security guards, all standing stock still like frozen marionettes in their gaudy robes.

"Oh, I think we can deal with all of them," he said, smiling, and wafted his staff towards the stationary goons. It unleashed further ribbons of sparks towards each one of them; this time, they were white in colour. Once more, as the sparks landed on each individual, they produced tiny golden flashes.

"When they waken up shortly, they will recall nothing about any of this," said Santa.

"What about Max Gris and Gris Corp? The organisation is all still here," said Tom.

"And Apotheosis. Don't forget about that," interrupted Jack.

"Oh, I've taken care of all of that, too," replied Santa. "No one will remember who she was, or the game and you'll find the name of the organisation has been changed and is now Lux Ludicrum."

"What does that mean?" asked Tom.

"Light amusement," said Santa. "A little play on words."

He turned to Merryweather.

"Now, I've used my magic on these people to turn them good. Every single one of them, but I'm leaving you in charge of them all, Octavia."

"Me? But I don't know how to run a global toy corporation!" exclaimed Merryweather.

"No, no, no, you won't need to. You're a wise woman. Ignatius here will do that," said Santa, pointing towards Slymington. "You simply need to give him direction and a nudge to start him off. The rest will take care of itself."

"Ignatius," mouthed Jack to Tom, who grinned. It was odd hearing anyone referring to Gris's right-hand man by anything other than his surname.

"Now, remember, your friends will wake up shortly. You'd best go look after them. They may be a little disorientated at first," said Santa.

"And now, I really must go. Gus, goodbye old friend. Until we meet again."

"Goodbye, Papa Nicholas," said Gus, with a hint of sadness in his gruff voice.

"Don't forget to put all of those relics back – and make sure you stay out of trouble, eh?" said Santa. Gus nodded.

Santa strode towards the main door of the church, his boots clumping on the stone floor, before turning towards them all one final time.

"A very Merry Christmas to you all and to all a goodnight! Ho, ho, ho!"

And with his customary greeting, Santa disappeared through the door and out into the night. Tom, Jack and Merryweather raced towards the door in time to see him settle into his sleigh and take the reins of his nine flying reindeer, who were already itching to be on their Christmas Eve travels.

With a single shout from Santa, the reindeer, led as ever by Rudolph, his nose blazing red, started to move, first into a trot, then building up to a gallop, and quickly gaining speed before taking off into the crisp, clear snowy Christmas Eve night sky. The three of them watched as the sleigh, pulled by the magical reindeer, grew smaller and smaller against the twinkling stars as it rose higher and higher into the sky until soon all they could make out was the tiny red dot of Rudolph's beacon-like nose against the blue-black sky.

A final "Ho, ho, ho…" floated through the air above the three of him, and then Santa Claus was gone.

As Tom, Jack and Merryweather walked back into the church, the three of them were beaming. Jack was agog and hyper.

"It was really, really, him!" he exclaimed.

Merryweather shook her head in disbelief. "Yes, it really was. If I hadn't seen it for myself, I would never have believed it."

Gus was hovering by the door as the three of them returned.

"Are you okay, Gus?" asked Tom.

The dragon nodded.

"Aye, laddie. I'll be fine," he replied with a slight sigh.

"I know you're sad, Gus," said Tom, "but I'm sure you'll see Santa again one day."

"I hope so, laddie," said the dragon.

"Gus, you'd better fly back to mine before everyone wakes up," said Merryweather. "We wouldn't want them to start asking lots of questions if Santa's just made them forget everything."

"Aye, Professor, you're a wise woman. Time for me to go, too."

He turned to Tom and Jack.

"Well done, laddies. Turns out you are both brave wee knights. I'll see you soon!" Gus gave them a wink and then bundled himself out of the main door, in his usual ungainly fashion.

There was a low groan from one of the cells on the far side of the church.

"Come on, you two. We still have some tidying up to do here," said Merryweather.

The three of them walked over towards the cells. Merryweather stopped en route to speak to Auld, who was sitting down in one of the church's few remaining undamaged pews, with his head in his hands.

"Are you okay?" she asked. Auld looked up at her. He was ashen-faced and looked overtired.

"Yeah, I'll be fine. Just need some sleep," he said hurriedly.

"You need to go home," said Merryweather.

"What about Dakers?" asked Auld.

"We'll find him and bring him with us," said Merryweather. "If you wait a few moments, I can give you a lift."

"It's okay. I'll walk. It isn't too far," said Auld.

"Are you sure, Nicky? It's bitterly cold out there," said Merryweather.

Auld nodded his assent.

"Can you bring Dakers to me okay?"

"Yes, of course," replied Merryweather.

With this, Auld wished Merryweather goodnight, raised himself out of his seat and began slowly walking towards the main door of the church. His head remained firmly down; his eyes fixed on the floor as he plodded out.

Tom and Jack reached the cells first. Both Katie and Sharp were waking up.

"Where am I?" asked Katie. "What's going on?"

"Hi, sis..." replied Jack, giving Tom a rueful grin. This was going to be tricky...

Merryweather crouched next to Atticus Sharp, who raised himself up on his elbows.

"Octavia?" He blinked his eyes several times. "Where am I?"

"It's a long story," replied Merryweather.

"Last thing I remember was leaving my flat with this young man here," said Sharp, pointing at Tom. "What on earth's been going on?"

"Best you don't know anymore. You'd never believe me anyway," said Merryweather.

"Try me," said Sharp, forcefully.

"All in good time," said Merryweather, helping Sharp to his feet. "We need to all get home; it is Christmas Eve, after all."

Sharp gave Merryweather a hard stare.

"You're not going to fob me off, Octavia. I shall want answers."

"As I said, all in good time," said Merryweather. "We need to get out of here now. Oh, and remind me I have a couple of keys in the Land Rover which I need to return to you…"

At this, she walked away from Sharp and towards a cluster of guards, who were waking up and looking very confused. In their midst stood Slymington, who was rubbing his eyes.

"Mr Slymington," said Merryweather. Tom walked over to her side.

"Yes?" said Slymington.

"You know how you are running Lux Ludicrum now," she began.

"Am I?" asked Slymington, quizzically, before a huge grin spread across his face. "Oh yes, of course I am!"

Merryweather turned to Tom and raised her eyebrows, an impish smile playing on her lips.

"You should return to making traditional games and toys. Be a bringer of light to the children of the world. Make the toys and games fun and educational," she suggested.

"Yes!" said Slymington, clapping his hands together. "That is an excellent idea!"

Tom couldn't believe what he was seeing or hearing. His aunt gave him a wink.

"Also," she continued, "you will find that the company has had a spectacularly good year this year – the run-up to Christmas has been particularly excellent. It has made more money than it could ever sensibly need, so I want you to donate all the excess profits to children's charities and to refund all the monies received from e-games, do you understand?"

Slymington nodded enthusiastically.

"Consider it the organisation's Christmas gift to the entire world," said Merryweather.

"Oh yes, that's a brilliant idea," said Slymington, who was looking happier – and younger - with each passing heartbeat.

"Have your Mr Rudderts announce all of this to the world with immediate effect," instructed Merryweather. "And then, everyone is to have the next few days off as a holiday for all of their hard work. In fact, you should give them all holidays until after the New Year. Once they're back, they're to help clear this place up, make it safe, then mothball it again. We need to preserve it but also quietly forget about it. Am I clear?"

"Absolutely, I shall put all of that into action straight away," said Slymington.

"Oh, and Mr Slymington... have a Merry Christmas," finished Merryweather.

"A very Merry Christmas to all of you, too," replied Slymington, and with this, he was off, bustling his way around the guards and giving out instructions. Tom saw the guards were all smiling, too – as though they had all been infused with the true spirit of Christmas.

Jack wandered over to Tom.

"How's Katie?" asked Tom.

"Oh, pretty much back to her usual self," grinned Jack, rolling his eyes. "Think we'd better get her home soonest."

He reached out towards Tom and gave him a massive hug.

"Thank you."

"For what?" asked Tom.

"Oh, you know, saving my life. All that stuff. You're my best pal," said Jack.

Tom grinned.

"Shurrup... I just did what pals do," he replied.

The two boys thumped each other on the back.

Merryweather looked at all the guards wandering about, looking happy, but rather dazed.

"Hello!" She clapped her hands together. The guards stopped and looked towards her.

"As Mr Slymington has doubtless already told you, it is nearly Christmas Day. It's time for all of you to go home and enjoy Christmas. So, turn off all the lights and then go and spend some time with your friends and families. And have a very Merry Christmas!" she shouted.

Two of the guards started extinguishing the lights in the old church and all of them returned the greeting. Gradually, they began filing out of the main door of the church.

Jack headed back over to the cell area to fetch Katie and Sharp and then led them towards the main door and they, too, left the building.

Now, only Tom and Merryweather remained inside the old building. It was eerily quiet and almost dark once again. Tom picked up a torch and shone it into the rafters of the old church. He looked upwards once more as the torch's beam picked out the newly created gargoyles of Gris, Krampus et al. and felt a shiver run up and down his spine.

"Auntieprof, do you really think that the entire world will simply forget about Max Gris?" he asked.

"I suspect so," replied Merryweather. "Santa used some extremely powerful energy here this evening. I doubt she'll be spoken about again for a very long time, if at all. It may be as though she never existed in the first place."

"Do you think she'll ever come back?" asked Tom.

"Perhaps one day," replied his aunt.

"If she does, I *do* hope she wakens up as a good person," said Tom.

"Hmmm," said Merryweather, gazing upwards at the gargoyle that had been Max Gris. "Only time will tell."

She flicked off the final light-switch. "Come on, let's get out of here and take everyone home."

"Time for this place to be forgotten about again, too," said Tom, pulling the door closed behind the pair of them with a final clunk.

CHAPTER FIFTY-TWO

Merryweather's Defender was rattling its way through the still snowy and icy city streets en route to its first destination: Atticus Sharp's flat. The start of the journey had passed in silence, but gradually, Sharp, in between staring out of the passenger window, began asking more and more questions. Merryweather had initially ignored these, treating them as Sharp having a monologue with himself, and then by giving monosyllabic answers to him, but even then, only if absolutely necessary.

Tom had been half-dozing on the back seat for most of the journey, but had heard enough to realise that Sharp, whilst he might inadvertently have also been subject to Santa's mind reset energy (or hypnosis, or magic or whatever it had been), could still half recall that something pretty big had happened; he just couldn't quite remember exactly what – but he knew things were somehow slightly 'off'. Tom heard his aunt becoming increasingly evasive in response to Sharp's questions.

The Defender finally slithered to a halt outside Sharp's abode. As he opened the passenger door to exit the vehicle, Sharp turned to Merryweather.

"Octavia, I'll let this go… for now. But understand that I am aware that *something* has happened, and I shall want a complete explanation as to precisely what it was once we return to the university in the new year. Understood?"

Merryweather nodded slowly.

"Good," said Sharp.

"Oh, I almost forgot," said Merryweather, fishing out a bag containing a package from the Defender's innards. "This belongs to you."

She handed the bag to Sharp, who peered into it.

"Thank you," said Sharp. He paused as he levered himself out of the vehicle and onto the pavement.

"We'll discuss this further in the new year," he reminded her and then poked his head back into the Defender to address the passengers in its rear. "I wish you a very Merry Christmas – and I hope Santa is good to you all," he finished with a slight smile.

You have no idea, thought Tom, as he joined in the chorus of Christmas greetings in reply.

As Merryweather pulled away, silence descended once more in the Defender's interior. Tom looked across at Jack and Katie. Both were half-dozing. He peered into the rear of the vehicle and could just make out a snoozing Labrador. Considering what he had been through in the past few days, it was remarkable how quickly Dakers had bounced back to being chilled-out. Or, more simply, to being a Labrador. Tom figured the canine snackables his aunt had procured had helped with this, as had making a fuss of him in general. By now, Tom couldn't keep his eyes open one moment longer. He didn't know for how long he had nodded off but was awoken by the jolt of the Defender shuddering and sliding to a stop, right outside the Wanless residence.

"Well, here we are," said Merryweather. "I should come in with the pair of you. Your parents will have been worried."

Katie was still dozing, but Jack, too, had woken up and now gave himself a shake and rubbed his eyes.

"Actually," he began, "it might be better if I handle the parentals on this occasion – fewer questions. But thanks anyway."

"Are you sure?" asked Merryweather.

"Yep. Quite sure," said Jack.

"What are you going to tell them?" asked Tom.

"Oh, I dunno. Something about having been out doing last-minute Christmas shopping in town and we both got a bit distracted," shrugged Jack.

He gave Katie a shake, and she began waking up.

"Wish me luck…" said Jack, rolling his eyes as he opened the door and led his half-asleep sister out of the Defender.

"Good luck," said Tom. "Oh, and Merry Crimbo, too!"

"Merry Christmas," murmured Katie as she staggered up the path towards the front door in a dwam[1].

"Better go – see you after Crimbo," said Jack.

He wished Tom and Merryweather a Merry Christmas with a big grin and then slammed the door shut before dashing after his sister.

Tom couldn't hear exactly what Jack was saying to Katie, but the gist of it was to let him go first and do all the talking. For once, Katie did not appear to be arguing with him.

As the front door of the Wanless household closed behind the pair of them, Tom pushed his way into the passenger seat, next to Merryweather.

"Time to take you home, laddie," said his aunt.

"Yes please," sighed Tom, nodding.

Merryweather started the engine and pulled off.

"Most of the power seems to be back," she said, indicating towards the houses and streetlights. Each house they passed seemed to be garlanded with Christmas lights, both indoor and outdoor. It was as though the whole world had returned to life just in time for Christmas.

"You should try your phone again. See if you can call your mother. She'll be fretting about you," said Merryweather.

"Good plan," said Tom, reaching into his jacket pocket for his phone. He plugged it into the car charger and flicked it on. The phone gradually powered up.

"There's a signal," said Tom, "and quite a lot of messages and missed calls..." He pulled a mock grimace, tapped the phone's screen, and called home.

The phone rang out a couple of times before his mum picked it up.

"Hi Mum, it's me."

"Tom! Are you all right? Where on earth have you been? Your nan and I have been worried sick because we couldn't get hold of you."

"It's okay, Mum. I'm okay. I'm with Auntie Octavia," replied Tom.

"Octavia? What are you doing with her? I thought you were at Jack's? I tried Jack's parents earlier on, but they didn't know where you or Jack were, either!"

"It's a long story," said Tom. "We're on our way home now – Auntie Octavia's driving. Should be back in about an hour."

"You need to learn to use that phone of yours, young man."

"Mum, there has been a big power cut..." began Tom.

"Even so, the power's been back on for ages," said Mrs Brightly. She let out a long sigh.

"Well, so long as you're all right, that's the main thing."

"Mum, I'm fine..."

"Good. Now, make sure you take care and stick to the main roads. They're the only ones that have been ploughed and gritted out here. And make sure you tell Octavia that they're still like a skating rink."

"We'll take it slowly. Don't worry, we'll see you in a wee while."

"All right, take care. See you soon."

"Bye," said Tom, ending the call.

"How did that go?" asked Merryweather.

"Could've been worse, I suppose," Tom replied. "I think we could be in for some more questions."

Merryweather smiled.

"Your mother's just been worried about you. Don't fret. Leave any questions to me when we get there. Come on, not too much further to go now. We'll get you home, and then I just have to drop off Dakers at Nicky's on the way back. Atticus's car will need to wait until after Christmas now."

Tom nodded, and then sighed. He lay his head back on the passenger seat and closed his eyes once more, as the Defender chugged along, making its way through the city streets and beyond, out into the countryside, driving deep into the night, under a canopy of the brightest, keenest stars, on this most wintry of Christmas Eves.

---

1. Scots: a state of semi-consciousness.

EPILOGUE

It was the day after the day after Boxing Day, one of the 'daft days' that marked the time between Christmas Day and Hogmanay [1] and the one time of year when everyone lost touch with the calendar as the world paused for a little while, leaving behind the normal hurly-burly of everyday life and replacing it with something slower, gentler and more in tune with the natural rhythm of the season.

For Tom and Jack, it had meant another opportunity to go sledging. The world had returned to normal relatively quickly after the solar storm and it was almost as though it had never happened. Almost...

After the festivities of the big day were done and dusted, the two boys had been itching to meet up again, to go sledging and to talk about everything that had occurred over the previous several days before Christmas.

The snow was still lying deep everywhere; there had been a couple of fresh falls to top-up the existing snow-cover and according to the weather forecast, the cold spell (which was now being talked of as a 'big freeze') was set to continue well into the new year.

Jack had arrived at Tom's house the previous evening and both boys chattered away for hours (carefully out of earshot of Tom's mum and nan), before heading to sleep with that rarest of feelings: the knowledge that all the snow would still be there on the morrow and that they could go sledging for as long as they wanted to.

Which, in Tom and Jack's case, was the whole of the morning.

As Tom zoomed down the hill behind his house for the last time before lunch, he flew along the hard-packed icy snow at a ferocious pace before skidding his sledge to a halt and exhaling. He stood up from the sledge and took off his helmet.

"That was definitely your fastest run yet!" shouted Jack. "If you carry on like this, you'll win next year's race by a country mile!"

"It was a decent run, wasn't it?" said Tom.

"Decent? That thing goes down the slope as though it's actually flying," said Jack, as he admired the sleek sledge.

"They didn't fib about it in the adverts," said Tom. "The Snowzoomer XL really is the *ultimate* sledging experience. Come on, let's go nab some lunch."

"Good plan," replied Jack. "Especially as I have now completely run out of snackables!" He theatrically turned his jacket pockets inside out to emphasise the point.

The two boys burst into the house and the warmth and immediately began taking off their many layers.

"Good morning on the hill?" asked Mrs Brightly.

"It was awesome," replied Jack.

"So, the pair of you will be ready for some lunch now? Perhaps some chunky soup and toast for starters?"

"100%!" said Jack, grinning at the thought of the incoming hot food.

"How's the new sledge working out?" asked Mrs Brightly as she busied herself over the stove.

"It's brilliant," said Tom. "I'll definitely be in with a shout at next year's school championship."

Tom paused and looked at his mum quizzically.

"Mum, where did the sledge *really* come from?" he asked.

Mrs Brightly stopped stirring the vast vat of soup on the stove.

"Tom, for the umpteenth time, it wasn't from me. There is no way I could have afforded that sledge. It was there, just as you found it, on Christmas morning. I'm as much in the dark as to where it came from as you are."

"Hmmm, said Tom, as he peered out the window at the sledge, parked in the snowy garden outside.

"Maybe it really was delivered by Santa Claus, after all," Mrs Brightly offered.

Tom and Jack shot each other a knowing look…

There was a metallic clang from the letterbox on the front door as the postman delivered the post-Christmas mail. Tom walked through to pick it up, with Jack following him.

"Late Christmas card?" asked Jack, as Tom scrutinised one envelope in particular.

"Dunno," said Tom, turning over the envelope, "but it's addressed to me."

He opened it up, pulled out the letter inside, and began to read it aloud.

"*Dear Tom,*

I hope you had a great Christmas, and that Santa was good to you (I'm sure he was).

You'll be pleased to know that Gus is now happily ensconced in the cellar and cheerfully using its alternative entrance (which comes out into the living room next to - or occasionally underneath - the sofa. Remind me to show you it next time you're over). It's less disruptive this way, and he seems to be getting used to his new way of life, though I have had to remind him not to snack on the neighbours' wooden outbuildings.

After our recent meeting, I am writing to outline the next steps of our project together:

You are hereby cordially invited to attend the inaugural meeting of the University of Time Travel. Class commences at 5pm on Thursday 10th January in my office. I look forward to seeing you (and Jack) then.

In the meantime, enjoy the rest of the school holidays and have a Guid New Year when it comes.

Love,

Auntieprof (Octavia)

Cc: Master Jack Wanless"

Tom handed the letter to Jack, who quickly scanned it, and then they both grinned.

The new year was going to be epic.

Scots: New Year's Eve

AFTERWORD

Tom Brightly will return in...

THE UNIVERSITY OF TIME-TRAVEL

Acknowledgments

Thank you to Leigh, Richard, Kate, Lisa, Lucy and Paula.

ABOUT THE AUTHOR

C. R. Stobo lives in a thin place on the southern edge of the Scottish Highlands with his young son.

This is his first book for children (and grown-ups who retain a childlike sense of wonder).